Praise for Sara E. Johnson

Molten Mud Murder
The First Alexa Glock Mystery

"The novel is a page-turner par excellence, with vivid characters and an enthralling plot, all wrapped up in a most charming evocation of New Zealand's landscapes, people, and local politics. I highly recommend this debut novel!"

—Douglas Preston, #1 bestselling co-author
of the Pendergast series

"Johnson gives us a compelling picture of modern New Zealand overlaid by Māori culture with its strict taboos and amazing artifacts. Alexa hopes to stay in New Zealand, and if this leads to a full series, my fingers are crossed that she gets her wish."

—Margaret Maron, *New York Times* bestselling author

"Johnson provides a fascinating view of New Zealand and insights into the Māori culture... Armchair travelers will have fun."

—*Publishers Weekly*

Also by Sara E. Johnson

The Alexa Glock Forensics Mysteries
Molten Mud Murder

THE BONES REMEMBER

THE BONES REMEMBER

AN
ALEXA GLOCK
FORENSICS
MYSTERY

SARA E. JOHNSON

Poisoned Pen
PRESS

Published by Poisoned Pen Press, an imprint of Sourcebooks
P.O. Box 4410, Naperville, Illinois 60567-4410
(630) 961-3900
sourcebooks.com

Library of Congress Cataloging-in-Publication Data
Names: Johnson, Sara E., author.
Title: The bones remember : an Alexa Glock Forensics mystery / Sara E.
   Johnson.
Description: Naperville, IL : Poisoned Pen Press, [2020] | Series: Alexa
   Glock Forensics mystery
Identifiers: LCCN 2020004703 | (trade paperback)
Subjects: GSAFD: Mystery fiction.
Classification: LCC PS3610.O37637 B66 2020 | DDC 813/.6--dc23
LC record available at https://lccn.loc.gov/2020004703

Printed and bound in the United States of America.
SB 10 9 8 7 6 5 4 3 2 1

To Forrest, with love

Prologue

Ocean Boy glided through the day in gradients of gray and green; occasional glittering light broke through the liquid world when his two-foot dorsal fin, notched and battle-scarred, cut the surface for a quarter hour, unaware he was a two-thousand-pound apex predator marvel. At gloaming, he rode the liquid slopes to deeper, deepest depths, specialized blood vessels keeping Ocean Boy's body temperature higher than the cold water pressing his organs.

The hunt was on. Night vision was activated. His black eyes rolled back to fibrous muscle as his jaws snapped the meaty squid, clamped rows of sharp teeth, his torpedo body impervious to struggling arms and suckers, to spilled ink blacking the already-black depths.

Sated, he headed northwest. Forty-three miles a day he averaged, intent on a destination his brain had mapped at birth, a magnetic and magnificent tug toward innate hunger for fatty seal and sea lion, for adding weight, for adding years, for adding fear.

At purple dawn, Ocean Boy's dorsal fin broke the southern sea surface. The scent of blood increased his speed.

Chapter One

Safe from the tempest, Alexa Glock dripped across the cement floor to the ticket counter. She scanned the price board: round trip Bluff to Stewart Island—$85.

"Stroppy, eh?" the agent said.

Alexa nodded, looking through the window at the pelting rain, slapping waves, and gusts that shook the building. The passenger ferry, tethered to the dock, challenged its restraints with each assault. It was dwarfed by a long, lean oil tanker one pier over. Alexa imagined the tanker breaking loose, crushing the ferry.

Mary, the one friend Alexa had made in her eight months in New Zealand, had called the whipping winds of Foveaux Strait *hau-mate*, Māori for "death wind."

Got that right.

"I need a one-way ticket." She hiked the crime kit strap securely up onto her shoulder and released the handle of her sodden suitcase, flexing her cramped fingers.

"Ferry is delayed." The agent, a wizened woman with sharp eyes, accepted Alexa's credit card. "No return, eh?"

The thought of no return induced a flicker of fear. "I don't know how long I'll be staying." She took the ticket and scanned the lounge. Her fellow passengers—locals, tourists, hikers—stared glumly out the window or at their phones. Alexa settled on a bench near a *Kiwi Experience* flyer. Stewart Island was a hot spot for the iconic birds. Another flyer advertised shark cage diving: "See Great Whites Up Close!"

Mary had planned to dive with sharks. "Come with me," she had cajoled. "*Mangōtaniwha.* The great white shark. Our guardian."

Alexa had laughed. "Yeah, right."

But now Mary was dead. She had died in a car wreck two months ago. Alexa mourned her new friend. And simmered with anger, too. Someone else leaving her.

A woman surrounded by a pile of shopping bags pushed herself up from the bench and came to where the flyers hung. She leaned in, frowning, and tore one down. "Rubbish," she said, crumpling it.

Kiwi Experience hung alone.

A tall man in gum boots and thick fisherman's sweater distracted Alexa. He shouted into his cell. "If they want it, they'll have to come get it." His halo of grizzled curls was a mini-storm, and he trailed the scent of salt and sea.

Struggling out of her raincoat, Alexa canvassed for coffee. No go. A caffeine desert. She had arrived late last night at the Vista Hotel and left it—and the breakfast buffet she had paid for—at dawn to catch the ferry. It had been a wild ride since yesterday when her boss at the Forensic Service Center in Auckland had popped into her cubicle. "Get packing. You've got your first away case. Stewart Island."

She had flipped a folder closed. "That's down south, right?" New Zealand was divided into two islands. Since moving here from North Carolina, she hadn't left the more populous North Island. Dan, her boss, explained that there was a third island. "Thirty kilometers off the tip of the South Island. Fly into Invercargill, bus to Bluff, ferry across Foveaux."

Dan Goddard, chief forensic examiner, had hired Alexa as a roving forensic two weeks ago. The six-month odontology fellowship that had lured her to Auckland was over, and she wasn't ready to leave the southern hemisphere. No one was waiting for her back home. She had completed a contract case in Rotorua—Detective Inspector Bruce Horne and his glacial eyes flashed in her mind—and then applied for a job at Forensic Service Center. Local police called FSC when they needed assistance, and she would travel to those places.

"What's the case?"

"Hikers discovered a decomposed body." Dan's eyes behind bookish glasses sparked with energy.

"Any idea who it is?"

"Ten months ago, Robert King, forty-four, from Christchurch, disappeared deer hunting. Never returned to the hut." Dan handed her a picture.

A fit-looking man held a dead deer by the antlers. His proud eyes stared directly at the camera. His hair—what little remained—formed a dark brown crown.

"That's King. The three blokes he was with looked for hours, then called it in. Massive searches, even recently with live tracking equipment. No sign. No body. Until now."

"Has the family been notified?"

"We need positive ID first. Get there ASAP. And…"

She waited, studying her boss, who wore red tennis shoes and untucked polos.

"…he has a bullet hole through the right zygomatic. The local ranger doesn't think it's self-inflicted."

Alexa fingered her cheekbone in the chilly waiting room. Out the window, the storm continued its vise grip on the harbor. Early December was the beginning of summer in the southern hemisphere, crazy as that was to an American, but the weather hadn't gotten the memo. She checked the time: almost nine. Sergeant Kipper Wallace of the Stewart Island Police Department was expecting her. First case of her new job, and she'd be late.

Dentals would be the quickest way to identify the remains.

She remembered what Professor McBride at the dental school had said. "Forensic odontology has the potential to bring the forlorn to justice."

Robert King awaited justice.

She texted Sergeant Wallace, but the message bounced back undelivered.

Wind slammed the entrance door against the wall, making her drop the phone. A man and woman in matching high-vis rain gear, pulling suitcases, blew in as she retrieved it from under the bench. Damn. The screen had cracked. She wiped the phone on her jeans and watched the couple at the counter. The man asked if the ferry was delayed. Americans, Alexa could hear.

"For now. Not to worry."

"We have a meeting at noon," the woman said, shaking her hood off to reveal blond tresses.

"Aye," the ticket agent said. "Might be a tad late. Round trip?"

The couple pouted like preschoolers. Alexa watched with mild interest as they arranged themselves and their belongings on the remaining empty bench and then sat back to back, huffed and sighed, and pulled out their phones.

To pass time in a more constructive way than judging the Americans, Alexa considered the missing hunter. She retrieved his dental records from her suitcase and studied his X-rays. The top film, a periapical, showed upper teeth from crown to roots snaking below the gum line. A chill danced up Alexa's spine. If King had not shot himself, who was the root of such evil?

Chapter Two

Alexa stood for the entire hour's crossing, holding on to the interior rail of the ferry and staring at the heaving horizon while the captain calmly picked his way through swells, some exploding over the bow. Her queasiness was barely abated by the ginger tablets she'd bought from the ticket lady. She vowed to fly back, instead of taking the ferry, even if it meant chipping in some of her own money.

Now on terra firma, passengers dispersed like sea spray in the wind. Alexa, jerking her roller suitcase through puddles, caught up with the man in the fisherman's sweater. "Excuse me. Is there island Uber?"

"Uber?" His nickel-colored eyes focused on her wet Keds.

"Or Lyft?" A raindrop hit her squarely in the right eye, blurring the world. She shifted the crime kit more securely on her shoulder and rubbed her vision back to normal.

"There's the one taxi." He pointed up the road at vanishing taillights. "Best way to get around is to ten-toe it."

She needed to dump her stuff at the hotel and get to the police station, pronto. "How far to the Island Inn?" She had reserved a room ahead of time, conscious of her *per diem,* and wasn't expecting a Ritz-Carlton.

"Five-minute walk." He pointed a long finger to a building perched above Halfmoon Bay. The rain distorted the inn into a cream-with-red-trim watercolor. "Heading that way. I'll drop you." Without waiting for an answer, the lean man strode toward a hulking black pickup truck in the parking lot.

What the hell.

Mr. Fisherman threw her suitcase in the bed of the truck, next to netting and rope.

The truck purred to life as Alexa arranged herself on the cold leather seat. She buckled up as the driver accelerated onto Elgin Terrace. Horsepower and rain drowned any chance of introductions. She glanced at the man's profile. Early forties, angular and weathered. In three minutes they arrived at the small two-storied inn.

"Thank you for the lift."

Mr. Fisherman nodded.

A group of people holding signs watched her from the patio area as she hauled her case out of the truck bed. It looked to be a mini-protest. Their screams of "Ban the cage, BAN THE CAGE" got louder as Alexa approached—as if she were going shark cage diving. Not. Happening. She squinted through the rain at the signs: *Paua Divers Aren't Bait,* CHILDREN SWIM HERE. Mr. Fisherman honked as Alexa scurried past and through the door.

An old-timey wooden reception counter stood at the far end of the lobby. The Americans from the ferry were already checking in. "I don't appreciate the greeting committee," the man said to the receptionist.

"Sorry about that," she replied, removing her glasses. "Caging is a bit of a stink on the island."

"The money we pay to dive with the sharks goes toward ocean conservation," the woman chimed in.

"Some of it," said the receptionist.

The high-vis couple snagged my taxi, Alexa concluded, unzipping her raincoat. Off to the right, a waiter carried a tray of fried fish and chips in the busy restaurant. Her stomach growled in protest. To the left an arrow pointed to Full Moon Lounge.

The Americans nodded at Alexa as they hurried off.

"*Kia ora*. I'm Constance Saddler, proprietor. Are you a shack diver too?"

"Shack diver?" It took her a second to decipher. "No. I'm not here to dive with sharks. I have a reservation. Alexa Glock." She fished her phone out to check messages. No bars. "Is there cell reception on the island?"

"Not to worry. On fine days." Constance looked a few years older than Alexa, early forties. Her blond hair, dark at the roots, needed a trim. "What brings you here?"

"Business. Can you give me directions to the police station?"

Constance's eyes widened. "It's number two View Street. A short hop." She took a map from a stack on the counter and circled a dot. "It's about the hunter, yeah?"

News had leaked. "I can't say."

"Right then." Constance checked the computer screen. "You've booked a studio. I'll take you there."

They exited out a side door, where a one-story wing had been added. "These are our private entrance suites." Constance unlocked Number Three with a key. "You have an en suite double, tellie, and wee kitchen." Constance cracked the window and approved when the curtain billowed. "Would you like standard or trim?"

Alexa was caught off guard again.

"Milk for your mini-fridge. Standard or trim?"

"Standard, thank you."

"I'll be back later with your milk." Constance paused. "It wasn't a local, you know."

Alexa watched through the window as Constance hurried away. She supposed on an island with fewer than four hundred residents that everyone would know everyone and there would be no secrets. She pulled hiking pants and socks from her suitcase and set her white Keds by the window—which she closed—to dry. She changed, combed her thick dark tangles into a ponytail, laced her boots, and grabbed a mini-package of biscuits next to the electric kettle. She would dine on her way.

The sea-green cottage at 2 View Street belonged in a children's picture book. Alexa checked the sign. Yep. *Police Station.* She climbed three steps to the front porch and turned toward the harbor. Through tapering rain, she could see the ferry leaving, causing her a flutter of panic. Stranded on a remote island. *And Then There Were None*, and all that. She swatted away such irrational thoughts of remote locales and killers among us and entered. Sergeant Kipper Wallace had expected her two hours ago. A uniformed woman in a cubicle turned. "Hello. How can I help?" Her name tag said Constable Elyse Kopae.

Alexa had learned Kiwis used the term "constable" instead of "officer." Same difference. "I'm looking for Sergeant Wallace."

"Are you from Auckland forensics?" The constable was young, maybe Māori, with dark, direct eyes. Her black hair was chin-length. She did not have a lip and chin tattoo like some Māori women. Neither had Mary.

"Yes."

"The senior is at the fire department. Waiting for the all-clear so he can take off."

"Senior" was another oddity. Instead of saying "sir" or "boss," police officers called their superiors Senior. Alexa couldn't bring herself to use it. "Take off?"

"To the location."

Constable Kopae pointed out the room's single window to another sea-green building. One side was an open garage housing an inflatable raft. Alexa's stomach flip-flopped.

She flew across the wet grass. A slightly overweight man opened the door before she knocked. "You made it. I'm Sergeant Kipper Wallace." He was mid-forties and wore a bright orange jumpsuit with SAR on the breast pocket.

"Alexa Glock." She put the crime kit down and extended her hand.

"Glock, eh? Like the gun?" Mostly bald, the sergeant had patches of sandy fuzz above each ear.

"Glock, paper, scissors. That's me."

The sergeant's shake was firm. "Call me Wallace."

"Sorry I'm late. The ferry..."

"The entire island knows when the ferry is late. We've got to get going," Wallace interrupted. "The tide." He looked Alexa up and down. "You'll need a search-and-rescue suit like mine and overnight gear."

"Overnight?" She had become an echo.

"No roads where we are going. We'll fly, land on the beach, hike a couple kilometers to the body. Bush is dense. We'll bunk at the hunter's camp. My constable will rig you."

Back across the grass, Kopae pointed to an orange jumpsuit hanging from a hook in the unisex bathroom. "It will keep you visible. Don't need you getting shot."

"Who would shoot me?"

"There are hunters out there. You can use my rucksack. I keep it ready. Lost trampers, that kind of thing. It's got a torch, compass, water, tooth powder, towelettes, space blanket, and jumper."

"Thank you. I appreciate your help."

"Are you from the States?"

Alexa nodded and pulled the generous-sized suit over everything but her boots, which she slipped back on and laced, glad for thick, dry socks. "How many officers do you have on the island?"

"We're a two-person station, me and Sarge."

"Two people? How do you get time off?"

"It's all good," Constable Kopae said.

"Don't know what I'm getting into."

"It's rugged. Beast practice for you to have a tracker." She handed over an orange-and-black walkie-talkie.

Alexa was alarmed. "Beast practice?"

Constable Kopae frowned. "You know, using latest knowledge and technology. Don't you have beast practices in the States?"

Oh, Alexa thought. *The constable was saying* best. "Of course. We follow best practice procedures back home too."

"That's the SOS signal," the constable pointed. "And it's waterproof."

The burn scars crossing her back tightened as Alexa studied the tracking device.

Chapter Three

Sergeant Wallace started the police SUV and pulled onto View Road without looking for oncoming traffic. "There are only twenty-nine kilometers of road. Most of them are around town. This one dead-ends at the airport. The rest of the island is National Park wilderness."

Alexa fastened her seat belt. "How big is the island?"

"Rakiura is seventy kilometers long and forty-five at its widest."

"Rakiura?" They zoomed past a quaint red-tin-roof chapel—no, it was a restaurant—on the right and a handful of cottages on the left.

"It's the Māori name. The Māori have come here seasonally—like our tourists—since moa times." Wallace looked at her. "Do you know about the moa?"

"A big bird, like an ostrich."

"Larger than the ostrich." He took a curve without slowing. "The Māori hunted them to extinction. Now they come for muttonbird. Rakiura translates as 'the great and deep blushing.'"

The road straightened. "Do you have beautiful sunsets?" Maybe she would send Dad and Rita, her stepmother, a postcard. She had called Dad last week to fill him in on her decision to stay in New Zealand longer. "But what about Christmas?" he'd asked.

"I'll be fine," she said, half true.

Her relationship with Dad was fragile as a glass Christmas ornament. How could it be otherwise when Alexa believed for many years his wife, Rita, had deliberately maimed her?

As a gangling thirteen-year-old she had skated the kitchen linoleum in fuzzy socks and slid into Rita as she poured boiling water from the electric kettle. The coldness in Rita's eyes as the water scalded Alexa's back, her shirt melting into her skin, was etched in Alexa's memory.

Or maybe that was a false memory.

"It was an accident. A terrible accident," Rita wailed to the EMTs.

She finally accepted Rita's story—even felt pity for all the times she had rebuffed her stepmother's overtures: hell no, she didn't need a ride to the mall or a new backpack or—God forbid—a makeover. Alexa had moved onward. Eight thousand, five hundred miles onward.

"The Māori probably named it for the Aurora Australis."

She guessed the Aurora Australis was equivalent to the Northern Lights. Northern Lights down under. Yep—she'd send a postcard.

The village was gone. Glistening green woods crowded the pavement, greedy to encroach.

"March is the best time to view the lights," Wallace said.

She'd be long gone.

"I was born here," he said as if Alexa had asked. "Had to leave for secondary and uni. Stayed away ten years. Thought I'd leave forever, but the place gets in your blood."

Small talk wasn't Alexa's forte. "So the remains are probably the missing hunter?"

"That's right. Hunting, tramping, birding are what bring tourists here. And, for the past couple of years, shark cage diving. We're dependent on tourism for the most part. Fishing, too." The sergeant raced down the middle of the road.

"What makes you think it wasn't suicide?"

"I haven't been to the scene. There's a ranger with the body. He has his reasons."

Alexa stared at the seamless blur of trees. The rain had stopped and the wipers were complaining.

"There were people protesting shark cage diving in front of my hotel," she said.

"Bet I know who. Julie from the lodge. Mason—he's a fisherman. Liz Chambers. She's a teacher. Tippy Jones. No, wait. Tippy was on the ferry." Wallace fished sunglasses out of his jumpsuit pocket and slipped them on. "We've always had plenty of white sharks—my grandfather fished these waters and never had a run-in—but the chumming has made sharks more aggro. They follow boats now. Cage diving is turning islanders against each other."

Alexa looked at the sea of foliage out the window. The thought of sharks following boats gave her chills. But sharks weren't the reason for her visit. "Is it easy for someone to become lost around here?"

"Too easy." Grunt. "Last week a sixty-four-year-old man from Timaru got off track hunting and set off his PLB. It happens out there."

"PLB?"

"Personal locator beacon. They transmit a satellite signal to the rescue center in Dunedin. They call us, we activate a search and rescue. It took forty-eight hours to find him."

Probably like the beast tracker the constable had given her. "Did King have one of those?"

"Supposedly, but it was never set off or recovered."

"Dan Goddard, my boss in Auckland, said it was hikers who found the body." She knew remains were often found accidentally.

Wallace switched the wipers off. "A couple. We're lucky we found King at all. We have a cold case—a tramper who went missing twenty years ago—never found. Heavy forest, manuka, leatherwood scrub, mud. Right now we have four alerts issued for higher-than-normal tides. Waves roll right up to the cliffs. The tracks get submerged. Hikers cut through bush, onto hunting land, get lost. Course, it's worse when they risk the tides and get sucked out to sea. That's my theory for the cold case."

"Dan said the wound was in the cheek."

"That's what the ranger reports." Wallace swung onto a dirt road. They bumped along until the road ended at a landing strip. Two small planes were visible, one tethered on the grassy shoulder, the other ready on the runway. A single gray shack was the only structure. A couple of men stood next to it.

"Ryan's Creek Airport. It's no LAX, is it?" Wallace laughed and parked next to a dirty jeep.

At the far end of the runway, a channel of blue-gray water churned uneasily. On the opposite side, undulating hills melted into haze. Alexa thought of her clean hotel room, a warm shower, a beer at the bar, and then shook off those longings and followed Wallace. She was thrilled to have this job. Moments later she was buckled into a six-seater Piper Cherokee and they were scuttling down the unpaved strip. Sergeant Wallace sat in the copilot seat, and the other man—a ranger—sat behind her.

This job allowed her to stay in New Zealand. She had resigned her job at the forensics lab in Raleigh, and Jeb, her ex-boyfriend, had most likely moved on. His biological clock and all. They had lived together almost two years, but she had turned down his marriage proposal. "You can't commit, can you?" he had said, his eyes full of hurt.

It had been for the best. Jeb hadn't been Mr. Right, and therefore she would have been Mrs. Wrong. She thought of Detective Inspector Bruce Horne, who had given her her first job in New Zealand. They had sparred during the case, Bruce's eyes flashing in anger more than once at Alexa's unorthodox techniques. But she *had* helped solve it, and sparks *had* arced between them. Last week Bruce had driven to Auckland, New Zealand's largest city and home of her new job, "for a meeting" he claimed, and afterwards they had met for lunch.

A date, she supposed. She was pretty sure he'd driven there just to see her.

Lunch at Lord of the Fries had been delicious, but they had argued over who would pay. Afterwards, he hadn't wanted to leave and suggested they rent scooters. Alexa envisioned crashing into the bay so they walked along Wynyard Quarter instead, bumping shoulders and ogling fancy boats. The wind kicked up whitecaps and turned her hair into a Medusa maelstrom. No way she could invite him to her two-bedroom apartment. Her new roommate, Natalie, a cop, worked the night shift and had been sleeping.

Aargh. Thirty-seven years old and she had a roommate. Auckland rent was twice as high as Raleigh rent, and she was earning half as much.

In parting, Bruce's cheek peck had slipped—warmly, delectably—to her lips. The memory heated her face.

A jolt of turbulence took her mind off Bruce. The pilot banked over the harbor and turned inland. The ranger behind her yelped. Maybe he was afraid of flying. He worked for the Department of Conservation, which she surmised was like the United States National Park Service. She hadn't caught his name. Out her oval window, a carpet of green stretched luxuriously, a river winding through it.

Wallace craned his neck and shouted. "We're crossing the island. Little Hellfire Beach is on the west coast."

Alexa nodded. No buildings, roads, signs of life. Just thicket, and then postcard golden sand, and an abrupt landing on a lonely beach. The plane juddered across the sand, avoided several large boulders, and stopped.

"I'll be back tomorrow morning at ten, weather permitting," the pilot said. "Tide'll be right. That give you enough time?"

Wallace nodded.

The pilot looked over his shoulder at Alexa. "She know about the mud?"

"What's to know?" Wallace unlatched the door and clambered out. The ranger contorted himself past Alexa's seat and followed.

"What about the mud?" she shouted to the pilot.

"Like quicksand. Watch your step."

God almighty. Quicksand. Saturated silt. You sink, but can't rise. Get prone and "swim" out if you get caught. She had read about it in a book when she was a kid. That was all she knew.

Crime kit on one shoulder and borrowed backpack hanging off the other, Alexa climbed out, scrunched through sand and shells, and turned to view the pilot swivel the toy plane round, past the boulders, nose it to the wind, and improbably lift off. She watched it turn inland and disappear. Just like that. Her flutter of panic came back. She searched for Wallace and the ranger. There they were—twenty yards past crashing waves, in the shadow of tangled mangrove-like bushes abutting forest. She hustled across the sand, hopping over emerald kelp, to catch up. A bellow—like an angered lion—stopped her midstep. What the? She whipped around.

One of the brown boulders was speeding at her like a tsunami mass.

Move, run! her mind shouted, but her legs stayed planted.

The ranger dude dashed from the forest and jumped to her side as the heap of muscle charged closer, flipping up a sandstorm, bellowing and barking. "It's a bull," he shouted.

God almighty. No boulder. A large marine mammal was using its flippers to propel itself, a bullet train so near she could smell the brine of its breath.

And see its teeth.

"Move!" the ranger shouted.

Alexa dropped the crime kit and ran at the trees, stumbling over driftwood. Wallace grabbed her arm, pulled her up. "A sea lion," he said.

She heard clapping and turned. The ranger stood like a schoolteacher and clapped again. As if that would stop the freight train. What was he thinking?

The sea lion didn't like the clapping. It stopped and quivered, opened its enormous mouth, and emitted an earsplitting roar that echoed off the bulwark of trees. Alexa believed the sea lion would eat the ranger or flatten him to death. A steamroller. Like one of those horrible nature shows where the lion takes down the gazelle.

The oceanic lion snorted, twisted its tree trunk neck like a wrung washcloth—left, right, left—then pivoted and humped toward the other boulders, which Alexa could now see were smaller sea lions.

The ranger dropped his hands to his side and bowed his head as if in prayer.

Wallace let go of her arm. "That was close."

"Jesus. What kind of place is this?" Alexa snapped, then wished she hadn't. Foot-in-mouth syndrome. Don't insult the locals.

Wallace ignored the snap. "Here's an opening." Without waiting for the ranger, he turned sideways, disappearing into the woodland.

She followed on his heels, wedging between clawing branches, her breath coming in spasms. On the other side, trees blocked sunlight and the sound of waves. Disoriented by the dimness and quiet, Alexa pressed against a tree trunk. Everything was happening so quickly. Wallace stood near, foraging in his pack.

Then the ranger appeared. Whipped the hair off his forehead. Halted. She started at him, but he lifted a hand. "I'm okay. A bull lion is all. The ruckus from the plane scared it. He was protecting his harem."

An insane desire to laugh bubbled up in Alexa's mouth. She choked it back. "Can it get into the woods?"

"No. I grabbed this for you." The ranger held out the crime kit.

How could she have forgotten about it? "Thank you." She forced herself to take yoga breaths, five counts inhale, three counts hold, five counts exhale. She remembered something she learned during her odontology program: you can tell a sea lion's age by counting the growth rings on a sectioned tooth—like rings in tree trunks. But it hardly seemed wise to check if that were true.

"Excitement over, eh?" Wallace said. He unfolded a paper and gave it to Alexa. "This is the permit King and his buddies filed last February."

She remembered why she was here—a dead hunter—and read the form. The ranger drank some water and moved close to her so he could see the sheet. Four names were listed, one of them Robert King, and the dates were February 2–8. *Six days of male bonding*, Alexa thought.

She pointed. "What does this 'block' mean?"

"A block is an area." The ranger was thirty years old, tops. A tumble of brown hair covered his eyes. His uniform was total REI: olive shorts, socks, boots, forest-green pullover with zip-pull. *Te Papa Atawhai* was etched at the breast. She wondered what it meant.

"Hunting areas are divided into blocks." He swept his hair back, revealing otter-brown eyes ringed with purple shadow. "King's block was Little Hellfire."

Wallace's radio squawked, making Alexa jump. He stepped aside to answer.

"I'm sorry, but I didn't catch your name," Alexa confessed. "Thanks for coming to my rescue out there."

He avoided her eyes. "I'm Stephen Neville."

"How do hunters know their boundaries?" she asked, getting back to business.

"Each party gets a map." The ranger's voice lowered. Alexa had to concentrate to hear. "Hunters have to know their boundaries. They take the block system seriously. Many spend their first day walking boundaries. If you shoot a deer outside your block or the open hunting zone, you have to pay a fine."

"How do you enforce that?" Alexa looked around—at the shrubbery and trees and weird ferns. And some bugs. She swatted one away.

"It's honor system." He put his pack down, unzipped a side pouch, and produced a folded map. "Take a look."

It was a combo map of Big Hellfire Block 13, Little Hellfire Block 14, and Open Hunting Zone. The back-to-back blocks bordered long stretches of beach.

"Here's where we landed," Stephen pointed. "We'll hike here, to the body." He pointed to a spot in the Open Hunting Zone.

There was no scale, so Alexa had no idea how long the hike would be. Each of the blocks had a hut: Big Hellfire Hut and Little Hellfire Beach Hut. She pointed to the beach hut. The map was made of waterproof paper. "Is this where King was staying?"

"Yeah," Stephen said. "He and his mates. On the second day King never returned."

Never returned. The thought gave Alexa chills.

Stephen folded the map and stashed it away.

"How many rangers work on the island?" Alexa asked.

Stephen shifted his backpack onto his shoulders. His hair hid his eyes again. "It varies. This time of year there are around thirty. Not all of them are full time, like me."

"Do phones work here?" Alexa patted her jumpsuit pocket where she had stuffed hers.

"No."

So, basically, she was cut off. She went back to studying the names and addresses on the form Wallace had given her. One guy was from Dunedin. Two were from Rotorua. She smiled; maybe the Rotorua connection would give her an excuse to call Bruce. Gun license numbers were listed for each hunter. She looked at the ranger. "What type of firearm is used for deer hunting?"

"Depends."

She waited.

"It depends on where and what you're hunting. Short-barreled rifles are best for Stewart Island deer. Certain shotguns. Game needs to be shot at close range, due to the dense bush."

Alexa nodded although, despite her last name, she didn't know boo about guns. As far as she could see, Stephen wasn't packing. "Do rangers carry guns?"

He frowned. "Only on special occasions."

"What? Shotgun weddings?" She laughed at her joke and slapped her ankle with the form. Wallace, his back turned, still jabbered on the radio.

Stephen didn't smile. "Do you have repellent on?"

"No."

He swung his backpack off again and unzipped another side pocket. "Spray all over. Sandflies are a bitch. Māori say when the gods created Aotearoa, the land was so beautiful that people stopped working. The goddess Hinenuitepo got upset no work was getting done, so she created the sandfly to get them going again."

"Works for me." She traded the permit for the repellent and sprayed liberally. "Was King's body found in the Little Hellfire block?" She loaded back up.

"Ah, no. It's in the Big Hellfire boundary."

Wallace rejoined them. "Let's get a move on."

Stephen followed Wallace, and Alexa brought up the rear.

Everything looked the same. Tall trees. Drooping leaves. Thigh-high ferns. Although she jogged several times a week, she wasn't exactly outdoorsy. The tangle of flora and fauna was freaky. Not to mention they were hiking toward a suspicious death. To calm herself, she caught up to Stephen and asked what a ranger's responsibilities were. "Besides warding off sea lions?"

"Every day is different." He skirted a mud puddle and didn't turn around.

"Like what?" she encouraged.

"Eh, well. Weed control. We're trying to get rid of the marram grass. And always pest control, track maintenance—that's a biggie—we have hundreds of kilometers of track. Yesterday I had a go with the chainsaw. We schedule the huts. Search and rescue. Boat safety."

He paused and looked over his shoulder before launching into a story about a stranded whale. "A little calf was in knee-deep water. Whales can't swim backwards, you know. We turned him round and rolled him onto a tarp so we could lug him to deeper water."

Alexa was listening so closely she stepped in a puddle.

The ranger swept the blowzy hair out of his eyes and waited while she wiped her boots on moss.

"Took twenty of us, even some school kids. The calf made it." Then Stephen's voice changed, lowered, and he stopped walking. "A month later eighty-two pilot whales beached at Big Hellfire Beach. Around the time the hunter went missing. A tramper girl from the States found them. Not too far from here. When I arrived—it was hard to reach—lots were dead, but others were thrashing, desperate, digging deeper into sand. Gulls were having a go at their eyes. While they were still alive, mind you." He rubbed his own as if to erase the image.

Wallace had faded into the forest, and Alexa shuddered, her heart thudding in her ears, drowning the sound of birds and insects.

"A calf—this baby—kept clicking and moaning."

Stephen obviously needed to vent, Alexa thought.

"They cry, you know. Whales look at you with their big eyes. Tears rolling into the sand. I pushed and shoved, even pulled one by the tail—that was dodgy, I could have been crushed—but I couldn't budge them." Life force drained from the ranger; he rag-doll slumped.

Alexa was immobilized.

"I—euthanized—I shot them, one by one, orders from the boss. That's an occasion where we can check out a Department of Conservation rifle—for euthanasia."

My stupid shotgun wedding comment. Alexa swallowed a whale-sized lump.

"The whales knew what was happening," he said. "They're intelligent. Probably smarter than me. You can see it in their eyes."

An urge to hold the ranger, comfort him, confused her. "I'm sorry," she stammered. "That must have been…"

"We flew in a Māori group a few days later. I led them to the spot. Some of the whales had already been carved up, and the elder got mad, yelled, I think, at the gods." Stephen sniffed like his nose was running. "The elder prayed, said the whales could now return to their ancestral home, and then they flensed the carcasses."

"Flensed?"

"Carved up. I wasn't around for that part. They remove the flesh, carve out the jaw and teeth, then they bury the carcasses. They couldn't flense them all—there were too many. The Māori will let nature clean the bones, and then return after six months or a year, and dig them back up and let them bleach in the sun."

Alexa now wished she hadn't asked about ranger duties.

"Using whale bone and teeth isn't illegal for Māori," Stephen said as if she had asked. "They make art with it."

Scrimshaw. Alexa had a scrimshaw brooch from her mother. Back in her Raleigh storage unit. It's not like she wore brooches with khakis or jeans. She was jittery to get moving.

"And now this—body retrieval. Add that to my list of duties." Stephen straightened, shook his hair back, and hustled ahead, his uniform blending into the woods.

Her innocent question about a ranger's duties had unleashed a tale of woe. Alexa followed slowly, as if space was a protective bubble from the horrors of nature and memory. The saturated ground muffled her footsteps, the canopy blocked wind, the birds twittered erratically. To take her mind off the whale tragedy, she began reviewing the four stages of decomposition in preparation for viewing the hunter's remains. A heel slipped in mud, but she caught herself before landing on her butt, and remembered the rate of decomp depends on heat and moisture.

Heat. Mid-fifties.

Moisture. The rain had ceased, but the canopy dripped from the morning's deluge.

Stage One begins four minutes after death when the body begins to self-digest.

She thought of the victim in Rotorua who had been thrown into a molten mud pot. He had melted instead of decayed. His teeth had remained.

Flies arrive almost immediately to lay eggs in eyes, mouth, ears, nose, vagina, and rectum.

She thought of the sandflies and hoped her bites didn't harbor eggs. Up ahead, Stephen scrambled over a tree carcass blocking the path. When it was Alexa's turn, she sat on the trunk a moment, her breath unnaturally loud.

Twenty-four hours after deposit, maggots hatch.

The bark was wet and slimy, probably housing and hatching its own maggots. She quickly swung her legs over and barreled onward, searching for Wallace's orange SAR suit. Her right foot sank in mud. She pulled it, but it wouldn't budge, sank further instead, up to the laces in viscous muck. She pulled again.

Something. Someone. Below the ground. Holding. Death grip. Quicksand.

"Hey!" she called. "I'm sinking."

An evil squawk echoed in the prehistoric forest. Now her left foot sank to the ankle, then shin. Alexa threw the crime kit and backpack to the side, went prone, grabbed at a grounded limb extending from the fallen tree and, throwing her upper body into the fight, began pulling forward, her legs in cement.

Pull. Tug. Strain.

The underworld let go, and in a squelch she freed her left leg.

Stephen reappeared. "You right?" He grabbed her armpits and pulled. He was stronger than he looked and freed her right leg.

"Hell, no. Something pulled me under." Her voice trembled as she assessed the damage: boots slimed, orange suit dyed java brown up to the knees, chest heaving. "You and Wallace walked over the same spot. Why didn't you go down?"

"You broke through a sink hole. The soil is shallow, only

supported by a web of roots. The rain, plus our footsteps, weakened the support. Camel's straw concept."   •

Alexa glared at the churned mud pot. "Thanks."

"For weakening the structure?"

"For coming back." *And trying to save the whales.*

A hundred yards ahead, the path faded. Alexa dodged and wove through thigh-high ferns. The purple-brown ferns were long, creepy, and scaly. The green ones looked similar to North Carolina ferns, but bigger. These were so thick that she surrendered and began stepping on the emerald fronds. Above all were the umbrella fern trees, the likes of which Alexa had never seen.

After fern valley, the ground became hilly, speckled with rock, moss, boulders paisley with lichen, and more umbrella trees, and then segued into a gully so that she was forced to walk with one foot on a narrow track and the other foot halfway up a steep bank. She had heard the Kiwi phrase *hard yakka*. This was a hard yakka. She refocused on her Stage One decomposition review. *The top layer of the skin begins to rupture and loosen.*

Alexa lowered the zipper of her jumpsuit.

"Take a break. Drink some water," Stephen said, suddenly next to her. Wallace stopped walking too.

"I'm fine," she said as sweat trickled down her chest.

"No. We should drink."

Alexa put down her pack, uncapped her water, and took a long swallow. "Listen to the birds."

Stephen scanned the trees. "Tui and bellbird. Keep a lookout for kiwi. Stewart Island is the only place where they forage during the day." He sipped water as his eyes continued to rove the tree line. "Botanists say the island looked like this before humans arrived. It's a forest primeval."

"Forest evil, more like it," Wallace called, capping his bottle. "For the hunter, anyway."

Alexa imagined Robert King's body as the forest darkened and the decaying wood and organic matter all around them released dank, fusty oxygen.

During Stage Two, the corpse will bloat and emit an odor.

The death stink. When Alexa was a newbie, the Raleigh police had called the forensic team to a dumpster at an apartment complex. A woman's body, enshrouded in shower curtain, was beneath garbage. It took Alexa three showers to wash the smell from her hair and body, but the combination of putrescine and cadaverine, chemicals released as a body decomposes, remained in her throat and taste buds for days.

She took a swig of water, swished, spit out.

Ten minutes later, the bank of a rushing, roaring stream stopped her. Stephen was balanced on a rock, halfway across, when he looked back. "No worries," he shouted over the din. "Hop rock to rock."

A hiker doing the famous Milford Track had recently been swept away crossing a rain-swollen stream. Her body, found two days later, had washed a mile and a half downstream. Alexa had read about it in *The NZ Herald*. She and Mary were scheduled to hike Milford in February. Now she'd have to hike it alone.

If I survive this.

She hurtled forward to the first slick turtle-back rock, balanced precariously, awed by the froth and frenzy, and lunged, toddler-like, to the next, and so forth. *Jesus.* Somehow she made it, her boots washed clean of mud.

"Piece of cake," she told Stephen and Wallace, who had watched impassively.

Up the path, something scurried in a leathery-leaved bush near her foot, making her wonder what critters feasted on King's remains. Back home it would be rats, coyotes, foxes, possums, dogs, birds. Vultures could strip a deer to bone in twenty-four hours.

"What scavengers do you have?" She trudged between the men now, Wallace leading, and when he turned, apprehension, maybe fear, was etched on his face.

"Rats, possums, and birds. Kiwi will eat carrion."

The sergeant had maintained a quiet reserve on the hike, so she was pleased to engage him. "How much farther?"

"Not far," he answered.

Fatty acids leak from the body, killing vegetation.

Wallace's walkie-talkie bleeped just as yellow caution tape near a giant tree caught Alexa's eye. She stopped to survey the area. First impressions were important. Why the hell had hikers been here, in the middle of nowhere? There was no trail. When she hustled to catch up, she stumbled over a root and fell forward.

"Crack-up entrance," a man said from behind the tape. "Who's the klutz?"

Chapter Four

Alexa righted herself and glared.

Wallace jumped in like a playground supervisor. "This is Miss Glock, forensics from Auckland." He handed Alexa the crime kit that had slid off her shoulder. "This is Ranger Gellman."

"Glock?" The ranger ran a hand through tousled blond hair. He looked to be in his mid-forties.

"Like the gun." *If I had one I'd shoot.*

"A Yank, eh? Call me Scratch." His green eyes slowly raked her orange-clad body. He held up the tape for her to enter and showed off Crest whites.

Alexa focused on the fact that the rude ranger was on the inside of the core scene boundary. "You need to step out here," she said.

He stepped toward her. "I like a Sheila who speaks her mind."

She didn't have time for macho crap. Ten yards past the ranger, a scarecrowish body wearing a camo hunting jacket was wedged against a fallen tree, a bright red tarp heaped next to it. She opened the crime kit, pulled on gloves and booties, readied the camera, grabbed evidence markers, and asked Wallace, "What's the timeline of the discovery?"

The sergeant paused before speaking. "Right. Yesterday at 11:30 a.m. we received a call from a tramper who discovered the body."

Stephen had said phones don't work out here. "How did the hiker call?"

"He and his partner hightailed it to Big Hellfire Hut. Another tramper was there, waiting out the rain. He had a satellite radio." Wallace flicked his chin toward Scratch. "Ranger Gellman hiked in to secure the area. That was yesterday, and Bob's your uncle."

Alexa looked at Scratch. "Why were hikers here? In the middle of nowhere?"

"Isn't middle of nowhere. Just there," Scratch pointed, "is the alternate North West Circuit track. It's the high-tide detour."

"Circuit track? What's that?"

Stephen broke in. "It's one of three main trails on the island. Takes ten days to hike it."

Ten days of mud, sandflies, and quicksand? No thanks.

"The alternate cuts right through the Hellfire block," Scratch said. "Kid who found the body was visiting the dunny."

"The dummy?"

Scratch snorted. "He almost whizzed on the deceased."

"What have you touched?" she asked.

"I moved the tarp to take a look-see. I didn't touch the, er, body."

She analyzed the taped-off area to make sure it was large enough, mindful of Dr. Winget's tenet: Go big. You can always shrink the perimeter later. Her mentor and former boss at the North Carolina State Bureau of Investigation often popped into Alexa's brain. Concluding that Dr. Winget would be satisfied, she ducked under, camera ready, eyes scanning left and right.

Scratch tried to follow, but Alexa put her hand up. "Stay back."

"But..."

"You need to wait outside the perimeter."

"Don't get your knickers in a knot," he said, stepping toward Stephen. "Yo, mate. Where you been? Didn't see you at the DOC bash."

Stephen mumbled something.

Keep an open mind, no jumping to conclusions, she thought. Her first photographs were wide angles. "Sergeant Wallace. There's a pad and pencil in the kit. Will you sketch the scene?"

"On it."

She nudged forward, aware daylight was diminishing.

Evidence needed to be photographed before it could be touched, but Alexa wasn't hopeful for much. Rain and time had done their dance. There could still be fingerprints, she mulled, adjusting the lens. Prints aren't as fragile as people think.

Her human decomp review had not progressed past Stage Two—the putrid bloating stage she had examined in the dumpster ten years ago. Alexa sniffed deeply. Only damp earth, loam, leaf rot filled her nostrils. No body gases.

During Stage Three, organs, muscle, and skin liquefy, leading to Stage Four—skeletonization.

It was Stage Four nestled against the tree. Alexa took time to form a general impression. The forest, the men, the strangeness of being in these remote woods collapsed to tunnel vision. The partly clad remains stretched full-length on its side. The skull faced the log as if the scene were too disturbing to witness. A rifle lay parallel to the buttock and back, less than a foot from the body. The left arm was concealed under the body, the right stretched at an awkward angle behind, hand resting near the hip. Scavengers had gnawed it to the bones. A gold band loosely encircled the metacarpal, or ring finger. The sight reminded her that a loved one would soon receive bad news. Hope would be jerked away.

She snapped photos, aware the position of the gun was important. Guns used in suicide were rarely recovered in the person's hand. More often they were found on or near the body, as in this case. Its underside was an area from which Alexa hoped she could extract fingerprints.

Of course the position of the gun could have been staged. She searched the ground for drag marks. Moss and vegetation appeared trampled. She stepped back, took more pics.

"Where did the tarp come from?"

"The bloke who discovered the remains covered the body with it," Scratch called. "Smart move, or I'd still be looking."

"There should be a spent cartridge if he was shot here. Start searching while I examine the body. Glove-up first."

"Glove-up? Who the hell are you?"

Alexa faced Scratch. Lots of times in her career, especially when she had been younger, male colleagues balked at being told what to do.

Wallace and Stephen complied. *Two out of three,* she thought—*not bad.* She turned back. Daylight was fading. A blood-curdling scream spliced the air. Another. Again.

"What the?"

"Female kiwi," Stephen said softly. "Maybe the male will answer."

She sucked a lungful of cool air. A boot imprint stopped her. She squatted, stuck a marker next to it, took close-ups.

"Probably the hiker who found the body," Stephen said.

"Take a cast," Alexa replied. "Supplies are in the kit." She searched for more, but the greedy ground withheld.

Body time.

King's skeleton—the parts exposed from sleeves, cuffs, and holes—would have made a perfect Halloween decoration back in the States. Alexa hadn't known whether Halloween was celebrated in New Zealand. It had been a relief, really, that the day had passed with no fanfare. Halloween hype was touchy business for a Never Married No Kids. She missed the leftover candy, though. A Nestlé Crunch would hit the spot.

She carefully rolled the body flat. King—if it was King—wore a jacket of synthetic material. It showed little wear after ten months' exposure to the elements. No visible tears that might indicate a struggle. The tip of a water bottle poked from a pocket.

The scream again. Closer. Evil. She had wanted to see kiwi but not now.

A bit of yellow caught her eye. She opened the jacket flap, revealing a wadded safety vest.

"Look at this," Alexa called to Wallace.

"Why would he have taken off his high-vis vest?" Wallace asked. At some point he had put glasses on.

"Don't know." She took photos. "Maybe someone didn't want him to be found."

A higher-pitched scream made her start.

"Eh, that's the male," Stephen said.

Add it to her thumbs-down list: children, dogs, now kiwis.

The pants were in tatters, exposing bone. Ankle knobs were visible through remnants of sock, probably wool, and appeared too delicate to support a grown man. They disappeared into large black boots, the toe of one wedged under the log.

She could hear Stephen talking softly to Scratch as they searched for the ejected cartridge.

Alexa crept forward and zoomed in on the rifle, a rusting Browning A-bolt, and took several photos, first without evidence markers, and then with. Finished, she asked Wallace to see if the rifle was loaded.

Wallace carefully lifted it in his gloved hands. "The safety is off," he noted. He set it and then removed the magazine, which he slipped into an evidence bag. "Okay. Safe now."

"What kind of ammo is it?"

"Point thirty-two, medium."

She needed to learn about guns and ammunition; Wallace's reply meant nothing to her. She gingerly turned the rifle over and set up her fingerprint powder.

"Prints won't be visible after all this time, eh?" Wallace commented.

Alexa ignored him and dusted the surface, hoping for a reward. The person who loaded the rifle, if not wearing gloves, would have transferred oils and sweat when pressing hard around the trigger or magazine chamber. She was let down; no identifiable marks appeared. "It might have been wiped clean." Then she brightened, remembering an article she read on scientists finding fingerprints on wiped metal. "The ballistics guys might be able to find prints using electrostatic process."

"Eh?"

"You can bag it now."

She cleaned up her print kit and then got on her knees to examine the back of the skull. It was cue-ball smooth, which surprised her. After ten months, she would expect patches of hair to still be present, but then she remembered the photo—King had been mostly bald.

A beetle crawled out of a jagged hole. With a start, Alexa realized it was crawling out of the exit wound. "Be searching for a bullet too," she said. Evidence like a gunpowder tattoo had decomposed long ago.

She set the camera down and maneuvered the skull for a frontal, grimacing when she discovered it was detached from the vertebrae.

The mandible was intact, but missing teeth created a macabre grin. "I'll be able to tell if it's King as soon as I can take X-rays." She searched the ground for the missing teeth but couldn't see them.

The entrance wound, smaller and neater than the exit, sat below the right eye socket. She imagined the bullet boring through the fragile skull-shell, perhaps somersaulting in deleterious assault on its fatal path through the brain, plowing through the jelly of King's thoughts, actions, memories, deeds, feelings—his very soul—before exiting. She fought the urge to peer through the hole like a periscope to see King's final thoughts. Had he thought of his wife or children? Had he known they were final thoughts?

What would my final thoughts be?

"Hand me the kit, please."

Wallace set it next to her and watched as she removed a ruler and took measurements. She shook her head, jostling a faint caffeine headache, and gave thanks for bodily needs, for protesting scars, for sore knees, for these signs of life. She looked at the sergeant. "The entrance wound is awfully clean to be a contact shot. There's no blow-out fragmenting."

"So not suicide?"

Alexa sat back on her haunches. "I don't think so."

"And don't forget that foot," Scratch added, coming over. "He didn't stick that boot under the log himself."

The thought of someone deliberately wedging the body against the fallen tree and hiding the safety vest gave her the creeps. She looked at the darkening woods and flexed her cold, stiff fingers. Another strangled kiwi call floated from the shadows. With the gloaming breathing down her neck, she hustled to inventory the pockets—mints, compass whistle gadget, Repel bug repellent. Alexa bagged each, wondering about the whistle gadget. If the hunter had been lost, or in trouble, wouldn't it have been in his hands? There was no phone or safety beacon. After gathering soil samples, she stood.

"I'm finished."

Goosebumps pushed the hair on her arms to standing as she realized how isolated she was, here with a dead body, soul departed, and three strange men, souls debatable.

Chapter Five

The forest chattered and the darkness thickened. Scratch's head-lamp cast a bobbing slice of light on the Northern Circuit Track. Behind him, Wallace and Stephen bore the body bag on a light-weight litter like Druids on the way to sacrifice. Alexa shadowed them a quarter mile until they arrived at a hut in a small clearing.

"Welcome to Big Hellfire," Scratch said. "Let's get the party started." He sprang up two steps to a covered porch, pulled his boots off with a grunt, and disappeared inside. Stephen and Wallace hoisted the litter onto a long wooden table on the porch, breathing hard.

"Place to butcher your deer, this is," Stephen said of the table, wiping sweat from his brow.

It looked like an autopsy table.

Wallace unlaced his boots. "Keeps the hut tidier to keep them out here."

Alexa set her stuff down and grimaced as she fought the filthy laces of her size-nine waterproof boots.

Wallace held the door and waited.

She blinked in lantern light.

"Basic, eh?" Wallace followed her in. "Huts save hunters and trampers from carrying tents, sleeping pads, that kind of stuff."

"Cozy." Alexa sniffed. Sweat. Musk. Mice. Something else.

"I stopped by earlier to kick out the hunters who booked it," Scratch said, lighting a second lantern. "Official business, I told them. Emergency. Full refund, but they were pissed." He started adding sticks from a neat pile into a potbellied stove.

"I have supplies for a meal," Stephen said from behind.

"Good on ya, bro," Scratch said.

Alexa's stomach rumbled. She couldn't remember her last meal. She wiggled her sock-covered toes on the cold plank floor, standing between four bunk sets, two per side, each with a thin blue mattress leaning against the wall. The other end of the hut had a counter, sink, and a table with wooden benches.

"Is there water?"

Stephen glided by to try the tap. "Straight from the rain tank." The trickle made Alexa aware of her full bladder.

"Long drop out back," he added.

Vision of walking off a cliff confused Alexa.

Stephen laughed. "A dunny. Take a torch so you don't get lost."

A couple times the men had slipped off the path and turned their backs, anointing trees she presumed, but she wouldn't be caught dead squatting in the woods.

Alexa claimed a bottom bunk and rooted in the backpack for the flashlight, aware of her bedraggled appearance. She unzipped and stepped out of the orange SAR jumpsuit, the sensation of cool air refreshing. She'd get chills as her sweat dried, so she pulled out the fleece pullover Officer Kopae had mentioned, pulled it over her long-sleeved T-shirt, and slipped her cell into the pocket.

"Back in a jiff."

On the porch she checked the phone for bars—none—and then photographed the right boot of each pair lined up obediently: a Scarpa, a Keen, and a Merrell, profile and sole. To compare and eliminate with the cast taken at the scene. *Should have worn gloves.* She grimaced again, wiped her hands on her pants, and slipped into her own.

The loo wasn't too bad. She savored the privacy, collecting her thoughts, the beam of her light agitating a spider in the ceiling corner. The daddy longlegs brought comfort. Something familiar. What was that song? *Eensy weensy spider crawls up the waterspout.* A memory flickered. She scratched at her sandfly bites and tried to focus. The older she got, the harder it was to see her mother, who had died when Alexa was six. Hadn't she sat on Mom's lap and sung the spider song? *Down came the rain and washed the spider out.* Her growling stomach broke her concentration.

She was about to sleep with three men.

Her friend Mary, the one who had recently died, would have laughed and said, "Enjoy it."

Lantern light and orange flames from the open stove created a *Little House in the Big Woods* scene. Stephen had water boiling over a miniature gas stove and was doling ramen noodles and freeze-dried cubes into bowls. A glorious sight.

"What can I do?"

"Cut up these carrots," Stephen said, his eyes downcast. "Straight from my garden. Use the greens too."

Alexa glanced at Scratch as she cleaned her hands with a wipe from the backpack. He was on his knees at the potbellied stove, blowing into the pile of burning sticks. Wallace stepped outside.

She got to work, turning her thoughts to DI Bruce Horne and the steak dinner they had cooked side-by-side in the wee warm kitchen of Trout Cottage a few weeks ago. It hadn't been a date, more an impromptu crashing of carts at the grocery store.

But it had whetted Alexa's appetite.

Stephen fiddled with the little gas stove, making the flame flare and hiss. The pot of simmering water hung over the edges. "Hut's nice, isn't it? Homey."

Alexa nodded to be polite. "My room at the Island Inn will be wasted tonight."

"That's a posh place," Scratch called.

Island Inn was nice, but not fancy, Alexa thought.

Stephen pointed to the medallions. "Add them to the pot."

She avoided boiling water. "You can do it."

He plopped the veggies and a package of seasoning into the water while Alexa sliced the last carrot with a dullish knife.

"Smaller will cook quicker," Stephen said.

"Too late."

They watched the carrots simmer. Stephen tugged at the zip-pull of his uniform fleece. Up. Down. Up.

She noticed the Department of Conservation logo again. "What does *Ta Papa Atawhai* mean?" Alexa asked.

Stephen laughed at her pronunciation and brushed the hair out of his eyes. "The caring father." He stretched the zip-pull closer to Alexa. "Everything on our uniform has meaning. The symbol on this pull is *manu*."

Alexa could make out spread wings.

"*Te Tini o te Hakuturi*," Stephen added.

"Do you speak Māori?"

"Just a few phrases. It means 'Spirit Guardian of the Forest.' That's my job. Take care of the forest." He poured broth into four bowls of ramen noodles and cubes.

The ranger was into his job. She appreciated that.

No one talked as they slurped at the table. The carrot, rehydrated chicken, and noodle soup almost sated Alexa's hunger.

After picking up his bowl to suck down the broth, Scratch produced a king-sized chocolate bar—Cadbury—and split it four ways.

Alexa forgave him his prior trespasses. The dark velvet coating her taste buds and the warm soup in her belly revived her curiosity. She started to ask Scratch about his name but realized she didn't care and turned to Wallace. "So King was married?"

"Wife and two daughters." Wallace wiped his mouth with the back of his hand and pushed his glasses higher on his nose. "Teens. I met them, the girls. Mary Hannah and Katie. They helped search, determined to find their pop."

The skeleton in the body bag ten feet away took on new status. Daddy status.

"People cling to hope," Wallace continued, removing his glasses and polishing them on his shirt hem. "Now we have to snuff it. You sure someone shot him?"

There were six causes of death: homicide, suicide, natural, accidental, undetermined, and pending. Natural and undetermined were out. "I can't be certain until I get him in a lab. But the bullet hole wasn't self-inflicted."

Stephen sucked in his breath.

"The soft tissue is gone, so that means powder burn evidence is too. That's a shame. But what's most important..." The three men watched her. Alexa pushed a wisp of hair behind her ear, enjoying the attention. "What's most important is how far away from the victim the gun was when fired. Based on the diameter of the entry hole, King couldn't have pulled the trigger."

"Knew it," Scratch said.

"What's worse?" Wallace asked. "Your pop kills himself or someone else kills him?"

"Never finding the body is worse," Stephen said. "Now they'll have closure."

"You sound like Dr. Phil," Scratch said.

Alexa leaned against the rough-hewn wall. "A ballistics expert will run the angles. I'm guessing King was killed close by and dragged to where the hikers found him. No one drags a body far." She took a deep breath. "We'll need to locate that primary scene of death."

"I'm calling it in now," Wallace said. "It'll take time to get a team here." He swung his leg over the bench and stepped out to the darkened porch with the radio.

"He's been waiting for this moment his whole career," Scratch said, his voice lowered. "First and only island murder," he looked at Alexa, "since 1927. Andrew Josey. Up at Horseshoe Bay. One night his landlady heard him screaming from his room. She rounded up police. Too late. Blood everywhere—on the walls, floor, linens. Josey was bludgeoned to a pulp. Murder weapon was a manuka branch. Tranquil spot turned ugly."

Alexa wrapped her arms around her torso. "Did they catch who did it?"

"Brought in detectives from Dunedin. Same thing will happen now. They'll bring in a detective from somewhere else. Eh, they caught the sucker. No place to hide on an island."

"Seems like there are plenty of places. All this jungle." She looked out the lone window through which she could see Wallace's reassuring back.

"House where he was murdered is abandoned. Stands near the edge of a cliff. I'll take you there." Scratch looked at her like they were alone. He stood, stretching hands to the ceiling, showing a patch of golden ab, and then padded to his pack leaning against Alexa's bunk. "You're not going to make me sleep on top, are you?" He snorted and rummaged.

The odor she hadn't been able to identify earlier hit with a jolt: male pheromones. Scratch produced a flask. "Help us sleep." He uncapped it, took a swig, and then sat down in Wallace's spot, smooshing against Alexa. He offered the flask.

Momentarily flummoxed, she held her hand out.

"Attagirl." Scratch brushed his fingers against hers as he relinquished his hold.

The whiskey slashed and burned a path to her belly.

Wallace returned. "Troops are called in."

Stephen mumbled something about duty and declined the flask, but Wallace had a swig, and when the talk turned to hunting, Alexa relaxed and settled back against the wall.

"Call 'em Grey Ghosts," Scratch said, sipping again. "Hardest NZ deer to hunt." He bumped his knee against Alexa, offering the flask. "The deer are imported from New Hampshire."

"Really?" One of New Zealand's wonders was that it had no indigenous land mammals. She took another swallow and nudged away from Scratch's thigh.

"It's Stewart Island, more than the species," Stephen said. "You can't get your bearings. Everything looks the same: flat, dense, low canopy, fern-covered. Hard to tell a deer from a tree."

"Best way to hunt is on your knees," Scratch said. "Slows you down."

"Just find a clearing and wait nine hours. That's the way to do it," Wallace said. "The ghosts are curious and come out eventually. One time…"

Scratch's thigh pressed against Alexa's, making her start. She must have drifted off. Standing quickly, she banged her head on a shelf.

Scratch laughed. Her cheeks flamed. "I'm turning in, gentlemen."

Sleep was impossible with Scratch on top—and sometime during the long night, maybe 1:00 or 2:00 a.m., a voice called for help. She didn't know whether it was real or a nightmare.

Chapter Six

Alexa clawed at her ankles under the crinkly space blanket as birds sang awake one by one. Stephen had told her there were 145 different bird species on the island. Reciting the funny names distracted her from her itches: kakariki, kereru, kakapo. Loud squawking made her sit up.

"Bloody nora, I'm coming." In gray light, a large form lurched from a bunk, took three giant steps to the table, grabbed the radio like a chicken neck. "Sergeant Wallace here."

"It's Constable Kopae, Senior," a voice responded.

"What is it?"

Muscular calves and calloused feet blocked Alexa's view. Scratch was dangling his legs from the top bunk. She scooted past his bare limbs and stood.

"Repeat," Wallace said into the radio.

Static filled the hut. "… a bloke, ripped apart, one leg…"

The radio went silent.

"Kopae!" Wallace shook the radio.

Static. "…on the shore. Jeannette's dog, Nanu, found him…"

"Dead?"

"Yes, sir."

A chill ran down Alexa's spine.

"Where?"

"Ringaringa Beach."

"Who?"

"...can't tell." Panic in the gargle. "People gawking..."

The cabin door creaked open and Stephen entered. "What's happening?"

Wallace held up a hand. "Don't touch the body. Close the bathing areas. Send a copter to Hellfire Pass. I'll be on scene in an hour." He clicked the radio off and studied his watch.

Scratch hopped down and pulled pants over his shorts. "Shark attack?"

Wallace's face had blanched. "A white death."

"The town will hang the chummers now," Scratch said. "A big-ass shark harassed me out near the Beak. Came right up, turned sideways, looked me over. Jesus—those teeth."

Stephen swept the hair out of his eyes. "I knew this would happen," he said almost joyfully. "I'll notify DOC headquarters."

On her way to the loo, Alexa was startled to see the body bag. She had forgotten why she was here. When she returned, Wallace told the rangers to take King's remains to the beach as planned. "Get him to the clinic." He turned to Alexa. "You come with me."

"But..."

"You'll have time for King later."

One of her duties as roving forensic was medical examiner. She could help the islanders by determining cause of death, not that it would be hard if Constable Kopae was accurate. But a shark attack was hard to wrap her head around. She packed up, zipped up, laced up, and caloried up via a power bar Stephen handed her—he was a thoughtful guy—and followed Wallace into the dawn woods.

Alexa kept quiet as they trudged over moss and mud and down through a ravine, muck making each step a challenge. She was aware the sergeant had much on his mind. Like the chief of police in *Jaws*, what was his name? Martin Brody had had to close the beach, deal with the public, with the fishermen, with the press, with the remains.

A low-hanging branch snagged her hair. "Dammit." What was in store? Visualizing a shark-ravaged body gave Alexa shivers as she jerked her hair free.

Three years ago she had entered a master's program in forensic odontology. Teeth are the most resilient part of the human body and sometimes the only body part left. Since earning the second master's degree, she had ID'ed several bodies using dentals—most recently confirming the identification of the mud-pot body in Rotorua. Her new area of expertise had led to the fellowship in Auckland and—one bite leads to another—to Stewart Island.

She pulled the zipper of the orange suit higher. Coffee. She craved coffee. Yesterday's niggling caffeine headache was now throwing a tantrum. She skirted a puddle and thought back to the lecture on shark bites. A shark expert from Florida was the guest lecturer. Bearded, salt-bleached hair, zeal lighting his eyes.

He had captivated Alexa and her odontology cohort with his "dirty bite" lecture. The memory flooded back. Virulent bacteria is transferred from sharks' teeth to humans through bites. Imagine surviving a shark attack, the scientist said, but having to be hospitalized for weeks because of infection. Doctors don't know what strain of bacteria it is, so they don't know what antibiotic works.

Her heart rate increased as she recalled that lecture in Bostian Hall. Dr. Dirty Bite and his researchers had set out to identify the strain. They'd manhandled sharks in the Florida surf and swabbed their mouths. Had the research with the unwilling marine participants led to determining what antibiotic worked?

But infection would not be a concern in this case.

Okay.

Dr. Dirty Bite had also explained how to identify the type and size of a shark through bite marks. She recalled graphic slides, a thigh with a half-moon of missing flesh, an amputated arm, gashes on a foot. Something about circumference and upper and lower jaw.

Wallace stopped. "What day is it?"

Alexa had to think. Friday? No. Friday was two days ago. "Sunday."

"Bloody hell. We have a cruise ship coming in. Once a week, weather permitting."

The helicopter liftoff felt like riding in an elevator. Alexa clutched the vinyl seat for twenty deafening minutes until they landed back at Ryan's Creek.

As they climbed out, the pilot yelled to Wallace that he was on his way to Invercargill to pick up Kana Duffy.

"From *Shark Shadow*? Who called that guy in?"

"Yeah, nah. Don't know, Sarge."

Alexa and Wallace watched the copter lift off and shrink to a gleaming toy buzzing below the stratus clouds. The airport was a ghost town.

Wallace marched to his SUV. Alexa followed, lugging the kit and backpack. Sinking gratefully into the front seat, she fished out her phone. Her boss needed to know about the second body. No signal. This island was giving her the creeps. She belted up as Wallace started the engine. "Was there a witness to the attack?"

"I don't know." He whipped the SUV around and accelerated down the lonely road while checking his own phone. "Shite," he said, throwing it into the cup holder.

"How long have you had shark cage diving on the island?"

Wallace rubbed his bristly chin. "We have two operations. They opened seven or eight years ago. Stewart Island White Dive out of Golden Bay Wharf and Shark Encounter out of Halfmoon Bay."

"What makes you think the attack is connected to cage diving?"

"The operators say they aren't changing sharks' behavior, but then they drop bait right offshore—our sharks like shallow water—and when the whites come running, they dangle tourists like lollies in front of a three-year-old. Most locals won't get in the water anymore, won't let their kids go swimming. Pāua divers are scared, but they still have to make a living."

"Pāua?"

"Abalone. Shellfish, eh. It's a way to make a living around here—divers sell pāua for food, the shell for art. They free-dive—no air tanks allowed. They pry the pāua off underwater rocks. Hell, might be a bloody pāua diver dead on the beach. Ringaringa is a popular spot. Jesus. I hope it's not Hal." Wallace accelerated as they approached a curve.

She had to ask.

"Hal is my neighbor Ann's lad. A twenty-something torn between leaving the island and staying. He ekes out a living pāua-diving. Ann has begged him to stop."

They were passing through the village. Two little boys in gum boots and a woman pushing a stroller walked down the middle of the street. "All right, Lydia," Wallace said under his breath and tapped the horn to get them to move over.

They drove past the little red-roofed chapel restaurant. At the next corner a man was hanging holiday lights round the Stewart Island gift shop window. "Are there lots of shark attacks in New Zealand?"

"Had a rash of them in the sixties. Since then, a few here, a few there. A white killed a surfer at Muriwai on the North Island two years ago. When the lifesavers reached him, the shark still had the bloke in its jaws, thrashing about. They bashed the shark with oars to get it to release."

It sounded like *Moby Dick* to Alexa.

Wallace pulled onto a grassy bank in front of a one-story white cottage, the windows trimmed in red. "Quick stop. I won't be a minute." He left the motor running and hustled to the front door.

She watched as he let himself in and then appeared through a large kitchen window. Wallace swung a child up in the air, a little girl, and then talked, gesturing with his hands, to a sturdy woman in a robe. His wife. Wallace was a family man. The scene tugged at Alexa's heart. *There's probably a dog, too.* The sergeant picked up a landline receiver hanging on the wall. The wife/woman vanished from the kitchen and the next second was striding to the car.

Alexa got out, a tad wary. "Hello."

"I'm Nina, Kipper's wife." She belted her robe more tightly. "Would you like a coffee or to freshen up?"

"I'm Alexa Glock. I'd love a coffee, but we're in a hurry."

"No worries, I have a full pot." Nina assessed Alexa with her pale blue eyes. "I'm straight up in shock."

Alexa nodded.

"Kipper won't tell me who it is."

"He doesn't know."

Wallace met them at the door with a mug in his hand. "Called headquarters in Invercargill. Filled 'em in. Let's go." He had removed the orange jumpsuit and added a police hat to his uniform.

"That coffee is for Miss Glock, right?" Nina said.

Wallace blushed and handed the mug to Alexa. "Er, hope you like it white."

Nina disappeared and returned with another mug for her husband.

"Daddy!" The little girl, all reddish curls and pink cheeks, flew out the door and clomped onto his leg. Behind her, a spotted dog barked.

"Careful, Shelly belly, I have a hot drink." Wallace freed his leg, pecked his wife's cheek, and ushered Alexa toward the car. His coffee sloshed as he looked at her. "I had to make sure they wouldn't go in the water."

The news had carved each middle-aged wrinkle in his pale face deeper. "My lad—he's nine—has rowing club."

"I get it." She did. The attack affected the entire community.

She gulped the milky coffee as woodland swallowed village. The one-lane blacktop climbed and curved past modest homes and tall fern trees, past inlets of choppy waves and small boats, past penguin crossing and kiwi crossing signs, past precipitous drops and hilly berms. Only once did they pass another car.

"Who will come from Invercargill?" she asked.

"I told them you're here. Volunteer rangers are en route to search for King's scene of death, and the higher-ups are locating a DI to take over the King case, eh. I'll have it up to here"—Wallace touched his checked-banded cap—"with the shark business."

Alexa knew in police hierarchy, a sergeant wouldn't head a suspicious death investigation.

They turned left on a thinner road. An arrow pointed to Ringaringa Heights Golf Course. Wallace pulled into a gravel lot. A Stewart Island Fire Brigade truck and ambulance took up most of the lot. Before Wallace could turn the car off, another car pulled in.

"Shite. Probably the press," he said.

Chapter Seven

The wind grabbed the car door. Alexa struggled to shut it as the crime kit slipped off her shoulder. Heart hammering, she followed Wallace across the parking lot to a steep vantage point overlooking a small beach bookended with cliffs. She saw a low and lumpy island offshore. A narrow path, swallowed by woods, headed downward. Alexa assumed it led to the beach. She stood with Wallace.

There were five bystanders—one a child—plus a cop on the beach. A dog gamboled along the wave-break, barking at gulls. "It should be leashed," Alexa said.

Past heaps of kelp, a caution ribbon encircled a tarp. She presumed the tarp covered the body.

The radio squawked. Wallace answered.

"Sergeant, where are you? The tide is turning."

Alexa recognized Officer Kopae's voice.

"I'm here," Wallace replied.

She watched the cop on the beach turn and look up.

Wallace waved. "Send someone up to secure the entrance," he said. He stuck the radio back in his belt pouch and walked to the head of the trail.

A car door slammed. Alexa turned to see a woman careening toward them. She didn't look like a member of the press.

"Kipper! Is it Hal?"

Wallace took the woman's arm. "Ann, I don't know who it is."

The neighbor, Alexa deduced, the one who had begged her son to stop pāua diving.

Raven hair whipped the woman's face as she pushed past him. Wallace tightened his grip. "You have to wait here. When did you last see him?"

"For tea. Friday." Her voice was ragged.

"Have you called him?"

"There's not been service!" She craned past Wallace's shoulder to see the beach. Shrubs and trees blocked the view.

"Try your phone again. From the lot." Wallace let go of her arm and squeezed her shoulder. "I'll let you know who it is as soon as I can."

A large man emerged from a curve in the path, huffing. A patch on his blue jacket read *Oban Volunteer Fire Brigade*.

Wallace pointed at him. "Dan will stay with you."

Alexa hurried after Wallace, her foot slipping on wet leaves. She grabbed a scraggly branch to keep from landing on her ass, launching a snowstorm of tiny white flowers. The path tunneled through more white blossoms and shiny greenery. Down and around a curve, the trees blocked sound and wind and view. *A calm before the storm*, Alexa thought, brushing a petal from her shoulder. After another steep turn, an arbor of branches framed the sea. She took a deep breath, scanned for sea lions, and walked through.

Constable Kopae was running toward Wallace as the bystanders watched. One of them, another man in a blue jacket, walked over to Alexa. "Jason Weaver. Oban fire chief."

"I'm Alexa Glock, forensic investigator from Auckland."

The unleashed dog sprinted straight at Alexa and stuck its sandy nose in her crotch. She kneed it.

"Nanu, come," its owner called.

"That dog needs to be leashed," Alexa shouted.

The owner, a fit woman in her late fifties, walked over and clipped the dog onto a lead. She was dressed in waterproof jacket, rain pants, running shoes. A ponytail poked out of her ball cap.

"This is Julie Stokely," Weaver said. "She found the body."

"Nanu found him," the woman corrected.

"Did you see the attack?"

"No, no. The body was washed up. I was taking my sunrise walk. My crib is there." She pointed to the right of the cliff path where a lone cottage nested in the trees. "Nanu started barking at the tide mark and I followed him."

The woman studied Alexa. "We tried to get them to stop cage diving. No one listened because our island is small and far away. This didn't have to happen."

"Yes, I see." Alexa wondered who *them* was. "What time was it?"

"Just after six. Barely light."

"Sergeant Wallace will want your statement. Who are those people?" Alexa nudged her head toward a man and boy staring at the surf.

"My son and grandson. They're visiting," Julie said. "Tony didn't want me coming back alone to wait for the police."

Alexa turned to the fire chief. "What time did you arrive?"

The fire chief checked his notebook. "We're all just volunteer, eh. Took me a bit after I got the call, I live in the wops, yeah? Arrived on scene at 7:00, pronounced the bloke dead at 7:06, covered him up."

"Thanks for that." Preserving a victim's dignity was important. "Make sure to send me your notes." Alexa set the kit down by a cluster of brilliant green kelp and dug business cards out of the crime kit pocket. "Were either of you able to ID him?"

Julie grimaced.

"Not a chance," the volunteer fire chief said. Alexa handed a card to each of them and then pulled on gloves, readied the camera, and willed her hands to stop shaking. "I'll have a look." Her every sense stood out like the hair on her neck. The sand squelched beneath her boots. She stepped on something that popped. A kelp bubble. Salt spray tossed from breaking surf landed on her tongue, explosive and gritty. Her nose pricked, caught a scent—something fishy and—dead.

Alexa ducked under the caution tape and approached slowly. Sand blew into her eyes as she scoured the ground, noting two sets of footprints stopping short of the decedent, and paw prints which didn't, all of which she photographed. They would soon be washed away. The body—when she removed the tarp—lay on a pile of kelp.

There was no kelp on North Carolina beaches. She had asked Mary about it. "It grows in cold water, close to shore," she'd said.

Her first impression of the remains was that of a mutilated seal. The torso, where not gashed or truncated, was encased in tattered nylon or polyester. There were no drag marks; the tide had delivered this gift on a bed of kelp. Maybe it was Ann's son. Had Hal seen a fin knifing toward him? Or had he been attacked from below, a sudden strike, a crimson bloom, and then dragged off to hell? The burn scars across her back tightened like a vise. She shook her head to erase the image and took stock of the victim's extremities. The head, in profile, was barely recognizable. Clumps of black hair interspersed with deep raking lacerations that exposed the skull. A hole gaped where the ear had been, water and body fluid pooled in the cavity. The eye was wide open, dull brown, gazing indifferently at the right hand balled inches away. Stubble near the torn jaw confirmed he was male. She moved to the limbs. The left arm ended in a mangled pulp at the elbow joint. Flies investigated strips of flesh and exposed humerus. A hunk of right forearm had been torn away and the right hand was clenched. Alexa shooed the flies away and looked at the left leg. Pants were tattered, and the leg ended at the ankle, the foot missing. The right leg ended in a purple stump at the thigh. Fatty tissue dangled like crab bait.

Jesus. A freaking savage did this.

Retching made her turn. Wallace was nearby, bending over. The sound made Alexa gag. She swallowed back acidic bile and focused on the body. What she had thought was kelp coiling below the abdomen were grayish-purple intestines leaking out of a massive crescent-shaped hole from the victim's waist. More bile flooded her throat and she had to fight hard not to vomit. One-third of the man's body had been torn away. She closed her eyes to regain focus.

Wallace joined her. "Sorry 'bout that."

"No judging," Alexa said. Lapping waves were seeping, creeping closer to the body. She watched a small shorebird run along the water's edge, taking solace from its sprightly zigs and zags, its feathered optimism that life continues. "How much time do we have with the tide?"

"Fifteen, twenty minutes."

The examination would need to be quick. Cause and time of death were her main goals. Massive tissue and blood loss, from the looks of it, for cause, and time of death? She looked for a watch on the victim's wrist. There was only one wrist left, and no watch—rarely was TOD that simple. Body temperature may have been influenced by water temperature. She gently lifted the man's right arm, noting rigor mortis was present. The man had been dead anywhere from six to forty-eight hours. It was a start, but she wondered how much of that time he'd been immersed or beached. Cold water would delay rigor mortis, so she guessed he had been beached for at least six hours. Probably washed up during the night.

She backed up and looked around, at the beach, at the bystanders watching, at the expanse of Pacific hiding the monster responsible for this carnage. She photographed the body from different angles. "Sketch the scene, please," she told Constable Kopae, who had joined them. A sketch would provide depth of field that photos couldn't.

Wallace interrupted. "Can you tell if the bloke was Māori?"

She could not tell by the man's skin tone. Cessation of capillary circulation—pallor mortis—had robbed him of color. The patch of chest poking through shreds of material was almost translucent. Alexa set the camera aside and brushed a clump of fine dark hair from the man's forehead, thinking of how a mother feels for fever, and gently turned the skull for frontal view. She gagged again, not expecting severe trauma to the face. The second eye was gone; the sandy hole leaked seawater and membrane. A face no mother should ever witness. "I can't tell by skin color. He has dark hair and brown eyes. Eye."

"Come on, she's up there waiting, thinks it's her boy," Wallace begged. "What else can you give me?"

"Does Hal have tattoos?"

"I don't know."

"Find out. Ask how tall he is, how much he weighs." A second material, royal blue, poked through the tattered pants in the groin area. Maybe a swimsuit, Alexa deduced. "And ask what color his swim trunks are. I need to get on with the examination."

Wallace sighed and looked toward the cliff.

"I'll go if you like," Constable Kopae said.

Wallace nodded and took the sketch pad.

Alexa knew this secluded beach was not the primary scene of death and looked again at the ocean. "Do pāua divers use boats, or do they wade in?"

"Both." Wallace added something to the sketch and then flipped the pad closed. "If it's a boat, it's usually small. Hal used a RIB."

Her expression conveyed her ignorance.

"Rigid inflatable raft."

"Get a search going for the, ah, RIB. Plus I'll need the water temp and tide information."

"On it." He stepped away to speak in the radio.

She took more photos, steadily closing in. Pictures were imperative since the scene would soon be underwater. Then she took rough measurements of the body—the man was an inch under six feet and weighed, she assessed from the subcutaneous fat globules around the stomach wound, 180 to 190 pounds. She measured the crescent-shaped bite, fighting the urge to return the man's mangled intestines to their rightful place. Nineteen inches across. This single bite would have caused rapid blood loss. A glint caught her attention. She leaned in, probing nimbly, lightly. Embedded in the bite was a triangular tooth. She extracted it, held it up, turned it.

Five centimeters at the base. Serration along the edges. Glossy.

An explosion of thwapping cut her reverence.

A helicopter plunged from the sky and hovered just where the waves crested, graceless as a pelican fixing to dive, the *thwap thwap thwap* deafening.

"Shite." Wallace waved his hands.

The copter pitched forward, zooming so close that sand blew. "For God's sake," Alexa screamed, bending low to protect the body. When she glared up, the pilot and a passenger nodded through the bug-eyed windows, and then the ugly bird backed up and off.

"Bollocks. That will be all over the internet before they land," Wallace said.

Alexa slipped the tooth in an evidence bag. Ten more minutes, max, until the body had to be moved. She looked at the decedent's fist, thought about unclenching it and taking fingernail scrapings, but there wasn't time. She secured a bag over it instead.

The other hand, and both feet, didn't need bagging. They were missing. Did that mean they were in the shark's stomach? Would there be a bloodthirsty shark hunt like in *Jaws*? Or would they wash ashore separately? What if Nanu had run around the beach with an arm in his mouth? Her mind raced. They would have to search the shoreline.

Officer Kopae ran up, her face red. *"Unaunhi."* She bent over, breathing hard. "A band of fish scales around his wrist."

Alexa had no idea what Kopae was talking about.

"The tattoo. Hal has a band around his left wrist."

"The left wrist is…missing. How tall is he?"

"Tall. Almost 180. He weighs eighty or so kilos. She doesn't know what color trunks." Kopae's wide young face was strained.

Alexa's mind blanked. As a scientist, she was accustomed to the metric system, but feet, inches, and pounds were still her first language. Deep breath. Okay. One inch equals 2.54 centimeters. One hundred eighty centimeters was almost six feet. "The height matches."

Kopae looked at the ravaged body and then at the hillside parking lot. Alexa followed her gaze to the silhouette of a woman, arms akimbo, a statue, on the rim. Wallace kicked sand.

"Wait," Alexa said. "Wouldn't her son have been wearing a wetsuit? This doesn't look like a wetsuit," she said, motioning to the body.

Kopae took off toward the woman again, her step lighter.

Five minutes. That was all the time left. Uneasy that her back was to the sea, she collected hair samples, body fluids, body temperature, and bundled the intestines close to the body, securing them with super-stick evidence tape. The waves lapped and hissed. She nodded at Wallace. "You can move him." Her final photos would be of the indentation left by the body before the waves erased it as if nothing but bird prints and sandcastles had happened. The sun was higher and she needed to switch to a different aperture. She looked at the ocean and her mouth dropped. A cruise ship eclipsed the offshore island.

Wallace summoned the fire chief and together they clumsily lifted the asymmetrical remains onto a black bag, tucked body parts in, and zipped death out of sight. The sparkling ocean mocked the sad funeral procession to the parking lot.

Chapter Eight

"I'll drop you at the health center," Wallace said as they followed the ambulance past the golf course. "King will be dropped off later."

The hunter. He has a family, people who are in agony not knowing if he's alive. "So I'll be pulling double duty. Do you have a doctor on the island?"

"Yeah nah. Doc retired five years ago. We have telemedicine and a couple of nurse practitioners, Joan and Matt."

"We'll need an autopsy on King because his death is suspicious. Who will perform it?"

"Bloke at Southland Hospital in Invercargill."

Alexa looked down, shocked to see she was still wearing disposable gloves. She slipped them off inside out and laid them across her orange thigh, limp and unprofessional. They were driving through the village now, tailing the ambulance. The cruise ship—a floating Gulliver—had made its way to the Lilliputian harbor.

Wallace noticed it too. "I've got to contact the activities director. A lot of island excursions involve the water, including cage diving. Gonna have to cancel the lot of them."

Alexa had never been on a cruise; she imagined a swarm of fat locusts disembarking and devouring a path through Oban. How did the island infrastructure handle the influx?

"Eh. I'll leave you here," Wallace said, pulling in front of Stewart Island Medical Centre.

"Thanks. I'll check in with you later." She stuffed the gloves in the pocket of the SAR suit—she felt like she had been wearing orange forever—and gathered the backpack and crime kit.

The center was locked. Alexa checked the sign: *Open Mon–Sat, 10:00 a.m.–12:30 p.m.* For real? Today was Sunday. Closed.

The volunteer firefighter, Dan, who had driven the ambulance, joined her on the porch. "I called Joan. She'll be right over." He rubbed his buzzed head and lowered his substantial self onto the steps with a grunt.

Alexa left her stuff by the door and sat as well, unzipped the SAR suit, and scratched her bug bites. Her night of tossing and turning under Scratch seemed a month ago. A burst of gray-green bird swooped from a tree and landed proprietorially on the porch railing. Large, with scaly claws and red breast, it studied Alexa as it scrabbled closer and squawked like Wallace's radio.

"Jeez. Is that a parrot?"

"A kaka. Watch it or he'll try to get in your kit."

"I thought a kaka was a canoe."

Dan laughed. "That's *waka*."

"I thought *that* was a war dance."

"That's *haka*."

"What the faka?"

They laughed together. The laughter felt good, a release, and then bad, a disrespect. She startled as a car door slammed, causing the kaka to fly off. A middle-aged woman, scraggly brown hair brushing her shoulders, rushed over. "Hello, Dan. Was that Wallace driving off?"

The ambulance driver nodded. "Known Kip since kindie." Joan unlocked the clinic door with shaking hands and introduced herself. "Joan Soucie, nurse practitioner."

"I'm Alexa Glock, from Forensic Service Center in Auckland."

Joan turned to Dan, her brown eyes wide through her wire frames. "Do you know who he is?"

"No. Can you help me haul him in?"

Joan nodded gravely. Her skin was pale. Alexa didn't know if this was normal or because of the grave task. The islanders carried the body bag by the corner handholds while Alexa held the door. "Put him in exam room one," Joan directed.

The clinic had a waiting area, two exam rooms, and an office. When Alexa spotted the restroom, she excused herself. After stepping out of the jumpsuit and leaving it in an orange puddle, she used the toilet, scrubbed her face and hands, and dug dirt and sand— remnants of jungle and beach—from her nails. As she studied her appearance in the mirror—windburned cheeks and disheveled hair—she considered the opportunity this first "away case" presented: A mere handful of people in the world have the opportunity to examine shark maul victims. Analyze the bite marks. Draw conclusions. Could she write an article about it? The *Journal of Oral Pathology* might be interested. The prestige of publication would help her secure a job when she returned to the States.

Later, of course.

She abandoned her reflection and bent, stretching, touching her toes and scratching the welts on her ankle—nasty and inflamed. Stretching eased the tightness of her back scars. Upside down in an upside down antipodean world. The blood rushed to her head. Joan was in pale pink scrubs and pulling the exam door shut when Alexa reappeared. "Dan's left. I...I've never seen..." Her words stumbled, ceased, and her shoulders sagged.

"I know. The body is in terrible condition."

"We...we placed it—him—on the exam table. Should I..." The nurse covered her mouth with a gloved hand as if she was going to be sick, or cough, or wanted to restrain the words behind her lips. Then she straightened. "Should I wash the body?"

Alexa remembered that clenched fist. "No. Not yet. I need to examine him more closely first."

They heard a rap, and then the door flung open. "Got here as fast as I could," a bearded man announced, setting down a leather duffel. Gold hair tumbled from his ball cap.

"Oi." Joan brought her hand back to her mouth. "Shack Man."

"Shack Man?" Alexa asked.

"Kana Duffy." The man smiled like sunshine. "I prefer shark biologist."

"I'm the island nurse." Facial pigment flooded back into Joan's wan cheeks. "I watched you on *Nightmares of the Deep*."

"I resuscitated a three-meter tiger shark on that show," he bragged.

"Why would you do that?" Alexa snapped. She did not know squat about any Shack Man, but she knew mouth-to-mouthing a shark was crazy.

"Why would you not?" Duffy's eyes were sea-glass green. "Ratbag fishermen left it for dead. Who are you?"

"Forensic investigator from Auckland." She figured he must be the guy the helicopter pilot had mentioned. "Why are you here?"

"He's famous," Joan gushed, stashing her glasses into her smock pocket. "He's been all over the world studying sharks and has his own telly program, *Shark Shadow*."

"Yes, terrific, but why are you here now?"

"I've been called in to assess the situation. To figure out what happened. And to direct a plan of action. This incident is going to set shark conservation back twenty years."

"Who requested your services?" Lack of sleep. Excitement. Exertion. They honed her tongue.

Duffy took the ball cap off and swiped his gilded bangs to the side. "Southland DOC." He pointed to the ORSC logo on his cap. "I'm with Oceans Research Shark Conservation. If we have to cull the shark, I can identify which one it is so innocent great whites aren't slaughtered."

Alexa thought "innocent" and "great white" did not belong in the same sentence.

"Would you mind if I got a selfie? For my son?" Joan interrupted.

"Joan—does the clinic have an X-ray machine?" Alexa snapped.

"Yes. A portable."

"I'll check in with Sergeant Wallace while you fetch it." Alexa left Joan tittering and entered the spare exam room. She guessed this was where they'd put the hunter's body when he arrived. One more victim, and there would be no room in the inn.

Her phone had bars for the first time in twenty-four hours, and Wallace answered promptly.

"I was about to call," he said. "A retired pathologist from *Sequin of the Seas* has offered to conduct the hunter's autopsy."

"From what?"

"The cruise ship in the harbor. *Sequin of the Seas*. He's a passenger. He'll arrive at 1:00."

Alexa frowned and looked around at the exam bed, stool, chair, wall cabinets, built-in desk with computer station, and sink. She was tempted to open the cabinets. "Is the health center equipped to handle an autopsy? Does it have the right instruments?"

"I don't know. What instruments?"

She thought fast. "Head block, bone saw, skull chisels." She opened a cabinet and inventoried paper gowns, paper covers, disposable gloves, cotton balls, and tongue depressors. At least they wouldn't need an organ scale since King's had decayed.

"Maybe this bloke carries his own."

She explained the reason for her call. "Is this Duffy man legit?"

"Department of Conservation have requested his services. He's got a PhD in sharks or some such and hosts a TV program. My wife loves the show. Or maybe she loves him." Wallace laughed, and then his voice went serious again. "They need an expert to figure out if we have an imminent threat to water users. As if we don't know, eh? What?" Wallace spoke to someone else. "Sorry about that. Press are calling, photographers, passengers. It's a bloody 'mare."

"No sign of King yet," Alexa said.

"We only have one ambulance. Dan is en route to meet

body number two at the airport. Gotta go," Wallace said and cut the line.

A shrill voice made her jump as she left the room. The mother. Hal's mother was standing in the waiting area. Alexa took a deep breath and barreled forward. "Hello. I'll be examining the victim. My first step will..."

"I want to see if it's my son," Ann screeched, looking toward the closed door of the second exam room.

Alexa tried to catch the woman's eye. "We have not been able to identify the remains, the victim. It might not be Hal." She stopped, worried giving the woman hope might backfire. "I'll take dental X-rays. Did your son receive dental care?"

"Let me see him. Please." Her eyes were crazed with fear.

"Ann," Joan said, gently tugging her arm. "Come with me. Let's call Dr. Keen's office. He's the one who made the oral care school visits. I'll make you a cuppa. Come, luv."

"He promised me he'd stop diving. Too many sharks coming close to shore. The cagers..."

Joan led her away. "I'll wheel in the X-ray machine," she said over her shoulder.

The situation was veering out of control. Perhaps already was. She entered the exam room and pulled on gloves as Duffy followed and closed the door. "Who is that woman?" he asked.

"A local. Her son is a pāua diver who's missing. She thinks," Alexa gestured toward the body, "it might be him."

"White sharks have always been here, feeding on the fur seals," Duffy said quietly, pulling gloves on. "Stewart Island is a hotbed. There's always been risk for divers."

She wasn't going to debate with Pretty Boy, didn't know whether he was for or against cage diving. She didn't know where she stood either. She was here to do a job but decided to give the dog a bone and removed a clear evidence bag from the crime kit, dangling it like a fish lure. "Is this tooth from a great white?"

Duffy lunged for the bait. "Carcharodon carcharias." He removed the tooth without asking and turned it this way, that way. "Broadly triangular." He ran a finger over the edges. "Serrated for tearing off chunks of flesh." He whistled. "This was from a massive shark. Probably male. The population of whites here is predominately male."

Joan and Dan, the ambulance driver, had done a professional job. They had removed the decedent from the bag, placed him on an exam bed, and covered him with a paper blanket. A briny and fruity odor had breached the paper barrier. Alexa lifted the cover, exposing the head, and recoiled, even though she had already witnessed the damage.

Duffy came close. "Mother of God." Against the white sheet, the plundered eye socket gaped like violent art. "The shark clamped the head in his jaws," Duffy said, his voice so close Alexa could feel warm puffs. "It's called the killing bite. Then comes the lateral head-shake, which ruptures the neck. It's broken, yeah?"

She reached her hands under the paper cover and gently manipulated the spinal cord. Rag doll snapped, the image of a shark with a man's head clamped in its jaws, body whipping back and forth, flashed in her mind. The floor undulated. She grabbed the exam bed to keep from crumpling.

"Take deep breaths," Duffy commanded.

The memory of fainting during her first autopsy flooded back. "I know what to do," she snapped. Head down. Deep breath in, hold, slow exhale. Repeat. She did this until the floor stabilized.

Joan wheeled in the adjustable-arm X-ray machine. "Ann is speaking with Hal Bennett's dentist in Invercargill. We'll have him fax the records."

"Good. Thank you." Alexa had regained her equilibrium and positioned the arm of the machine for a frontal. They'd have post-mortem dental X-rays within seconds. Teeth wear and tear, size, shape, and dental work glowing in ghostly black, gray, and white. Point, aim—"Step behind the screen," she told Duffy—shoot.

She took a side view, a close-up, and one that would include the neck, and then left Duffy and the body to find Joan. A friend of Ann's had arrived and was sitting with her in the waiting area, both with cups of tea, untouched, on the side table. Ann began to rise, but Alexa shook her head.

She and Joan studied the X-rays together. Nothing like a chipped tooth or gold inlay stood out. Couple cavities, one impacted wisdom tooth, the other three established.

"I'm still waiting on the fax," Joan said. "I'll let you know when it comes in."

Alexa hoped the decedent wouldn't be Hal and wheeled around. Time to find out what the clenched fist might reveal. When she returned to the exam room, she found the victim uncovered and Duffy leaning over it, his gloved hand probing the amputated elbow. "What are you doing? Step back," Alexa commanded.

Duffy turned toward her, his face pale and his golden eyebrows scrunched together. Another shark tooth gleamed between his fingers.

"What's wrong?"

"This man was ripped apart by multiple whites."

"A pack of sharks attacked him?" The thought was horrifying.

Duffy nodded. "This tooth was embedded in the elbow area. It's smaller than the tooth you found, so it's from a different shark." Duffy shook the tooth. "And look here." He pointed to the large chunk missing from the left calf. "This bite mark is even smaller. See how the… "

"But I thought great white sharks hunted alone."

His authority reasserted itself. "Not always. We've spotted up to eight whites in one area. Something, like a seal colony, attracts them."

Alexa tried to connect the nightmarish remains on the table with caging. "When people go cage diving, do they ever see more than one great white at a time?"

"Sure. Whether they were already in the same area, or brought together by the fish guts the cagers ladle or pump into the water. They're triggering a response from any shark in the vicinity. But the chum, by DOC code, must be finely minced so that the sharks can't feed on it. It attracts them and doesn't provide payoff."

"Jeez. Would that get them all riled up to attack?"

"Sure. Sharks bite for six main reasons: predation, aggression, defense, mating, hierarchy, and curiosity. This looks like predation or aggression. The press will run with this. Blame it on the sharks."

"Shouldn't they?"

"Not if the sharks were set up."

Alexa began measuring bite marks. After talking to Wallace, she had located a scientific article titled "Determining shark size from forensic analysis of bite damage." It had to do with bite circumference and interdental distance, or IDD.

"I'll be able to give you type and size shark that inflicted this bite," she told Duffy, pointing to the man's side.

"No worries. I can tell it was a large white."

She hid her disappointment. "Why don't you document how many different sharks you suspect were involved?"

"Sounds like a plan."

Duffy's movements were lithe and underwater-fluid as he glided around the body. Alexa watched while a grim movie flickered in her head: multiple sharks attacking a man from different angles. A horror movie. She took a deep breath and returned to her measurements. She'd feed the data into the computer later. Come up with a *Wanted* poster of the shark.

Finished with bite marks, she removed the bag covering the decedent's remaining hand and strained to break the rigor stiffness of the clenched fist. *Let me read your fortune.* She unfurled the palm, wincing as contracted muscles—the result of the coagulation of proteins—fought back and then relinquished with a sickening pop.

"Your lifeline is short," she whispered.

Duffy froze. "What?"

"Talking to myself." She bent forward, her attention lured by a bright strand. A blue fiber was embedded in the fingernail of his remaining index finger. Before she removed it, she fetched her camera.

"What is it?" Duffy asked.

"I don't know." She took a couple photos and then extracted the fiber with tweezers, held it up to the light, a small braid, frayed at the tips, and then bagged it. Fiber analysis was almost as exciting as teeth. Cloth? Rope? Netting? The color indicated it was man-made. A stereomicroscope would help her examine it. She thought excitedly of the fully equipped lab at the Auckland Forensic Science Center as she set it in an evidence envelope and scraped a trace from beneath the nails. Had he scratched a shark? Fought back? His ring finger was missing the nail. She winced. A nail ripped off hurt like hell.

Idiot, she scolded herself.

His whole body was ripped apart. He didn't notice one fingernail. A smaller strand of the fiber was under the pinkie nail. Her curiosity was roused. Where had the fiber come from? She combed the tattered remnants of black material left on the torso for more blue fiber. A partial logo—half a circle, the tip of an arrow—stopped her. "Do you know this brand?" she asked Duffy.

He put his camera down and leaned in. "Sure, yeah, Swazi. Skux."

"Swazi Skux? That's a brand?"

The shark expert grinned. "American, eh? Swazi is the brand. Made here in New Zed. Skux means, well, flash. Swazi makes top-of-the-line rain gear. Maybe he's a fisherman, fell overboard."

"Why hasn't someone reported a missing person?" Alexa began removing pieces of the jacket with scissors when Joan ran in, her face flushed. Scissors midair, Alexa frowned. "What?"

"The fax came in." Joan looked at the body. "He's not Hal."

Chapter Nine

Alexa studied the side-by-side X-rays at Joan's desk as Ann watched from the adjacent waiting area. "You're right, it's a negative match," she told Joan. "Hal has a gap here, between the front teeth. The decedent doesn't. And the fillings don't match."

Joan yelled out the good news.

Ann covered her face with her hands and fell into the arms of her friend.

Alexa smiled, removed her gloves, and walked into the spare exam room—still no King—to let Wallace know. "The victim wasn't wearing a dive suit. It's a New Zealand–made raincoat and rain pants."

"Who can it be?" His voice sounded stunned. "A surf fisherman? Someone who fell out of a boat?" His voice was strained. "I'll check with DOC and missing persons in Invercargill."

It took ten more minutes to finish the exam. "I'm done," she told Duffy.

"Me too."

Her stomach growled as she labeled evidence bags, tidied up, washed up, and left the room.

"I'm glad for Ann," Joan said. "She still doesn't know where Hal is, but he's twenty years old. Why should she?"

"Can you distribute the X-rays to local dentists? See if you can get a match?"

"I'll send them to all the dentists in Bluff and Invercargill. What if it's a tourist? Someone on hollies?"

"One step at a time. I'll be back at 1:00 to meet the pathologist."

"For the body in the bush, right?"

A body in the bush is worth... No. A body in hand is worth... No. A bird... "I've got to eat." She visualized the fish and chips at her hotel.

Duffy appeared, making Joan go bug-eyed. "Did someone say food?"

"Miss Glock did," Joan said. Her lively eyes flicked from Alexa to Duffy. "You should eat before the restaurants are chocker with cruise ship passengers."

"I'll be grabbing a bite at my hotel," Alexa said irritably.

"That's cracking." The sunny smile was back on his face. "Island Inn?"

She had been planning to review her notes as she ate. "Yes."

"I'll report my findings to DOC first—save me a seat. Is there a desk I can use?" he asked.

"Oh, use mine," Joan gushed.

Alexa left the crime kit and mounting pile of evidence in the spare exam room. She would add more with the body of the hunter, and then she would write reports, draw conclusions, and release the findings and evidence to the Stewart Island Police Department.

She stuffed the orange SAR suit into Kopae's backpack, swung it on her shoulder, and—eager to leave death behind—stepped into bright sunshine. Where was she? From the porch, no kaka, she spotted her hotel overlooking the bay, two blocks' walk. A breeze-swept walk would clear her mind. The village sparkled; it was like seeing it for the first time. Fuchsia blossoms gleamed from a tree across the street, their vivid color yelling, "Welcome to the southern hemisphere. Summer in December!" A life-sized chess set stood on a grassy patch by the seaside. How had she missed it before? A toddler wrestled a pawn to a new square. A woman with spiky purple hair sat on a picnic table watching him.

Alexa nodded as she passed.

"G'day," the woman said. "Are you from the ship?"

"No. I'm…I'm staying on the island."

The woman's eyes hardened. "Here to dive with the sharks?"

"No way."

The toddler toddled over and grabbed his mom's leg. He studied Alexa with seal cub eyes.

The woman scooped him up and kissed his head. "Stay out of the water, right?"

"Right." Alexa waved and hurried on, eager for a shower and food. She passed a tiny grocery store, with wildlife cruise and fishing-trip flyers posted on the window, and a museum open 2:00 to 4:00 p.m. She was glad she didn't have to walk through the inn lobby—she looked, and probably smelled, a mess. She panicked until she located her key, side pouch of backpack, and opened Room Three.

Cozy and plain. Someone had cracked the window again—New Zealanders loved fresh air—and this time Alexa didn't mind. Whoever had done it—the maid or the proprietor, Constance—must have noticed she hadn't spent the night. She opened the mini-fridge, and there stood a tiny bottle of milk. All alone. *Like me.*

The warm spray of the shower was heaven, the water pressure excellent. It eased the sandfly itching of her ankle and the tension camped in her neck. She washed and conditioned her hair and then soaped her body. The rough skin of her back was secret: scars no one could see. Unless that someone was a man she chose to be intimate with. Jeb had said he didn't mind, hardly noticed. She thought of Bruce, of how it would feel to have his large hands explore her body, coming to a dead halt as they encountered the damage. What would her life have been like if the scars had marred her face or arms or legs? Wasn't their placement a blessing? Nonetheless, they were her albatross. She thought of the striking Calder-like mobile in the lobby of the Rotorua Police Department. Six large albatrosses floating slowly in an undulating circle, their triple-jointed wings rippling on invisible currents. Every time she had walked under it, her scars had tightened.

Alexa turned off the water.

It would take forever to dry her hair, so she combed the dark tangles into a wet ponytail. She cast her eyes at the pile of dirty clothes, which included the muddy SAR suit and Officer Kopae's fleece. She wrote a note asking for laundry service, added a few other items, and then checked her cell phone. Two bars—good, she would call Auckland and fill her boss in—and one message: "Bruce Horne here. I have another meeting in Auckland. Why don't I stop by afterwards and take you scootering? Give me a ring."

She laughed. Bruce would have to scoot without her. She was dangling off the most southern tip of New Zealand, away from any exploration of new territory.

She left a voicemail explaining she was working a case on Stewart Island. "How about a rain check?"

Private joke, rain check.

Satisfied, she called her boss, Dan Goddard, and let him know about the second body.

"Are you kidding? A shark attack?"

"It's true. There's an expert here who claims the victim was attacked by multiple sharks."

"It will be all over the tellie, internet. They have the right man—I mean woman—for the job with your odontology background. Was it a surfer?"

"The victim wasn't wearing a wetsuit. I'll keep you apprised. The victim had some fiber under his fingernail. Where is the closest lab for analysis?"

"Closest forensic lab would be in Dunedin."

Might as well be Timbuktu.

Chapter Ten

Duffy had nabbed a harbor-view table in the busy restaurant. Through the window as she approached, Alexa could see the sidewalk crowded with cruise passengers lined up like school-children. At the head of each line, a guide held a sign: *Kiwi Journey, Ulva Island Birding, Guided Tramp.*

Duffy noticed her gaze. "The cage diving group are on the piss in the bar."

What was on the piss? Despite the shower and fresh clothes, fatigue squeezed Alexa's brain. Calories would rev her up to face the hunter's remains. Her findings could launch a homicide investigation.

"Pulling your leg."

"What?"

"The cagers. They aren't drowning their sorrows. They're doing a scenic boat tour instead, if the local sergeant gives permission."

"His name is Sergeant Kipper Wallace." She imagined Wallace was tired too. "Would a boat tour be safe?"

"The boat is large enough. They'll be fine. I've already ordered, eh. I'm in a hurry."

Alexa flagged a waitress and ordered beer-battered blue cod and chips. "And an L&P. With ice." She had become fond of the lemon soda but not fond of the no-ice custom.

"Yours will be right up," the waitress told Duffy.

"Ta." He looked at Alexa. "There's a press briefing at the ferry terminal. My pronouncement is required."

The scene in *Jaws*, in which half of Amity launched small boats loaded with harpoons and dynamite, flashed in her mind. "What's your pronouncement?"

"Stay out of the water." Duffy's green eyes regarded her. "They also want my opinion on culling."

The opened top buttons of his oxford shirt revealed a tawny pelt. Three women at the next table stared. "What is culling?"

"Capturing and killing sharks. There were two white shark incidents off Queensland in September," he said. "Bite and flight. Probably different sharks each time. It's counterproductive for a white to feed on a human. They're energy maximizers and hunt prey with high blubber content. People are too low-fat."

Alexa thought of the massive sea lion charging her on the beach. "Do they eat sea lions?"

His eyes gleamed. "Ah, yeah. High in fat. And seals, squid, tuna."

"What did the authorities in Australia do about the attacks?"

"Incidents, not attacks. Watch your terminology."

"What does it matter?" Her nerves were frazzled.

"Shark language is biased," he explained. "Stalking, attacking, lurking, shark-infested. The media feed people's fears to sell advertising. "

"Mmm. Never thought of it that way."

"The Australian government knee-jerked and hired fishermen to bait drum rolls to catch sharks, yeah?" His eyes narrowed. "Snared over one hundred. Shot and killed eight big sharks, loads of small ones. When they shoot them, they throw them overboard to attract more sharks. There's no evidence they killed the right sharks or that it made swimmers safer, although whites are smart enough to leave the area for weeks. It's barbaric." He fiddled with his phone and handed it to Alexa. She studied the photo of a listless shark impaled on a big hook.

"Cage diving lures sharks to certain areas too, right?" She handed him back his phone.

"That's debatable."

"Really?"

"Cage operators claim different sharks come each time. And operators are meant to change locations regularly. And there are strict rules about attracting them."

"Such as?"

"The New Zealand Code of Practices says no mammalian-based products can be used as bait, and like I told you earlier, chum has to be finely minced so that it doesn't actually feed the sharks. Bait can't be pulled or dangled in front of the cage when divers are in it. Things like that."

It was a lot to digest. She had been lured to this restaurant by scent and would be pissed if no one fed her. "So sharks aren't actually being fed?"

"No. Just attracted by the scent."

"That hardly seems fair to the shark. Are you against cage diving?"

Duffy frowned. "I prefer free-diving with sharks, not hiding in a cage, but the answer is not simple. Ecotourism has lined local coffers, eh. People rely on that money, especially since the oyster blight closed the area aquafarms."

Alexa felt lightheaded as she watched a nearby teen masticate French fries. "What does that have to do with cage diving?"

"The closure hit islanders hard. People lost their jobs. Some jumped ship to work for the caging industry. And when tourists see whites in their natural habitat, it casts a spell on them. They end up high on adrenaline, and they turn that energy into wanting to protect sharks, protect the oceans, ban finning."

"Finning?"

"The most barbaric offense of all, for a bowl of soup. Millions of sharks are slaughtered every year. Slice the fin off and toss the still-living fish into the sea, where the shark either suffocates or is eaten by other predators."

"Millions?" Alexa couldn't believe it. "Does the United States allow finning?"

"The States banned it in 2000, good on ya."

"Is finning allowed in New Zealand?" She frowned at a woman taking Duffy's picture.

"We banned it a couple years ago. Sharks are key to healthy oceans. If we exterminate them, the marine ecosystem collapses. Other species will die off." Duffy sounded reasonable, Alexa thought, but there was a mutilated body at the health center.

"When you spend time with sharks," he continued, "study them, you fear them less and are amazed more. Did you know they can see in the dark?"

"I thought they used vibrations, like thrashing, and smell—like blood, to locate their prey." The smell in the restaurant was driving Alexa crazy. Where was her food?

"True, but their eyesight is really sophisticated, even in the dark. They have tapetum lucidum tissue—you know, same things cats use to see at night."

"So, don't bleed, move, or swim at night, right?"

A waitress delivered Duffy's meal. He took a bite, looked out the window, chewed slowly. "Ahh, lovely. Cold water produces the best cod." He put down his fork and fiddled with his phone again, handing it to her. "There's a photo on Instagram. Did you know?"

Alexa studied the picture. The body on Ringaringa Beach. The waves. The top of her head. The orange jumpsuit. "A helicopter flew low over us while I was examining the body," she murmured and tapped the link:

Great White Rips Man to Pieces

The shark-shredded remains of an unidentified man washed ashore on Stewart Island's Ringaringa Beach this morning. The victim succumbed to massive bites and severed limbs. Great whites congregate around the island, and locals have warned authorities that an attack was imminent due to the cage diving industry's use of chum and bait.

"It was just a matter of time," local bach owner Julie Stokely said. "The cage operators have changed the sharks' behavior. Baiting sharks, teasing them—how is that not asking for trouble? And no one put a stop to it. The sharks were out for revenge, and here's your bloody evidence."

Sergeant Kipper Wallace of the Stewart Island Police Department halted all water activities and closed bathing beaches. "Contact the department if you have any information about the victim's identity," he said.

Department of Conservation authorities flew in shark expert Kana Duffy to assess the situation and determine a plan of action. Duffy, who holds a PhD in marine biology from the University of Melbourne, is host of *Shark Shadow* and runs the Oceans Research Great White Shark Program.

"Our island of tranquility is no longer tranquil," local fisherman Rex Cooper said. "The cagers have turned whites into man-hunters. It's *Jaws* down under."

The language—revenge, man-hunters, *Jaws*—was inflammatory. Alexa watched Duffy scrape his plate.

"I don't like this *incident* one bit," he said, his emerald eyes glowing. He looked around the crowded room and leaned forward. "Sharks have been set up. This man was killed due to human interference. Meet me in the pub tonight. We can discuss it, eh? Come up with a plan."

Alexa, jolted by "meet me in the pub," didn't answer and watched Duffy pay at the counter and leave the restaurant. No denying he was a lovely specimen. He reappeared on the street and pushed through the Ulva Island Birding group. They parted like a school of fish around a reef.

———

Energized by scarfing the best-ever fish and chips, Alexa arrived back at the medical center. A silver-haired man paced impatiently on the porch. "Do you work here?" he asked.

"Temporarily." Alex tried the door.

"It's locked. I'm Dr. Edward. Geoffrey Edward. From Perth."

"The pathologist?"

He nodded.

"I'm Alexa Glock, forensic examiner." She extended her hand.

"Do you have a permit for that name?"

Oh, brother. She dropped her hand.

"I'm coming, I'm coming!" Joan, a coat over her pink scrubs, scurried across the lot and up the stairs.

Alexa introduced the Kiwi to the Aussie.

"Oh, good," Joan said to the doctor. "I thought you were another reporter. I sent one on his jolly way. I was afraid he would follow me to the Four Square." She held up a grocery bag. "Had to get lunch."

"Have the rangers delivered the remains?" Alexa asked.

"Yes. The ranger with floppy hair and Dan hauled him in. The ranger asked for you."

The whale ranger. Stephen.

Dr. Edward interrupted. "The shark victim. He's here too, right?"

"Oh, yes. In there." Joan pointed. "We don't know who he is."

"Everyone on the ship is spotting fins," Dr. Edward said. "Even the ones who can't see worth a joey. I'll take a look at him, if you'd like, to confirm your findings."

"Let's get to the hunter first," Alexa said. "A wife and kids have been waiting a long time." They entered the room, washed up, and gloved up. "There won't be much cutting since the soft tissue has decayed. Cause of death is obvious."

She unzipped the body bag, releasing earthy scents, and

continued. "The remains match the ten-month time frame since Robert King disappeared. Clothing slowed disarticulation of the major joints."

She parted the top section of the bag and jerked. The skull, wedged like a pet owlet on the skeletal shoulder, stared at her.

"The head has detached." It reminded her of the skull sold on the black market in her last case. According to the Māori, the separation of body and soul unleashed demonic destruction.

"Was a weapon recovered with the body?" the doctor asked.

"A rusting Browning A-Bolt. Sergeant Wallace has it."

"I'm a Browning man too. Use the T-Bolt."

"What's the difference between A and T?" Did Browning go through the alphabet like Sue Grafton, Alexa wondered.

"Both are bang-up rifles." The doctor wore chinos and a garish Hawaiian shirt. He had accepted the disposable apron Joan handed him and was securing it with a bow. "A-Bolts hold a higher resale value. The T is more accurate."

King's remains, once they removed the bulky jacket, tattered pants, and large boots, had shrunk. The doctor brushed debris off the bones. Alexa lifted the skull, surprised by its lightness, and reminded herself that evolution designed as lightweight a container as possible for supporting and protecting the brain. *Our thoughts are heavy enough.* "I'll take dental X-rays and then get out of your way."

"Teeth are like fingerprints," Dr. Edward said. "No two are alike."

Alexa smiled. "Every tooth has unique characteristics."

"A molar masher, are you?"

"A forensic odontologist." Alexa placed the skull on a paper-covered tray and deftly manipulated the jaw. An upper incisor and premolar were gone, resulting in a meth mouth appearance. The remaining—she counted—twenty-six teeth (the wisdom teeth had been removed) were intact. Alexa spotted a lower left tooth restoration. She had studied King's antemortem records while waiting for the ferry; this looked like a match.

She positioned the arm of the portable X-ray machine.

"Take left and right lateral, as well," Dr. Edward said, stepping behind the screen.

Alexa bristled. She had planned to take laterals. Posterior, too. After taking the images, she left to find Joan. They studied the right lateral—a full view of the entire skull—on the computer screen. A chill ran through Alexa as she noted the dead end where the skull should have attached to the cervical vertebra. How could people go about their business if they knew how tenuous this connection was? Joan held the antemortem films. Their heads went tennis-match mode: both films showed lower jaw teeth crowding, one restoration, similar interspacing, four fillings, and wisdom teeth extraction.

"It's him," Alexa said.

"Came here for a hunting holiday and never left, out there all this time, rotting in the bush," Joan said in a husky voice.

Alexa left a voicemail for Wallace—he would need to notify next of kin—and then returned to the exam room to watch the doc. Well, to check on him. Make sure he wasn't a quack. Dr. Edward was bending over King's skull with a magnifying glass. "Do you carry a Glock?" he asked. "Most Yanks pack, right?"

Her list of comebacks was at the ready, aim, fire. She sighed. "No. I don't own a weapon. Let's finish up."

The pathologist straightened. "We have a mature male with Caucasoid traits and age indicators compatible with your missing hunter."

Alexa watched his wrinkled face. This probably wasn't how he anticipated spending his holiday.

"With the biological tissue gone, we can't be one hundred percent certain. There could have been lesions involving soft tissue. However, I conclude COD is bullet trauma to skull. If you locate the spent bullet, it can provide clues to the model and make of weapon."

Alexa nodded.

"The size and shape of the entrance wound indicate the shot

was fired from five to seven meters away," he said. "This man did not take his own life."

This confirmation caused goosebumps to pop up on her arms. Someone had deliberately or accidentally killed King. Either way, the body was left to rot.

Dr. Edward threw his apron and gloves in the trash. "Now, about that shark victim." He washed his hands.

"I'll meet you in the other room. I need to call the sergeant again." She washed up too and stepped out of the room into the waiting area.

Wallace didn't answer, so Alexa left another voicemail. "The pathologist confirmed my findings. King didn't take his own life." She hesitated and then added, "Kana Duffy has concerns about the shark victim. Since the pathologist is here, I am asking him to autopsy for cause of death." Autopsies were performed for various reasons: to check for the presence of and extent of disease, to evaluate medical care, to advance medicine, to reassure family members. And—like now—if the circumstances were suspicious.

Decision made. But was the medical center equipped? She found Joan. "Does the clinic have a bone saw?"

Joan blinked rapidly. "Dr. Bennett, he's retired, had one for emergencies—amputations or if you had to massage the heart."

"Find it. And do you have a baby scale?"

"Oh, sure. A digital." She collected the equipment, and they joined the doctor.

He pulled back the blanket, exposing the mauled remains. "Oi."

"If you don't mind," Alexa said, trying for charm, "I am requesting an autopsy."

"Pardon me?" the pathologist said. "I just want a look-see."

"I have the authority to request an autopsy on this John Doe."

Dr. Edward's white eyebrows rose. "Well, if you deem it necessary. COD appears obvious. I can be more specific with time of death when we check the contents of his stomach. There's indication of lividity on the chest and face. He floated facedown

while in the water. Before washing ashore." He scanned the decedent, his eyes resting on the raw thigh stump. "My ship leaves in
an hour. That gives me time to do a partial. You've completed
the external examination?"

"Yes."

He noticed Joan holding the scale and saw. "I'll need a steril-
ized scalpel, forceps, and sample containers."

Joan fulfilled his requests as he tied on a fresh apron.

Most of the one and a half gallons of blood circulating in the
victim's body had disgorged into the ocean. That was fortunate
because the exam bed did not have an attached sink and spray
hose to wash away body fluids like a standard morgue table does.
It wasn't stainless steel, either.

Joan helped them position a plastic sheet under the body.
"Blimey. We've never had an autopsy here."

The doctor ignored her and asked, "What's your estimate of
height and weight?"

Alexa checked her notes. She had measured the decedent from
head to the one remaining foot and based weight on the amount
of body fat visible for that height. "He's about 180 centimeters
and weighs approximately 85 kilos."

"Brain or chest?" he asked.

A partial autopsy was neck-up or neck-down. Cause of death
was her objective. Could it be anything other than massive bleeding? The organs would reveal more. "Chest, please."

"A no-brainer, then."

Joan laughed, and Alexa forced a smile for the doctor's benefit
as she carefully removed the tape securing the seeping intestines.
Joking was a coping mechanism. This was only the fifth autopsy
she had attended in her life, and she had fainted during the first
one. Examination of skeletal remains, like the hunter, was different. Easier.

"The decedent has shallow lacerations and punctures in the
upper chest," Dr. Edward said, getting right to business. He used

the largest scalpel to make a Y-incision from armpits to the pubic bone, and then pulled the chest skin back in a sickening squelch. "Hand me the saw."

Joan solemnly put it in his outstretched hand.

Dr. Edward studied it and pressed the On button. "This will do nicely." With the motor making a low, steady thrum, he cut through the breast plate and ribs, exposing the neck, heart, and lungs. He switched from saw to scalpel and proficiently cut and removed the four-inch trachea. "I need more light."

Joan fetched a flashlight and held the beam so the doctor could see more clearly.

"Hold it just there," the doctor directed, examining the gray-pink tracheal tube. "Hmmm. Do you see?"

A sickly sweet stench emanated from the windpipe as Alexa peered into it, trying not to gag. The body was ripening, and there was no air filter in the room. "What is it you're seeing?"

"Fluid and foam," the doc replied.

Foam was a symptom of drowning. Alexa was confused.

The doctor set the windpipe in a sample container and studied the heart and lungs. "They're in good shape. It will save time if I remove them en masse." He sliced through connective blood vessels, reached in, and removed the major organs together.

Alexa watched as he separated the heart from the lungs and examined the arteries. "Clear. No sign of heart attack." He placed the mass on the scale. "Three hundred forty-two grams. Slightly heavy for his body weight."

Next he examined the left lung. Then he weighed it. "Strange," Dr. Edward said, frowning. "Do you see?"

"What?"

"Eh? It's enlarged, distended. Weighs more than normal."

Alexa studied the waterlogged organ on the baby scale. "There's hemorrhaging, too." She pointed to a red cluster on the grayish lung.

The doctor nodded. "Cause of death could be drowning. Not blood loss."

"I don't understand," Joan said. "He was eaten by sharks."

Could John Doe have drowned before he bled to death, Alexa wondered? Her phone barked, making her jump.

The doctor looked up in alarm.

"It's my cell phone. I need to change that ringtone." She let it go to voicemail.

"My wife's phone quacks," Dr. Edward said, shaking his head. "I recommend a diatom test in the lab. And full toxicology screening."

"Diatom. That's microscopic algae, right?"

"Yes. It's found in open bodies of water. Now I'll check the lower organs. Never overlook the liver, eh?"

Alexa watched as he probed the meaty organ and explored the tattered abdominal cavity. "I see partially digested food in the stomach and upper intestine," he offered.

"So…you know how long since he ate?"

"Digestion ceases with death. I'd say three to six hours between his last meal and time of death." He leaned closer toward the stomach, scowled, and adjusted the light. "What's this?"

"I don't know." His rhetorical questions were becoming tiresome.

Dr. Edward pried loose and lifted the abdominal aorta. "Look how the vessel has been cut."

"By shark teeth?"

"There are no bite wounds in mid-abdomen. This was severed by a bullet."

Alexa froze. "What?"

"I'm seeing bullet damage."

Drowning. Bleeding. Bullet. What the hell?

The doctor fingered the small intestine still attached to the stomach and leading—like a bluish snake—out the crescent bite at the man's side, piling in a coiled blob on the exam bed.

He probed, inch by inch, then stopped. "Here." He lifted a nearly severed section. "Bullet damage. See?"

Alexa nodded, amazed.

Dr. Edward finished examining the viscera. "The entrance wound is missing." He pointed to the crescent bite on the man's side. "Let's see if there's an exit wound."

Joan helped the doctor turn the body on its side, and all three of them scrutinized the marred skin. "There," Dr. Edward said, pointing.

Above the left buttock was a red-rimmed hole.

"Easy to miss among the puncture wounds," he said kindly.

"Blimey," Joan whispered.

Alexa stared with disbelief. "So, the bullet didn't lodge in the body?"

"No."

"Can you tell what type of weapon or the caliber of the bullet?"

"Doubtful. There's a lot of damage from the shark bite wounds. I do know that the bullet to the abdomen wouldn't have killed him instantly, but it would have caused him agony." He paused. Maybe the ramifications were solidifying. "This is a case for law enforcement."

"I'll call Sergeant Wallace and let him know."

"I need to sew him back up and be on my way. The wife might have issued a man-overboard."

"I have to take photos and video first. Sergeant Wallace will want to speak with you." She pictured Dr. Edward back on the cruise ship, decompressing with an umbrella drink at the tiki bar. "Don't tell *anyone* what we've discovered."

"Doctor's oath," he replied.

Joan promised to get the two bodies airlifted to the morgue in Invercargill. Alexa's mind was a whirling dervish as she called Sergeant Wallace. When he didn't answer, she hung up. This news was better delivered in person.

Chapter Eleven

Murder bullied its way into her mind as Alexa left the clinic. Could someone have shot John Doe and thrown him to the sharks? The wind tugged her ponytail as she hustled to the one-room police station on View Street. A pair of women blocked her way.

"Our guide said they're the most aggro sharks in the world," one said, swinging her Stewart Island Gift Shop bag.

Alexa stepped around them.

"Serial killers is what I heard," her companion replied.

They joined a throng of tourists heading to the ferry terminal. Down the hill, Alexa spotted *Sequin of the Seas,* dwarfing a motley fleet of fishing boats in Halfmoon Bay. Where was *Sequin* headed next? Get away from this island, she wanted to shout.

The little village, isolated and wild, reminded Alexa that she was alone. She had cut ties with her family and colleagues back home and didn't have a single friend alive in New Zealand.

She broke into a run—eager to share urgent news—despite the heavy tote that contained her laptop, bumping her side. Maybe the new DI had arrived.

At the station, Sergeant Wallace and a young woman, her auburn hair subdued in a frizzy braid, sat at a table in the center of the square room. Constable Kopae's desk was empty, as was the rest of the station.

"Miss Glock." Wallace stood. "Did you get my message?"

Alexa remembered she had ignored a call during the autopsy. She shook her head, set her tote down, and tried to catch her breath. The gunshot surprise ricocheted through her brain. Take away drowning. Take away sharks. If treated quickly—transfusions, tubes, surgery—the victim may have survived.

Her urgent news would have to wait. Wallace looked miffed. "This is Lisa Squires. She and her partner, Andy Gray, run White Dive."

"Hello," Alexa said, trying to be patient. "What's White Dive?"

"I told you earlier. We have two shark cage companies on the island. White Dive and Shark Encounter. Miss Squires says Andy is missing. He never came home."

Alexa's attention piqued. Twenty-six, twenty-eight, Miss Squires was dressed in a T-shirt and yoga pants. A tattooed fin poked from the scoop-necked tee at her right clavicle.

"Miss Glock has just come from the medical center," Wallace added.

"Call me Lisa. Andy can't be the bloke who was attacked because our dives were canceled yesterday." Lisa squeezed her cell phone. "All the rain. The seas were rough. He sent the crew home. He was due back this morning."

"Give me the names of the crew members," Wallace said.

"You know John Lynch and Squizzy Koch," Lisa said.

"When did you see him last?" Alexa asked.

"I took him a sammie yesterday, one-ish, 'bout the time it quit raining. I drove over—we share a car—and we ate on *The Apex*."

"The apex?"

"His boat," Wallace explained.

"She's a beauty. A high-tech, custom-built catamaran." Lisa's face relaxed for a second and then reverted to worry. "Andy slept onboard, did equipment checks and paperwork. He had deposits to refund because of the cancellations. He promised he would walk home for Sunday tea. I had the jug on, waiting. He doesn't answer his phone." She caressed her abdomen, and Alexa could see a bulge. "We're expecting a babe. He's so excited. Please find him."

A stab of sympathy or regret or something she was unwilling to identify jabbed Alexa's gut. "Can you describe your partner?"

"He's all about the sharks, yeah? Like he could look for fins all day—the whites spend two-thirds of their time on the surface, and Andy can spot a fin a kilometer away. When they dive he can spot them on the fishfinder. Our boat has all the latest gear. Yeah—he can lose track of time. Whites are his passion."

Alexa interrupted. "I meant what does Andy look like?" The ravaged body flashed in her mind.

A sliver of a smile formed on Lisa's lips. "He's easy on the eye. Tall, fit, dark wavy hair."

Wallace took over. "I've sent Constable Kopae to check the vessel. We have your permission, eh?"

"Yes," Lisa said. "Anything to find him."

Wallace looked at Alexa. "Andy is Caucasian, thirty-two years old. He and Lisa live on Kaka Ridge."

"That's here on the island?"

Wallace nodded.

Alexa pulled out a chair and sat. "What was he wearing when you saw him last?"

Lisa's eyes widened. "It's not him, right? It couldn't be."

Alexa stayed quiet.

"I think, um, his track bottoms and a pullover."

"What color were the pants?"

"Black."

"Would he have worn a raincoat?"

Lisa brightened. "I gave him a keen one for his birthday. A black Swazi anorak."

Oh, crap, Alexa thought, *that's John Doe.* "Did Andy have fingerprints on file?" She had fingerprinted the deceased, the left hand anyway, since the right was missing.

"What do you mean 'did'?" Lisa's hands went to her belly again. Alexa gave Wallace a slight nod. He went to Lisa, placed a large hand on her shoulder. "Andy's from Australia, right? His prints will be on his immigration records. Go home while we check things out. Call a friend to come round, sit with you. Or your mum. We'll stop by as soon as we know anything."

Lisa looked stunned as he ushered her out. "It can't be him," she said plaintively.

As soon as the door shut, Alexa said, "Get me those prints, so I can confirm."

"God almighty, a babe on the way," Wallace said. "Lisa's a local girlie, grew up on-island, but Andy Gray is an Aussie. I met him once. He came in to file a complaint."

"About what?"

"Lots of the islanders are against shark cage diving, right?"

Alexa nodded, remembering the protest in front of Island Inn.

"Someone threatened him. Chummed his porch and left a message."

"What was the message?"

"'Ban the cage, or else,' written in blood."

Chapter Twelve

"Are you kidding?"

"I'm not kidding," Wallace said. "Ironic, he was killed by the whites he lured for tourists."

Alexa cleared her throat. "I have some important information from the autopsy."

"Autopsy? Who needed an autopsy? The hunter was all bones." Wallace sat back down.

"I requested an autopsy on the shark victim. And…"

"Why? Cause of death is obvious. Blood loss. I saw that body. Andy's body, if it's him. Sharks tore it limb to limb."

"The pathologist discovered bullet damage in his abdomen." It came out in a whoosh. She was still in shock, like a rip current had her in its grip.

The sergeant flinched. "That's a good yarn."

"It's not a yarn. A bullet traveled through the victim's stomach. It was camouflaged by the extreme condition of the body. From the shark. Or sharks." To prove it, she pulled up a photo of the exit wound on her phone and held it in front of Wallace's face. "You need to notify that DI, get him here stat. Now we have two suspicious deaths."

Wallace continued talking as if he hadn't heard. "A bad accident. Andy Gray probably fell off his boat. Let me see that." He seized the phone and studied the photo, frowning. He set it down and pulled glasses out of his pocket. Once he had slipped them on, he tapped the photo, enlarging it.

Alexa waited, watched, wondered why Wallace was resistant to the truth. A wall clock she hadn't noticed ticked loudly.

He stood abruptly. "I need to call this in."

"Good idea."

The station door swept open. "Kipper, g'day," bellowed a tiny woman in a purple cardigan. She carried an umbrella and small cooler and strode to the table. "Is it true? A shark attack?" Sun and age had carved topographical lines on her face.

The sergeant's face flushed. "Yes, Maumau. Stay out of the water."

"Humph. Never in my life. Who is it?"

"We aren't certain, but this is a bad time. Go on home."

"All my life sharks never came close to shore. Arthur saw them northwest, around Seal Rock. It's those cagers, Kipper. They brought this on." Her pinpoint eyes honed in on Alexa. "Well, who's this?" She set the cooler on the table but kept a gnarled grip on the handle.

"A colleague, Maumau. Miss Glock from America. She's helping."

"Helping what?"

"Miss Glock, this is my granny, and Arthur was my grandfather. Maumau has lived on-island all her life."

"Pleased to meet you." Alexa stood, her five feet, seven inches towering over Maumau.

"Humph. She the bird you went tramping with?"

Wallace's flushed face deepened to beet. "That was business."

"The hunter bloke. I know all about it."

No secrets on an island, Alexa remembered. How long would the bullet stay secret then?

Wallace picked up the cooler. "You need to leave, Maumau." He walked to the door and held it open. In a softer voice he said, "You're coming for tea tonight, right?"

"Bring her." Granny Maumau pointed her umbrella at Alexa.

"Seven thirty. And give me my chilly bin." Wallace looked pained as he handed over the cooler.

Maumau said "humph" and slammed the door behind her.

Alexa compiled reports as she listened to Wallace drop the bombshell of news on his superiors. "Yes, Senior, that's right. Bullet damage," he repeated. He listened gravely to the voice at the other end, said, "Yes, Senior. No, Senior," and then ended the call.

Constable Kopae let in a paper-blowing gust when she opened the door. "*The Apex* is docked in Golden Bay. I poked around onboard. No Andy Gray."

"Any signs of disturbance?" Wallace asked.

"Dirty dishes in the wee sink is all."

Alexa hoped the constable hadn't touched anything.

Wallace told Kopae about the bullet.

Her mouth dropped. "Eh?"

"You heard me."

Kopae's dark eyes got wide. "Gone to the dogs, sir. The island has gone to the dogs."

"The ship is a possible crime scene," Alexa interjected. "I need to go there."

"It's not a ship," Wallace said.

"Say what?"

"It's in the size. A ship can carry a boat, but a boat can't carry a ship."

"Oh, for God's sake," Alexa snapped. "I'll go to the *boat* now."

"My orders are to keep the news to ourselves and wait for the DI to arrive in the morning."

"The longer we wait, the more chance evidence will erode."

"I'm calling the shots," Wallace said. "We'll wait. No chance of mucking things up this way. Constable, go back and secure the premises with caution tape."

Alexa fumed and shoved a stack of papers toward him. "My preliminary reports are ready. I'll head to the inn." She shoved her laptop into her tote.

Wallace cleared his throat. "Do you remember the way to my house?"

She wanted to decline the forced dinner invitation, but maintaining a working relationship was important. She steadied her voice. "Are you sure it's all right?"

"Maumau gets what she wants."

"I'll find my way." She checked the time on her phone as she walked, high strung, to the Island Inn: 6:00. A run was what she needed. Her last one had been four days ago, too long. A run would give her time to think about what was happening. Laundry was stacked neatly on the double bed of her room. Alexa rummaged through it and her suitcase for a sports bra, running tights, T-shirt, and pullover. After changing, she swished the curtain back, peering at the sky. No rain. She did a minimum amount of stretching as she picked a route on the town map Constance had given her: up Golden Bay Road to Phil's Sea Kayaks and circle back on Raroa Walk, which looked like a hiking trail. Maybe forty or forty-five minutes, giving her time to return, rinse, report to Wallace's. After dinner, she'd meet Kana Duffy in the bar. She locked the room and walked to the front of the inn.

Three bearded men in short sleeves sat on the patio drinking beer, gesturing with big hands. She heard "sharks" and "bloody hell" as she passed. Locals, she guessed, each capable of using a gun. One man caught her eye and lifted his tallboy. She turned away, toward the harbor. *Sequin of the Seas* was receding toward a bruised-cloud horizon. She lifted her hand in a wave, as if Dr. Edwards could see her, and then started to run. Other than two muddy trampers with big packs, the street was empty. There weren't many cars in town. Or on the island, period. Kinda nice, Alexa decided. She quickened her pace, causing free-ranging chickens to flutter out of her way. After five minutes of passing modest bungalows, she was out of town. The road curved and opened to Golden Bay, dotted with islands and moored boats. A postcard scene.

She gulped tangy air, challenged herself to a burst of speed, cognizant of climbing, cognizant of beauty, willing to concede to the island's allure, passing boat houses and cottages on the waterside and tangles of green opposite. How was it that such a tiny place harbored evil? The bay glinted and shifted, and as she crested a hill she spotted the sign for Golden Bay Wharf. Home to *The Apex*. She jogged in place as she looked down the hill at the "wharf." It was no fancy-schmancy yacht club. There was a single pier leading to three boats. A fourth moored in the harbor. No sign of people. An island at the mouth of the harbor probably sheltered the harbor from the worst sea thrashings. A flutter of yellow caution tape waved to her from the single pier.

Wallace was wrong to bar her from the scene.

A car barreled toward her. The driver honked as Alexa hopped aside. Across the narrow road she saw the sign for Raroa Walk.

The track started muddy. After the first bend, the forest crowded in, and the only sound, besides her steady breathing, was a cacophony of birds: clonking tuis, tinkling bellbirds, meeping fantails, squawking parrots. Everything—the light, the weird birds and trees—was different from Umstead Park in Raleigh. She stiffened as a fantail alighted on a branch ahead, spreading its tail like a deck of cards and watching her with beady eyes. A dead one had been left in her rental cottage during her last case—as a threat.

"Shoo," Alexa yelled.

The path was gravel now, allowing her to speed up until a felled tree—maybe from yesterday morning's tempest—severed the route. She fought her way over the slimy trunk, a sharp branch snagging her tights. She got untangled, wiped her hands on her thighs, and jogged ahead, the path turning into a curving boardwalk, the wet wood forcing her to slow. As she approached the end of the boardwalk, she heard the crunch of footsteps. Someone was coming. She hadn't expected this. Thought she had the path to herself. Alexa turned and searched through the tunnel of green. No one in sight.

A loud flapping and whopping made her whip around. A fat green-and-white bird, big as a chicken, flew at her, careening at the last second, brushing one limb and crash landing on another, the branch bobbing under its weight.

What the hell?

The bird—like a pigeon on steroids—blinked red eyes, cocked its emerald head, and ponderously ascended, *whump, whump* through the trees.

She shook her head, flicked sweat from her brow, checked over her shoulder again, and took off herself—back on gravel— until another oddity slowed her. A tree trunk ten feet off the path leaned sideways and was shaped like a horse's head. She jogged in place for a moment and then sidled off-trail, breathing hard, and explored the trunk. Yep. It looked like a horse's head. She patted the fuzzy wood between the ears, ran fingers through the ferny mane, and cupped below the stumpy muzzle as if offering grain.

A crunch, louder this time, made her slip behind the horse tree. Someone *was* coming. She shooed an insect away and listened for more. Held her breath, aware the birds had stopped singing. After a minute of silence, she realized how stupid this was and crouched behind a tree. She peeked above the stump, her nose brushing tickly moss, to make sure everything was okay, and gasped. At the curve stood a lone man, his dark clothing blending into the tree behind him. He stayed motionless, staring into the path she'd just run. The hair on her neck stood. Someone had shot the shark victim. Someone had shot the hunter. *Someone might know I know.*

Evidence. Look for evidence. She stayed still, aiming her eyes on the target, glad her dark hair blended in with the stump and that she hadn't worn her red ball cap. The man's head slowly turned…

Alexa ducked before his eyes could snare hers and groped for her phone. Dammit. All she had in her pocket was the room key. She squeezed it, the metal protruding like a switchblade. Go for the eyes, the eyes. She listened.

Crunch. Coming closer. *Crunch.*

The man passed without looking in her direction. His neck stayed craned upwards toward the trees. One hand rested on binoculars hanging from his neck.

A birder. She was a fool. Alexa backtracked and sprinted to the inn. When she returned to her room, the door was ajar.

———

The hair on her neck stood again. She was sure she had locked up. Then she chastised herself for being paranoid and pushed the door open. "Hello?"

No answer.

She stepped in and canvassed the room: clothes strung over chair, open suitcase and toppled laundry stack. Alexa dashed to the bed. Her tote wasn't next to the laundry. Laptop, passport, wallet, notebook, phone—her world was in the tote. Maybe she hadn't left it on the bed. She opened the closet—empty—and then dove to look under the bed like a kid checking for monsters. There, in the middle, a sock. A balled up white sock, forever alone, but no tote. From her knees she spotted the tote leaning against the chair, her khaki pants obscuring the N.C. State Crime Lab logo.

Sweat from her sprint, gone cold, trickled down her back as she rummaged through the tote. All items were accounted for. But she hadn't left the door open. If someone had broken in, why? What could they have been looking for? Something to do with the cases? Reports or evidence? They were either on her laptop, protected by password, or at the medical clinic or police station. Constance, or someone from housekeeping, must have entered, maybe to deliver fresh towels, and not pulled the door shut when he or she left. She would stop by the front desk. Give a little hell.

Stepping out of the shower minutes later, she didn't like it that the towel was damp from earlier. Housekeeping had not been here. Rubbing dry did not ease her goosebumps. She dressed quickly and double-checked that the door was locked when she left, stuffing the room key in her pocket.

She stood on Wallace's front stoop and didn't knock, debating whether to tell him about the cracked door. She wished she had a confidante, someone to talk over matters with. Or even tell her when her outfit was wrong. Constance had looked blank when Alexa complained her door was left open, said housekeeping wouldn't have made such a mistake—was it possible she hadn't pulled it tight? The wind, you know. The wind on the island is notorious.

The door opened. Wallace's wife, Nina, smiled like it was normal for someone to stand there without knocking. The spotted dog pushed past Nina and stuck its nose into Alexa's crotch.

"Come in, Miss Glock."

"Ms. Glock. I prefer *Ms.* Glock." It was better late than never to make this preference clear. She kneed the dog and stepped inside. She could hear a pot lid clanging and a TV ad. "But call me Alexa." She should have brought something. Wine. Flowers. Cookies. Bruce Horne had brought a box of TimTam cookies when he had come for dinner in Rotorua.

"Maumau—you met her earlier, right?—is in the kitchen. Helping me." Nina made a face that made Alexa like her. "Having you for tea is an occasion. We don't have a lot of off-island visitors. Living here can be a wee lonely."

"Mummy," came a squeal. "Don't let Spot out."

"Shelly is worried because Spot hasn't had kiwi training," Nina explained. Before Alexa could ask about kiwi training, Wallace appeared, his little girl riding piggyback.

"Is this Merica?" the girl asked.

"No, Shelly belly," Wallace said, "this is Miss Glock *from* Merica."

"Ms. Glock, hon," said Nina. "But call her Alexa."

"It's been a long day, eh?" Wallace said, sliding Shelly off. A boy's head peeked from around a corner.

"This is Sam," Wallace said. The boy ducked his head shyly. "Speak up, lad. Say hello."

"Hello," Sam mumbled.

Alexa smiled at him. "How old are you? Thirteen?"

Sam grinned. "I'm nine."

"Come with me," Nina told her.

The children scattered, and Alexa followed Nina into a cozy yellow kitchen. The aroma—garlic, stew or soup, something fishy—caused her stomach to growl. Maumau, even tinier without her bulky purple sweater, stood at the counter nimbly breading oysters.

"Nice to see you again," Alexa said.

"Humph." Maumau pointed to the blob at her fingertip. "Best oysters in the world."

Alexa nodded, but she didn't like oysters.

"Maumau, sit down. I'll do it," Nina said.

"You make lumpy batter. You sit down."

Nina's face stayed passive as she lifted a pot lid, freeing more enticing smells. When was the last time Alexa had had a home-cooked family meal? Sadness, like the released steam, engulfed her. She and Jeb had played family, but heart and soul had been missing. "We'll leave the chef and have a drink in the den," Nina told her. "Would you like a glass of wine? Beer?"

"Wine, thanks."

Chilled sauvignon blanc in hand, Alexa sat on a worn couch, Spot sniffing her Keds. Sam turned off the widescreen TV and left the room. Nina sank in a recliner and let Shelly, who held a pink tennis shoe, climb on her lap. "I want to practice my shoes," Shelly said.

Another twinge of sadness fluttered as Alexa watched Nina guide the little girl through shoe-tying steps. Had her mother taught her to tie shoes? Mom had died when Alexa wasn't much older than Shelly. A wet nose nudged her from her funk. Spot wagged hopefully. "Tell me about kiwi training," Alexa said, patting the dog's head.

Nina loosened a knot for Shelly and explained how unrestrained dogs kill kiwis. "It's aversion training, using a shock collar. One sniff of a kiwi or penguin or weka, and *zap*." She helped Shelly pull the laces evenly. "We're trying hard to protect our birds, yeah. Sometimes I let Spot off-lead when we're on the beach, and I don't want her to hurt one."

"Or bite its head off," Shelly added.

"I saw a giant pigeon in the woods," Alexa said. "It was flying like it was drunk." Probably shouldn't say "drunk" in front of a kid, she realized. She gulped the savvie.

Nina laughed. "It was. That's a kererū. They feed on fermented berries. Get silly clumsy. Sometimes they fall out of trees."

Now Alexa laughed and relaxed into scratching Spot behind the ear.

"Over, under," Shelly said and then sighed, pulling the laces straight again. "Over, under...pull it tight, bunny ears. See, Mum?"

Alexa could see a loopy bow. "She's precocious."

"What do you mean?" Nina looked puzzled.

"Isn't it amazing that Shelly tied her shoe?"

"Ah. No. It's normal. She's almost five. Don't you have children?"

"I have two nephews." It was her ready answer. "Benny and Noah."

Nina knit her brows. "You still have time."

Alexa tamped her anger with another sip. Why did people assume she wanted kids? As if happiness were a ring and a diaper. She loved her work. She didn't want to compromise her ambition, her daily schedule, to align with a daycare holiday. She'd rather assist in a postmortem than a postpartum.

But this Shelly was a smartie.

Wallace came in. "You don't mind if we go over a few updates, do you?"

"Let's go help in the kitchen," Nina said to Shelly, giving Wallace her chair. Alexa watched the child skip off.

Sam popped back in. "Can you tell me about the shark attack now, Dad? Was he eaten alive? Was there blood?"

"Later, lad. Go finish your schoolwork."

"No one tells me anything," he said, stomping off.

Wallace turned to Alexa. "The bodies are on the way to the morgue, and we have positive ID on our shark victim. Your fingerprints match Andrew Gray's. We aren't releasing his name until the DI arrives, decides what to do. Constable Kopae and I stopped by to tell Lisa Squires. We did not mention the bullet—DI's orders."

"Is someone with her?"

"Her mother. Judy Squires is a book club friend of Nina's. Judy's afraid Lisa might miscarry."

Alexa knew research on rats showed high levels of stress during pregnancy could adversely affect the baby's brain function.

"Lisa wants to see him. She doesn't believe it's Andy."

"Fingerprints don't lie. Did you catch who chummed their front porch?"

Wallace scratched his chin. "I had suspicions, but no proof. Everyone alibied everyone else. 'We were at the pub.' 'We were having a barbie.' 'We were fishing from the wharf.' Bit odd no one was alone, eh?"

"Write down the names of those suspects for the DI."

Wallace narrowed his eyes.

She squirmed on the couch. "I'm sure you've already done that."

He let the comment slide. "Come to the station tomorrow morning at 7:30. The DI is holding a briefing. I spoke with him by mobile. He said to act like this is an unfortunate shark incident. No mention of foul play."

"Good call. That shark guy, Kana Duffy, wants to meet me tonight in the pub. To talk about what would entice multiple sharks to attack. Do you think..."

"Go. Act normal."

"Normal?"

"Go along with his recommendations," Wallace clarified. "After the morning meeting I'm flying to Invercargill, weather permitting, with Lisa and her mum."

"I don't think it's a good idea for Lisa to see Gray's body."

"That's her call," Wallace said. "Robert King's wife and daughters will be arriving at the morgue, too."

"Have you reached Gray's crew members?"

"Squizzy and John are stopping by first thing."

The hunter was on her back burner, and she was glad of the reminder. "I need to get to a forensic lab."

"There's a lab in Dunedin. I can see about getting you there." His shoulders slumped. "What in God's name is happening around here?"

"Come eat," Maumau called.

They squeezed around a circular kitchen table, Alexa between Sam and Shelly. "It's seafood stew," Nina explained, passing out bowls. "Cod, crayfish, mussels, and scallops."

"And these are wild oysters," Maumau said, passing a platter. "My husband was an oyster man for thirty years. I've eaten my share of oysters."

Sam stabbed three and passed the platter to Alexa. "Dad, did the shark bite off the man's legs?"

"What shark?" Shelly asked.

"Not now, Sam," Nina said.

Alexa felt a muzzle press on her thigh. She wondered if she could slip Spot the oyster she spooned to her plate, but Maumau was watching, so she forced herself to eat it. She chewed, tentatively at first, and then with gusto. "Wow. It's good."

"Because of the clean, cold saltwater, the taste," Maumau said approvingly. "Not like farmed oysters."

"We don't farm oysters on the island anymore," Wallace explained to Alexa. "Because of a parasite."

"*Bonamia ostreae,*" Sam said excitedly. "It kills ninety percent of oysters that get it."

Alexa glanced appreciatively at the boy. Was knowing scientific names normal for nine-year-olds, or precocious? She didn't know.

"Good riddance. Wild is always best," Maumau said.

"People lost their jobs," Wallace said.

"Like Mike's Dad," Sam said. "Mr. Warren."

Wallace, Nina, and Maumau argued about sustainability, Shelly and Sam made faces at each other, and Alexa finished her stew.

Nina offered coffee, which Alexa declined, and Alexa offered to help with dishes, which Nina declined.

"I'll drive you back," Wallace offered.

"No, thank you, I'll walk."

———

Buttoning her cardigan on the street, Alexa realized she knew exactly where she was. Ten-toeing it created a clearer mental map than darting around in a car relying on GPS. At the corner of Golden Bay and Dundee, she lifted her face to the moonless and murky sky, feeling wispy sea air graze her cheeks. Or maybe it was fog. She was glad to be alone. The fury of the long day was ebbing like the tide, allowing her thoughts to migrate through the debris left in its wake. To the right, the Island Inn shone like a lighthouse in the dark village. Kana Duffy might be waiting in the bar. To the left it was tar black.

The wisps of moisture—she ran a finger across her cheekbone—were no longer ethereal.

Rain.

Rain would wash away evidence, especially blood, on the cage-diving boat docked at the wharf. She headed left on Golden Bay road. Toward *The Apex.*

Screw Wallace.

Her tote banged against her side as she trotted. What was in it? She had left her laptop at the inn, so it was lighter. She had a Maglite, a couple of plastic baggies, a magnifying glass. Cell phone. Disposable gloves and booties. Never knew when they'd come in handy. But what good could she do with limited supplies? She thought of the bullet that had streaked hotly through Andy

Gray's abdomen. She would search for blood spatter, a spent bullet. The plan made her speed up.

She was impatient for her eyes to dilate, to let in more light as she canvassed overhanging banks on the sides of the road, searching for tiny pricks of blue-green light, glowworms, to lead the way. *Titiwai*, the Māori called them. Living lights.

The overgrowth was black, vacant. Maybe glowworms didn't live on Stewart Island.

The scent of ocean strengthened on the hill crest. Briny like the oyster she had swallowed under Maumau's watchful eyes. No cars, no streetlights, no birdsong. The glowing window of a cottage high on a hillside reassured Alexa that she wasn't alone in an apocalypse. Her eyes had adjusted, and she could make out the Golden Bay Wharf sign and arrow. She followed it, descending a steep single-lane road enclosed in a tunnel of tangled overgrowth. It dead-ended in a dirt parking lot. She stood still, panting slightly, and made out two boathouses flanking the beach. A sign above one said *Water Taxi Tickets*. A sign on the other said *White Dive Check In*. Tiny boats—maybe the kind people used to ferry to shore from bigger boats—nosed into a steep bank between them.

She scanned the shore. Lapping waves churned pebbles on a beach. A pier, made leggy by low tide, cordoned off with caution tape, still had three boats tethered to it. No one had set sail since this afternoon. Again she thought how rinky-dink the wharf was. There were no security lights, no CCTV. She rummaged for her cell and checked for a signal. None.

At least the camera would work. She slipped the phone in her pocket and took out the Maglite. It was time to review her plan. She would board the vessel and look around, search for any sign that Andy Gray had been shot. Or abducted. She was doing the right thing.

Alexa scrunched through sand to the pier, canvassing the perimeter for movement.

A chicken-sized bird with a long beak stood at the water's

edge. Its head nodded like the drinking bird Professor McBride from the dental school had on his desk. "The methylene chloride produces heat to extract motion," he'd explained.

The wooden gangplank was slippery and steep, though the rain had ceased. Her Keds didn't have much tread, so she grabbed the rail and clung until the gangplank leveled. She ducked under the caution tape and straightened. The water below churned and slopped against pilings, and there was no more railing. She padded ahead, taking deep breaths of fishy air. A squawk made her jump. She watched a gull circle above and veer off. The pier split into a *T*. A fishing boat and a small motorboat were on the left. *The Apex* was to the right, farthest out.

It was time to choose a search pattern: spiral, line, grid, quadrant, or wheel. Alexa preferred the quadrant. She came to the *T* in the pier and pivoted toward *The Apex*.

Alexa had no idea how to gauge a boat's age, but this one looked newish. And expensive. *The Apex,* a catamaran like the dead man's partner had said, was maybe thirty-five feet long. A second floor loomed above. A lookout for shark fins. The main deck was three feet lower than the pier. Because of the tide, she figured. She looked for a gangway. Nope. She'd have to jump down and over an eighteen-inch gap of black water.

The front half of the boat appeared to be an indoor cabin. She sidestepped to the stern. Three big Suzuki engines lined the rear. On her opposite side, past back-to-back padded benches, a pulley contraption was attached to a raised stainless-steel cage pressed lengthwise against the boat's side. The cage. It was big enough for several people to stand in, and it stole Alexa's breath. To think the cage was lowered into the Southern Pacific, and people willingly climbed in. Mind-boggling.

It occurred to her that if someone had shot Gray in his boat, and thrown him overboard, that great whites had probably lingered below the black surface, hoping for more. She had read somewhere that sharks never sleep.

Chapter Thirteen

The gap yawned wider. Not only would she have to jump the gap between pier and boat deck but also over a knee-high railing.

She forced herself to turn in a slow circle, to check for movement. The coast was clear.

Don't trip, she prayed. Then she lunged.

She thudded onto the deck. She took a deep breath, congratulated herself for not falling, and stayed still, listening to the hungry lick of waves against the hull. When her heart ceased drumming in her ears, she sat on a bench seat and pulled on gloves, covered her Keds with protective booties, and readied her light. As if by magnetic pull, the beam lit the metal cage secured to the boat's side. She walked slowly over, reaching to touch the side, running a finger over the door latch.

A notch was built into the side of the boat so that when the cage was aligned, tourists—three or four at a once—could step right in. Steel handgrips lined the side of the cage, and a viewing window on each side looked large enough for a shark to stick its nose in. The image gave her chill bumps.

She backed away and searched the no-skid deck surface for blood, sweeping the beam of her Maglite back and forth. Maroon droplets near a large cooler along the rail stopped her dead.

Bingo.

She tugged, and with an *oof*, the cooler lid opened. A vile stench assaulted her nose. The Maglite beam turned black goop contents to blood red.

Chum.

If she had had a proper container, she would take a sample. Damn. She slammed the lid and concluded the droplets were fish blood. She entered the cabin through a skinny unlocked door. The Maglite illuminated a snug room flanked with padded booths. The table of the right booth was messy with papers, a can of V—a New Zealand energy drink—and some sort of bulky black belt. Alexa figured this was Andy Gray's office. She lifted the belt. What the heck? It weighed ten, twelve pounds. This baby would sink like a stone.

The sea is salty, and salt equals buoyancy, she deduced. People who got lowered in the cages needed to weigh themselves down.

She illuminated the stack of forms. The top one read: *DOC Great White Shark Sighting*. Date, Time, Location, Vessels in Area, Weather, Description—filled out in cramped scrawl. *23 November, 5:15 p.m., Lee Bay, Strait Up, choppy, four meters length, followed alongside boat thirty minutes.* She checked a few more: all shark sightings. Why did Andy Gray have Department of Conservation documents? She set them down and surveyed the rest of the cabin. There was a galley kitchen with everything tucked and secured in nooks, a couple dishes in the tiny sink, and two closed doors: Head and Change Room.

Just a general snoop, she reminded herself.

"Cramped" came to mind when she inspected the bathroom. But functional and clean. A phone booth shower. No blood smear in the drains. When she opened the other door, she almost dropped the light. Lifeless black suits hung from a rack. Frogmen faces stared from a shelf. Jesus.

Wetsuits and dive masks. Her heart drummed in her ears again as she set her tote on the bench and sifted through the suits, checking for moisture. She didn't like the way the suits undulated from the hangers. She lifted a random dive mask, held it inches from her face, dangled it from the strap, and set it down. Life jackets were stacked on the bench, and underneath were ten pullout storage bins. She checked them, one by one, not sure what she was hoping for. Her reward was mildewing swim trunks.

A clang on deck made her twirl.

She turned off her light and waited. One Mississippi, two Mississippi. No more sound. She cautiously left the cabin area and shone her light on the deck. Yellow eyes reflected back. A jumbo gull squawked from the cage top, spread monstrous wings—was it an albatross?—and flew away. She didn't want to be stuck in the cabin anymore and began inching her fingers along the gunwales, searching for bullet damage.

Be methodical, she reprimanded herself. Inch by inch. When she crawled adjacent to a spiral staircase, it enticed her to explore the viewing deck. The metal railing was cold and slippery through her thin gloves. She stuffed the Maglite in her pants pocket so she could use both hands to pull upwards in a claustrophobic coil.

Spiral staircases were always cooler to look at than maneuver. She popped up like a bewildered gopher.

With a sweep of the Maglite she saw the top deck had back-to-back benches and waist-high siding. Up front, in a small enclosed area, was where Andy Gray steered the ship. Boat. The high swivel seat looked comfy, and the console was all high-tech screens and gadgetry. The latest in shark detection.

She checked the deck for blood. It looked clean, but some stains on the inner knee wall caught her attention. Next to a nasty spear with a hook at the end—a gaff, she thought—she spotted little dots and bigger blots. Maybe blood. Would they chum from up here? She'd have to come back with the crime kit. Take samples. The three-inch overhang of the rail would protect the samples from rain, unless it came in slantwise. She checked the sky, relieved to see a partial moon peeking from a scudding cloud.

Now on her knees, she felt along the ridge, inch by inch past the stains. Her fingers felt a knothole. She rubbed over it, snagging a glove tip. She pulled back too quickly, felt the latex rip. Crap. It was important not to contaminate the evidence. She shone her light closer to the nick. It was a perfect burrow. She leaned in, could hear her breath. The light glinted back, bouncing off something copper. A stone. No. Her heart raced. An embedded bullet. Andy Gray had been shot here. Her hands shook as she traded flashlight for camera, focused, zoomed, clicked, dazed by flash. Wallace would be glad she had disobeyed him. She stuffed the phone back in her pocket. Maybe…

She heard a clang. Before she could react, a muscular arm clamped across her chest, and hot sour breath rasped in her ear, "Don't scream."

Alexa screamed and jabbed her elbow to the man's gut. The man *oofed* like the cooler lid, dropped his arm, grabbed the gaff. Alexa, still on her knees, lunged sideways and felt the breeze as the gaff smashed the railing inches from her head. She jumped up as the man raised the gaff again. The hook pierced her cardigan as she jumped ship.

Chapter Fourteen

Her mouth—mid-scream—clamped shut as she smacked the water face-first, plunged downward.

Cold.

Shock.

Cold-shock to freeze her heart.

She commanded her eyes to open. Open wide. Wider. Didn't matter. Underwater was black. Pitch black. No surface or bottom. No left or right. No up or down. Fourteen feet. Forty feet. Cold and black. She would die.

The taste—salt—made her think buoyancy. She spread her arms, surrendering, and felt them drift upwards. She thrashed in that direction, kicked her feet, kicked the thought of someone pushing her, kick-boxed adrenaline into action, kicked ass, and broke the surface. A wave slapped her, flooding her nose and mouth. Gasping. Heaving. Coughing. Clothes so heavy. Anchor clothes.

She sank.

No one would save her. No one in the world knew where she was. The cold squeezed her chest, lungs. She was drowning. Alone. She thought of Charlie, her baby brother. He had had apricot curls and followed her like a duckling after Mom died.

"Go away, Charlie. Leave me alone." She'd wallowed in grief, no

comfort to spare for the two-year-old. Now Charlie would never know how much she loved him. How sorry she was.

Alexa kicked again, resurfaced, kept her nose high. Inhaling water would kill her. She hadn't been swimming since she was thirteen. The thought of wearing a bathing suit and exposing her ugly back scars had stopped her, but the summers of swim lessons before the accident infused her limbs. How stupid she'd been— limiting life for vanity. Who fucking cares? She spit, treaded water, glad Keds were lightweight, and craned her neck toward *The Apex*, a hulking, slippery giant eight feet away. The man—how could she have forgotten the man?—was a dark outline leaning over the rail, watching.

"Help," she screamed.

He reached for something.

A whoosh of warmth, of slick oil, of putrid rot, coated her head, blinded her, splashed heavy around her. She blinked, flailed, pawed at her eyes. A disposable glove, disgusting and slimy, flew off.

Chum.

The man had doused her with chum.

Sharks.

Hot panic flooded her veins. The sharks were awake, swim-ming below, their sense of smell activated. *Get away from the chum.* She ducked, back-paddled frantically. She inhaled tainted seawater, coughed, sputtered, surfaced, kicked out. Don't kick. Movement attracts them. Something brushed her calf. Something solid, leathery. A white. She screamed, went down.

This is it.

Fight back. She scrambled for eyes to poke, gills to rip, her arms thrashing, hands groping, feet punting, waiting for the body slam, for the massive jaws to clamp her torso, arc into the air, rag-doll shake, to die a white death. But something had roped her. She couldn't kick. Her foot was tangled, snared. Rubbery blades grabbed and wrapped her ankle. Strands encircled her. What the hell?

Seaweed. She was snared in a bed of seaweed. Kelp. It was all around her. Disgusting, massive, beautiful kelp. She ducked under, pulled her leg out of its grip, pushed up through the thick fronds.

When she popped up, she was facing the beach, thirteen, sixteen yards away. In silvery moonlight a figure ran across the beach to the parking lot. From the cold clutch of the kelp, Alexa watched headlights brighten the parking area and then fade up the hill. She put her face down in the black, kelpy water and stroked with every muscle, kicked free the last strands until she felt the whip-like tips relinquish, and stroked like a machine, until her foot—there, no, yes—touched bottom.

Chapter Fifteen

Alexa bob-stepped in waist-high water until a wave slapped her flat, shoved her forward, spit her out. The beach was open arms, and she was the prodigal child. She scrambled on all fours past the tide line, flopped into a child's pose, pressed her cheek against the sand, raked grit and shells through her fingers. She was safe. No sharks could get her.

What if the man came back?

She jumped up, ran, stumbled, caught herself, limped toward the closest boathouse. Her left hand hung heavy, swollen. The remaining glove had filled with water.

Charlie. She would call Charlie if she made it out of here. She pushed against the rough wood of the boathouse, tore off the bloated glove, wiped sand from her face, edged around the side. Droplets ran down her back, making her want to squirm, but she stayed still and peered from around the corner—at the beach, pier, boats—alert for movement, shadow, footsteps.

The serene view did not compute. The water could have swallowed her whole and left not a ripple. Her mind jumped to footprints. The man had dashed across the beach. She could photograph his footprints. She reached into her pocket for her phone.

"Shit."

Her cell, stashed in her pants pocket, its outline leaden, was a goner. And her tote was on *The Apex.* No way she was going back. The man might be coming back. She didn't think his attack had been premeditated, because her decision to search the boat had been split second.

He had probably been surprised when he climbed those stupid spiral stairs and seen her.

She studied the sandy stretch between her sodden Keds and the pier. Maybe she could spot a footprint anyway, make mental notes of size and pattern. She began to shiver. Her sweater was gone. It must have been ripped off by the gaff, was probably on *The Apex,* or floating in the water. As if she had drowned. Only a wet, no-iron button-down between her and cool air. The thought of her North Carolina-light cotton sweater, a tear at the shoulder, floating on an ocean current—all that was left of her—made her cry.

Get a hold of yourself.

The shivers would fight hypothermia until she got warm and dry.

Alexa turned and skulked behind the boathouses to the parking area. No car. She jogged the steep hill to warm up, ready like a deer to jump into the thicket at the sight of headlights. The weight of sodden, sandy clothes made it hard and slow. She was heading straight to Wallace's, even though she knew she was in for a lashing. Bruce Horne had told her during a heated exchange in the case they worked together that her brash actions had put herself and her colleagues in jeopardy.

Yep. Old dog. Old tricks.

No porch light. Nervously, she knocked.

A bathrobed Wallace looked incredulous at her drowned-rat appearance at his doorstep, and he was furious when she spewed her tale.

"I told you to wait until morning."

Nina, from behind his shoulder, took Alexa's hand, leading her to a hall bathroom. "Your hand's ice. Use that towel," she said, pointing. "I'll wash your clothes, get them to you tomorrow. Let me find something for you to wear."

In the mirror Alexa saw a raw scrape on her right shoulder, near her neck, where the gaff had nabbed her sweater, whipped it off. The wound made her gasp. She leaned into the sink and gingerly washed sand and salt from it, her hands shaking, and then rinsed her face and arms.

Outfitted with dry undergarments, too-short pants, socks, and snuggly sweatshirt, Alexa towel-dried her hair and reset her ponytail. She extracted her phone from her sopping pants, double-checked for a pulse by pushing buttons and shaking it. Nada. Photos, proof, and her contacts list, down the drain.

Unless photos live in the cloud. The thought gave her hope.

Voices—Wallace's angry and urgent, Nina's calm and soothing—penetrated the bathroom wall. She wondered if she'd be fired, lose her new job. What a mess. A door closed and footsteps passed the bathroom. Alexa folded her sad, wet clothes and left them on the bathroom floor. Nina was in the kitchen, pouring boiling water into a mug. The scent of hot chocolate made Alexa want to cry again. Dammit.

"Drink this, luv," Nina said, putting the mug in front of her.

"Thank you."

"It's only powdered," Nina said. "Kip is changing into his uniform."

Alexa sipped cautiously. The dishes had been washed; a few pots drip-dried in a rack. She pushed her back against the wood slats of the chair, grateful for the tableau of home and hearth, the lingering scent of fish stew, the heavenly hot cocoa. She set the mug down and put the ruined phone on the table.

Nina noticed. "Too bad—that. Do you want me to try ricing it?"

"It's dead. Do they sell phones on the island?"

"No. You'll have to go to Invercargill."

"I appreciate the clothes."

"Ah, yeah, glad to help. Don't mind Kip. The hunter, the shark attack. It's not been a box of fluffies for him."

Spot pressed a muzzle on her thigh. Alexa scratched the silky spot behind the dog's ear. She opened her mouth to say something, anything to fill the awkwardness, but Wallace reappeared, dressed in uniform. "Let's go," he said. "Constable Kopae is meeting me at the station."

"Hold your bones, Kip," Nina said. "Let her finish her cuppa."

Alexa stood. "We need to go back to the ship now. Process the..."

"It's late, almost eleven," Wallace said. "You're in no condition to go back. I'll drop you at the inn. The constable and I will search the area and keep watch on *The Apex* until morning."

"I'm fine. I can go back."

"No. You are off the case until I speak to the DI."

"I found a bullet lodged in the upper deck railing. Secure it, but don't remove it. And will you bag that gaff, the one he swung at me, and bring it to the station?"

"He probably tossed it."

———

As if she hadn't had enough excitement for a day that had started a hundred hours ago, Alexa decided to hit the pub after Wallace's car disappeared, see if Kana Duffy was still there. She wasn't ready to be alone, and maybe she could snoop out some information from Shark Man. Redeem herself.

Jukebox music—Tom Petty, maybe—penetrated the empty lobby when she entered. The restaurant was closed, and through the windows, a harbor light flashed on and off.

I nearly drowned, she thought, watching.

But I didn't, she thought back.

The gaff gash felt leaky, sticky, hot. As she opened the door to the Full Moon Lounge, it occurred to her that the man who had tried to kill her could be here. Toasting his victory if he didn't know she'd escaped the jaws of death.

The bar was half-full. Three bearded men sang with fervor into beer bottle mikes. They were—what was the expression? three sheeps? ships? sheets?—to the wind. A woman with long yellow hair and tattooed arms danced in a circle and extended a hand.

"No thanks," Alexa mumbled, pushing past. She squeezed behind a fishy-smelling man in gum boots—he might have been the man who gave her a lift from the ferry—and bumped into a guy in a ball cap. "Pardon," she said, searching for Duffy.

He was still here, talking with a couple at a nearby table. She waved like she hadn't had a near-death experience and approached the bar. "Speight's," she called to the bartender.

"Eh?" A pen dangled like a cigarette from his mouth.

"Speight's." Alexa jabbed the rubber Speight's bar mat.

"The bump, eh. Classic move," said a voice from behind.

She whipped around.

Ranger Scratch from the hut grinned sleazily. The missing hunter—the reason she had been sent to Stewart Island—had slipped her mind again. The bartender pushed a cold bottle into her hand.

"I'll treat the lady since we've already slept together," Scratch said.

Blood rushed to Alexa's cheeks. "It was business," she yelled to the bartender. "Put it on my tab." Her wallet was in her tote. On *The Apex.*

The bartender suppressed a smile. Alexa signed the receipt, glared at Scratch, and hustled to Duffy's table.

"Ah. Here you are. I was about to give up." He looked her over and pulled out a chair.

"Long day." She sloshed some beer as she sat. The man and woman sharing the table, in their forties, had vitamin-and-sunshine looks.

The woman smiled. "I'm Meredith Hall. We saw you on the ferry."

"I'm Alexa."

Meredith flicked a blond tress over her shoulder. "This is my husband, Theo. We're from Santa Monica. Where are you from?"

It was the couple who had snatched her taxi. "North Carolina. But I live in Auckland now."

"The Halls were telling me about their cage dive," Duffy said. "They went out yesterday afternoon."

Yesterday afternoon she had tramped with Wallace and Stephen through the bush to the hunter's remains. And Andy Gray supposedly canceled Saturday dives due to weather. Maybe he had gone out after all. "Did you go with White Dive?"

"No," Meredith answered. "We went with Shark Encounter on *Glowing Sky*. Lucas, our captain, was brilliant."

"What time did you get back?"

Meredith concentrated. "Six thirty, I think." She looked at her husband for confirmation. "We were lucky. Dives have been suspended. Everyone is talking about the attack."

"Yes." Alexa looked around at the pub patrons. Two of the drunk bearded men were leaning against the bar now. Scratch caught her eye and lifted his beer bottle. She turned back to the couple and spoke loudly. "The man on the beach died from shark bites. The body is in terrible condition. The attack was horrible."

There. She had cast information and misinformation. Let the tide carry it away.

Meredith looked at her curiously. "Was your cage dive canceled?"

"I'm not here to dive."

"Oh, you're a birder. That's too tame for me."

Alexa didn't correct her. "So you went down in a cage?" She wished she had her notepad.

Meredith beamed. "Lucas knew where to find the sharks."

It occurred to Alexa that it might be the other way around—the sharks knew where to find Lucas and *Glowing Sky*. "Were there other tourists in your group?"

"There were supposed to be, but they canceled due to the storm. We had calm seas and the sharks to ourselves."

Duffy interrupted. "How far from shore did *Glowing Sky* anchor?"

"We could see the beach. Twenty or thirty yards. Lucas said the great whites round here hang out in the shallows."

Alexa choked on her beer. "What beach?"

Meredith looked to Theo. "I think it was Frenchman's," he answered.

She didn't know if Frenchman's was close to Ringaringa, where the body washed up. Or Golden Bay, where she swam with the sharks. She needed a map.

"How did Lucas lure the sharks?" Duffy asked.

"The first mate chummed," Theo said, wrinkling his nose. "Blood soup. That stuff reeked. When we anchored, he threw more chum and some tuna over the side."

I was the big tuna a little while ago.

"Being below is a religious experience," Meredith said. "I'm still in a trance." She saw Alexa's confusion. "You're somewhere you don't belong. It's clear and cold, and when that massive gray torpedo comes at the cage, this immense force—jaws open, rows of jagged teeth—and turns at the last second, you are saved, redeemed. Life and death in the underworld, and you are a witness."

Theo nodded. "Eye level with a killing machine."

"What did you mean by 'you are a witness'?" Alexa asked.

"It probably was the same shark that ripped that man apart." Meredith's brown eyes sparkled in dim bar neon. "We could have been witnesses."

"Sixteen, maybe eighteen feet she was," Theo said. "A big swell came up when I was getting into the cage. I nearly fell in the water. She'd have eaten me alive."

"The shark was probably male," Duffy said. "The population around here is mostly male. How many sharks did you see?"

"Two," Meredith said. "The giant and later a smaller one."

Duffy leaned forward. "Did you notice if the sharks had been tagged?"

"Tagged?" Theo asked.

"An electronic tag. They look like large darts, near the dorsal fin. The data can show where the sharks have been, how deep they dive, when they surface. A tag could—well—provide an alibi. Prevent someone from hunting him down."

"Wow," Meredith said. "I didn't know to look."

Raised voices made Alexa turn. One of the three-sheets men was leaning, palms flat, on a nearby table, arguing heatedly with a seated man. His buddies swayed behind him.

Duffy scowled at Meredith. "Luke—your guide—should have explained. The goal of cage diving should be shark conservation and education."

"I took photos. There's a place in the cage with no bars. I leaned out so I could get good shots," Theo said.

Perhaps Theo's gene pool needed culling, Alexa thought.

"Can I see the photos? Might save the shark," Duffy said.

They exchanged emails so Theo could send them.

"I'll need your copy of the photos as well, and contact info," Alexa said. "The sergeant or DI will need to talk with you." She didn't have a pad, or anything to write with, and shoved a bar napkin Theo's way.

"About what?" Meredith asked.

"In case there are further questions about your cage dive. Maybe you saw another boat?"

"One or two," Theo said. He pushed the napkin away and handed Alexa a business card. "I may have taken snaps of them. Fishing boats—so quaint."

"The big shark had a long slash over his eye," Meredith added. "I remember that."

John Mellencamp started rocking about small towns, and the bar patrons sang along as Meredith and Theo stood. "We leave in the morning," Theo shouted. "Onward to Queenstown. Bungee jumping."

Duffy raised his bottle. "Good on ya."

Theo and Meredith snaked toward the exit. Alexa watched as Meredith's hair bounced alluringly down her back—how did she manage? Her own hair was stiff with drying salt water. The bushy-bearded man who had been arguing cut in front of the Americans, blocking the exit. "You got balls going down in a cage," he snarled inches from Theo's face. "Don't need the likes of you here, turning our whites into packs of hungry dogs!"

Theo placed a hand on Meredith's arm. "Small Town" ended on the jukebox, and the bar went quiet.

A broader man appeared by Bushy Beard. "Are you brain dead?" he bellowed at Theo. "The whites aren't entertainment. Go on, take your Yank money, leave."

"Hold on," Theo said. "We respect..."

The first dude's fists were balled up. "How about I slice you open, chum with you?"

The bartender swung around the counter and bounded across the floor. "Stormy, Isaac—back off. These are paying customers."

A chill coursed through Alexa's blood. Could one of these men have been angry enough to shoot a cage dive operator? Might one of these men have been her own *Apex* predator? She glanced at Duffy, who appeared riveted.

"Hell. I'm a paying customer," yelled the first guy. "And your bloody neighbor."

Across the bar, the woman with long yellow hair called, "My children swim here. What do you say about that?"

Theo looked stricken, Meredith defiant as they scuttled to the exit. Their Santa Monica cheese-and-wine party might be marred. Or perhaps enhanced. Alexa imagined Meredith laughing and recounting her shark safari: "The townies are a bit unpredictable and defensive. They don't understand how diving with sharks protects the ecosystem and educates clients."

Several bar patrons clapped when the door shut.

"It's over, folks," the bartender said. "Next round is on the house."

Alexa and Duffy exchanged glances.

Duffy shrugged. "I believe in putting people in the water without cages and without chumming. Pure diving."

"Jesus. Are you crazy?"

Duffy ignored her remark and started riffing on Shark Encounters. "That sounded like dangerous conditions when Theo entered the cage. He should not have had any body parts outside the cage bars, and the boat anchored too close to shore. Three violations."

Alexa reminded herself that Duffy didn't know about the bullet in Gray's gut. "Could *Glowing Sky* anchoring close to shore have contributed to the attack?"

"Maybe. I'm going to arrange a cage dive in the morning," Duffy said. "See what's going on out there. Come with me."

Not. Happening. "I need to go off-island tomorrow and get to a lab. There are some findings I need to follow up on."

Duffy leaned so close Alexa could see the pores along his nose. "I'll wait until you get back. I think the victim was killed because of human interference. I've never encountered multiple whites causing a fatality. It's almost always a single shark and a bite-and-flight."

She drowned a bit in his pretty face and almost told him his "human-interference" theory was right. Blood from a bullet wound triggered the attack, and someone was willing to feed her to the sharks to keep that a secret.

Duffy took out his phone, probably checking Instagram for how many Likes he had. The jukebox blared again. Alexa looked around, thinking of dueling worlds: tourist and local, predator and prey, good and evil. Three women stumbled to their table, phones poised, squealing for selfies with Duffy. Alexa yelled good night and—fingering the sharp edge of her key—headed to Room Three. She didn't exhale until she was inside, leaning against the locked door.

Chapter Sixteen

Being bereft of tote, phone, and sleep caused Alexa's feet to drag the next morning. The aroma of sausage when she entered the restaurant brought them to life. She'd stuff her face—a last meal before the gallows. A man in a navy blazer, his broad back to her, was filling his plate at the breakfast bar.

She surveyed the offerings. Scrambled eggs, baked beans, stewed tomatoes, fruit, yogurt, granola, Canadian-style bacon, and lightly browned and glistening sausage. She grabbed a plate.

The man turned. "Alexa. Good morning."

She looked up. Confounded. "Bruce?" Had he been dragged in to fire her? Could he fire her? She worked for the Forensic Service Center now, which was contracted by, but not run by, the police. The empty plate slipped from her hand to the carpet. It spun and wobbled like her heartbeat. "What are you doing here?"

Detective Inspector Bruce Horne of Rotorua Police Department kept his patient eyes on the plate. When it stilled, he retrieved it, set it on a counter, and turned to her. "I flew in last night. I'm taking over."

Heat flooded her face. "But…"

Bruce's blue-sky eyes stayed steady. "Aren't you happy to see me?"

He didn't appear to be angry. But if he wasn't here to somehow fire her, what was he doing? "I...I...don't know. It's just a surprise. Stewart Island is a long way from Rotorua."

She had lain in bed last night, shivering under two blankets until she remembered the heated mattress pad. It helped with the shivers, but not with the Netflix horror binge-playing in her mind. When she'd finally fallen asleep, a nightmare—she had been locked out of an underwater cage, banging to get in, sharks circling—jerked her upright at 2:00 a.m. "Why are you here?"

"Sergeants don't lead murder investigations," Bruce said. "That's true in the States, right?"

Rank wasn't the issue. Distance was. "But why are you here, and not someone from Buff?" *Is it because you wanted to see me?*

"Buff?" His smile turned warm and sexy. "*Bluff* is another two-person station."

"Well, Invercargill or Dunedin." Clearly, Bruce wasn't mad. Wallace must not have informed him about her disobedience. Yet.

"Two of Robert King's hunting pals live in Rotorua. I interviewed them, offered my services—here I am." He held out a clean plate.

She could confess, tell Bruce about searching the boat. How rain might have destroyed evidence, and that it was the right thing to do. She brushed a wisp of sable hair out of her face. In truth, she had acted without thinking. She kept her mouth shut and accepted the plate.

Constance arrived with a coffeepot. "Morning. Can I pour a cup?"

"Ta," said Bruce.

"Thanks," Alexa said.

"I'll put you here." Constance righted the cups at a table for two. "Toast? Juice?"

"Yes," they answered as one.

Oh, brother.

An elderly couple traipsed in, looking chirpy, and stashed guidebooks and binoculars on a table. "I expect there will be a massive shark hunt today," the man said.

"Oh, my. I hope our bird tour is still on," the woman said.

Bruce leaned toward Alexa, his voice low. "Sergeant Wallace told me about the bullet in the shark victim's body."

She could smell his aftershave—something woodsy and fresh. "Not in the body. It passed through. I'll send you a copy of the pathologist's report."

Alexa buried her plate in food. Bruce followed her to the table. "I'm starved too," he said. "Between flying from Auckland to Dunedin to Stewart Island, I lost a meal."

She tamped the flutters in her stomach by forkfuls, and they ate in silence. From all appearances they looked like a couple, tourists, maybe, like the gray-haired birders anticipating the day ahead. There was much to share about the cases, but her tongue hadn't caught up with her mind. When Theo strode into the restaurant, she waved him over.

"You'll want a statement from Mr. Hall," she told Bruce. "He and his wife are visiting from the States and were on a shark dive in the vicinity of the attack. He's got photos for you, too."

Bruce's eyes narrowed. "You know where the attack took place?"

She had misspoken. "Well, the general watery area." *Watery area?* She was the village idiot.

"Meredith and I are leaving this morning," Theo said. "We'll need to hurry."

Bruce wiped his mouth and stood. "No time like the present. I'll see you," he said to Alexa, "at the seven thirty briefing."

She watched as he followed Theo to the breakfast bar where the latter filled two bowls with yogurt and granola. Bruce offered him a tray. Maybe Meredith was getting breakfast in bed. Alexa decided she wouldn't mind breakfast in bed either. With Bruce.

Don't jump the gun, Glock.

Back in her room, alone with coffee, she turned on her laptop. In a click, the pathologist's reports were in Bruce's inbox.

The door of the police station was ajar, even though the temperature was sixty degrees. Alexa took a fortifying breath and pushed it open. Bruce, conferring with Sergeant Wallace by the coffee maker, caught her eye, frowned, and looked away. Wallace turned his back to her. This was not a good sign, Alexa thought, pulling the door closed.

Constable Kopae waved and turned back to a man in a soft green Department of Conservation pullover. He had flipped up the collar, and his hands were burrowed in his pant pockets. Another ranger, Alexa guessed, setting down the crime kit.

The door banged open, and a young cop in a short-sleeved uniform hustled in and whipped his checkered cap off. "Am I late? The ferry…"

"You're fine," Wallace interrupted. "We'll start in a moment."

Wallace was calling the shots, Alexa noted. She wondered how the changing of the guard would play out. Would the sergeant resent relinquishing control? Or be relieved?

She was drawn to a map mounted to the wall under the clock. The station buzz faded as she studied Stewart Island's shape: It bulged in the middle and was almost severed (the image made her cringe) by Patterson Inlet. The shoreline was nooks, crannies, jags. The island tapered to South West Cape at the bottom and Mt. Anglem at the top—or was the top actually the bottom? Alexa located and followed Golden Bay Road to Golden Bay Wharf, harmless when mounted to the wall. To the east, she located Ringaringa Beach, where Andy Gray's body had washed up. If Gray had been shot in Golden Bay Wharf and thrown overboard—her theory—the current must have dragged his body around Muttonbird Beak. Odd. Would a body wash around a spit of land jutting out?

A rapping sound made her jump.

"Let's get started," Wallace announced and gestured to the table. He stood at the head, Bruce at his side.

Alexa scooted a chair next to Constable Kopae, who nodded

and handed Alexa her tote. "Found it in the locker area on *The Apex* when we searched the boat," she whispered. "Figured you might need it."

Alexa clutched it to her chest. "Thank you. My passport and wallet..."

"Still there," Kopae said. "I thought you were right to search the vessel. Lisa—Gray's partner—gave permission, so entry wasn't an issue."

Alexa sat straighter. Kopae's words provided hope that her transgression would be forgiven. The ranger and new cop sat across from them.

Wallace cleared his throat. "As you know, I'm Sergeant Kipper Wallace of Stewart Island Police. It's my honor and duty to introduce Detective Inspector Bruce Horne from Auckland Central..."

"He's from Rotorua," Alexa blurted.

Wallace looked flummoxed. "Senior?"

"I'll get to that in a minute," Bruce said. "Continue, Sergeant."

"As per protocol, the DI has been brought in to assume responsibility for these cases." Wallace stepped aside for Bruce.

"Thank you, Sergeant." He paused and looked at Alexa. Heat jumped between them. "I am formerly of Rotorua Police Department, as Ms. Glock interjected. In a fortnight, I will be commander at Auckland Central. This was supposed to be my holiday time."

Alexa's jaw slackened. Bruce was moving to Auckland? What the heck? Why hadn't he said so at breakfast? He kept speaking, but Alexa wasn't hearing. What about his teen daughters? There were two of them—braces and sports and needing a dad.

She supposed Auckland Central was a promotion. Rotorua was small potatoes compared to Auckland. *And I live in Auckland.*

"That's all about me," Bruce said, penetrating Alexa's thoughts. "Please introduce yourselves."

The ranger guy went first. Ian Lowell was a Department of Conservation supervisor. "Been super for five years," he said.

"Conservation and people manager." His short dark hair stood at gelled attention. Alexa figured he must be Stephen and Scratch's boss. "I stopped by to see if I could assist in any way."

"Supervisor Lowell knows the bush inside and out," Wallace said, taking a chair.

"How many staff do you have?" Bruce asked.

"I have twelve permanent staff," Lowell answered. "Busy season is starting, so in addition to my regulars, I have sixteen temps and ten volunteers."

"We'll need to tap into them," Bruce said. "Thank you for offering your assistance."

Alexa explained who she was.

"Ms. Glock and I worked together on a previous case," Bruce added.

"Like CSI, eh?" said the young cop. He was Constable Bobby Briscoe, a twenty-something loaner from Bluff. His delicate nose was at odds with his beefy tattooed biceps—a swirling of fern fronds.

"I brought Constable Briscoe over. More hands on deck," Wallace said.

Alexa wanted to fix Briscoe's collar—one side stood at attention while the other lay flat.

When the intros were completed, Bruce continued. "Sergeant Wallace is to be commended for his handling of the situations thus far. Look around the table. We are now a team, 24/7, until these cases are resolved. Are we in agreement?"

Everyone but Lowell nodded. "Why cases, plural?" he asked. "I heard about the bullet hole in the hunter's skull. I get it—he couldn't have shot himself. But how is a shark attack a case that needs solving? Are you going to cuff the sharks?"

No one laughed.

"Good question." Bruce uncapped a marker and drew a line down the middle of the board. "We'll start with the alleged shark attack, since you brought it up."

"Nothing alleged about it," Lowell insisted. "I saw the photo on the internet."

"The victim has been identified through fingerprints. His name is Andrew Gray. He owned White Dive Tours." Bruce wrote the name at the top of the left column of the white board.

"My God, I knew Andy," Lowell said.

Everyone knows everyone around here, Alexa remembered. The charm of a small island. Or curse.

Lowell stiffened, like a beagle at scent. "Did he fall overboard?"

"Let's hold off on speculation." Bruce's blue eyes caught Alexa's. "Is time of death established?"

"His partner, Lisa Squires, took him to lunch at 1:00, and they ate together," she replied. "Contents of his stomach…"

"A simple answer," Bruce interrupted.

Bye-bye, breakfast buddy. "The pathologist's T of D estimate is between 5:00 p.m. and 8:00 p.m."

"That would be Saturday, right?" Bruce asked.

She nodded stiffly.

"And this is Monday morning." Bruce twisted off the marker cap and wrote the time of death on the board. "Ms. Glock made a surprise discovery during the autopsy that will answer Supervisor Lowell's question. Please continue, Ms. Glock."

"Gray had a bullet wound in his abdomen," she said. "He was shot."

"What did you say?" Lowell asked.

Alexa watched the DOC man. "He was shot in the gut. The pathologist said the wound wouldn't have killed him instantly."

"What do you mean?" Lowell looked incredulous. "It wasn't a shark attack?"

"Not solely a shark attack," Bruce said. "Sergeant Wallace communicated this unusual discovery to me late yesterday. That's when the situation on the island went from one case to two cases. I gave him orders to not divulge this information. I'm giving everyone in this room the same order, understood?" He paused, looked at each of them.

Lowell jumped on board quickly. "The pāua divers and shark cagers have been going at it. The pāua divers say the chumming is making their dives more dangerous. They go down, close to shore—no air tanks—and pry the pāua off the rocks. The courts are debating a cage diving ban. It's been dragging on years. Maybe a pāua diver got tired of waiting. Took matters in his own hands."

"Stormy Parker is the local PāuaMac rep," Wallace said.

Alexa perked up at "Stormy." Where had she heard the name?

"Mac? What's that?" Bruce asked.

"Stands for management action committee."

Bruce wrote *motive* under Gray's name and *paua diver*. "Get those men to the station for an interview. What's the name of Gray's competitor?"

"Shark Encounter. Owner is Lucas Grogan," Wallace said.

Bruce added *business competition* to his motive list. "Others?"

"Islanders who hate cage diving," Constable Kopae said. "Lots of locals want cage diving banned. And Andy and Lisa's porch was chummed." She shoved a hank of dark hair back into her stubby ponytail.

"I made a list of suspects," Wallace said.

Bruce added *local opposition* and capped the marker.

"Who was the last to see Andy alive?"

"His wife, we think. Lisa Squires," Wallace said. "He sent his crew members home that morning. Squizzy Koch and John Lynch. They're stopping by at 9:00."

Bruce wrote the names on the board. "Last people to see the victim alive are always first on my suspect list."

"So the shooter doesn't know we know about the bullet, right?" Constable Briscoe said. "He thinks we think the bloke died in a shark attack. Brill."

"Until fifteen minutes ago, that's what I assumed," Bruce said. He turned his gaze to Alexa. She knew what was coming. Her heart drummed a minor-key funeral march.

"I learned that Ms. Glock conducted a preliminary search of Gray's vessel. Last night. She discovered a lodged bullet and then was attacked by an unidentified assailant."

"The search was against my orders," Wallace said, his face triumphant. "She jumped overboard to get away."

"Blimey," Constable Briscoe said. "So the bloke knows we know."

Alexa spoke up. "My search last night was unauthorized." There. Out in the open. The truth. "I was afraid rain would destroy important evidence, and that the unusual circumstances warranted my actions."

Everyone stared at her. The minute hand on the clock ticked accusingly.

"Unusual circumstances?" Bruce asked.

Alexa shifted, feeling like a third grader in class who called out the wrong answer. "We didn't have a DI running the case. I believed that if we had one, searching the murder scene would have been first response."

"Did you know *The Apex* was the scene of the murder?" Bruce's expression was cold.

"No way to know that," Wallace broke in.

Her heart skipped a beat. "I found blood spatter and a bullet lodged in a rail indicating it *was* the crime scene."

"Did you know it was the scene of the murder *before* you searched?" Bruce repeated.

"No, sir. I only suspected."

Bruce took a tissue out of his pocket, covered his nose, and blew an angry honk. A delay tactic, Alexa suspected, as he figured out whether to fire her on the spot.

Constable Kopae pushed back from the table and walked to the coffeepot. "Anyone for a cuppa?"

Bobby Briscoe started giving instructions, "Two sugars, ta," but his voice petered out as Bruce threw the tissue into the trash and placed both hands on the end of the table.

"Ms. Glock, you *did* have a commander." His voice was calm. "Sergeant Wallace was in charge until I assumed responsibility. I'll speak with you privately about disobeying an order. Cases are weakened when an officer takes matters into his or her hands. Is that clear?" Relief washed over her. "Yes, sir." She glanced at Wallace, but he refused to meet her eyes. Kopae gave her a discreet thumbs-up.

"What's done is done," Bruce said. "Let's reap the benefits. Describe what happened on the vessel, Ms. Glock."

Alexa was glad someone had propped the station door open again. The breeze, carrying salt and sea, refreshed her memory. "I discovered a bullet lodged in the rail on the upper deck. I took some photos, and someone grabbed me from behind as I was putting my cell back in my pocket." She hadn't remembered until this moment what she had been doing when hands grabbed her. A tremor infused her voice. "I elbowed him to get away, and then he came at me with a gaff." Her hand went to the wound on her shoulder. "He swung once, hit the rail, swung again, grazing my shoulder. I jumped overboard. I think jumping in the water, uh, saved me." She swallowed, trying to moisten her throat. "He threw a cooler of chum on me."

"Blow me over," Constable Briscoe said. "That's harsh."

"Were you hurt?" Bruce asked.

Darts of pain emanated from the gash. The horror hadn't diminished by the telling of it. "I'm okay."

"Report. File a report," Bruce said. "Do you have the photos?"

"No. My phone drowned when I was in the water."

"Were your backup and sync activated?" Kopae asked.

She had no idea.

The team members continued staring. "How did you get out of the drink?" Constable Briscoe finally asked.

"I swam to the beach." As if it had been easy—the terror and loneliness.

"That water is fifty degrees," Lowell said. "You're lucky hypothermia, or sharks, didn't kill you."

She smiled weakly. "Well, the kelp tried to."

"Kelp probably saved you," Lowell said. "The sharks stay out of it."

Saved by seaweed.

Wallace took over. "We ensured Miss Glock's safety and then searched the boat. No sign of anyone. The area on the upper deck where Miss Glock thinks she saw a bullet was vandalized—gouged out—and there was no gaff."

The bullet and gaff. Gone. Alexa worried the team wouldn't believe her. If she hadn't searched the boat, no one would have known the bullet had ever existed. Right? She was conflicted. Right. Wrong. Up. Down. It was like being in the cold black water again, disoriented.

"The attack was attempted murder," Bruce said. "Could you identify the assailant?"

Alexa closed her eyes, conjuring the scene, but the attacker stayed in the shadows. "It was too dark, and it happened quickly. Black clothes, dark hair. Taller than me." She could feel the man's hot breath in her ear, the scratch of stubble grazing her cheek. "No beard. He didn't have a beard."

Bruce didn't dwell. "Someone shot Andrew Gray—for what reason we don't know—was he innocent, or was he involved in criminal activities? And then the perpetrator dumped his body..."

"He might have been still alive," Alexa said.

"...threw Gray overboard. He was attacked by sharks, washed ashore. And now Ms. Glock has been attacked. Let's take a ten-minute break before we jump into the case of the missing hunter."

"Ha," Constable Briscoe said. "Jump in. Like Miss CSI did."

Chapter Seventeen

On the porch, the tongue-lashing from Bruce was severe and brief. "Follow orders, is that clear?" His blue eyes were ice daggers. "You could have been killed. Another fatality. One more transgression and you're banned."

She stepped backwards, against the rail, ashamed. It wasn't the time to bring up his move to Auckland. She'd most likely sabotaged their nascent relationship anyway.

Bruce turned sharply and entered the station, pulling the door shut.

A closed door was a punch to her stomach. She preferred to be the one who shut the doors—years of men like Jeb floating in her wake testified to this preference. Being left behind made her feel like a powerless kid. Like someone was never coming back.

But hey, her job—for the moment—was intact. The morning air was brisk, and after a moment's glance at the harbor where the ferry was departing, she squared her shoulders and flung the door wide.

Damn if the talking didn't cease when she stepped inside.

Bruce was ready. "Let's go. Case two." He scribbled *Robert King* on the right side of the board and waited until the team settled back at the table.

"Robert King, aged forty-four, from Christchurch, went deer

hunting with three friends in the Little Hellfire hunting zone in Rakiura National Park last February. On the second day, three February, he left the hut early and never returned. He has not been seen since, despite full-scale searches," Bruce summarized.

"This was shortly after the massive whale stranding," Supervisor Lowell said.

That piqued Alexa's attention. The ranger Stephen had tried to save the whales but ended up shooting them. Euthanasia was more humane than slow suffocation. *God, that must have been horrible,* she thought.

"Is the whale stranding relevant?" Bruce asked.

"Frame of reference," Lowell answered. "Myself and a few of my rangers had to deal with the aftermath. It diverted our attention."

"I see," Bruce said, scribbling *whale beaching* in the corner. "Last week King's body was discovered by bush trampers. One of your rangers stayed with the remains until Ms. Glock arrived. You've been busy, Ms. Glock. What can you add?"

She was back on terra firma. "The remains were consistent with ten months of decomp. I used dental records to identify the deceased as Robert King."

Briscoe knocked a knuckle against his incisors.

"We recovered a Browning A-Bolt next to the body," she said. "The diameter of the entrance wound in the cheek is consistent with a greater firing distance than self-infliction. We need that shotgun in a ballistics lab—to see if it's the same weapon used to kill King." She looked at Wallace.

"It's bagged, tagged, ready," Wallace said.

At least he responded, she thought.

"I'll handle the rifle," Bruce said. He wrote *motive* under King's name and looked at the team. "Round two. Motive?"

"Life insurance for the wife," Constable Briscoe said.

"There's no policy," Bruce said. "I checked."

"Maybe nobody planned to kill him," Wallace said. "It was

probably an accident, and the shooter panicked. Main suspects would be his hunting buds."

"I agree with Sergeant Wallace," Constable Kopae said. "Accident and cover-up."

Bruce raised an eyebrow. "I interviewed the two from Rotorua yesterday. They claim they've been close friends since uni and were devastated by King's disappearance. They were willing to be fingerprinted. The third man is from Dunedin. Get him to the local station. Any other motives?"

No one said anything.

Bruce studied his team. The room went hushed, nothing but the wall clock ticking away the time, and a growl from someone's stomach.

"Here's what I've been wondering," Bruce said. "Is there anything to link Robert King and Andrew Gray? Could the deaths be related?"

The team stared back, silent.

Supervisor Lowell broke it. "I believe we're looking at unrelated incidents."

"'Course we are," Constable Briscoe chimed. "The deaths are months apart."

Nonetheless, Bruce drew a line connecting the names. "I don't see it that way. Two victims, both shot, on a remote—I emphasize remote—island that hasn't had a murder since 1927." His voice went low and grave. "Occam's razor."

"Eh?" Constable Briscoe asked.

"He means go with the simplest solution," Constable Kopae said.

Bruce nodded. "The simplest explanation is that this is the work of one man."

Chapter Eighteen

Bruce directed Lowell to lead the rangers back to where King's remains were discovered to establish where he was shot. "It can't be far from where the body was," he said. "Cross-check all DOC records—which rangers had been near, what hunters and trampers were on-island."

The desk phone rang, and Kopae jumped at it.

Bruce continued firing orders at Lowell. "Stop by the ferry office. Get passenger lists for the past week and have one of your rangers stationed at the terminal. I want to know who is going and coming."

Alexa noted the ranger supervisor was taking notes.

Constable Kopae hung up the phone. "Reporters, Senior," she said to Wallace. "I told them bathing beaches are still closed."

"I called Kana Duffy in to assess," Supervisor Lowell said. "I'll have him make a statement to the press."

Bruce turned to Kopae. "Constable, I'd like you to canvass the Golden Bay area. Who heard the sound of a gun Saturday afternoon? Who saw anyone around the wharf? Who owns the boats docked there?"

"Also—sir—I could follow up on islanders with gun permits."

"Good thinking." To Wallace, Bruce said, "Get Gray's partner in here. I want to interview her."

"Lisa Squires and her mother are meeting me at the airport at half past nine," Wallace said. "Miss Squires wants to view the body at the morgue. King's family will be there too."

"Round her up now." Bruce looked at his watch. "It's only eight. Bring her in before Gray's crew gets here. She needs to know her partner's death wasn't a simple—if there is such a thing—shark attack. I'm releasing Gray's name to the press, but nothing about the bullet."

Bruce was working the room. Alexa could understand why he had been promoted. He swung around to her.

"You're booked on the same flight as Squires and Wallace," Bruce said. "We're getting you to a lab."

"I need to get back to *The Apex* first," she said. "With your permission."

"Granted."

She collected her belongings but lingered; she needed a ride.

Constable Briscoe was sent to interview Lucas Grogan, owner of Shark Encounter. "See if there was animosity between the rival companies. Was there enough business to go round? Check the books, the owner's whereabouts." Bruce threw orders like darts. "Then dig into Gray's finances and phone records. How much does a vessel like *The Apex* cost? Where did he get the money? Get me a report by noon."

Briscoe's collar was messed up again—half up, half down. "Sweet az," he said.

Alexa was picking up Kiwi slang and knew Kiwis used "sweet as" when they were pleased. She stepped over to Kopae. "Could I get a lift to Golden Bay?"

The constable looked startled, then agreed. "Short on cars, we are. Let me file this report first."

Uncomfortable with Bruce's proximity, Alexa waited on the station porch. She let the early morning breeze off the harbor cool her cheeks, calm her mind. No cruise ship blighted the postcard vista. Kopae told her the cruise ships showed up only once a week, weather permitting. No approaching or departing ferry either, only a figure rowing a dinghy toward a moored sailboat. The rower's progress was jerky, making her think of the cases. Advancement in crime investigation was often jerky, hard to identify. She thought of her impending return to *The Apex*. The Alpha Predator. The wound on her shoulder throbbed.

Showing fear triggered attack—right?

She thought instead of Bruce's theory that the cases might be the work of one person. She understood Occam's razor theory— but considered an article she had read in *Psychology Today* that said people who believe two variables are related tend to see connections in the data when it doesn't exist. People are fallible. She might have to become the voice of reason for Bruce.

Constable Kopae appeared, zipping her navy police vest. Her checkered police cap hid her stubby ponytail. "Let's go."

Kopae's car was a slightly rusted gray sedan—a Holden Commodore. Alexa shook her head; the make sounded like the captain of a yacht. She stuffed the crime kit and her tote in the back and climbed in as Kopae lowered the windows. They stayed silent until the station was out of view.

"So…" Kopae said.

"I want…" Alexa said at the same instant.

They laughed. Alexa tried again. "Thank you for getting my tote."

"Ah, yeah," Kopae said. "Good to stick together. Me Too movement, and all?"

Alexa bit her tongue. #MeToo was about sexual harassment and didn't apply.

"Did you see the stack of Shark Sighting forms in the galley," Kopae asked, "when you were on *The Apex*?"

Alexa nodded. "They were from the Department of Conservation," she said. "I wondered why Gray had them."

"Me too. Wallace put in for a warrant so we can confiscate them."

That was the kind of Me Too Alexa could support.

They glided through the village. A light was on in the Four Square grocery store, and a man, newspaper tucked under his arm, yanked his yellow lab along the sidewalk. In a blink the town was gone. Alexa recognized Wallace's house and craned her neck to see if Nina was in the kitchen window.

Kopae slowed to let a large parrot hop across the road. "So you've worked for DI Horne before? What's he like?"

The bird stopped, faced them. "Cheeky fella," Kopae complained, honking. "Sometimes kakas perch on top of my car and slide down the windshield." The parrot fluttered large green wings and stalked to the shoulder.

Alexa watched the bird show and thought of how Bruce had masterfully taken the reins at the briefing. "Bruce is dogged and smart. A bit single-minded…"

"Bruce?" Kopae interrupted. "I heard Yanks were casual. I'd be given bus fare to Te Anau—that's where I grew up—if I used his given name."

Oops. "Yeah. We are casual in the States. I meant Detective Inspector Horne. He'll do a good job."

Kopae turned off Golden Bay Road. A rosy palette of wharf spread below as the constable pulled next to a rusting Toyota Vitz. "That's Ryan Kern's car. He runs the water taxi. I'll be back in sixty mins."

Alexa yanked her stuff out and said goodbye. She turned her head, retracing last night's steps: down the hill, through this lot, onto the beach, up the pier, onto *The Apex,* into the water, through the chum, swim to shore. She was thankful to be alive and remembered her vow to call her brother. Tonight.

Wait. Her phone was ruined.

She focused on the work ahead. In Raleigh she would process a crime scene with a team, but New Zealand was too sparsely populated, spread too wide for forensic teamwork. Usually she preferred working alone.

I'm not alone. The rusted Toyota dude was here somewhere, and a figure in a floppy hat walked the shoreline. Alexa readied the digital camera and began clicking. The world seen through a viewfinder was governable. Yellow caution tape still barricaded the pier and fluttered from *The Apex*. Alexa took several stills, including the beachcomber, a woman, and then hung the camera around her neck and trekked to the White Dive boathouse. She tried the door and window. Locked. She'd remind Bruce to have it searched.

"No dives today," called a bushy-haired man from the water-taxi boathouse. He leaned out the ticket counter ledge.

She walked over. "Good morning. I'm Alexa Glock, working with the police."

"Eh, I saw Elyse drop you off. What's with that caution tape barricading the pier? I have customers arriving. Need to get to my boat."

"I'll remove it in a sec. Constable Kopae said your name is Ryan Kern. Is that right?" Alexa took out her notepad.

"That's me. This have to do with the shark attack?" He was fifty, maybe, tall and lean.

"We're taking precautions."

"The attack will shut the cagers down, eh?" His chestnut eyes were sharp. "'Bout time. Tormenting sharks for profit. Makes me sick."

The team would have to look into this guy. "Where are you headed this morning?"

"Ulva Island." He pointed to a green mass in the bay. "Pristine predator-free bird sanctuary. No one lives there—just the birds."

She followed his gaze. The morning sun peeked above the cloud, the air was cool, the waves docile. She wasn't fooled, though. Ulva Island might be predator-free, but Stewart Island wasn't.

"'Birds and Bamboo Orchids.' That's the name of my tour. I'm the guide, too." His eyes softened. "Do you know who the victim is?"

"Not yet," she lied. "Were you around Saturday?"

A car crunched across the lot. They watched it park and a couple get out. Alexa recognized the birders from the breakfast bar.

"It was pissing guts Saturday. I stayed home." He stepped out from the boathouse and doused his ankles and neck with bug spray.

"It cleared up later." Alexa scratched her sandfly bites. "Where do you live?"

He pointed up the hill and slipped on sunglasses.

Alexa could make out three cottages partly hidden by woods. The birders were walking this way. She turned to the fishing boat docked past Kern's water taxi. "Whose boat is that?" Rust stains wept from two small portholes, staining the gray painted hull. A winch and netting lined the stern.

"*Darla Jo* belongs to Sean Warren."

"He around?"

"He comes and goes." Kern grabbed a key from his pocket and locked the boathouse door. "His schedule is irregular since he lost his job. The oyster farm shut down, eh? He does odd jobs now. Can you take that ribbon down?" Kern turned toward the birders. "G'day," he said jovially.

"Is 'Birds and Orchids' still on?" the man asked.

"Is it safe?" the woman asked, eyeing the yellow tape.

"It's all good," Kern replied. "Let's fill out paperwork. Last week I saw a saddleback."

Alexa didn't know if a saddleback was a bird or an orchid. She walked to the pier, scanning the sand. High tide and rain had erased footprints. She removed the caution tape at the end of the pier—Kern had to make a living. The tape barricading *The Apex* waved, but she turned away for the moment and focused on the beachcomber who appeared to be taking notes on a clipboard.

She was young, early twenties, and wearing green-and-purple-striped pajama-like pants tucked into gum boots, and a black pullover pinched tight by backpack straps. Her floppy blue hat clashed. A thrift store bargain hunter, Alexa decided, approaching. "Hi," she said.

The woman studied her clipboard. Alexa tried again. "Hello. I'm with the police. May I ask you some questions?"

Her pale green eyes darted everywhere but at Alexa. She finally spoke. "No policemen are with you, and you aren't wearing a uniform."

Alexa unzipped her all-purpose lightweight jacket. She could hear the girl's American accent. "The police are at the station. I am helping them with an investigation. I'm from the States, too. What's your name?"

The woman—maybe a college student—turned sideways and studied the shore. In a monotone, she said, "I'm Madalyn Smith from Annapolis, Maryland, United States of America. I am collecting data." She pointed to a strand of seaweed stretching half the length of the beach. "This is number forty-four. *Macrocystis pyrifera.*"

"It's kelp, isn't it?"

"Giant kelp is the world's largest seaweed. It can grow two feet per day." Madalyn tapped her pencil against the clipboard. "Giant kelp can reach one hundred feet long. That is equivalent to thirty meters."

"There's a lot of it around here," Alexa offered. She wondered if Madalyn was on the autism spectrum.

Madalyn marked her spreadsheet. "There are fifty-six varieties of brown kelp on Stewart Island available to aid me in my dissertation: Kelp Forest Ecosystems. I have collected data on forty-six."

Alexa perked up. "Is it true that sharks stay out of kelp?"

"That is false." Madalyn spoke loudly. "Researchers in South Africa attached cameras to the dorsal fins of eight *Carcharodon carcharias*. Seven swam into the kelp forests. That's eighty-seven percent. The experiment is recorded on YouTube."

The waves hissed, and the water was clear and green. Ten feet out the kelp undulated lazily. She hadn't been safe from the sharks when she thrashed through it last night. Kern caught her attention—he was leading the birders to his small boat. Would a great white shark attack a small boat? Were the birders safe?

Madalyn removed a ruler from her backpack side pocket and walked away.

Startled, Alexa followed. "Do you come here every day?"

"No. I work six days a week. I begin at 9:00 a.m., which is 4:00 p.m. yesterday in Annapolis, Maryland. I stop to eat lunch at 12:30. I begin again at 1:00 p.m., which is 8:00 p.m. yesterday in Annapolis, Maryland."

"Were you here this past Saturday?" Alexa asked. The sound of a motor caught her attention. Kern had started his boat and was zipping off, tailed by a frothy wake.

Madalyn's brow, barely visible under her sun hat, scrunched. "Saturday morning the island received 2.5 inches of precipitation." She did more tapping. "I stayed at Stewart Island Youth Hostel. At 2:00 p.m. I walked here."

Was this young woman safe? Smart, yes. But safe? No. Not with a killer on the loose. Alexa worried for her. "Did you see people around?"

Madalyn's pale green eyes ricocheted off Alexa's.

Alexa clarified. "Did you see people on this beach, or on the pier Saturday?"

"No."

"Did you see anyone in the parking lot or in the boathouses on Saturday?"

Madalyn spoke so loudly that Alexa had to step back. "At 5:00 p.m., a black Chevy truck drove at a high rate of speed and parked in the lot."

An ice pick jabbed Alexa's heart. This was within Andy Gray's time-of-death window. "Did you see the license plate?"

"Yes."

Alexa waited for more, but nothing came. "Do you remember the license plate number?"

"No."

Alexa wrote down Madalyn's contact info and a description of the truck. "Could you describe the driver of the pickup truck?"

"He was a man with dark hair and light skin."

Alexa searched the beach. They were completely alone. "Thank you for talking to me. Good luck with your kelp work. And be careful."

"Be careful," Madalyn repeated, looking confused.

Chapter Nineteen

The tide had leveled *The Apex* with the dock. No downward leap like last night. Sergeant Wallace and Kopae had wrapped caution tape along the rail and posted two *Keep Out* signs. The warning might work on people who followed rules.

Graceful as a gymnast in hiking boots, she hopped aboard and settled on the bench to suit up. *I've got this.*

She photographed the scene, aware that the flat, lazy sea surrounded her. The cooler, once full of blood slurry, lay on its side. A whoosh of breath escaped from her lungs as she swabbed a sample of leakage. The stench lingered as she dusted the lid for prints.

She had less than an hour and worked industriously, calmed by procedure.

The knothole on the second level was now a crude irregular gash, and the gaff was, indeed, missing.

The knee-wall blood spatter she had spotted last night was gone, but Alexa smiled. Trick's on you, buddy. Blood is almost impossible to eliminate. Even chlorine bleach only erases it to the naked eye. BLUESTAR FORENSIC spray would illuminate hemoglobin left behind. But dim light or darkness was necessary for the trace to glow. Stewart Island was good for darkness. She had read the island had recently been named as a Dark Sky Sanctuary. There was such a thing, and Alexa thought it was cool. In the daytime, anyway.

She'd come back at night.

The bullet evidence could not be brought back. The proof in her head that it had been here, lodged and lethal, didn't count. But she did have photos of the exit wound on Gray's body. And Constable Kopae had mentioned that the photos she had taken on her phone might still exist in the cloud, if her phone had been synced.

Fat chance. When in her life had she ever been synchronized?

She had waved to Madalyn and was walking up the hill when Constable Kopae crested it and pulled over so Alexa could get in. "Senior said to bring you straight to the airport," Kopae said.

She had a busy day ahead examining evidence in a lab. "Stop by the medical center on the way. There's more evidence I need to pick up."

"Roger."

Alexa filled Kopae in on Madalyn's description of the man and truck.

"That sounds like Sean Warren's truck," Kopae said. "He owns the fishing boat. Bunks there, too, sometimes."

"Do you know him?" She glanced out the rear window at Madalyn, a small figure against the ocean and sky.

"He's going through a rough patch. No job, his wife kicked him out, I heard."

A bad feeling kicked Alexa too. "Madalyn could be in danger if the truck driver had anything to do with Gray's death. Get one of Supervisor Lowell's rangers here to keep an eye on her."

Chapter Twenty

A half hour later Alexa was squished in the rear of a six-seater plane flying over Foveaux Strait. Wallace looked solemn in the copilot's seat. He'd taken Alexa aside at the airstrip and told her the list of Stewart Island residents with guns had been faxed to the station and included Andy Gray. "Did you find a gun on *The Apex*?"

"I would have told you."

"Lisa says Andy carried it for protection."

People who owned guns had an increased chance of being killed by one—be it homicide, suicide, or accident. This was looking like the Big H, Alexa thought. She studied Lisa Squires and her mother, huddled by Wallace's SUV as they awaited the pilot. "Can anyone verify where Lisa was Saturday evening?"

"Her mum, Judy, came round, that's all," said Wallace.

Maternal alibi was almost as weak as a spousal alibi, Alexa thought.

"Here's the Death Investigation report on Andrew Gray. The DI said to give you a copy. You can read it on the plane. We put a rush on his bank and phone records."

Wallace would fly with the mother and daughter to Invercargill, and then the pilot would take Alexa to Dunedin so she could use the university lab.

Now mother and daughter were in the middle row. Alexa didn't want to stare, so she looked out the window. The sea was kicking up whitecaps, and the plane dipped and shuddered. *Death winds.* Wasn't that what Mary had called them? She clutched the armrest.

Lisa spoke. "Sergeant Wallace, I know who wants Andy dead. Stormy..."

The whining engine made it hard for Alexa to hear.

"He... Stewart Island pāua divers," Lisa said.

Alexa leaned closer, watching the back of Lisa's head, her hair clumpy and unkempt.

"It's true, Kipper," Lisa's mother said. "I told Nina at book club that PāuaMac needs to back off. They don't own the ocean."

Wallace had turned his solid body around. "Ta, Judy. I'll let the DI know. We'll haul Stormy in for questioning."

That name again—Stormy. Alexa's stomach lurched as she reviewed that pāua diving was a way to make a living on the island and that the cage diving industry was making it dangerous. The thought made her dig in the crime kit for the larger of the two shark teeth extracted from Gray's body. She palmed it and stared at the beauty and savagery of its serrated edges and crown point sharp enough to pierce her skin.

"Andy. I want Andy," Lisa mewled. "His mum and dad are flying from Perth. And I've never met them. What will happen to the boat? Our business?" Her mewls turned to wails.

The plane vibrated and shuddered. Alexa stuffed the tooth in her jacket pocket and squeezed the armrest.

In Invercargill the two women stumbled out, Wallace following. "A flight back to the island leaves at six. That enough time?" he asked at the threshold.

She gave him a thumbs-up and didn't envy his tough job ahead: loved ones viewing remains. On the puddle-jump to Dunedin she read the Death Investigation report on Andrew Elkin Gray that Wallace had given her. She skimmed DOB, height, weight, and race. Gray's "Nationality" was listed as Australian. "Marital Status" snagged her eye. New Zealanders used "partner" regularly, and Alexa wasn't sure if Lisa Squires and Andy Gray were married. Nope. The "Never Married" box was checked. "Next of Kin" was Harry and Louisa Gray of Perth, his mother and father.

Who made that dreaded call, Alexa wondered? Lisa? Did Andy's parents know they were going to be grandparents?

"Date" and "Time of Death" concurred with her forensic findings. "Last Seen Alive" was marked Saturday, 7 December, 1:55 p.m., by Lisa Squires.

But besides Lisa—who was last to see him alive? In case Lisa was lying.

"Nature of Injury" was marked as "Multiple". "Manner of Death" was marked "Pending". "Place of Incident" was marked "Other", and *vessel* scrawled in the blank. Alexa felt clammy thinking of *The Apex*. She looked out the small window. How did a young man raise the capital to start a cage diving business? *The Apex* must have cost a fortune. Was Andy in over his head?

Alexa snorted.

She skimmed a second report entitled Solvability Factors. This was information about the crime that could help determine who committed it—like witnesses, serial numbers, mobile phones, photographs, CCTV, fingerprints. The fewer solvability factors listed, the less the chance of solving the crime. The bullet hole in the deck railing—which she had seen with her own eyes—was an example of a solvability factor. Too bad the perp had obliterated it. Most of the report was blank at this point.

Alexa wondered what had happened to Andy Gray's phone. Not that it would have saved him—the service on the island being sporadic, and that was kind—but where was it? It had probably been in his pants pocket and had joined Davy Jones's locker.

Momona Airport on the outskirts of Dunedin had a real terminal and a dozen planes. On the tarmac a young cop held an

Alex Clock sign. "You're on time, ha ha, but you're not a bloke. I'm Constable McFee sent to drive you to the lab."

McFee talked nonstop on the way, left hand on the steering wheel, the right gesticulating. "I hear it's not a one-off, eh. The sharks down there are primed from all that chumming, yeah."

He was winding up, and Alexa let him spin.

"When sharks get a taste for blood, they'll lurk about, wait for more, just like any animal." He glanced her way. "No more pāua diving for me, that's right. I'll switch to whitebait up the river, New Zealand caviar, eh—have you had some?"

"Had some what?" Rolling countryside had vanished, and they were in a city with Baroque-style buildings. The scent of sea slithered through the officer's open window.

"Whitebait? Where are you from? Canada? Juvie fish, that's what whitebait are. Traditional way to eat 'em is in a fritter, but my wife and I fry 'em in omelets."

Alexa's stomach was queasy from the plane ride, and fish in an omelet wasn't helping.

"My senior isn't closing our beaches, but I think he should. TV bloke said the shark lifted the man a meter high, shook him like a rag, left a cloud of blood."

"The newscaster witnessed the attack, did he?" She tightened her fingers on the crime kit and spotted a mobile phone shop. "Do you mind stopping? I need a phone."

If she purchased another iPhone, the clerk promised her data and contacts could be restored. "What about photos?"

"Yeah nah. Shouldn't be a prob. And you can keep the same phone number."

Yes, she would purchase a screen protector. And insurance. The bottom line made her cringe. Everything was more expensive in New Zealand.

The forensic lab was two blocks from the mobile store, so she didn't have time to check her photos. "I'll pick you up at half past five, eh?" McFee said.

In the lobby she found a directory. Forensic Science Laboratory: basement. Figures. Most labs were in basements, as if the work carried out belonged in the underworld. She took the stairs and entered the room at the bottom. A man looked up from his computer.

"Alexa Glock," she said, striding toward him.

He stood, short and wrinkled, and ran fingers through sparse gray hair. "Dr. Stanley Kisska. How can I help you?"

"I believe you've heard from Sergeant Wallace? Stewart Island?" She hefted the crime kit and evidence bag on a table and fished out a business card.

Dr. Kisska stared through bifocals. "From Auckland? Is Daniel Goddard your supervisor?"

Alexa smiled at the mention of her new boss.

"I taught Daniel in Instrumental Analysis. He had issues with liquid chromatography."

Issues? "You have a good memory," she said. "Do you still teach?"

"Forensic Chemistry. Keeps me young. What brings you here?"

"Did you hear about the missing hunter on Stewart Island?"

"I'm surprised he's been found. Trampers and hunters go missing in the bush. Many are never heard from again."

He said this as a matter of disturbing fact. "Well, his remains have been found, and there are circumstances I need to check out. Stewart Island doesn't have a lab. Plus tests I need to run on the shark victim case."

"I heard about the shark death. Bloody sad, reminds me of the sixties when I was a teen." Dr. Kisska bowed his head. "Three fatal attacks here in Dunedin. Great whites. It was all we talked about, thought about. It might have been one shark, come back year after year. First attack was Les Marks. I went to primary with his brother. Just a lad out for a surf one morn. His leg, gone. His mates got him to shore, the white circling the whole way. He died from blood loss. Ever since, I spend time *on* the water, not *in* the water. Lots of us who were around back then feel the same way." The scientist's eyes had a faraway look.

"I understand."

"Stop by the Harbor Museum. You can see the jaws of a white hauled in from the harbor a couple years later. Looks like a train tunnel. Lots of people believe it's him, the killer, because the attacks stopped. Let's get you registered, and then I'll show you around." Dr. Kisska pointed to a visitors' log.

Intrigued by the museum jaws, Alexa signed in and had a tour of the windowless lab. A large workstation formed an L-shape in a corner. Cubicles—one equipped with a microscope—jutted from the opposite wall.

"Evidence lockers and storage are in here," Dr. Kisska said, opening a door. "A free computer is there."

The blue fiber from Andy Gray's palm was on her mind. "Do you have a stereomicroscope?" This microscope provided different viewing angles so that a sample looked three-dimensional.

Dr. Kisska smiled like a proud parent and pointed to a closed door. "In the supply room. Let me know if I can help. I'll be grading end-of-term exams."

Alexa removed her jacket, scratched her bug bites, and washed her hands. The hunter, Robert King, wedged his way into her conscience and turned her thoughts to the constellation Orion, or The Hunter. Orion was visible in the northern *and* southern hemisphere; Bruce Horne had told her this on the dark night they had sat on her cottage porch in Rotorua, admiring the sky. "Make you feel at home, right?" he'd said, sparks fluttering like fireflies between them.

Had a hunter tracked a hunter and denied two daughters a father?

She started with fingerprints from the water bottle and the high-vis vest stuffed under the camo jacket of the deceased. Who had stuffed it there? She guessed the person who dragged the body, not wanting it to be seen. She had used go-to black powder on both, and single-use brushes so there was no cross-contamination, lifting tape and backing cards on which to press the tape. Every kid's I-wanna-be-a-detective dream.

Alexa smiled. Her throbs and itches faded. Labs were her happy place.

Forty minutes later she had a print from the vest that didn't match King's classic whorl. There was no duplicate for the unidentified print in the database. King had been hunting with three men. Had their prints been taken? She jotted a note to ask.

Up next: the cast of a Merrell boot print she had instructed Stephen to make at the scene, size ten, spattering dried mud on the paper-covered specimen tray. She logged into the computer and located the uploaded photos she had taken at the hut of Wallace's, Scratch's, and Stephen's boots.

Scrape the Keen.

Scrape the Scarpa.

The third set were Merrells. Her eyes flicked from photo to cast, back, forth. She couldn't make out the size of the boot in the photo and hadn't recorded which boot belonged to which man. Alexa chided herself for sloppy tagging. It had been a long day: storm, ferry, flight, hike, scene investigation. But mistakes were inexcusable.

She'd call Sergeant Wallace to find out. If the boot print matched a hut-buddy, what did it prove? They had all been there. Tramping about. It occurred to her that the rangers Scratch and Stephen could be suspects. Where had they been that day King failed to return?

Let the evidence guide you, her mentor's voice reminded.

Dr. Kisska interrupted. "Your phone is ringing."

She hadn't recognized the ring tone. No barking dogs. "Oh, yes, sorry." She whipped off her gloves and answered. "Hello?"

"I need you to stop by Dunedin LandSAR offices. Check records on King's PLB."

Bruce Horne. Alexa held the receiver a little farther from her ear.

"You there?"

She stayed quiet.

"Alexa?"

"Hello, Bruce."

"Yes. Hello. Er, sorry."

She could hear an intake of breath. "What's a PBL?"

"PLB. Personal locator beacon," he answered. " Robert King's wife gave him one for Christmas. He had it with him, and it's never been located. It sends a signal to the LandSAR rescue center any time it's activated. The center is in Dunedin. I'd like you to go, um, please, and pick up all records associated with it. Where and when it was activated. We've faxed the paperwork."

"Hasn't someone already done this?"

"Not since two weeks after King disappeared. It's worth another look. Any lab news?"

"I lifted an unidentified fingerprint from King's vest. We need to compare them with King's hunting partners."

"We took prints yesterday when I spoke with the two in Rotorua. I'll fax them. The other gentleman is from Dunedin. Hold on." She heard a ruffle of papers. "His name is James Reilly. I'll get someone to print him today." Bruce gave her the address of the rescue center. "Get those records. See you tonight."

It was time to switch to Andrew Gray, the man who would never have the chance to hold his child. (How could Bruce leave his girls behind and move to Auckland?)

The prints she had lifted from the cooler were too degraded to be of use. The blood sample from the chum leakage did not test positive for human blood, so she discarded it.

Two steps back, no steps forward.

She debated whether to complete a diatom test on Gray's lung tissue. Did it matter whether he was (a) killed by sharks, (b) drowned, or (c) died from a bullet? It might matter to his partner and his parents. She located a beaker to add equal parts sulphuric and nitric acids, sliced a sliver of lung for a negative control test, and added distilled water to both samples. The results—either absence of or presence of diatoms in the tissue—would be ready in twenty-four hours.

She washed up and pulled on new gloves. Fiber time. The inchworms of blue fiber nestled in the evidence envelope. Alexa removed the larger of the two with tweezers, hoping it would reveal answers.

The smell of tuna pierced her concentration. She looked up from the stereomicroscope to see Dr. Kisska munching a sandwich. He must have seen her hungry look. "Would you like the other half?"

"No, thanks. I'll pop out to get a bite."

The doctor looked relieved.

Alexa finished the fiber examination, recording length, diameter, luster, dye, and cross section pattern, and then switched back to the computer. New Zealand was the second country in the world to set up a DNA databank, following the UK, but she couldn't locate a fiber databank. Darn.

Dr. Kisska was munching on an apple.

"Is there a marine shop around?" she asked. "One that sells roping and netting?"

"Of course." He chewed, swallowed. "We're a fisherman's paradise. Fresh and saltwater. Trout, salmon, flat fish, red cod."

She hadn't asked for a fish report. "So is there a nearby marine supply store?"

"Taylor's Rig is my favorite. Two blocks past the corner."

"Thanks. I'll be back in an hour or two. Will you still be here?"

"Eh. Be here until five."

———

The streets in the South Island's second largest city were rush and scurry. No one stared at her. Alexa felt safe. She popped into Percolator Cafe for chowder, bread, and flat white coffee. Tanked up, she dodged tourists and college students as she searched for, and almost passed, Taylor's Rig.

Bells jangled as she entered and stepped past fishing rod displays. A quick skim of three tight aisles revealed scales, knives, bait buckets, hooks, buoys, and, toward the side, roping, nets, fishing line, and—her gut went queasy—gaffs. Some had hooks, others ended in spears—all meant to stab, and lift, if the poster was correct.

A thirty-something woman in a tight *I'm So Fly* T-shirt appeared. "G'day. How can I help?"

"I'm looking for rope, or netting, anything that matches this." Alexa dug out the sample and held the clear bag up for Fly to see. The fiber looked like a blue inchworm.

"Why?"

Alexa showed her ID and explained the fiber was important evidence.

She held out her hand, and Alexa gave her the bag. "It's a wee bit. Where did it come from?"

"Stewart Island."

"There was a shark attack there. Great white. Customers have been talking about it all morning. Two blokes bought shark gaffs. I hope they know what they're doing." The woman's face was speckled and windburned. "I think it's netting. We don't carry much in blue."

Alexa and the saleswoman scanned the netting display. White and black nets were most common. "It's polyethylene, if that helps," Alexa added. She had discovered this under the stereomicroscope. Polyethylene fiber was strong and light.

The closest to a match was a turquoise cast net. "Let's check the catalog," the woman said and reached under the checkout counter, producing a thick *Quality Marine* catalog. After licking her finger and thumbing through, she showed Alexa two blue fishing nets. "This one is for trawling," her finger moved to the adjoining page, "and this is a drag net."

Alexa had never been fishing. "What's the difference?"

"Trawling nets get towed behind a vessel, and the drag net is thrown by hand. It spreads out, then sinks."

She thought of the fishing boat docked at the wharf. She'd seen netting attached to a winch. What color had it been? "Do you have these in stock?"

"This drag net will take two weeks. It comes from China."

No Amazon Prime, Alexa thought. "What about the trawling net?"

"It's made local. Van Kees Nautical Nets on Cliff Hanger Road."

Bingo.

"Does Dunedin have Uber?"

———

The netting factory, located on the aptly named Cliff Hanger Road, was up, down, and around several hills and perched on a cliff shadowing a rock-strewn bay. "Do you mind waiting?" Alexa asked the Uber driver.

"I'll have to charge."

"That's fine."

Alexa couldn't believe her luck. The fishing net was manufactured right here.

She opened the front door of the single-storied factory, noting *Van Kees Nautical Nets* etched in the glass. The throttle and hum of automated spinning drums assaulted her ears. A technician was monitoring spools of fiber—maybe polyethylene—being woven into an origami of netting cascading onto a conveyor belt. To the left were two similar machines, each with a technician. She stepped forward to inspect the netting, disappointed it was white. Maybe the dyeing process came next.

The female technician smiled at her and pointed to an office to the right.

Alexa nodded, walked over, and knocked on the closed door.

A burly man, maybe fifty, opened it and held out his hand. "Guy Van Kees, owner. How may I help you?"

"I'm Alexa Glock, a forensic investigator, and I have a sample of netting that I need to match. It might be one of yours."

"That's an odd request." Van Kees looked at his watch. "I have an appointment."

"This won't take long. Look at this." She cracked open the fiber evidence envelope and let him peek.

Van Kees crossed his arms. "Who do you say you are?"

She closed the envelope and fished for a business card. "I'm working on a missing persons case. Another case as well. The shark attack on Stewart Island."

He accepted her card.

"This fiber was found on the victim, and I am trying to match it."

"On the shark victim? How on earth? Come in. I can spare a moment."

She followed Van Kees into the office. "Do you mind if I turn this on?" she asked, clicking on a desk lamp before he could answer. She extracted a plain white index card from her tote and slid the fiber on it. "Here's a magnifying glass."

Her father had given her the glass when she was accepted to the NC Sciences Forensic Institute. It lived in her tote, sheathed in fawn-soft leather. "Look hard at the world around you, Alexa," Dad had advised, his button-down buttoned to his neck. "But magnifying people's faults is unbecoming."

Her father had been in a hard position—married to a woman his daughter despised. The magnifying glass felt hot and heavy in her hand.

Van Kees watched silently. "You don't want me to touch it?"

"That's right. Does it match the nets you make here?"

The factory owner took the magnifier, leaned in, and studied quietly.

"It's two millimeters wide and just short of two centimeters long," Alexa said. She forced herself to stand still, breathe.

"One of the benefits of polyethylene is that it weighs the same, wet or dry," Van Kees said. "No absorption. Makes lifting and hauling easier and reduces fuel costs. Stronger than steel, too. No breakage." He beamed like a proud father. "It's ours. A trawling net. I believe it's our Polyurethane Stealth Glider."

Alexa exhaled a whoosh of air. "I'll need your contact information, sales records, and a sample, please."

Van Kees frowned. "Our sales records? What? I can't give you my sales records."

She considered calling Bruce, get him to order the guy. She shrugged—it was best to be self-reliant. "I know you want to help with our investigation. What about the past three years in Southland?" She had a map of New Zealand's sixteen regions on the wall of her new office at the Forensic Service Center so she would know where she was being sent as cases arose. Southland included Stewart Island, Bluff, and Invercargill.

"No. I know my rights. You'll need a warrant."

"You're not a doctor protecting patients," she snapped.

"I am protecting my customers from harassment."

This time she did call Bruce. He listened and then asked to speak to Mr. Van Kees.

She left with no sales records. Bruce was no more successful than she had been, which for some reason was satisfying, and would rush the warrant. At least she had confirmation that the fiber was Van Kees's. The Uber fare was thirty-four dollars. She looked at her watch 2:00—and had the driver take her to Harbor Museum. She could spare a few minutes to see that shark jaw Dr. Kisska had mentioned before she stopped by LandSAR.

The museum was free. "Where can I find the shark jaws?" Alexa asked the woman at the information desk.

"In the maritime section on the second floor."

When she got there, Alexa's attention was snagged by a 1968 photo of capsized *Wahine Ferry* in Wellington Harbor. The caption read: *One-hundred-and-fifteen-knot winds and enormous waves thrust the ferry, within sight of land, onto the reef.* She thought of her Foveaux Strait ferry ride two days ago: the seething waves breaking over the bow, the fierce wind, sharks lurking below. She knew it wasn't on her agenda but couldn't stop herself from watching a five-minute black-and-white clip of the disaster, which killed fifty-four people. *"Beneath the turbulent waters, like a row of shark's teeth, was Barrett Reef,"* the announcer droned, *"subject of many nautical fears, now deadly in fact."*

"Like a row of shark's teeth," Alexa murmured, creeped out and backing away. She searched the area for the jaws. There they were, in a glass box so they could be viewed from all angles, hinged wide open. Enormous and gaping. A woman and two little boys stared at it.

"A monster mouth," the littler boy piped.

Alexa moved closer and read the placard: *From Great White Shark* (Carcharodon Carcharias) *Caught in Otago Harbor, 1975, Length: 5.2 Meters, Weight: 1,840 Kilograms, Female.*

The trio moved to a fossilized shark's tooth as Alexa stood rooted, calculating that 5.2 meters was seventeen feet. Jeez Louise. *Three of me.* The white teeth had maintained their calcium phosphate, so they hadn't fossilized and turned black. They would cut like a knife straight through flesh and bone. She analyzed the teeth. The upper anterior ones were large and triangular, the coarse serrations slightly irregular. The lower teeth were skinnier, pointier, needle-like, and would pierce the hide of a seal—or person—and snag it. When those jaws snapped, anything in its path would be severed. Jeez Louise again—she understood why Andy Gray was missing an arm and a leg. She could be too. As the family moved away, she dug the tooth out of her jacket pocket and held it against the glass.

Definitely from the top jaw, Alexa concluded, and similar in size, indicating at least one shark involved in the Stewart Island attack was close in size to this shark. A voice interrupted her thoughts.

"Where did you get that?" A college-aged boy with spiked hair stared at the tooth she was pressing to the glass. "Is it from a display?"

"No," Alexa assured. "I brought it with me."

"Did you find it?"

"Well, ah, yes." In a body.

"Where?"

"I can't say."

He looked at her suspiciously. "I'm in the marine biology department at uni. That's not fossilized. It's fresh. Can I have a gawk?"

"Sure."

"This is worth a lot of money," the boy said, holding it like a gem. "You could sell it on eBay. Did you know that when one tooth falls out, another spins forward to replace it? Sharks have rows of backup teeth."

"I'm learning a lot about sharks," Alexa answered vaguely.

"A whopper, this white was," the boy said, handing it back and turning his attention to the gaping jaws. "There's a friggin' black market for jaws."

"Really?"

"Are you a Yank?" he asked.

"Yep."

"White jaws this size would sell for eighty thousand U.S. dollars on the dark web. That tooth you have would go for three or four hundred."

She squeezed tight the jagged triangle and then slipped it back in her pocket. "Um. So, selling shark teeth and jaws is illegal?"

He looked at her with earnest eyes. "Absolutely. Since 2007. It's illegal to hunt for white sharks in New Zealand, as well as illegal to trade in any white shark parts like teeth or fins or jaws. If you accidentally catch a white, you need to release it unharmed."

"Good luck with that. How do you accidentally catch a white anyway?"

"Sometimes they get caught in nets and drown. Or they might get hooked by a fisherman."

Great. So now she had contraband in her pocket.

———

Alexa's phone map showed the LandSAR office was two blocks from the museum. She walked briskly, her mind a whirl of fiber, shark jaws, boot casts.

Another glass door, another etching: New Zealand Land Search and Rescue, Inc. This door opened into a wood-paneled room void of people. Adventure posters brightened the walls: people snowboarding, river rafting, glacier climbing, bungee jumping. The theme must be different ways to die, Alexa surmised.

A stack of Personal Locator Beacon guides was on a shelf below the bungee jumping poster. Alexa opened one. The gadgets looked like palm-sized radios. They could be clipped on, worn around the neck, or stuffed in a roomy pocket. There were different brands: RES-Q, FastFind, and rescueME, with different prices—from $350 to over $500. Alexa wondered which type Robert King had. She stuffed the brochure in her tote and moved to a large map of the South Island pricked with blue, orange, and red pin flags. Alexa studied it: Certain areas, like Stewart Island, were pin-magnets.

"Each flag is a SAROP," a voice said.

Alexa whipped around to face a young woman. "What is a sarop?"

"LANDSAR Search and Rescue Operation. Last year we had 495 SAROPs. How can I help you?" Her blue polo was tucked into hip-hugging khakis.

"I'm Alexa Glock, forensic investigator, here to pick up PBL records."

"PLB," the woman corrected. "Personal locator beacon. I'm

Juta Fowlkes, support officer for Lower South." She had a whole-
some frosting of nose and cheek freckles.

Alexa had met so many people that day that her mind blurred.
"I'm here to pick up records from Robert King's PLB. He's…"

"…the missing hunter. I heard his body has been recovered."
Fowlkes stood eye to eye with Alexa. "That's why his flag is red
now." She pointed to Stewart Island.

"Red means dead?" Alexa asked. Damn. Red flags were scattered over the map.

"We refer to them as premature fatalities. I need to stay in the
control center room. I'm on call." She pointed to a hallway. "Do
you want to come with me? We can talk there?"

"Yes, thanks," Alexa said, following.

A row of computers lined the control center. Fowlkes pulled
out a chair for Alexa and sat in another. "I am familiar with the
case. About a month ago Sergeant Wallace contacted us to search
the bush again for the missing hunter, with live transmitters."

"Live transmitters? What are they?"

"It's dense bush in Rakiura National Park. Gullies, ravines,
creeks, mud."

Check, check, check, check, Alexa thought.

"Our every move was being tracked back at the station. That's
what live-tracking is. We were wearing transmitters so none of us
got lost. Or if we did, someone knew where to find us."

"Like Google."

"Yeah nah. We took a fresh look at the missing person, figured
in factors like King's age, experience, fitness level, the weather
and terrain—helicopters are of no use out there because of the
canopy—and created a search grid."

Fowlkes's phone buzzed; she checked the screen, stuffed it
back in her pocket. "But in the end, we didn't find King. How
did you do it?"

"Hikers found his remains. The DI asked me to pick up King's
PLB records."

"I haven't had time to pull it," Fowlkes said. "I got busy with a class-three Otago Pennisula rescue. Tourists are overdue from a boating expedition. Had to send in Coastguard and a copter."

"Jeez. Hope they get found."

"No sign yet. Visitors don't understand how quickly the weather changes." Fowlkes moved to a computer monitor and typed. She rocked back and forth in the roller chair, making it squeak. When a report appeared on the screen, she stilled. "The PLB is registered. That's fortunate. Some blokes don't bother to register, and then the locator is worthless."

"What date did King register his?" Alexa had pad and pen ready.

Fowlkes rocked again as her fingers tapped. "January 2018." Then she stopped rocking. "This is odd."

"What?"

Fowlkes double-clicked a link, and another window opened. "King's beacon was activated ten days ago."

Chapter Twenty-One

"What do you mean?" Alexa asked. A dead man can't send an SOS.

"On 28 November, the PLB was activated." Fowlkes studied the screen. "Whenever a beacon is activated, our first step is to call the emergency contact info on the registration form and check things out." She read from the screen. "That would be Danita King, the hunter's wife. But before my operator could do that, the owner called and said it was a mistake. There was no emergency."

"Did you notify the police?" Alexa's voice was sharp.

Fowlkes's face hardened. "Around a third of our calls are accidental activation. It's good the owner called before a rescue team was assembled." She paused and read the screen. "It says the bloke apologized and assured the operator he was fine. He bought the PLB from a friend and hadn't registered it yet. The operator took his name and number, called back to verify. That's our procedure."

"Didn't the operator know the beacon belonged to a missing person?"

"That connection wasn't made. We're not police."

Morons, Alexa thought. "Give me the name and number, please."

Fowlkes read the name of the caller: Doug Clifford, and number.

Alexa whipped out her new cell and punched the numbers before formulating a plan.

"Hell Pizza."

"Hell Pizza?" Alexa repeated.

Silence.

"Ah, is Doug working?" she asked.

"Who?"

"Doug Clifford."

"No one by that name works here. Do you want a pizza or not?"

"No." Her stomach rumbled. "Do you keep a record of customers?"

"You'll need to speak with a manager," the person said and hung up.

Alexa punched Bruce's number, but she got a "no service" message. Urgency swirled in her mind. What good was a three-hundred-twenty-seven-dollar phone if there wasn't service? She shoved the worthless device in her tote and stood.

Someone had activated King's beacon. Maybe the person who shot him.

Alexa regarded Fowlkes. This woman spent her days helping people, rescuing them. "I know your operator did her best."

"His best," Fowlkes said. "I can tell where it pinged from. Would that help?"

For real? Alexa fought to keep her voice nonchalant. "Yes."

Fowlkes jumped into action. The ping had come from Fern Gully Road on Stewart Island.

———

Alexa returned to the lab and intermittently interrupted her work to call Bruce. She never got through. *Dark ages*, she thought. *Total dark ages*. At 5:00, she thanked Dr. Kisska for his lab hospitality.

"I'll email the results of the diatom test in the morning," he said.

On the way to the airport she had Constable McFee reach Sergeant Wallace by radio. "King's PLB pinged," she shouted.

"What?" Static, static.

"From Fern Gully Road."

"Can't hear you," Wallace replied.

She repeated, slowly. "Tell Bruce," she added and then cringed. "I mean, tell DI Horne." Out the car window, trees twisted in a stiff wind.

McFee dropped her off at the airport. The pilot—his name was Joe—paced by the Cessna. "Rough ride ahead. Fasten your seat belt." He unlatched the plane's door and pulled down the steps.

She must have looked stricken.

"Storm coming," he elaborated. "No landmasses between us and the South Pole to block the high winds and rain coming, eh, it's the roaring forties. If we leave now, I'll be able to return home after dropping you off."

With foreboding she clambered into the middle row. How much excitement could she take in one day? Bruce showing up this morning, her confession to the priestly team, the jaws at the museum, lab tests, beacons pinging. Who lived on Fern Gully Road? The first ten minutes of the flight were normal, but then gusts and judders knocked the plane about like a shark's tail hitting a cage. With each slam, she squeezed her eyes and inhaled sharply. Bumper cars collided in her stomach. She couldn't bear to speak with the pilot—what if panic infused his voice?

Twenty-five minutes later they touched down. Her grateful smile changed to a frown. The airstrip was deserted. This morning there had been a couple cars, two planes, and six people. Now—no one.

"Any chance of a lift to the station?" she joked.

Joe laughed and unlatched the door. "I'll radio—let 'em know you're here, lass."

Before she could thank him, he yanked the door closed. The

plane turned, wobbled down the runway, lifted like magic, banked left, and, frail bird that it was, headed toward the mainland above the infamous strait. "Be safe," she whispered.

When the plane vanished, panic descended. She tried her phone again.

No connection.

Cut off, that's me, Alexa thought, turning in a circle. The grass blew slantwise, the wind carried threats of rain, the gray shed stood empty as the oyster shell at her foot, which she kicked. Nothing was like it should be. Phones should work. Airports shouldn't be deserted. Dead people's PLBs shouldn't ping. Shark victims shouldn't have a bullet in their gut.

She was in full-temper mode like a little kid.

Buck up, Glock.

She hitched the crime kit to one shoulder, tote on the other, zipped her jacket to the chin, and set off on the one-lane road, her pace spurred by impending rain. Forest encroached on either side, shielding her from the worst of the wind. Oban was four or so miles away. After a few minutes, a dark gray bird landed a few feet ahead of her, cocked its head, puffed its white belly, and said, "Chuk, chuk, chuk."

"I know," Alexa answered. "It's going to rain any second."

"Chuk, chuk, chuk."

"I know. It's getting late." *It must be almost seven,* Alexa thought, too encumbered to fish out her cell and check. She worried suddenly about the young woman on the beach she'd met, Madalyn the kelp expert. Kopae had promised to get a ranger to watch over her. Had she remembered?

As soon as Alexa got within a few feet, the bird flew ahead, landed, puffed, cocked, chukked. After the fourth time Alexa paused, and her little friend hopped close, cocked its head, and pecked at her boot with its tiny black beak.

"I'm hungry too," she said.

She heard an engine. In a sound wave, panic was back, and the bird was gone. Someone on this island still wanted her dead. She checked the tangle of trees to her left—ready to dash and dive—as the Stewart Island Police SUV rounded a curve.

Wallace screeched to a halt. Bruce was riding shotgun, so Alexa climbed in back, cringing at Wallace's jerky five-point U-turn.

Bruce's half-smile didn't erase his worry lines.

"Fern Gully Road is Stephen Neville's address," Wallace said. "We're on our way."

"Whose address?" she asked.

"Stephen Neville—ranger from the woods, eh?" Wallace caught her eyes in the rearview mirror. "The one who hiked with us to retrieve Robert King's body. King's PLB was activated from his address."

Alexa pictured the shaggy-haired ranger. He had saved a baby whale, had rescued her from the sea lion and quicksand. She searched for the seat belt buckle, her hands shaking. Rain began pelting the car. Maybe the storm that the pilot, Joe, had been trying to out fly had arrived. "Why would Stephen have King's locator?"

Trees flashed by. Wallace was flying. She looked at Bruce, who stayed facing forward. The skin visible between his dark hair and shirt collar looked tender and touchable.

"Lowell checked the records," Wallace said, turning on the windshield wipers. "Stephen Neville was in the Hellfire area the day King disappeared. There are witnesses—the Māori group who came to carve up the beached whales. Stephen led them."

"But that doesn't prove he shot King," she said weakly.

Bruce turned, his eyes bright. "He had a DOC shotgun checked out, from euthanizing the whales two days earlier. Never returned it. Therein lies the opportunity."

"He told me about euthanizing the whales." About their big eyes and tears.

"Probably mistook King for a deer," Wallace said.

Out the window, ferns drooped. Alexa couldn't wrap her head

around the idea that Stephen had shot the hunter, stolen his PLB, and hidden the body.

"Then he didn't man up," Wallace continued. "Skulked off like a coward." The radio squawked, and he grabbed it. "Eh?"

"Constable Briscoe and I are here, Sarge," Constable Kopae said.

"Stay back until we arrive." Wallace pressed the SUV's pedal a notch. "ETA five minutes. Neville is armed."

Chapter Twenty-Two

Wallace screeched to the narrow shoulder of a winding side street and cut the engine. "His house is around that bend—12 Fern Gully."

Alexa unbuckled and fumbled for the door handle.

"Wait with the car," Bruce barked.

"But…"

His eyes tangled with hers, reddened her cheeks, held her prisoner. His "one more transgression" warning from this morning made her release the handle.

Wallace left the key in the ignition. "Turn the engine on if you get cold."

Through the rain-drizzled rear window she watched tall Bruce and solid Wallace recede around the bend. When they were gone, she scooted out, closed the door softly. "Wait with the car" didn't mean wait *in* the car. As long as the car was within sight, she was compliant. She pulled up her hood and scurried to the side of the road, glad there were no other houses where an occupant might question her actions, and ducked under a leafy tree.

But she couldn't see anything. She dashed forward to the cusp of the bend. She could still see the SUV, and now she could see Bruce, Wallace, Briscoe, and Kopae in rain ponchos, huddled twenty yards ahead. Alexa pressed against the trunk of another tree, its limbs catching and pulling her hood off, and watched Bruce's mouth move. He was hatless and appeared impervious to the rain. She wanted to hear his words. Injustice jabbed. Hadn't he said this morning they were a team?

Like a mini-choreograph, Bruce and Wallace walked up a flagstone path, while Kopae and Briscoe split, ponchos billowing, to either side of the single-storied bungalow.

A bird squawked.

Jesus. Alexa searched and spotted a kaka eyeing her curiously from a branch above. It was large—eighteen inches tall, maybe— and its sharp, scaly claws could grab her hair. "Go away," she hissed.

The parrot considered her request, ruffled its wings, and hopped to a higher branch, causing raindrops to splatter Alexa.

She wiped her eyes, pulled her hood back up, and faced Stephen's cottage. Overgrown shrubbery and cabbage trees blocked the front windows. She wondered what a ranger earned— and how expensive houses were on the island. Was Stephen in debt?

A similar house stood catty-corner across the road, with a car in the driveway. No other houses were visible. No sign of Kopae's vehicle. She watched Bruce knock on the front door. Wallace stood a few feet behind, to his left, police baton clutched in his hand.

Bruce banged, harder, as if the door were a drum.

Alexa sensed movement. The parrot? But no, it was scratching its beak with its reptilian claw. Through leaves she saw the front door of the *other* house, the house across the street, open. Stephen Neville stepped onto the stoop. He looked across the street and quickly backstepped, closing the door softly.

Had they gotten the wrong house? Alexa burst from the tree like a flushed pheasant and ran down the middle of the road, waving her arms. She didn't want to scream; that might warn Stephen that he'd been spotted.

Her crazy flailing jog worked. Bruce pivoted, recoiled. Wallace looked flummoxed.

Alexa barreled onto slippery grass. "I saw him," she whispered. "Over there." She pointed crossways.

Bruce's eyes blazed. "What the hell?"

"What's going on, Senior?" Kopae said from the side yard.

Alexa pointed a wet finger. "I saw Stephen in *that* house."

Bruce hissed, "You were supposed…"

A revving engine and squealing tires silenced them. Briscoe sprinted to join them as Wallace tore across the yard, into the street, and jogged around the curve. "My ute," they heard him scream. "The bastard stole my ute."

Briscoe's and Kopae's mouths dropped.

"It's a goddamn snafu," Bruce shouted.

Wallace reemerged, huffing, his arms held up in surrender. "My car is gone. Neville's done a runner."

Crap. Her tote and crime kit were in the car. She groped her pocket, relieved to feel the outline of her new phone, and then fixed her hood, stuffing in wet hanks of hair. "He came on the porch, then darted back inside," she said. "He must have run out a back door."

"What? We had the wrong address?" Constable Kopae asked.

Briscoe blanched. "The rental form I checked said number twelve, I'm sure."

Bruce honed in on Alexa. "If you had stayed in the car this wouldn't have happened."

"That's insane," she shot back.

Wallace leaned over, hands on knees. Rain ran off the back of his slicker in rivulets. "I don't know, Senior. Neville could have jumped in the ute, taken her hostage. This is my fault for leaving keys in the ignition. We have to get him."

Bruce scowled and gestured to the shelter of a cabbage tree. "Let's think this through over there."

They gathered round and Bruce continued. "Where can he drive? There are barely any roads on this island, right?"

Kopae bounced on her toes. "Twenty kilometers. That's all."

Alexa converted—that was only twelve miles.

"Most circle the village or dead-end," Wallace said. "Everyone will recognize my ute."

"Neville should be considered armed and dangerous," Bruce said.

"He wasn't holding a gun when I saw him," Alexa said. Movement caught her eye. She pointed across the street.

The front door had opened, and a young man hovered under the eaves on the stoop where Stephen had stood moments before. He looked up and down the road and then did a double take as he spotted them under the tree. "What's happening?" he called. He stuck a hand out to test the rain.

"Who are you?" Bruce shouted.

The man flinched, backed into shadow.

Bruce pulled out his badge and squelched across the soggy grass.

Kopae caught up with him. "I recognize him, sir. He's a seasonal ranger."

"Your name, please," Bruce demanded.

The man popped back out. Wallace gripped his baton and joined Bruce.

"I'm Henry Fokisi."

"Does Stephen Neville live at the address?" Bruce asked.

Alexa and Briscoe crossed the street and watched from the edge of the yard.

"Eh, yeah." He swiped at his eyes as if the sheer number of cops and strangers—five was an illusion. "I was playing *Super Mario* when Stephen looked out the door, came running through, took off." The ranger's shorts ended at knobby knees, and he had the kind of beard that refused to thicken. "Where did he go?"

Bruce ignored the question and beckoned to Constable Kopae. "Stay here. Get Mr. Fokisi's information. I'll take your keys. Meet us back at the station." He turned and locked eyes with Alexa. "Glock, stay with Kopae."

As the three men stalked off to commandeer Kopae's car, Alexa thought, *Too many cowboys, not enough horses.* A raindrop hit her nose. She heard Wallace calling someone on his radio. Who? As far as she knew, the station was empty.

Inside, cola and beer cans, dirty plates, muddy boots, chip packages, and gaming controllers cluttered the room. Super Mario was scaling a castle wall on the TV while irritating synthesizer music beeped.

Constable Kopae whipped her poncho off, hung it from the doorknob, and slipped out of her boots. "Don't want to muss your floor," she said while Alexa stood dripping on it. Kopae crossed to the TV and turned it off. "So we can hear each other?" She brushed some crumbs from the couch, sat on the edge, and pulled a pen and notebook from her vest pocket.

Henry Fokisi looked dumbfounded.

"You don't mind if I call you Henry?" Kopae patted the spot next to her. "Have a seat. I've seen you on weed patrol at the waterfront. Where are you from?"

Kopae was self-assured and disarming, Alexa noted.

Henry sat at the far end of the couch and crossed an ankle over his knee. "Christchurch. What's going on?" His jandal—that's what Kiwis called flip-flops, Alexa had learned—dangled from his big toe.

"You're a temporary ranger, eh?" Kopae's pen was poised over the pad.

"I'm here December through March. Busy season."

Alexa walked to the back window and nudged aside a brown curtain. She spotted Stephen's garden plot and a clothesline with a long-sleeved shirt soaking up the rain.

"How many people live here?" Kopae asked.

"Stephen and me, that's all. It's his crib. I'm letting a room."

Kopae looked around, her brown eyes alight. "Why did Stephen run off?"

Henry rubbed his wispy beard. "I don't know."

Kopae kept silent.

Alexa sat in a wooden chair across from the sofa and studied the fidgeting Henry. His jandal fell off. He didn't seem to notice. She reminded herself that jitters were as common in truth-tellers as in liars. Maybe he was just gathering his thoughts.

Henry's foot stilled. "Stephen is odd. Stays up all night, reads his books." He pointed to one on the floor, spine up. *Field Guide to New Zealand Cetaceans.* A breaching whale photograph was on the cover.

Alexa picked it up and turned it over to see what Stephen had been reading. "Stop the Snoring" was a sidebar story. She skimmed it. In 1840 there were so many right whales in Wellington Harbor, she read, that the Wellys complained the whales' spouting, which sounded like snoring, kept them up at night. Stephen had been reading about snoring whales. Had it been right whales that Stephen euthanized?

No—Stephen had said pilot whales.

"Sometimes he sobs in the loo," Henry said.

Alexa looked up.

"Sobs?" Kopae said. "About what?"

Henry shrugged.

"Didn't you ask?"

"Not my biz. I only pay my rent. But his mum called me."

Kopae clicked her pen. "Why?"

"She got my mobile number from the DOC office. She hadn't heard from Stevie. Was checking up on him. I don't want to talk with someone's mum. I'm not a nursemaid."

"What did you tell her?"

"That Stephen was fine. What else would I say? I'm sure she's calm as, now. Stephen went home—his sis is doing the big OE."

Odontology exam? Alexa perked up at the thought of Stephen's sister joining the field of dentistry.

"Did my OE across the ditch," Kopae said.

"London, myself," Henry said. "Worked in a chip shop."

Alexa had to ask. "What's an OE?"

"Overseas experience," Henry said, shaking his head, probably at Alexa's ignorance.

Kopae took down Henry's contact info while Alexa looked up pilot whales in the index of the guide and turned to the correct page. Highly gregarious, dark gray to black, live in groups, eat squid, 18–19 feet long—*hardly bigger than white sharks*, she thought. The sobbing in the loo comment made her think of Stephen telling her the dying whales had been crying. She searched "eyes" in the index and thumbed to the page. Whales have eyelid glands that secrete oily tear-like substances to remove debris from their large eyes. She read further down: Whales are sometimes seen or heard crying or moaning when they lose a loved one or feel alone.

Stephen's whales were crying, she thought, setting the book back on the floor.

"Does Stephen have a gun?" Kopae asked Henry.

His eyes darted to the kitchen. "A shotgun. In the pantry. It belongs to DOC."

Alexa went to investigate. The kitchen door was open— Stephen's escape route. She visualized him dashing past the garden and up the road, being surprised by Wallace's SUV, keys in the ignition. The ranger had acted on impulse. *Like the person who attacked me last night.* A gust of wind blew rain into the kitchen. Alexa shivered and shut the door. The pantry was a large cupboard, door ajar, next to the oven. A white plastic compost bucket on the floor reassured her. Murderers don't compost. She lifted the lid and saw a slurry of carrots, eggshells, coffee grounds, slime. Bacteria and fungi at work. Stephen was doing his bit to save the planet. She replaced the lid and glanced around. Three cans of Wattie's beans and an unopened bag of Value Choc Chip cookies sat on the shelf. A broom leaned in the corner.

Alexa returned to the den. "The pantry is clear. No shotgun." She noted a small hallway. "Which room is Stephen's?"

"His is on the left." Henry slipped his jandal back on and pressed his feet to the floor.

The bedroom door was open. Alexa knew she couldn't search the room or touch anything without Stephen's consent. But taking a peek didn't infringe on his rights. If she saw something incriminating—like Robert King's personal locator beacon out in the open—that was different.

She stepped inside, a foot or two, and smelled sweat and damp. Maybe mold. The bedroom was small and dark. One shaded window, a lamp on the nightstand. She wished she could turn it on but didn't want to leave her own DNA behind. The fitted sheet of the single bed was half-off, exposing the mattress. A blanket heaped at the foot.

No PLB in sight.

Half the sliding door of the tiny closet was open. A DOC pullover hung from the rack, and sneakers were strewn on the floor. That reminded her to check the muddy hiking boots in the den. Maybe they would match the Merrell boot cast she had studied in the lab. Size ten it was. Funny, though—it had been Stephen, following her directive, who had taken the impression at the crime scene. The cast was in good condition. It didn't appear as if it were evidence he wanted to hide, or he could have tampered with it.

Constable Kopae was flipping her notepad closed.

"Did Stephen ever mention Robert King?" Alexa asked Henry. She stood by the boots, one up, and one lying on its side, mud caked to the tread. They weren't Merrells.

"Nah yeah. We all know about the missing hunter. Most of us thought he carked it in the sea. Those trampers tripping on the skeleton? A surprise, for real."

Alexa had heard a lot of "yeah nahs," an irritating Kiwi habit, but never a "nah yeah." She hated it. "So did Stephen mention Robert King or not?"

"Eh?"

God almighty. "What about Andy Gray? Did Stephen ever mention him?"

The temporary ranger stared at Alexa as if she were batty. "Who?"

"The man who washed up on the beach yesterday. He ran White Dive caging company."

"The shark attack—damn bad luck. I never heard Stephen mention Andy Gray."

A straight answer, finally.

"Do you know where Stephen might have gone?" Kopae asked.

"He in trouble, then?"

"Yeah nah," Kopae said.

"Stephen loves the bush. That's where I'd look," Henry said.

The rain pattered with less gusto as they started toward town, carless. What had that fishermen said when she first arrived? Ten-toeing it was the best way to get around. It had been raining then, too. Kopae, encased in her yellow police poncho, looked around suspiciously as if Stephen, armed, might jump out from behind a bush. The cinched hood of her poncho gave her a pie face. Alexa tightened her own hood and felt untethered without her tote and crime kit, now joyriding with Stephen.

"You're a good interviewer," she told Kopae. They passed the spot where Wallace's car had been parked. Alexa scanned the trees, spooked by Kopae's leeriness.

Kopae ignored the compliment. "I asked Henry about the PLB while you were in the bedroom. You didn't touch anything, did you?"

"No. Of course not." Her cheeks flushed despite the cool air. She wanted to be the kind of person who inspired trust, not doubt.

"Henry saw Stephen in the garden with some kind of radio device. Thinks it could have been the PLB." Kopae's voice was anxious. "I think Stephen might hurt himself. Or someone else. He's burned some bridges what with stealing Sergeant's ute, and that's dangerous."

Kopae will make a good DI someday, Alexa thought. She explained Stephen's crying whales and the mass euthanasia.

"Yeah nah, it was sad," Kopae said. "But don't let sympathy for a suspect cloud up your judgment."

"If you ever want to work in Auckland," Alexa blurted, "I might have a few connections. Did you get someone to watch over that girl on the beach? Madalyn?"

"Aye. Supervisor Lowell positioned a temp ranger in the parking lot."

They picked up their pace and after a ten-minute half-jog arrived at the station, both surprised to spot Kopae's car parked in front.

"Maybe they caught him," Alexa said.

Bruce, Sergeant Wallace, and Constable Briscoe were inside. Bruce was barking orders into the phone. Briscoe was scribbling a report, and Wallace—arms akimbo—stood at the map.

Kopae rushed to his side. "I thought you'd be combing the island? What's happening?"

"The DI is ordering a helicopter. My ute will be easier to spot from the air," Wallace said. "What did you find out from the temp?"

"The DOC shotgun is usually in Neville's pantry, but it's missing," Kopae said. "Henry saw Stephen messing with a radio in the garden. Probably King's beacon locator."

Bruce's eyes narrowed when he spotted Alexa dripping in the threshold. Surely, he couldn't still be mad she left the car? Would he rather Stephen had taken her hostage? He hung up and said, "Copter will be here shortly. Sergeant, you and Constable Kopae get back out, take the sedan, cruise around. There's an hour of daylight, and you know the island."

Kopae straightened. "That would leave you with no vehicle, sir," she told Bruce.

"Use the constable's. We'll take the wife's car," Wallace said, setting keys on the table.

When the door closed, Bruce glanced from Briscoe to Alexa, his expression now neutral. "We've got a few minutes, Ms. Glock." He gestured to the table but remained standing. "Are there any significant lab results?" His square jaw was shadowed with stubble.

"Yes, sir." She hung her jacket on the chair back, aware she looked a sodden mess. Briscoe shoved his report aside and drummed his fingers.

"Take notes, Constable Briscoe," Bruce said.

"Yes, Senior." He grabbed a notepad and looked expectant.

Alexa was glad Briscoe would record this impromptu meeting. Even with a small team, there were still a lot of moving parts. Keeping everyone up to date was the oil that kept the investigation running smoothly. "I'll start with Robert King."

"No," Bruce said. "Andrew Gray is more immediate. He was shot three days ago, and you were attacked last night. Start with Gray."

"The photos I took on board *The Apex* were backed up in the cloud. They showed a bullet buried in the railing." *And prove I was telling the truth.* "I emailed them to you."

"All good," Bruce said. "I forwarded them to Auckland."

She explained for Briscoe's benefit about the fiber that had been embedded in Andy Gray's fingernail. "It's from a trawling net and made in Dunedin. Van Kees Nautical Netting. Specifically, a Polyurethane Stealth Glider trawling net."

"Does it match netting on *The Apex*?" Bruce asked.

"I didn't see any netting," Alexa said.

"Trawling nets are used on fishing boats," Constable Briscoe said. "I spent a couple summers on my dad's boat out of Bluff. We used Van Kees. Best in the biz, hardly any drag. I don't think a cage diving boat would have a trawling net."

"Maybe they stuff it with bait to attract sharks," Bruce suggested.

"It's too big," the constable said.

"The fiber could have been transferred to Gray during a

struggle," Alexa said. "Van Kees refused to give me his customer information."

"I've filed for a warrant," Bruce said. "Identifying the fiber is still useful evidence. You can tell whether a particular net matches, right?"

"Yes." She was explaining about the diatom test when her new phone rang. "Pardon." She dug it out and checked the screen. "It's the shark guy, Kana Duffy."

Bruce nodded. "Answer. I need to talk with him."

"Hello?" Alexa said.

"We have a date for 7:30 a.m.," Duffy said. "We're meeting Captain Luke Grogan at Halfmoon dock."

"A date?" Alexa's eyes flickered to Bruce.

"Lucas Grogan will take us cage diving if we get permission from your sergeant fella," Duffy said. "I need to figure out what's going on with the sharks and whether to continue the ban on water activities. Put me on to him."

Alexa thought fast. A couple hours in a ship—boat—with Andy Gray's single competitor, also a suspect, might yield answers, but no way she was diving with the sharks. She held her hand over the phone and explained.

Constable Briscoe jumped in. "Grogan was cagey when I interviewed him, Senior. He wouldn't show me anything, wants a warrant for his client list and financial doings. Said he barely knew Gray, that they operated in different shark grounds."

"Shark grounds?" Bruce said. "Sounds like a coffee drink."

"I'll go," Briscoe offered.

Bruce snorted. "This isn't a circus. I'm not having my team get in a cage with sharks." He held out his hand. "Let me talk to him."

While the DI talked, Briscoe opened the station door. Cool air whooshed in. "Can't hear the copter," he reported.

Alexa was trying to decipher Bruce's conversation with Shark Man and ignored Briscoe.

"Invite the press," Bruce said. "Make your pronouncement."

He handed the phone back to Alexa, looking satisfied. "All set then. Briscoe, you'll go with Grogan and Duffy in the morning."

"Sa-weet az," Briscoe said.

Off the hook. Alexa felt relief, then cringed. The thought of hooks made her gaff wound throb, pulsate.

Bruce scowled at Briscoe. "Make sure the cager is following DOC's code of practice. Keep an eye on Grogan, get him talking about Gray, the biz, whatnot."

"Yes, Senior."

Bruce looked out the sole window. Darkness was falling. "Where is that bird?"

Briscoe opened the door again as Bruce turned to Alexa. "We got good news from Supervisor Lowell. The rangers located the scene of King's death."

"How did they do it?" Alexa asked.

"They used string to measure the shortest route from the clearing where the body was, to the North West Circuit track where the hikers were. The bloke stepped off the path to take a—er—bathroom break, remember?"

She nodded.

"They found a spent cartridge. From a shotgun."

"Nailed him," Briscoe said.

"Excellent," Alexa said. "Did anyone take soil samples? There might be blood…"

"The ammo is good for now. Lowell said the cartridge was similar to the type used by DOC shotguns."

"Double nail," Briscoe said, "in Neville's coffin."

She hated the thought; she wanted Stephen to be innocent.

"Supervisor Lowell knows which of his rangers, temps, and volunteers were in the area around the time King went missing," Bruce said. "Neville is one of them." He paused, maybe listening for the copter. Then he said quietly, "Keep in mind that once you've killed one person, it's easier to do it again."

The sound of chopper blades made Alexa jump.

Chapter Twenty-Three

Alexa watched from the shelter of the porch as the copter followed the curve of roads, searching for prey, more dexterous than she thought possible. Constable Briscoe stood at her side, and Bruce, despite the rain, stood in the street for a better view as the copter hovered, dipped, rose, then swooped like a hawk after a rabbit.

"That's near Observation Rock," Briscoe said.

"What's that?" Alexa asked.

"There's a fancy lodge and a trail to an overlook. Tourists love the view. Rangers maintain it, so Stephen would know about it."

The radio in Bruce's hand blared. "Horne here," he answered. His feet were hips' width apart. At some point during the day he had switched from a navy blazer to a black windbreaker. Alexa thought he looked FBI handsome.

"Wallace here. My ute is parked at the Rock."

"We're on our way." Bruce stashed the radio into his jacket pocket. "Briscoe, come on. You wait here," he told Alexa. "Understood?"

Before she could protest, they were screeching past in Kopae's sedan, running the stop sign at the corner.

She paced the porch, furious at being left behind. Again.

I am not a police officer, she chastised. Bruce had made the right decision.

The adrenaline circulating in her bloodstream didn't dissipate.

It pinged around like Super Mario, taking corners, moistening her armpits, pulsating her gaff wound, shortening her breath.

What was happening to Stephen?

A gust chased her inside. She pulled the station door shut and leaned against it, breathing slowly, deeply. Too quiet now. She viewed the small room—the conference table, Wallace's desk, Kopae's cubicle, the coffee maker, file cabinets, the map, the minute hand on the wall clock reminding her she'd been on the go over twelve hours.

Then she remembered being alone in the Rotorua Police Station lab. A scary man had pressed his face against the glass, had tried the door.

Someone had attacked her last night. Someone had hoped big-ass sharks would rip her apart in a sheen of chum. This station might not be safe either. She searched the door for a lock.

The deadbolt made a reassuring click.

She caught sight of her reflection in the window glass: A pale, frizzy-haired woman stared back. Who was that? Her image of herself was more Viking—strong and tall. She tucked a hank of damp, tangled hair back into her ponytail and squared her shoulders. That was better.

Be of use, she thought.

On the conference table, the stack of *Great White Shark Sighting* forms, the ones that had been on *The Apex,* caught her attention. Obviously, Kopae or Wallace had thought they were important and brought them here. She borrowed paper and a cheap pen from Sergeant Wallace's desk, missing her Pilot G-2 gel pen stashed in her tote, gone again like it had a life of its own. She began reading, intent on taking notes.

Halfway down the form was *Description of Encounter With Shark.* There were four choices: 1) Observation only (no interaction), 2) Swim-by (came and went, casual), 3) Interest (swim-by, return, circle, bump, mouth), and 4) Attitude/Aggression (fast swimming, biting, shaking, ramming).

Ramming? A mental image of a ramming great white made her throat go dry.

Compiling data calmed her. Ten forms marked *Observation*, nine had circled Swim-bys, four circled Interest, and one—filled out by an Alistair Foster—was marked Attitude/Aggression. "Shark took my bait, butted stern, followed with intent. Visible laceration on head." Duration of encounter had been twenty minutes.

Twenty minutes of terror, Alexa imagined.

There were twenty-four forms in all, with names and contact numbers. None were filled out by Andy Gray, or his competitor—Lucas Grogan. Were the cage operators not expected to fill out sighting forms? Why had these forms, already filled out, been on *The Apex*? Was Gray using them to find sharks?

Was this illegal?

She made a note to ask Supervisor Lowell. Then she saw ranger Scratch Gellman's name. His "since we've already slept together" remark in the pub last night infuriated her all over again. She should have had a comeback: In your dreams. *Lame.*

Never sleep with a loaded Glock. *Better.*

Scratch had spotted a five-meter white on 3 November, 7:00 p.m. Weather had been calm, location off Muttonbird Beak. She remembered seeing Muttonbird Beak on the map—a jut of land between Golden Bay and Ringaringa Beach, where Gray's body had washed ashore. Scratch had noted a fishing vessel in the vicinity but hadn't been able to identify it. He'd classified the encounter as *Interest* and added, "circled my roundabout twice, came alongside, disappeared." The duration was six minutes.

Beyond creepy.

The wall map helped her locate the areas white sharks were spotted. Besides Muttonbird Beak, two sharks had been sighted in Halfmoon Bay, a couple near a place called Seal Rock. Figures, she surmised. Sharks eat seals. One off Ringaringa Beach, and two between Golden Bay Wharf and Ulva Island, where the water taxi had been headed. The rest of the places she couldn't find on the map.

She ignored her growling stomach and dove deeper into the data. Time factored in. Early morning or dusk accounted for three-fourths of the sightings. One-third of the sightings included another vessel in the area. She listed the vessels: *Aotearoa, My Happy Place, Oh Bugger, Three Sheets* (that's the expression she'd wanted in the pub when she'd seen the drunks), *Gloria. Darla Jo* appeared three times. Alexa remembered *Darla Jo* was the fishing boat moored next to *The Apex.* What had the water taxi driver said about the owner? Lost his job on the clam farm, that was it. Tough luck.

Alexa shuffled through the stack to see if the owner of *Darla Jo* had filled out a sighting form. She'd recognize his name if she saw it.

No. This was odd. If the fishing boat had been in the vicinity of white sharks on three separate occasions, why had the captain not filled out a form?

She heard a rattle and lifted her head.

The wind. Just the notorious wind.

She would look for the list of Stewart Island gun owners, compare the names with those who filled out…

Creak. Footsteps on the porch.

Alexa, immobilized, watched the doorknob rattle, twist.

Chapter Twenty-Four

The door rattled louder, followed by rapping.

Alexa jerked back in the chair, fumbled for her cell, tapped Bruce's number with shaking fingers.

No service.

Godforsaken island.

She was halfway to the landline on Wallace's desk when the rapping moved from the door to the window. White knuckles knocked against the pane. *Rap, rap, rap.* "Open up," said a man.

The voice jarred Alexa. This was a police station. Someone needed help. "Who is it?" she called.

Garble, mumble.

"Who?" She stabbed 1-1-1 on the landline.

The windowpane rattled. A face moved in. "Stephen Neville."

It couldn't be Neville. Bruce and Wallace and the team are hunting him down at Observation Rock. But the ranger's face solidified like a mugshot through the glass. She hung up before an operator answered and moved to the door, undid the deadbolt, pulled it open.

Stephen, gaunt and diminished in wet jeans and T-shirt, longish hair plastered to his skull, stepped from the window.

Alexa scanned the street. "Where's Sergeant Wallace's car?"

His eyes were as vacant as the street. In slow motion he reached for a shotgun perched against the siding. Lifted it. Turned.

Alexa slammed the door, lunged for the phone. Bruce was right. Stephen was armed and dangerous.

But wait—Stephen hadn't been aiming. He'd balanced the shotgun like an offering in his outstretched hands. Had she overreacted?

Wailing seeped through the station walls. Alexa froze, listened, hoped it was a siren and that backup was coming. But no. The wail was human. Stephen was crying. She flicked the porch light on and cracked the door. Stephen sat on the top step, head bowed to his knees, his keening like chalk scraping a blackboard. The shotgun was laid like an abandoned baby on the doormat.

She inspected it: *870 Remington* was etched in the steel butt. Below the brand, a tag said *Property of DOC.*

"Crying won't help." She backed up, over to the coffee counter, and grabbed napkins in lieu of gloves, since the crime kit was in Wallace's SUV. She returned and gingerly lifted the shotgun, its weight awkward. What if she dropped it? "Is this loaded?" she called.

The ranger's back stiffened. She could see the bumps of his spine against the wet fabric of his T-shirt. Gulps and blubbers continued.

God—he was useless.

She kept the muzzle pointing away from herself or Stephen and carried it into the unisex bathroom. She stared at the lethal weapon, imagining what might have been lined in its site, and tried to remember something about unloading. Didn't shotguns fold in half? She had no idea. She searched the bathroom and settled on the shelf above a row of hooks. She shoved aside toilet paper and paper towels and put the gun on it. It was the best she could do. The bathroom door could only be locked from the inside, she noted as she left, which was crap luck in case Stephen changed from Wailing Winkie to Trigger Tim.

Before insisting Stephen come inside—she could see him through the open door, slumped on the steps—she walked to Wallace's desk phone and dialed Bruce's number.

Voicemail. She fished out her phone and sent Bruce a text: Stephen @ po station. Then she called 1-1-1.

"Are you in danger?" the operator asked after taking her location.

"I don't think so. No." Alexa knew the 1-1-1 operator was based at a call center somewhere off-island, probably in Dunedin or Christchurch.

"What is the nature of your emergency?"

"Well, I have a missing person," she lowered her voice, "a suspect. He turned himself in. At the Stewart Island Police Station." She wasn't sure the operator understood.

"Is he hurt?"

"No. The whole department is searching for him, and he's here," she reiterated. "Call Sergeant Kipper Wallace or DI Bruce Horne. Let them know." She hung up before the operator could tell her to stay on the line.

Another crazy mess. Her eyes landed on the electric kettle. She shoved boiling memories aside as she filled it with water and clicked it on. Hot tea to the rescue.

"Come inside," she called. Stephen rose and followed her, his wet boots squelching.

Hiking boots.

Alexa pointed to a chair and studied Stephen's shoes, thinking of the evidence cast. Were Stephen's boots Merrells? He sat like an obedient dog.

She couldn't see the brand and went back to making tea.

How long would it be until Bruce looked at his phone? Would he get her text? Would the 9-1-1 operator—well, 1-1-1 operator—get through? She poured the steaming water into a Best Dad mug—her back scars tightening—added a tea bag, and, with care, set it in front of the ranger.

The station phone rang. Stephen stiffened as she answered. "Alexa Glock."

"This is the 1-1-1 Emergency Call Center. I have a report of a missing person..."

Alexa interrupted. "I'm the one who just called you. Get in touch with Sergeant Wallace or Bruce Horne, I mean DI Horne. Get them to the Stewart Island Police Station STAT." She hung up.

Stephen shivered. Alexa, thinking shock, looked for a blanket or spare coat, no go—and grabbed hers and draped it over his shoulders. "You're in big trouble stealing the sergeant's SUV. Why did you do it?"

He shuddered, wilted. Her jacket slid to the floor. Perhaps her technique needed refining. She sat opposite him and tried again. "Um, Stephen, what's going on? Are you okay?"

A wail escaped from his mouth.

She leaned back—he didn't appear dangerous. She watched him gasp and sob. Comforting people wasn't her nature. No one had comforted her when Mom died. Physical needs—check. Emotional needs—empty box.

Where the hell was the team? She nudged the mug closer to Stephen. "Here. Take a sip."

He hiccupped and then obeyed. His fingers were boyish and pale. Alexa thought of his mum, how she loved her Stevie boy, and grabbed a napkin from the counter so the ranger could wipe his snotty face.

The tea seemed to unclog Stephen's vocal cords. "Supervisor Lowell called me in because I was closest," he sputtered. "He said the whales were doomed. We'd be doing them justice. The tide had turned, and they hadn't refloated."

Stephen seemed to be flashbacking to the whale beaching, Alexa realized. He ignored the napkin and wiped his nose with the back of his hand.

"I saw them from the copter. Masses and masses of whales. Thrashing and heaving. When I got out, I could hear the clicks and cries and see them desperately trying to swim. The ones that were still alive, anyway. The whale I was sitting with watched me. Her big tears made tracks through the sand on her face. I tried to wipe the sand away." He stared into the tea as if the whale's beseeching eyes looked back. "My dad, when he slaughtered our lambs, he always covered their eyes by folding down their soft ears. It calmed them. But I couldn't cover the whales' eyes. And there was blood." He wiped his hands on his pants. "So much blood."

"You were helping them," Alexa said. Her heart thumped as if it would split in two.

Stephen shuddered and reached for the mug, sloshing tea. "Supervisor Lowell could have ordered sedation. He should have, to calm the whales. Pentobarbital works. I've researched it. A shot in the tail. But it takes time to work, and there were so many, and I was alone, so what's the difference? They watch me all night long, the whales. I can't sleep."

Alexa strained for sounds of Bruce and the team, but all she could hear was the patter of rain. She took her phone out, checked for a signal, texted Bruce again: Hurry- Stephen at station. Her gaff wound ached, seeped. She could feel her shirt sticking to it and thought of the other time her shirt had adhered to her skin. Melted into it, really. She shuddered, pushing those thoughts under the rug, and changed the subject. "Did you take Robert King's PLB?"

"I didn't mean to."

"So that's a yes? You took it?"

"The day of the flensing."

"The what?"

"When I was leading the Māoris to the dead whales so they could do their thing, you know, pray for the whales, carve up the bodies. Send them home. Māori believe whales are *taonga*."

Alexa knew from the Rotorua case that *taonga* meant treasure.

"Zeke Harata and the other elders walked all around the dead whales, up and down the beach. They called them *upokohue*, talked to them, prayed for them. I watched them before I left." Stephen seemed to inflate. He used the napkin to wipe his face. "Harata said whales used to be land animals, and they lived in wet places, like rivers and marshes. The god Tāne gifted whales to Tangaroa, the ocean god, and that's why whales came to live in the sea." He paused, got a faraway look in his moist eyes. "Maybe the whales got mixed up and thought the forest was their home. Maybe that's why they beached themselves."

"Maybe." Back home, whales occasionally stranded along the Carolina beaches. Scientists thought it was because of underwater sonar pulses, but Alexa didn't think that was the case here. But she was getting off track. "What about the beacon locator?"

"I saw it on the path, just lying there. Harata saw it too. King must have dropped it. I picked it up and meant to turn it in."

Footsteps stomped on the porch, and the door slammed open.

Chapter Twenty-Five

Bruce barreled past the team, pulled Alexa up, swung her behind his body. A human shield.

"I'm okay," she stammered, stepping back.

The DI turned, his eyes blazing a blue heat. "What happened? How did you find him? Did you leave the station?"

Kopae, holding Alexa's tote and crime kit, stared curiously.

"He found me." The spot on her upper arm where Bruce had grabbed her throbbed. She didn't like being manhandled and didn't need Big Strong Man to protect her. She'd been doing a good job as therapist-interrogator. "Stephen turned himself in."

"But my ute is at Observation Point," Sergeant Wallace said from the doorway.

Stephen pushed back from the table and stared at his feet.

"Stay where you are," Bruce commanded.

Wallace walked over. Stephen looked up, his eyes like a cow's in a slaughterhouse. "You're under arrest for stealing a police vehicle. Additional charges are pending upon investigation." Wallace searched his pocket for his wallet, extracted a card, and squinted at it. "My glasses. Wait." He strode to his desk and searched in a drawer. He came back with reading glasses perched on his nose.

The Miranda rights sounded about the same as they did back home, Alexa thought.

"You have the right to speak with a lawyer without delay and in private before deciding whether to answer any questions. We have a list of lawyers you may speak to for free," Wallace finished.

Alexa doubted any lawyers lived on the island.

"Thank you, Sergeant," Bruce said. "Cuff him."

Stephen stood obediently as Wallace cuffed his wrists behind his back.

"The shotgun is in the bathroom," Alexa said. "It might be loaded."

"Why didn't you unload it?" Bruce snapped.

"I didn't know how," Alexa shot back.

Kopae sprang toward the bathroom, Briscoe on her heels.

"Sit down," Bruce told Stephen. "Would you like a lawyer present while I ask you questions?"

Say yes.

Stephen hesitated and then shook his shaggy head. "It won't make a difference."

Bruce turned on his phone's recording app and started with date and those present. It didn't take much prying for Stephen to spill his guts—euthanizing whales, finding the PLB, night sweats, the whole waterworks. "I didn't shoot Robert King. I never saw him until we hiked to his body."

"Why do you still have the shotgun?"

Stephen didn't answer Bruce's question. Alexa wondered if he might have considered taking his own life.

Kopae returned from securing the shotgun. "Why did you set the PLB off? Didn't you know it would show your location?"

"I didn't think about that. I...I wanted to see if it worked," Stephen stammered. "I thought the battery would be dead."

"Where is it?" Bruce asked.

"At my mum's." Stephen hung his head.

An overgrown kid with an electronic. Alexa wasn't surprised to see him dissolve into tears again. *I'd blubber too if I screwed up my career.* She half-listened to the interrogation and began to write down everything she had learned from her time alone with the distraught ranger. She underlined the name of the Māori elder, Zeke Harata, who had led the whale flensing. The team would need to see if he had witnessed Stephen finding the PLB on the beach path as Stephen claimed. Otherwise, people would assume Stephen had shot Robert King and taken the PLB off his body.

Alexa didn't want this horror to be true. She thought back to when she first arrived on the island three days ago. It felt like a month. Stephen had charged between her and the bellowing sea lion, so that she could escape. Risked his life in front of one thousand pounds of pissed-off blubber.

Her ears perked when Bruce asked Stephen when he last saw Andy Gray. Not *if* he knew him. Stephen's face stayed blank as if he hadn't heard who the shark attack victim was. Bruce needed to let go of his Occam's razor theory.

There was no jail on the island. Wallace radioed Supervisor Lowell, who agreed to take custody of Stephen. The shotgun, disarmed by Kopae, would be flown to the ballistics lab in Auckland.

Bruce ended his recording with time and date. "We'll talk more in the morning."

Alexa went over to Bruce and whispered in his ear.

He turned the tape back on and said, "One final question, Mr. Neville. What brand of boots are you wearing?"

He looked surprised, then lifted one as if he didn't know. Alexa could see they weren't Merrells.

"If the results prove it's the same gun that shot Robert King, you'll be off to jail for good, Mr. Neville," Wallace growled. "Either way, you've stolen a car and obstructed justice by withholding evidence."

Stephen looked like a kicked dog. Alexa wanted to pat him and tell him everything would be all right. But that wasn't true. She had a theory that his irrational behavior was due to post-traumatic stress disorder.

"Constable Briscoe and I will stay with him until Lowell gets here," Wallace continued. "I'll start on the reports, Senior. Then it's home to the missus. Briscoe, you'll bunk at my crib."

"Who needs a ride to the inn, then?" Constable Kopae asked. "At least the rain has stopped."

Bruce stood and stretched. "Everyone meet back here at 7:30 a.m.," he said.

———

The wet earth smelled violently of sea and humus. Alexa's heart wouldn't stop pounding as she and Bruce stood side by side, backs to the inn, watching Kopae's taillights fade into darkness.

"I think Stephen has PTSD," Alexa said.

Bruce shifted closer. "You may be right."

The relief of being safe settled like a cloak around her shoulders. Maybe she had been more scared than she admitted. Alexa gazed upward, stretching her tight neck muscles. The multitude of peacock-tail stars made her gape, made her wonder where the rain and clouds had gone, swished away like a magic trick, made her wonder if some of the stars might shake loose and fall like sparkler sparks into the sea.

She looked sideways. Bruce was staring heavenward, a quarter-smile at his lips. She had an urge to touch those lips, taste them. He shouldn't be so near. She hitched her tote higher on her shoulder and set the crime kit on the ground.

Bruce caught her eye. "The Stewart Island Town Council replaced all the streetlights with dimmer lights. To welcome the dark."

She looked back to the sky and sea. The only luminance besides the multitudinous stars was a nautical warning blinking in the inky harbor. "They must be dimmed. I've never seen so many stars. It's like a glowworm cave." That was as poetic as she could get.

Bruce's breath hitched. "Geographic isolation has its perks."

"A dark sky sanctuary," she whispered, "all around."

They turned to each other as if the geographic poles of their births were opposites attracting. Bruce tilted forward; Alexa leaned in. Their lips touched, settled, the pressure hard and soft simultaneously, Bruce's tongue prodding Alexa to part her lips, her heart, shift her body, lean closer.

Tinny music from the pub escaped when someone opened the door. "Having a smok-o," a voice called.

Bruce pulled back. "Er, um." His arm that had been around her waist fell as he scanned the perimeter. They saw a flare of a lighter on the patio. Bruce scowled at the smoker and then looked at Alexa as if her lips were toxic. "I shouldn't have done that. Entirely unprofessional. I apologize."

"But..." She took a disappointed step back and stumbled against the crime kit.

Bruce grabbed her arm. "Don't fall."

"Too late."

———

There were only six people in the pub. "Time After Time" blared from the jukebox. Catch you if you fall. *Right.*

The pen-chewing bartender from the night before tore his eyes from horse racing on TV as Bruce ordered two burgers and two pints. He hadn't asked, but a burger and a beer was exactly what Alexa wanted.

And another kiss.

"It's past 9:00, mate," the bartender said. "Kitchen's closed."

Bruce showed his badge. "See what you can do."

The proprietor, Constance, came out a swinging door. "I heard, Rob. You pull the beer, I'll fry the burgers."

"Ta," said Bruce.

Alexa grabbed the first beer and sat at a table. She stared into the foamy suds while a meteor shower streamed across her brain.

Each bright streak—longing, lust, anger—flared for attention. She couldn't catch hold of any one. Bruce's kiss disintegrated with each passing moment. He was right. Kissing the boss was verboten. She gulped her beer as Bruce pulled a chair out and sat. He avoided her eyes. "I'm knackered."

So, he was going to pretend the kiss hadn't happened.

She stared into her mug and warned herself to slow down, take smaller sips, fewer risks. In her peripheral vision a bearded fellow in a black knit-cap weaved toward the jukebox. Alexa held her breath, would bet money on the Eagles, but Pearl Jam from her high school days blared.

"I, well, em," Bruce started and then stopped.

He was at a loss. Alexa liked this.

Bruce tried again. "I'm sorry for what happened. Word got out, it would put my new position in jeopardy."

Alexa's nostrils flared. "I have my own career to protect. Why didn't you tell me you were moving to Auckland?"

Bruce looked surprised.

"You didn't say anything at breakfast." She regretted the words as soon as they escaped. He didn't owe her an explanation.

"It only just happened. I was going to mention it, but then you called that American bloke over. Theo Hall. The one who went cage diving with his wife. He sent me his photos from the trip." He pulled out his mobile and started scrolling, but then his hands went still. "It was a hard decision. Sharla is furious."

The ex, Alexa concluded. What kind of name is Sharla?

Pearl Jam was making conversation difficult, so they settled back against their chairs and sipped their beers until it ended, and the pub reverted to hushed tones and a TV ad. The knit-cap man said, "Be seeing you, mate," to the bartender and left, letting in a gust strong enough to ruffle the napkins on their table.

Bruce leaned forward, his eyes sad. "She thinks I'm shirking my parenting responsibilities."

"Are you?" Alexa had no tolerance for dads who abandon

their kids. Once their dad had recoupled a few short years after her mom died, Alexa and Charlie had been shoved to a distant third and fourth place, barely visible.

"I'll be earning more. Marriage dissolution is expensive."

"Money isn't..." Stupid cliché. Alexa shut up.

Constance came bearing plates heaped with burger, fries, and side salad. "Long day, you two?" She fetched a bottle of Wattie's Tomato Sauce from the next table, swiped it with a towel, and set it down. Alexa grabbed it.

"No longer than yours," Bruce said kindly.

Constance's apron was spattered with sauces, her hair had escaped its top knot, and mascara was smudged under her pale eyes. "I heard it was Andy Gray killed by the shark," Constance said. "Odd twist, that. Will this end the shark cage diving?"

"That's for the courts to decide," Bruce replied.

Alexa delicately dipped her fry in the ketchup, then scarfed it.

"Caging brings tourists," Constance said. "It's not...well, it's not that I support it—I say if we leave them alone, they'll leave us alone."

"Whom are we referring to?" Bruce asked, also eating a fry.

"The sharks. We've always coexisted with them. But the cage diving rents my rooms, fills my restaurant, helps me pay off my expansion."

"Expansion?" Bruce asked.

"The wing where you and..." She looked at Alexa. "I've forgotten your name, I'm sorry. But the en suite wing. She's in Room Three, and you're in Room Four."

Bruce coughed.

"The tourists pay six hundred dollars to cage dive, so dropping more money for accommodation and grub is nothing to them. They come here—to the pub—to toast their bravery. They help me pay my loan, eh?" Constance lowered her voice. "Lots of my neighbors want it banned. Hold it against me for catering to them."

Bruce interrupted. "Anyone in particular?"

"No names will pass these lips. They drink here as well. Only pub on the island. Cheers." Constance surveyed the room and hastened to the bar.

Alexa gazed at Bruce as he gazed at the proprietor, one eyebrow slightly higher than the other. Was their relationship doomed? He caught her looking and grinned. "Penny."

"My thoughts are worth a quarter." She smiled back, and the tension between them lifted. They attacked their meal with mutual gusto.

After a moment, Bruce said, "I have a meeting with the local rep for PāuaMAC, a Mr. Stormy Parker, at 11:00 tomorrow. His association has been trying to shut down the caging companies. He says sharks are protected, but pāua divers aren't."

"They can protect themselves by not going in the water," Alexa said.

"And we need to check up on your fiber. Go around, check fishing boats for similar netting. Might lead us to the killer."

"There are a lot of fishermen on the island, right?"

"Briscoe said it was a trawling net. Not all fishing boats are trawlers. That narrows it down. I'll get Wallace to make a list." His left eyebrow rose as he studied Alexa. "I heard what you said about Stephen suffering PTSD. I'll interview again in the morning. Before we have him flown to Invercargill."

"Good," she answered. The calories were a needed energy boost. But then Alexa almost choked. "Dammit." She set her burger down.

"What?"

"I need to get back to *The Apex*. Now."

"Why?"

"There was blood splattered near the lodged bullet. I took photos of it—remember?"

Bruce picked up his napkin.

"When Wallace and Kopae returned later, the blood had been

wiped away. I want to go back in the dark and use BLUESTAR to take samples."

He wiped his mouth. "Not to worry. BLUESTAR will detect blood trace weeks and months after blood is cleaned up."

She relaxed and picked up the burger. "You're right. Centuries even. I read a report about BLUESTAR FORENSIC spray illuminating blood shed from the Battle of Gettysburg in 1863." Would a Kiwi know about Gettysburg?

"Your war between the states, right?"

Sexy *and* smart. "Tomorrow night, then. I promised Constable Kopae she could come with me." She resumed operation burger, and when it was complete, she wiped her face and fingers. "May I see Theo's pictures?"

Bruce twiddled with his phone, frowned as he read a text, then scrolled. "Here are the ones dated Sunday—the day they went caging."

The first photo showed a shark swimming below the cage, the top of its sleek gray body stippled with sunlight. In the next, a monstrous white swam straight at the cage, its black eyes emotionless. Had it veered at the last second, or rammed? Theo had had his thrill factor, caught it on camera to show back in Santa Monica with cheese and crackers. Alexa enlarged the photo and was surprised to see a gash on the shark's snout. A stab of sympathy for the creature surprised her. Lured by blood, its instincts activated for naught.

Exploitation, the water taxi man had said.

Was caging taunting the sharks? Causing them harm? No one chummed with dead cows to lure lions on a safari. And in the North Carolina mountains, fed bears were dead bears. Did the same apply here?

"The public doesn't know about the bullet wound," she said. "I hate that the sharks are getting all the blame." Her sympathy continued to surprise her. The next few photos were also of the shark, farther away, turning, coming back, then just a tail in liquid green.

Alexa realized she was scrolling backwards, looking at the last photos first. One photo was Theo and his wife—Meredith—embracing on board. Another showed Theo pulling on dry-suit gloves. Then there were scenic photos: the horizon dotted with islands, the shore, a fishing boat. Alexa touched the screen. She enlarged the boat's name: *Darla Jo*. Again.

"Odd," she said to Bruce.

He hiked an eyebrow.

"When I was alone at the station and y'all were searching for Stephen..."

"Y'all?"

"Yes. You all, whatever." She paused, making sure Bruce was listening. "I read the DOC shark-sighting forms. This boat, *Darla Jo*, was mentioned several times as being in the vicinity of shark sightings. It's the same boat docked at Golden Bay Wharf."

He took the phone, studied the photo. "What are you thinking?"

She covered up a yawn. "It's just something I noticed."

Bruce's forehead bunched. "Sometimes it's small details like this that solve a case. I'll look into it. What's the owner's name?"

It had been a long day with about a thousand new names. "I don't remember. I think the water taxi man said the fisherman who owns the boat lost his job at the clam farm."

"Clam farm? You mean oyster farm."

Something else niggled. "The *Darla Jo* owner has a truck, and I have a witness—an American girl studying kelp—who saw a truck coming down the drive to Golden Bay Wharf the day Andy was killed." She got out her notebook and gave Bruce the information.

"Worth looking into." He rubbed his eyes, told her to get some sleep, and excused himself to ask the bartender who owned *Darla Jo*. Alexa was relieved. If he'd walked her to Room Three, she would probably have invited him in.

Chapter Twenty-Six

Alexa hoped the hot, robust shower spray would wash away her longing for Bruce's lips, hands, and all the rest of him. She wiggled her toes and watched the whirlpool vanish, like the kiss, down the drain. A small sign in the bathroom pleaded with guests to conserve water. That seemed strange to Alexa, what with all the rain, but she turned off the faucet instead of lingering and reached for a towel, dry this time.

She wiped the foggy mirror and examined her gaff wound. She'd have a new scar to add to the old one cascading across her back. The edges of the lesion were pink and puffy. She rummaged for her ancient tube of Neosporin and rubbed some in. The sting as the ointment went to work felt good, medicinal, an answer to a problem. She dabbed some on her sandfly bites for good measure.

Standing naked in front of the mirror, she took care combing out tangles and blow-drying her hair. Dad claimed she was the image of her mother. Mom had been only thirty-nine—two years older than Alexa now—when she died.

Crappy unfair, Alexa thought. Every day is a gift, and all. *Is a glioma brain tumor in my future?* Thinking of Mom made her think of her brother.

If she were the image of Mom, Charlie looked nothing like Dad. She pictured her brother in rumpled khakis and plaid flannel shirt. Shy of six feet, affable face, thinning hair, glasses. Charlie was a geotechnical engineer in Asheville, North Carolina, and liked to drill holes in the earth. His wife, Mel, bossed him around.

How old were Benny and Noah now? Seven and four, she guessed. Dammit. She hadn't remembered to send them Christmas presents.

What time was it back home? She subtracted seventeen hours. Five a.m. yesterday. Charlie wouldn't like it, but when else was she going to call?

She pulled on her pajama shorts and red N.C. State basketball T-shirt.

Her new phone surprisingly had a signal. She punched his number before she could chicken out. The phone rang and rang. Every time it went to voicemail, she hung up and dialed again. It rang across Foveaux Strait, across the Pacific Ocean, across the equator, across datelines, across time zones, across the United States, across the Blue Ridge Mountains, across loss and sorrow.

After four separate calls, Charlie answered.

"It's me," she said brightly.

"Who? What?" His voice was thick, groggy.

"Alexa. Me."

"Lexi. Where are you? Is something wrong?"

Charlie was the single person on earth allowed to call her Lexi. "No. I'm in New Zealand. I wanted to say hello. See how you are."

No way she could tell him that she was sorry for being mean to him when they were kids, that she missed Mom, that she had no one to love on the brink of death but him.

"But..."

Alexa could hear rustling and sighing.

"Okay. I'm in the kitchen—didn't want to wake Mel. Why are you calling?"

"I told you," she said cheerfully. "I wanted to see how you were doing. And the boys."

"But it's five a.m."

"I know it's early, but this is the only time I had. I'm busy."

Silence.

Crap. She had offended him. "I know you're busy too. How's work?"

"Really?" Charlie said. "You wake me at five a.m. to ask about work?"

Alexa shoved her dirty clothes to the floor and sank into the chair. "I'm going down in a shark cage. I thought I better tell a family member in case I don't survive." Why in the world had she lied? What was wrong with her?

"Must be nice. I thought you had to work for a living."

"I've always worked," she spat. "No one paid for my graduate schools like they did yours." This wasn't going according to plan. Brotherly love was careening off a cliff. "How are Benny and Noah?"

The strain in Charlie's voice lifted. "He wants us to call him Ben, not Benny. He's reading chapter books. Like *Magic Tree House* and *Nate the Great*. I don't think I could even read in the first grade."

"Because no one read to you after Mom died. You made up for it. And Noah?"

"He says whatever comes into his head. He asked a man at the grocery store where his hair was."

Alexa laughed. "How's Mel?"

"She's...well, things aren't great. She has us seeing a counselor."

"No way." Charlie and Mel were her Norman Rockwell illustration. Their little family was proof of an ideal. Even if she didn't aspire to that ideal, she liked to know it existed.

She waited for him to say something. Ask about her job maybe. As a kid, Charlie had perfected the wall of silence. He was still good at it. She counted to ten, tried to wait him out. "W h y don't you come visit?" she finally asked. "New Zealand has great hiking, and there's crazy geothermal stuff on the North Island."

"I actually looked into fares. I can't afford sixteen hundred dollars a pop."

"Well, I just wanted to say hi. Tell Benny and Noah I love them."

I love you too, Charlie.

She stared at the curtain-covered window of her cozy room. Her mind was wired; no way she could sleep. Why had she told Charlie she was going down in a shark cage? What would it be like? She grabbed her computer and Googled shark cage diving YouTubes. There were loads. People liked to share their death-defying feats. Some were a minute or two long, and poorly filmed. She clicked on a twelve-minute one from Cape Town, South Africa, featuring a nauseatingly cute couple. "Hi. I'm Kara. This is my boyfriend, Nate. I can't believe we're doing this," all young and sunglasses and bonhomie. The cage boat wasn't as fancy as *The Apex.* There appeared to be two crew members and six or seven tourists. When the boat arrived at the shark grounds ten miles off the coast, the operator explained it could take minutes to hours to spot a shark. To lure them, he ladled chum overboard, and another crew cast a bloody fish attached to a buoy into the water and slowly reeled it back, over and over. Alexa laughed at Kara and Nate struggling into their wetsuits, thrusting and zipping, wiggling toes and teasing each other about hyperventilating and deathtraps. The crew members threw the cage, attached by ropes, overboard, and pulled it close to the side of the slightly rocking boat.

It looked flimsy.

The suited-up Kara leaned over the boat railing, pointing at a bird. A crew member yelled, "Back, back, back." A great white shark erupted from the water, lunging for the bait, making Kara scream and Alexa jerk in the chair. Kara's hands were shaking as she buckled her weight belt and strapped on her mask.

Nate, looking like a fat black seal now, sat on the side of the boat. A crew member shouted instructions: "Put your bum there, swing your feet over, get your left foot to touch that second bar." Nate hovered over the cage. "Tell my mother I love her," he goofed to the camera. He took a breath and slithered into the cage, which was three-fourths submerged.

The camera went with him and caught a damn white coming at the bars, jaws wide, ramming the corner, the camera jerky and whirling. Nate popped up like a seal head, and the crew asked if he was okay.

God almighty, Alexa thought. *Say no.*

Then the woman dropped down, and the crew lowered mouth-pieces attached to tubes leading to the boat. The air. So, no scuba tanks, just hoses. The couple lowered their heads beneath the water, camera following into murky green. Their gloved hands grasped handles inches from the cage bars, and they tucked a foot each in a bar at the bottom. A crew member dropped a fish head on a line in front of the cage. Hadn't Kana Duffy said baiting the cage was illegal? A shark swam straight at it and veered at the last moment, showing a massive ivory belly as it arced away.

The sharks were being teased. Alexa didn't have the stomach to watch anymore and closed her laptop. She slumped in the chair, too tired now to bridge the floor to the bed and fell asleep. Her dreams were peppered with Bruce and Charlie and sharks and whales. A soft *scritch*—was it a knock?—startled her into stiff-necked alertness an hour later, according to the glowing numbers on the clock. A jolt of joy—Bruce was tapping to be let in. But what if it wasn't Bruce? Fear made her heart gallop. She strained her ears, listened for more, heard only her rapid breath.

The wind, she thought. *Must have been the wind.* She stumbled to the bed, crawled in, and pulled the covers to her chin. Bruce was only a scream away.

Chapter Twenty-Seven

Her gaff wound was hot to the touch in the morning. Little red lines emanating from the nasty slash pointed to infection. After rubbing on Neosporin, she checked the tube's expiration date. Long gone. She'd stop by the medical center—what were those crazy hours?—ten a.m. till noon. Joan would hook her up with antibiotics.

Before she left for a bite to eat—and maybe a tête-à-tête with Bruce over scrambled eggs—she checked her email. A message was from her boss. A spark of fear: Had Wallace complained about her rogue tactics? But, no, Dan had registered her for three upcoming courses: Bite Mark Analysis, Courtroom Testimony for Forensic Practitioners, and Advanced Latent Ridgeology. Score. Bite Mark and Courtroom Testimony would be repeats, but she knew she'd learn something new. Or could show off. The important thing was that Dan was investing in her. She replied with an update on the cases and suggested that she would benefit from a gun-safety class.

A second message was from the ballistics lab in Auckland and was cc'ed to Detective Inspector Bruce Horne and Sergeant Kipper Wallace. She read rabidly. They had completed firearms examination on the Browning A-Bolt rifle found with King's body. They concluded the rifle had been wiped clean, but technicians had been able to use an electrostatic technique to produce a print. Washing the metal, applying volts of electricity, using toner. Alexa tried to remember the steps in this process—she had never done it herself. She read further. The fingerprint matched Robert King's.

Damn. The print didn't help solve the case.

The final paragraph made her heart sink: The bullet wound in King's skull did not match the medium-sized bullets taken from King's rifle. It was caused by a larger caliber, like a shotgun.

Bruce wasn't at the breakfast buffet. Alexa fought disappointment by filling her plate but then had no appetite. The sausage was fatty and unappetizing, the eggs rubbery. *What if he's avoiding me?*

She left her almost-full plate, pushed back from the table-for-two, shook her head at Constance hastening toward her with a sloshing coffeepot. "No thanks. I'll get some at the station."

Constance's eyes darted around the room as she spoke softly. "One of my waitresses heard a tale that might be important."

Like a Pavlovian dog, Alexa dropped the crime kit and searched for her pen and pad.

"Andy Gray killed a white shark and didn't notify DOC."

Live sharks had been Gray's business. "Why would he do that?"

"Accidentally. It happens. One of his crew started talking merry hell—too much drink, eh—said the motor sliced up a white. Instead of letting it swim off trailing blood—sure to be torn apart by other sharks—Gray shot it."

Grisly, but maybe humane.

"They hauled it onboard," Constance continued. "The laws say Gray had to notify DOC, turn over the carcass for research, but the hand doesn't believe he did."

"I'll let the DI know. Who was the crew member?"

"Trina doesn't know his name. She's new, aye, spending her summer hollies here." Constance took a pencil from behind her ear and asked for Alexa's pad. "Here's her mobile number."

Alexa thought about Gray's crew members as she left the inn.

What had the team found out from interviewing them? She was out of the loop.

The sweet-smelling breeze blew her hair—hanging loose because it had looked nice in the bathroom mirror—into a curly halo. She rummaged through her tote for an elastic band and wrestled it into a ponytail—down boy, she commanded. A boat in the harbor, slightly blurred by a soft morning mist, wended toward open water, a flock of gulls or maybe mollymawks in pursuit. She had read a sign about mollymawks—they were a subspecies of albatross that frequented the island. The vessel they were tailing was too small to be the ferry. Was it Briscoe and Duffy on *Glowing Sky*, ready for their cage dive expedition? The YouTube last night helped her visualize the process. Part of her wanted to go, turn her lie to Charlie into the truth. The lie had been a pathetic way to see if he cared about her. And it had backfired.

Some of us have to work for a living.

She shrugged off her annoyance and pulled out her phone. Duffy had said meet the *Glowing Sky* crew at 7:30, and it was only 7:10. She decided to walk to the harbor before heading to the station—she didn't want to look too eager to see Bruce. She crossed the grassy lawn where they had kissed, wishing the replay in her mind would erase.

Traipsing across the grass in front of the inn, she checked over her shoulder. Someone had swung that nasty gaff as if she were a fish to brain. Paid to be cautious. Coast was clear.

What was the gaffer doing right now? Something as mundane as eating breakfast? Had he left the island? Had he killed Andy Gray?

Upended rowboats in sun-faded colors and large rocks marked the high tide line. She scrunched past them and kicked an oyster shell. A spray of sand blew in her face. *Figures*, she thought, spitting out grit: Her life was a series of rash mistakes and backfires. Like last night's kiss. It had backfired.

Two terns played tug-of-war with fish entrails, and a crab

skittered over a pile of kelp. The swishing and sucking sound of small waves calmed her down, soothed her ruffles. She watched a shell somersault backwards with a wave's gentle retreat. A football field to the right, the beach curved into tangled trees and a derelict boathouse. Halfmoon Pier—twice as large as Golden Bay Wharf pier—was to the left. A huddle of people stood halfway down, maybe waiting for the ferry. Lucky for them the water was calm this morning. She wondered if the group was watching her watch them. She waved, but no one waved back. Alexa turned and located the sea-green police station up the hill. It looked like a pretty doll's house.

Would one murder, or both, be solved by sunset, she wondered, hitching the crime kit and her tote on opposite shoulders. She winced. The strap hurt. *Better start antibiotics soon*, she thought, trekking across the sand.

The station door was propped open. What was it with these New Zealanders leaving doors and windows open all the time? Alexa pulled it closed. Only Wallace, at his desk, and Bruce, making coffee, were in the room.

"Sleep well, Ms. Glock?" Bruce said.

The quarter smile played on those lips she had kissed. Alexa looked away. "Very well, thanks."

"Coffee?"

"Yes. Where's Constable Kopae?"

Wallace looked up. "On her way. Briscoe is at the dock. He'll be sniffing out Lucas Grogan and his cage business."

"I hope the constable has finesse," Bruce said. He was wearing what Alexa considered his FBI outfit: pressed khakis and a black windbreaker with the New Zealand Police logo embroidered at the breast.

"Shark Man will snag all the attention," Wallace said.

Alexa dropped her things and accepted a mug from Bruce. How did he know she added milk? He must have paid attention at breakfast yesterday. She sat at the table, the mug warm and comforting in her hands, and told them what Constance had said about the dead shark.

"I'll report it to Supervisor Lowell," Wallace said. "Department of Conservation violations are his jurisdiction."

"Any news about Stephen?" she asked between sips. The firearms report weighed heavily on her mind.

"One case solved is the way I look at it," Wallace said. "That firearms report? Read it with my porridge. The bullet in King's skull came from a shotgun. Just waiting for the gun to get to the lab so they can confirm it was Stephen's."

"Maybe it was his. Maybe it wasn't," Bruce replied. "Keep an open mind. The shotgun is on its way. We'll know if its ammunition matches the hole in King's skull by afternoon. I'm going to have another go at Stephen." He nodded at Alexa. "Before we fly him to Invercargill."

She nodded back. If Stephen didn't shoot King—accidentally or on purpose—who did? The prime suspects were King's pals. "Did we rule out the men hunting with King?" she asked.

"I met them," Wallace said. "When King disappeared, they joined the initial search. Devastated, all of 'em. Their holiday ruined by tragedy. Ever since uni, the four of them would take a yearly hunting trip." Wallace dug through his file and pulled out a list. "Let's see. James Riley from Dunedin, and Hal Moore and Ken Wilson from Rotorua. We Skyped individually with them while you were in Dunedin. They alibi each other, said they were together like Musketeers when King went missing. They've provided fingerprints and turned over their guns for comparisons to their local police."

"Make sure to coordinate with ballistics in Auckland," Bruce said. "We don't want loose ends sabotaging the case."

"Right, Senior," Wallace said.

Could be a *Murder on the Orient Express* scenario, Alexa thought, where instead of a lone killer, all the suspects took part in the murder. She had enjoyed the movie but hadn't liked that in the end, justice had not been served. "What about Andy Gray's crew members? Are they still suspects?"

"We're still tracking down John, but Squizzy Koch is off the hook—he spent the afternoon at the salmon farm, plenty of witnesses," Wallace said. "Afterwards, he was seen at the pub. He provided information on those shark-sighting forms we confiscated from *The Apex*. Andy used them to figure out where to chum. One of his buds works at the main office and made copies for him. Gray shouldn't have had them."

"They would give him an advantage over Grogan," Alexa said. "What have you found out about the *Darla Jo*'s owner?"

"Sean Warren?" Wallace asked.

"Ms. Glock noticed his boat was in the vicinity of several white-shark sightings, and he may have been in the area of *The Apex* the afternoon Gray was killed. A witness saw his truck."

"*Darla Jo* is docked at the same pier," Wallace said. "That's probably why."

"Get him in here," Bruce ordered. He swung his eyes to Alexa. "Let's talk fiber." He looked at the wall clock: 7:35. "We'll start without Constable Kopae. I'll review. A strand of fiber was removed from Andy Gray's fingernail. Is that right, Ms. Glock?"

She nodded. "The fiber matches trawler netting made by Van Kees Nautical Nets in Dunedin. Brand called Stealth Glider."

"We surmise Gray came into contact with this netting— possibly during an altercation," Bruce said. "Sergeant Wallace has produced a list of fishing trawlers on the island, and their captains. Ten blokes. Stormy Parker is on the list. He's the PāuaMAC rep. I'll talk to him when he comes in."

"Lucas Grogan is on the list too, sir," Wallace said. "He had a trawling boat before he sold it to buy a shark boat."

Bruce looked interested. "Gray's only competitor?"

Wallace nodded.

They divided up the list. "Team up with Kopae," Bruce said to Alexa. "I'm short-staffed, what with Lowell guarding Neville, and Briscoe taking a cruise. Ask for permission to see the netting. Shouldn't take long to see if it's Van Kees' brand, right?"

Alexa hid her smile and silently vowed to follow all the rules.

The station door pushed open. Andy Gray's partner, Lisa Squires, and her mother walked in. Bruce and Wallace stood.

Lisa's mother strode to the conference table. "We have some information you might be interested in."

Lisa, red-eyed, held a form and followed meekly. "I don't know if it's important." She glanced at Alexa.

"Please sit," Bruce said. "You've met Ms. Glock?"

Lisa pulled out a chair and sat, but Mrs. Squires remained standing. "You were on that awful plane ride yesterday," she said to Alexa.

"Yes. I continued on to Dunedin. Did you make it home before that rainstorm hit?"

"We were home for tea. Not that either of us was hungry—Lisa is staying with me. The sight of Andy's body in the morgue—barely human."

Lisa made a gurgling noise from the back of her throat.

"And that other family—all tears and hullabaloo. The young lasses. I'm glad they found their dad after all this time," Mrs. Squires added.

The hunter, Alexa speculated.

"I know it wasn't easy for you," Wallace said. "My condolences." He sat, fished reading glasses out of his shirt pocket, and turned to Lisa. "When are you due, lass?"

A soft smile tugged at her lips, and she looked down. A baggy sweatshirt hid her rounded belly. "Early May."

"Lovely. How are you feeling?"

Her smile dissolved.

"Eh, well." Wallace adjusted his glasses and took the sheet from Lisa. "Bank statement, eh? You shared finances?"

"Andy is, was, a good man." Her chin quivered. "Nothing to hide."

Alexa was relieved to hear her use "was." Viewing her boyfriend's brutalized body had cured her of denial.

"Tell them what you told me," Mrs. Squires said. She squeezed Lisa's shoulder and took the seat next to her. Bruce sat as well.

"It's that, um, Andy's mum called me. She was hysterical, right? She and his dad are flying here, to meet me, and I guess since Andy and I weren't married, they have the right to Andy's things. They'll arrive tomorrow."

"Not fair, that," Mrs. Squires said, smoothing her tousled graying hair. "Lisa and Andy have been together three years. You should have made it legal."

Lisa jerked. "Why would you say that?"

Mrs. Squires sniffed. "Tell them what you found out."

"Andy hadn't told his mum and dad—their names are Harry and Louisa—that I'm preggers. It was all awkward like when I thanked them for their generosity. They didn't know what I was talking about."

"Well," Bruce said, "perhaps Andy hadn't found the right time."

"Maybe he was waiting to tell them at the hollies," Wallace suggested.

Or maybe he wasn't keen about becoming a father, Alexa thought.

Lisa's voice strengthened. "Yes, but…" She took the paper from Wallace and pointed at a line. "Andy told me this deposit was a baby gift from his parents."

Wallace leaned in. "Five thousand dollars, dated 9 September. Two months ago, eh?"

"We used the money to update the shark cage. Add tubing over the steel, to comply with the latest DOC rule. So the sharks couldn't get hurt if they crashed the cage."

Also known as ramming. Alexa's marine biology knowledge was accumulating.

"We added vinyl roll-down sides, too. Passengers don't like wind spray. We want to keep the boat comfy. Good for business."

"How was your business?" Wallace asked.

"You can see the balance of our loan." She pointed to a column on the statement. "We were making our payments."

Wallace whistled. "Those are hefty payments. You must not have had much left to live on. I'll make some copies, eh."

Bruce leaned forward. His black jacket darkened his eyes to navy. "You're saying Andy lied to you about the origin of this deposit?"

Tears gathered in Lisa's eyes. "He hadn't told his mum and dad about our news. So how could that money have been a baby gift?"

Alexa handed her a napkin. She heard Wallace softly curse and open the paper drawer of the copier.

"Since you're here," Bruce said, "I'd like to ask about the gun Andy possessed." He turned and called to Wallace, "Let me see that list of Stewart Island gun owners."

Wallace closed the drawer, pushed a button, and popped over to Kopae's cubicle. He shuffled through a stack. "Here we go." He gave Bruce the list and went to collect the copies. "Need an assistant, I do."

Bruce scrolled the list with his finger. "Andrew Gray had a Ruger handgun?"

Lisa nodded. "For protection. After our porch was chummed, he didn't feel safe."

"Were any other threats made to you or Andy? Besides the porch vandalism?"

"People give us dirty looks, say things under their breath in the Four Square. 'Leave the sharks alone,' 'Go back to Aussie, convict,' that kind of thing. We don't go to the pub anymore. We were planning to move to Bluff." The gathered tears crested and rolled down her pale cheeks.

"So, he bought it for protection," Bruce said. "Where is the gun?"

Lisa's hands cradled the swell of her belly. "I guess on *The Apex*. In the console box."

"No gun was found on the boat," Wallace stated. "Have you searched your house?"

"No. Andy carried it with him."

"I'll stop by, have a look, if you don't mind," he said.

Lisa shrugged.

Alexa wondered if ballistics tests could determine if Gray's wound was from a handgun.

The station door yanked open. Constable Kopae popped in. "You're needed at the wharf, Senior," she said out of breath. "There's trouble on the pier."

Chapter Twenty-Eight

Bruce stood. "You did right by sharing the bank statement."

"What now?" Lisa swiped at her face. "What does it mean?"

"We'll get back with you as soon as we know."

Mrs. Squire's nose tipped upward. "Andy was hiding something."

"No he wasn't. You never liked him, Mum."

Kopae ushered the mother and daughter out. When they left, she turned toward the team. "It's the cage protesters. Blockading the pier. A crowd is gathering to watch."

"You stay here, Constable," Bruce ordered. "Glock can explain about the deposit. I agree with Mrs. Squires. Gray was up to something." He motioned for Wallace to join him and left.

Alexa walked to the window and watched them hop in Wallace's SUV.

"It's my island. I should be down there," Kopae said.

"I hear you." Alexa returned to the table and sipped her lukewarm coffee.

"Idiots," Kopae said. "The pier is private property—belongs to Stewart Island Charters. The protesters don't have a permit." She laughed. "I would know if they did. I'm the one who would issue it." She leaned on the table and began jotting a list of names.

Alexa watched. "Who are they?"

"The protesters I saw on the pier."

Julie Dreyer
Hani Kawata
Mason Star
Stormy Parker

Alexa pointed to Stormy. "DI Horne said Stormy Parker was a pāua diver rep, and coming to the station this morning." She was sure he was the same guy who had threatened Theo in the pub. What had he said? "I'll slice you up and chum with your guts."

"Stormy is vocal about ending cage diving. A lot of pāua divers wade in from shore, and he's afraid for their safety."

"Is pāua diving popular around here? Like hunting and fishing? Or is it business only?"

"It's both." A gleam came into Kopae's eyes. "I've gone pāua collecting with my uncle and auntie at Butterfield Beach. I only wade, stand on rock. But Johnnie takes the snorkel, swims out past the breakers. Shows the missus who da man. And he does right—makes sure pāua and kina are the right size, doesn't take more than he should."

"Kina?"

"Sea urchin. But Johnnie quit diving since he saw a white up close and personal. He was prying a pāua off the rock. A shadow blocked the sunlight. He looked up and saw a white flick its tail, come straight at him. 'Taking a look,' Johnnie said. They're curious. But now...with the chumming so close to shore, he's afraid next time it wouldn't be just a look."

Kopae wrote another name, Liz Chambers, and dropped the pen. "Have you ever cared enough about something to protest?"

Alexa had joined the Save the Earth club in high school— they had snipped plastic six-pack rings and made *Turn Lights Off* posters, but they hadn't protested like young people today. She admired that young climate-change activist from Sweden, what's her name—Greta Something. But caring too much led to disappointment. "No. Have you?"

"I care about law and keeping people safe." Kopae walked to the window.

Alexa joined her. Side by side they stared down at the harbor. Alexa noticed smudge marks where Stephen had rapped against the glass. Trace evidence. The panes made the station feel like a jail.

Be of use, she thought. She told Kopae about the deposit in Andy and Lisa's bank account.

Kopae perked up. "The money trail. He lied to Lisa. What was he hiding?"

Maybe a dead shark. Alexa told Kopae what she had learned from Constance about Andy Gray killing a shark.

"Anyone who hurts or kills a great white has to report it," Kopae said. "Big fines if you don't. Andy Gray wasn't all lightness and lollies." She hung her cap on a wall hook and walked to her cubicle.

"What would you do with a big dead shark, anyway?"

"Well. Black market. Jaws and teeth. Fins. But that hardly makes sense. Andy needed live sharks for his business, not dead ones. He should have reported it."

"Sergeant Wallace said he'd tell Supervisor Lowell." Alexa came over and leaned on the cubicle partition, her mind jumping to money being the root of evil. "How will you follow up on that deposit? Is there a bank on Stewart Island?"

"Ah no. There's an ATM at the Four Square. We do online banking."

Alexa had only been in her Auckland bank once, to open an account. Everything else was mobile banking.

She explained how the DI had teamed them up to investigate trawling fishermen. "He gave us four names."

"We'll do that later. The DI had said to stay here. He was worried about you last night. About your safety. He drove my car like a hoon when he got the call from 1-1-1."

A hoon was a reckless driver. Usually young and male. "I was fine."

Kopae smiled. "Both of you staying at the inn, eh?"

Alexa's new phone rang. She dug it out of her pocket and turned sideways, hiding her pinking cheeks, even though she and Bruce had nothing to hide. Professionalism was something she admired about Bruce: he would toe the line instead of tow her to bed. "Hello?"

"It's Kana. I have information that might pinpoint where the shark attack took place. Meet me at the Halfmoon Pier. I'll be there in three minutes."

"There's some kind of protest..."

Duffy hung up.

Alexa fingered the sleek phone and rationalized that Bruce had ordered Kopae to stay in the station, not her. So leaving wouldn't break her new pledge to follow rules. "That was Kana Duffy. I need to see him about the case." Before Kopae could respond, she grabbed the crime kit and opened the door. "As soon as I get back, we'll start on the trawler list."

Kana Duffy had said to meet on the pier, so that's where she headed.

She retraced her earlier route: View Street to Golden Bay. The back of her neck tickled when she passed the smoked salmon shop; a figure watched her through the window, but she couldn't make out who it was. The crime kit knocked her thigh with each quick stride, and her gash throbbed with heat. At the bottom of Elgin Terrace a small gathering stood in front of the ferry terminal, including Wallace's wife, little girl, and grandmother. Alexa scanned the area for Duffy. Something poked her.

"You," Granny Maumau said, wielding her umbrella.

"Put that down," said Nina, grabbing Maumau's wrist.

Alexa wanted to rush by, but it would be impolite. Nina had fed her and clothed her. "Good morning," she said. "I'll return your clothes later today."

"I'm washing yours now," Nina said. "What's happening?"

Alexa had to take a step forward to let a woman walk by.

Wallace's daughter jabbed the crime kit. "Is that a doctor bag?"

"Shelly, don't poke," said Nina. "You're teaching her bad habits," she scolded Maumau.

"No, it's not a doctor bag." Alexa fumbled in the side pocket for her forensics ID badge and hung it around her neck. "It's for crime scenes."

Shelly's copper curls blew into her face. She used her pudgy hands to hold them back as she stared expectantly. "What's a crime scheme?"

There was no time to explain.

"We dropped Sam off at school and saw the commotion," Nina said. "Is Kipper okay?"

"More caging shenanigans, that's what," said Maumau.

"Wallace is fine," Alexa said. "I have to go." She wanted to get to the root of why all these people were gathered and find Duffy.

The water taxi operator nodded at her as she stepped onto the pier. She had last seen him headed to Ulva Island with the birders. Alexa spotted the woman with purple hair whom she had spoken to after the autopsy. Locals were becoming familiar, she realized. They appeared here and there like actors in a play. *Dial M for Murder* or something. The purple-haired woman's toddler was straining to break free of his mom's hold on his arm. The water between the planks looked deep. Had to be, if this was the ferry pier. If she had a child, not that she wanted one, she wouldn't take him onto a crowded pier where he could break loose and fall off.

A singsong chant—something about the cage—floated through the crowd. No sign of Duffy, or Wallace and Bruce.

She dodged hikers with bulging backpacks and wedged between birders with binoculars. A grungy man in gum boots and overalls— well, maybe fishing bibs—stared at her. He was familiar—maybe she had seen him in the pub. Past him she saw the main attraction.

Five people, arms outstretched, hands clasped, formed a chain across the pier. No one could get through. "Caging kills, caging kills," they chanted. Alexa recognized a few of the protesters— especially the one in the black knit-cap. He liked Pearl Jam. Another woman held a blowup of a white shark bursting from poster board. *Be My Chum* was written in red. A man next to her waved a *Ban the Cage* sign. Droplets of blood ran from the letters.

Bruce, his back to her, stood in front of the protesters. Constable Briscoe was to his right: his collar was askew. Wallace stood behind the protesters, facing the crowd.

"Ban the cage," the protesters yelled. "Ban the cage."

"Caging provides jobs," a man from behind Alexa screamed.

She whirled. It was the man in fishing bibs. Every time the protesters yelled "Ban the cage," he yelled "Jobs."

Behind the fisherman she spotted Scratch, the asshole from the bar, in full ranger regalia: khaki shorts, forest-green pullover, ankle socks, boots. She intended to ignore him but reconsidered. She edged past the fisherman and approached him. "How are you?" she said perkily.

"Missing you," he said.

Alexa studied his feet. She could see an orange label on the side of his boot: Merrell. The boot imprint at the scene where King's body was discovered had probably been his—a case of classic crime-scene contamination. Same thing had happened in Rotorua. "You need to come by the station, drop off your boot." She walked away as he protested. She'd deal with him later.

Movement in the harbor caught her eye.

Glowing Sky was moored to a piling. A short staircase ramp led from the pier to a boarding bridge. But no one could board. Two men with grim expressions stood on deck, the steel cage glistening behind them. Alexa figured one was Lucas Grogan, Gray's competitor. The other man she had seen before. He was the fisherman who had given her a lift to the inn when she first arrived.

A boat half the size of *Glowing Sky* motored past. The skipper called through a bullhorn, "I'm ready for the hunt." Three industrial-looking fishing poles and an enormous gaff were racked across the stern. A few people on the pier clapped as the boat broke the no-wake rule and circled in a flourish of wake.

Alexa turned to Bruce, wondering why he wasn't calling a halt to the protest. She could see the 8:00 ferry entering the harbor.

A tap on her shoulder made her jump. Kana Duffy gave her his best movie star smile, but she couldn't hear what he had to say because Bruce was yelling for the protesters to stop.

"We have a right to protest," the woman with the Chum poster screamed.

"You don't have the right to interfere in someone's business," Bruce said, pointing. Three people pulling luggage were trying to get through to meet the approaching ferry. "This is private property. Dismantle, or we will begin making arrests."

No one could argue that the protest was interfering with business, Alexa thought, if passengers couldn't reach the ferry. It blared its horn. What would happen, she wondered, when passengers tried to disembark?

"I have some information for you," Duffy told her.

Her attention ricocheted to the shark poster the angry woman was waving five feet away. The blowup of the shark showed a slash across its snout. If she wasn't mistaken, it was the photo Theo had taken and shared with Bruce.

Wallace tapped the tallest protester from behind—the black knit-cap guy from the pub. "Mason," he said. "I don't want to have to cuff you."

"Then don't," Mason responded. "Cuff them instead." He pointed to the men on *Glowing Sky.* "Chumming is responsible for Andy's death. Your own kin might be next."

Duffy pulled papers from his backpack and shook them to get Alexa's attention. "These are tagging reports."

The hullabaloo—that's the word Lisa Squires's mother had used—continued and she ignored Duffy.

Granny Maumau broke through the spectators. "Kipper," she called.

Sergeant Wallace's face went red.

"You can't arrest Mason," Maumau said. "Where will I get my pāua?"

Wallace yelled at Maumau to leave the pier. He turned back to Mason. "Come to the station. Fill out the forms for a proper protest."

The ferry was swinging broadside to tie up. A man on the deck appeared to be filming the commotion.

"That's my film crew," Duffy announced.

"Everyone leave," Bruce yelled at the crowd. "Unless you have legitimate business."

The ferry horn sounded again, causing circling gulls to squawk and fuss.

The protesters dropped hands, grumbled, and followed Wallace, who ushered Granny Maumau slowly along. Spectators parted to let them through, then followed, talking animatedly.

Alexa spotted the young mother, her toddler safe and heavy in her arms.

Bruce strode to the *Glowing Sky* ramp and called to the crew, "All good now. I have a constable ready to join you. Make sure everything goes okay."

The captain—the man Alexa figured was Lucas Grogan—hopped from the boat and ran up the stairs to meet him. "Sir," he said to Bruce, "please lift the ban on water activities. I had to refund twelve customers today."

Bruce's eyes narrowed. "Are you Mr. Lucas Grogan?"

"In the flesh."

Alexa thought that was odd to say, given that the only flesh exposed on Grogan was his nose and mouth. He wore long-sleeved sunscreen shirt, pants, gloves, wraparound sunglasses, and a hat with side and neck flaps.

"You want to take passengers out, knowing what happened to your competitor?"

That's hardly fair, Alexa thought. *Andy Gray was shot.*

"My caging practices are one hundred percent safe."

"Mr. Kana Duffy is here to represent the Department of Conservation." Bruce waved Duffy over. "He will assess the situation from your vessel and make his pronouncement of whether to discontinue the ban on water. I have an officer also accompanying you."

Briscoe hustled to his side. "That would be me, captain."

Alexa hugged the crime kit and stepped closer.

Bruce scowled. "What are you doing here?"

"She came to meet me," Duffy said.

Bruce's left eyebrow hiked up.

"I have information for her. About the sharks."

"If this information relates to our case, you'll share it with me. I'm the commanding officer."

Duffy shrank in stature a bit. "I have shark identification data. From NIWA."

"What is knee-wah?" Bruce asked.

"National Institute of Water and Atmospheric Research," Duffy said. "They're the ones tagging whites around here. They've tagged over a hundred."

Alexa scanned the harbor for fins.

"They've got acoustic data-logging platforms set up all around the island that record the time and date of a tagged shark when it swims by."

"Get to the point," Bruce told Duffy. "I don't have all day."

"I can use pings to see what sharks were in the vicinity of the fatal attack," Duffy said.

Duffy didn't know about the bullet wound, Alexa reminded herself.

"That's well and dandy," Bruce said. "But we don't know the vicinity of the attack. All we know is where Gray washed ashore."

Grogan swiped his sun hat off. "The attack had nothing to do with our cage dive operation."

A scraping clang made Alexa jump. The ferry employees were lowering the gangplank.

"We know Mr. Gray was attacked by more than one shark," Duffy said. "I think from the bite marks that it was three different sharks. I can use ping coordinates to locate where two or more sharks breached the surface at the same time." He smiled at Alexa like they were in cahoots. "Alexa can come with us and make note of the location."

Bruce shook his head slowly. "Share your information with Constable Briscoe. I have other plans for *Ms. Glock*."

Alexa's heart missed a beat, but she spoke up. "Since I'm here, I'll take a look on *Glowing Sky*." She lifted the crime kit. "Before it sets sail."

Bruce considered and then nodded. "Do we have permission to see what type netting you use on board?"

"What?" Grogan asked. "My nets?"

"Netting. It's part of our investigation. Unless you object?"

Grogan sighed. "I have nothing to hide. Come with me." He did an about-face and boarded his vessel.

Permission granted in front of witnesses. Bruce called her over and lowered his voice. "Briscoe will tell Duffy about the bullet wound."

"Good," Alexa said. "He needs all the facts."

Two men holding video recorders, tripods, and lights barreled toward them. Duffy waved and pointed to *Glowing Sky*. "My lads, fresh from the ferry," he said. "You missed the excitement. Small town gone wild. Might make a good show. Let's board."

She guessed they were Duffy's camera crew. She caught up with Grogan and boarded.

Glowing Sky outsized *The Apex*. There were two rows of benches instead of one, and four engines. A platform jutted above the engines. Alexa craned her neck as she slowly weaved through Duffy and his crew. She gauged the distance from the upper deck to the sea to be eighteen feet: a high dive at a swimming pool.

Her belly flopped at the thought. But it was the stench of chum that stopped her cold.

There it was. A cooler of blood gut soup, ladle at the ready, against the rail. The fear and despair of being in the cold, black water coated with chum. Bile rose in her throat.

Alexa regrouped and approached the fisherman. "I'm Alexa Glock, helping the police with their investigation. Thanks for giving me a ride from the ferry."

He nodded, shifting in his tennis shoes, his pewter-colored eyes landing on the crime kit.

Grogan called, "Show her whatever the hell nets we have on board, will you?"

She followed the fisherman, who apparently worked as crew when he wasn't fishing, up the narrow stairway to the upper deck. He pointed to safety netting stretching from railing to deck. His longish curls defied the breeze as if stiff from salt. She nodded and scanned the pier. The sight of Bruce's broad back caused her a pang as he left the pier. A giant white bird flew by at eye level, an albatross. It landed in the water, turned and stared up at her, its dark eyes calculating.

Are you good luck or bad luck?

She had to turn sideways in the cramped stairwell to let Grogan pass. He had wrinkles around his eyes and sandy hair under his hat flap. "Hurry up," he said. "We're getting set to leave."

Below, the fisherman pointed to two nets attached to poles. Not even close to a trawling net. More for butterflies.

"That's it," he said.

She said thanks and went to tell Briscoe goodbye. He stood at the cage, which Alexa noted was attached to a cable—no flimsy ropes like in the YouTube—and big enough for three or four people to stand upright and still have ceiling space.

"I can't believe I'm going down," Briscoe said.

She envisioned the cage sinking in the cold water. Herself stuck inside. A thin blue line, perhaps an eighth-inch in diameter, was threaded through a bar at the bottom. She knew from the YouTube that it was a foot bar, to keep the tourists from floating. The line snaked to the far side.

Alexa's heart skipped a beat. The line wasn't netting, but it looked like polyethylene and the color matched the Stealth Glider. Could the same fiber be woven into rope? She used her phone to take photos and then pulled on gloves and stretched her hand through the bars. It was out of reach. "Where's the door?"

A shadow loomed over her. The fisherman had returned. She hadn't heard a peep.

"Where's the door?" she repeated.

She followed his strange steel eyes to the top of the cage where hinges indicated the entryway. "I need to get in."

"You can climb up," he said. "No time to lower it over the side, so you can drop down."

Alexa took this as a challenge. She dropped the crime kit, tore off the gloves, and grabbed as high as she could. The bars were perfect footholds, and the steel supported her weight without give. She winced as the pull on her trapezius and deltoid muscles made her gaff wound gape. On top she turned two latches, heaved the door open with a clang, and lowered herself in.

Easy-peasy.

Briscoe and the fisherman stared like she was a zoo animal. "Give me gloves, scissors, and a plastic bag," she commanded the constable.

"Evidence, eh?" Briscoe's brown eyes sparkled. He pawed through the kit and passed the items through. She gloved up, snipped off a strand of the line, and held it close to her eye. Damn. It was interwoven with specks of white. All this trouble and no match.

The cage rattled, vibrated. The growl of engines filled her ears. The fisherman laughed. What the hell?

Her blood turned cold. She was trapped in the cage, and the boat was leaving.

Chapter Twenty-Nine

When she stormed into the station ten minutes after Lucas Grogan, smirk on his face, had watched her scramble out of the cage and disembark, she'd had to plug her volley of complaints. Bruce and a bespectacled Wallace were speaking to a man whose bushy beard and moppy mustache must have never experienced a comb-through. Stormy Parker, the PāuaMAC representative, had arrived at the station. She recognized him as the drunkard in the pub who had threatened to slice and dice Theo. He scowled at her. Alexa's gaff wound throbbed in response. Had he been the one who attacked her?

No. She would have remembered those wiry bristles against her neck.

"Don't mind me," she said.

No one introduced her, so she parked herself at Wallace's desk, noticed Kopae was absent, and powered up her laptop. She had an email from Dr. Kisska from the Dunedin lab with the subject line: Diatom Results.

She listened to Bruce establishing that PāuaMAC was a countrywide agency, divided into five regions, and represented the commercial pāua fishery's interests.

"Yeah. That's us," Parker confirmed.

She opened Dr. Kisska's email. There was a brief explanation of diatoms: monophyletic group, single-celled heterokont algae, yadda, yadda. She skimmed to the results: the test was negative. No diatoms present in the lung sample. Andy Gray had not had time to drown. The multiple factors contributing to his death had dwindled to blood loss prior to being submerged. Dying from a gunshot to the abdomen was notoriously painful but maybe more toothsome for Lisa and his parents than torn limb to limb by sharks. She composed a thank you to Dr. Kisska as Parker's voice rose in decibel.

"Pāua are important to Stewart Island's economy. Caging is interfering with production. I've got four or five boys won't dive. Our quotas aren't being filled. If that continues, MAC will give another region more quotas and take ours away. You need to ban the caging."

She didn't grasp all the stuff about quotas, but Parker sounded sober, not soused.

"The shark cage diving permits come from the Department of Ministry. It's their decision," Bruce said calmly.

"They won't listen, and you're passing the buck."

Alexa watched Parker turn his glare to Wallace. "This DI bloke isn't an islander. He doesn't care, Kipper. You've been here all your life. You know what's going on. How caging is tearing the village apart. Who is going to help us if you won't? Do you want a second death on your bloody hands? One of my boys?"

Parker's plea hung like fog across the room.

Wallace looked stricken. Alexa knew he cared about his flock of islanders.

"Andrew Gray wasn't killed by a shark," Bruce said softly.

Parker swiveled his eyes to Bruce.

"He was shot and thrown overboard."

Parker squinted as though it would enhance his hearing. "What the hell did you say?"

Bruce explained about the gunshot wound found in Gray's abdomen. "This is confidential information."

Parker tugged at his beard. "Someone shot Andy? Who?"

"That's what we're trying to find out," Bruce said patiently.

"The newscaster said he was torn up by sharks," Parker argued. "Says so on the internet, too. And everyone at the pub is going on about it." His voice trailed off.

Bruce moved his chair closer to Parker's. "Did you chum Andy Gray's porch?"

A huge Adam's apple appeared and disappeared from below Parker's beard. Like a pale mouse venturing out of its burrow, then dashing back.

Bruce looked at Wallace. "How long ago did Gray make that complaint?"

"Mid-October."

Parker looked panicky. "You can't pin this on me."

"Where were you Saturday afternoon and evening?" Bruce said.

"I don't bloody know where I was, do I? Mostly at the pub with my mates." He whipped a phone from his jacket and started scrolling.

"All afternoon and evening?" Wallace asked.

"Can't say, can I?"

"Do you own Van Kees netting?" Bruce asked.

"What?"

"Just answer the question," Wallace interjected.

"Look at these," Parker said, handing his phone to Wallace. "You might find your killer in the comments."

Wallace studied the screen. "Facebook comments, from a group called Ban the Cage. Damn print is small." He nudged his glasses up and read out loud:

> "**Quim Hilton:** The courts are dragging their butts. If they don't ban caging, we will.
> **Michael Patterson:** As long as cage-dive operators keep throwing blood and guts in the water within the sight of

my crib and tormenting white sharks for fun and profit, I
will fight."

"Patterson lives up the way. He's one of my boys," Parker said.
Wallace cleared his throat and continued.

"**Jane Garrand:** It is barbaric that a protected species can be
   baited and harassed for the tourist dollar.
Liz Chambers: I take my eight and nines class kayaking in the
   bay. A shark followed us.
Keri Barret: Hello. Bloody audacious that apex predators
   are being trained to associate boats and divers with free
   feeds, right on our doorstep.
Jo Head: Chumming affects migration patterns of marine
   megafauna.
Leonard Wilson: So wait. You're telling me the whites haven't
   been coming here for 100s of yrs?
Ed McAdam: If the courts won't shut them down, we will.
Hani Kawata: DOC allows cage diving boats to teaz and
   torment sharks in Foveaux Strait so big-money clients can
   film them smashing into the cages. OUTRAGEOUS."

Wallace looked up from the screen. "Hani was protesting on
the pier. And Liz."
"People in the community are angry," Bruce interrupted. "I
hardly..."
"Wait," Parker said. "Read more."

"**Nina Wallace:** Stewart Island might seem like a faraway..."

Wallace looked up, reddened, then back down. "It's the wife.
I didn't know she belonged to this group." He read silently, then
cleared his throat and read aloud:

"…seem like a faraway place to lawmakers in Wellington, but this is where my boy swims. This is where I live and work and play. Ban the cage.

Colleen Diddles: Totally Objectionable. Kiwis are protected, but whites can be taunted.

Nathan Rawner: Paua divers unite. Kill the cagers."

Wallace went silent.

"Keep going," Bruce said.

"**Tony Adams:** When I lived there I remember the great whites—they were huge bastards!!! They are intelligent and keen to learn. You chum, they learn the sound of a boat means a feed.

Andy Gray: Sharks are after the seals, not chum, which is so finely minced that sharks can't feed on it. The seal population has exploded and the whites keep them in check."

Wallace looked up. "Fark me dead. It's Andy." He pushed his glasses up his nose and leaned in. "The initial comment is dated 2 December, just days before he was killed. The replies aren't dated."

"Read the next comment," Parker said.

"**Ed McAdam:** I'd like to see a white keep you in check."

No sound but the clicking of the minute hand on the wall clock as they digested this information.

Parker reached for his phone and pushed back from the table. "See? What did I tell you?"

"We'll look into it." Bruce stood abruptly. "We'll be round to check out your netting. Don't leave the island."

"Ha," Parker said. "Storm's coming. No one will be going anywhere when it hits."

Chapter Thirty

Alexa was the only one with a Facebook page and hadn't checked it in a month. She vacated Wallace's desk and moved to the table. As Bruce hovered over her shoulder, she logged in on her laptop. Wallace was checking the weather.

"Stormy was right. MetService says 120–140 kilometer-per-hour gusts by 6:00. Periods of rain, squally storms, followed by a cold front."

Bruce bumped her shoulder.

"Ouch."

He stepped away. "What's wrong?"

"Nothing." The pain reminded her to stop by the medical center. She looked back at the page and could barely remember who half her forty-nine "Friends" were. A few high school ghosts, a smattering of undergraduate acquaintances. Mel, Charlie's wife, who posted pictures of Noah and Benny. Rita, her stepmother, who shared artful table settings. Her friend Mary. Mary was dead, but her account lingered. A lump lodged in Alexa's throat.

"You have a friend request," Bruce commented.

Alexa wished she couldn't smell his woodsy aftershave. She clicked to see who wanted to be friends. Shark Man. Kana Duffy himself. She smiled slightly, confirming the request, and then searched for Ban the Cage and quickly joined. More heated or heartfelt comments. Bruce pulled up a chair, and they read silently, shoulders almost touching, Alexa clicking and scrolling:

> **Dick Shanley:** Cagers playing with killing machines. What did you expect? The locals have suffered long enuf.
>
> **Miles Smith:** DOC dickheads.
>
> **Roger Trubeck:** Sharks injured when they r taunted by bait and ram cages. One had eye gouged out.
>
> **Carolyn Parker:** A shark got in a cage with divers in South Africa. Guess who was hurt? The shark.
>
> **Sue Griffiths:** Don't tease these beautiful creatures that my ancestors loved and respected.
>
> **Theo Hall:** As tourists, my wife and I were greeted by anti-caging protesters. We paid $$$ to dive. We were stared down by locals, attacked in the pub. In Queenstown no one threatened to cut me up for bungee jumping.

Alexa pointed. "Theo is the one who gave you the pictures from his dive," she said to Bruce. "The American."

"Look at the response," Bruce said. "From Lucas Grogan."

A low burn simmered in her chest as she read Grogan's comment. She was still angry he had started the engines while she was in the shark cage.

> **Lucas Grogan:** Sorry you weren't treated well. Glad we saw some big ones down under.
>
> **Ed McAdam:** Footage has emerged of a 6m great white shark lunging at a dinghy in Halfmoon Bay, your competitor torn apart, and you still take people out? Ought to lock you in your cage.

Bruce scooted closer. "Start a list of any people who made threatening comments, and put McAdam at the top."

The landline rang. Wallace answered. "Eh. Right. All good." He called to Bruce, "Gray's mobile company for you, Senior."

Bruce jumped up. Alexa listened to the conversation with interest.

"Yes," Bruce confirmed. "Section 88. Plausible reason."

In the U.S., the police had authority to search cell phone records if exigent circumstances were present. The same rules applied here. The wiped-up blood and gouged bullet hole were exigent circumstances. And her life had been threatened.

Bruce hung up, sat at the head of the table, and opened his laptop. "Should be in my inbox. If anything, the records will help us formulate a timeline."

Alexa returned to scrolling and trolling, using her Pilot G2 gel pen to add names of people who had posted threatening comments. While she was lost in her task, a tap on her shoulder made her start.

"Senior says for us to start visiting the fishermen," Constable Kopae said.

"I didn't hear you come in," Alexa said.

Wallace nodded from his desk. "Let's see your Facebook list first."

It had five names.

"I know two of these men," Wallace said.

Kopae studied the list. "Yeah nah. I know Ed McAdam. He's on our trawler list."

"Do you know Nathan Rawner, Mr. Kill the Cagers?" Wallace asked.

Kopae shook her head. Alexa scrolled back for the "Kill the Cagers" comment and clicked on the name. Rawner's profile was marked private. Alexa sent him a friend request—figured it was worth a try—and shut down her computer.

"Speak with Whale Man first," Wallace instructed.

Alexa thought Stephen was the whale man. "Who?"

"Zeke Harata. He's the Māori elder who Stephen claims saw

him pick up the PLB. Harata doesn't have a phone, so just stop by. It's on your way to McAdam's place."

"We have three lists," Kopae said. "Trawling fishermen. Gun permits. Facebook. Did any name make all three?"

The sergeant and constable cross-checked for a hat trick. No luck.

Bruce spoke as Alexa and Kopae opened the door. "Ask permission to see the nets. Is that clear?"

"Yes, sir," Kopae said.

"If you see something suspicious—identify, determine significance, photograph, record."

Kopae nodded and Alexa patted the crime kit.

"If there is any danger, call us and leave immediately. Get back before the storm hits."

"Radio is right here." Kopae patted her belt.

Alexa did a mental eye roll.

"Methinks he's worried about you," Kopae said on the porch stairs.

Alexa refused to engage. Her story about Grogan's shenanigans on *Glowing Sky* burst from her mouth. "He started the engines to scare me," she said. "While I was in the shark cage." She suspected all of them—Duffy, his film crew, Grogan, the fisherman, Constable Briscoe, maybe—were in cahoots. They had watched her storm off the pier. Probably laughing.

Not. Funny.

Kopae swiped fingers through her hair, settled her cap firmly, and looked to be suppressing a smile. They walked across the soft grass to the car. Kopae picked a leaf off the windshield before opening the car door. "Why were you in the shark cage?"

Alexa explained about the fiber as a jeep pulled up. Supervisor Lowell nodded to them. Stephen, head down, sat in the back. Part of Alexa wanted to stay, listen to the interrogation, and another part was glad to leave misery behind.

Shoving the crime kit in the back seat caused her to grimace.

She told Kopae to stop by the medical center. "I might be getting an infection. I'll run in, get some antibiotics."

"We better move. The clinic closes in ten minutes. I'll drop you, hit the Kai Cart, pick us up some lunch. We'll chow on the way to Zeke's."

The thought of food occupied Alexa all the way to the clinic.

Joan, the nurse practitioner, was pulling on her jacket when she arrived. Alexa explained about her wound.

"Let's take a looky."

She removed her jacket and ushered Alexa into the same exam room where they had conducted the partial autopsy on Gray's body. It smelled of disinfectant. "Took me an hour to clean it," Joan said. "It's not like we have a cleaning crew." She washed her hands, pulled on gloves, and asked Alexa to remove her shirt. "Sit here, love."

Alexa hopped onto the exam table and dangled her Keds.

"What have we got?" Joan pushed Alexa's bra strap out of the way and gently prodded the inflamed skin surrounding the laceration. "All the classic signs, even producing pus. What happened?"

"I, um, ran into a gaff."

"Blimey. Looks more like someone tried to catch you with one. Bacteria from fish guts is the problem."

"Gross."

Joan's wire-frame glasses caught the overhead light. "Does your running into a gaff have anything to do with Andy Gray being shot?"

"I can't say. Thank you for keeping quiet about the bullet."

"It's been hard," Joan said earnestly. "My husband is ready to lead a shark hunt. He'll be gutted if Shark Man says no to culling. But he will, right? We can't blame Andy Gray's death on the sharks."

Alexa nodded. "Um, my shoulder?"

"I'll clean it and start you on amoxicillin. I keep some stocked.

When was your last tetanus shot?" Joan stuck a thermometer in her mouth.

"I'm 'ood," Alexa mumbled.

Joan was efficient. Alexa's temperature was 37.3 degrees Celsius. Slightly high. Pill bottle in hand, she was on the clinic porch searching the sky for storm signs when Kopae honked.

Chapter Thirty-One

The sedan smelled heavenly. "Got us fish bites and chips," Kopae said, a dab of red sauce at the corner of her mouth. "And L&Ps."

"You're my BFF." Alexa rummaged in her tote for her wallet and pulled out a colorful New Zealand tenner. "This enough?"

"Yeah nah." She kept the motor off.

Alexa opened the L&P and swallowed her first pill with the lemon fizzy drink. She ate a fry and vowed to run soon. She'd been running for over ten years. And practiced yoga to keep flexible. Her burn had been subcutaneous. Her doctor's anger way back when was seared in her brain. "Why didn't you get treatment quicker? Cold water would have reduced the damage."

Jesus. I was a kid, writhing on the floor.

Running and yoga kept her scars from tightening with age. "Are you a runner?" she asked Kopae, envisioning girl time jogging along a beach.

"Eh? Not me." Kopae dipped a fish bite in ketchup and popped it into her mouth. "I stay fit by playing squash and lifting weights. At the community center. Joined soon as mum and me moved here five years ago." She wiped her hands with a napkin and started the car. "It's fifteen minutes to Zeke's."

Stewart Island floated past. Alexa chewed contemplatively, awed by the lush foliage and peeks of emerald water. She inhaled the scent of brine, battered fish, clean air. The island was invading her soul, taking hold like tendrils of ivy. Houses were spread thin, weathered, modest. An occasional fancy one preened from a hilltop, and she imagined renting it, holing up, watching the sky change from dusky blue to purple and gray. The car threaded along Horseshoe Bay Road, past lowland, shrubs, and trees yielding to bay and boats. A car approached from the opposite way. Kopae lifted her hand in a wave.

"Hard to believe a storm is coming," Alexa said, savoring her last fish bite.

"No wind, and temperature's warm." Kopae's right elbow rested out her open window. "Those are sure signs."

"What do you know about Zeke Harata?"

"Not much. He might be a great-uncle, something like that." She pulled out her mobile and hit speed dial. "Eh, Mum," she said, casting Alexa a sheepish grin. "I'm on my way to visit Zeke Harata. Is he a rellie?"

Fragments of animated reply. Out Kopae's window Alexa saw a tall rock formation on a beach. Like a Jenga tower. The green water stretched to the horizon and then was gone, blocked by trees.

"Auntie Helen's brother?" Kopae listened some more, frowned. "No, that's all good. I don't have time for a story. I might be home late. Ta."

Kopae looked straight ahead. "She wanted to tell me the whale rider legend. It's not like I haven't seen the movie." She slowed the car and turned away from the water onto Potiki Road, a one-lane strip wending through a canopy of trees. "Harata is a great uncle, but I've never met him. He summers here. The rest of the time he lives on the North Island. Near Auckland. Mum says he helped change the Marine Mammals Protection Act so that *iwi* could harvest beached whales."

Iwi, Alexa knew, were Māori tribes. "Is there an *iwi* on Stewart Island?"

"The Waitaha *iwi* came here way back, during the moa hunting age. But most Māori come here seasonally. Like Harata. He goes around the country and leads whale flensings. Tries to keep our Māori culture alive." She slowed the sedan to a crawl. "It's along here somewhere. Mum says he owns a lot of hectares."

A carved wooden whale marked the driveway. Kopae turned and weaved through the woods on a claustrophobic track. Branches swiped the doors. Kopae tried to dodge mud holes. The car bottom scraped a gravelly mound. "Don't like the sound of that," Kopae said.

Ahead, Alexa spotted a dark brown chicken-sized bird tapping a mud hole with its long beak. The bird seemed to have hair instead of feathers. "Is that..."

"A kiwi," Kopae said, stopping the car. "A southern brown."

The kiwi shuffled off. Alexa had trouble reconciling the pear-shaped bird with the scream she'd heard while examining King's remains.

The driveway ended in a round clearing. The dwelling, to the right of the clearing, was more shack than bungalow. Kopae parked next to a rusting oil drum. "I'll do the talking."

It was quiet. There was no other car, no sign of life, no birdsong.

Kopae must have noticed. "The calm before a storm, eh?" She swished her hair back with her fingers and settled her cap. "Doesn't look as if the house is hooked to electricity. Off the grid. Let's go."

Alexa checked her cell phone. No signal. She followed through the stubby grass and waited as Kopae stood on a rubber mat and knocked. After a few seconds, she tried again. "Not home. Let's look around back."

As they turned the corner of the house, Alexa saw a broad, bald man, head down, emerging from a shipping container shed. She nudged Kopae.

"*Kia ora.* I'm Constable Kopae, Stewart Island Police."

He froze like a deer.

Kopae started over. "We would have called, but you don't have a phone."

The man, dressed in flip-flops, jeans, and a gray T-shirt that bulged over his stomach, stepped to meet her. Dusky spirals were tattooed on his cheeks. He replied in Māori, and Kopae shook her head. "How may I help you?" he asked in English.

"Are you Mr. Harata?"

"I am."

"We have questions about the whale flensing at Hellfire Beach."

He lifted his chin. "I had proper permits."

"Yes. I know," Kopae said. "I have questions about who you were with."

"It was a long time ago," he said. "I will return soon to harvest the bone."

"Is there somewhere we can sit?" Kopae looked at the house, but Harata beckoned for her to follow him into the container. Alexa wondered how the container had gotten here.

Harata pulled open a double glass slider. Inside the metal rectangle were a stove, lanterns, bench, messy wooden worktable, tools, two folding chairs, and bone. Lots of whale bone. Light from the slider illuminated a broad, brownish jaw with pointy teeth on the table, surrounded by a drill, small saw, a plush work mat. Alexa stepped over and peered at the jaws. Whale, she decided. Not shark. She counted the teeth: forty-two. Sparse for such a large jaw. The teeth looked capable of grasping and holding prey, but not slicing and ripping flesh.

"My mum, Nicki Kopae, says we are relatives," Kopae said to Harata.

"We are all *whānau*."

"It's about the day of the Hellfire Beach flensing," Kopae said.

"So many whales," he replied. "There was much work to do."

Alexa walked to a shelf spanning the length of the wall and touched a huge cream-colored vertebra the size and appearance of an airplane propeller. She imagined this vertebra attached to the next and the next, each vertebra diminishing in size all the way to the tail. The bone was porous and rough to her finger pad. "Is this from a pilot whale?"

"We'll ask our questions over here." Kopae looked sternly at Alexa and patted a chair. "Mr. Harata, this is Ms. Glock. She's a forensic investigator from Auckland."

"I know who she is."

Alexa tried not to react as she sat, but how the heck did he know who she was?

Harata observed her with dark eyes. "A pilot whale's vertebra is smaller. That is from a sperm whale. Do you know that a whale formed Foveaux Strait?"

He was older than she first thought. Mid-seventies. "How's that?"

A leather strand disappeared into his T-shirt. He pulled it free and dangled a fishhook made of bone. "Kiwa, our ancestral navigator, was tired of crossing the long land between the South Island and Rakiura." He rubbed the pendant between his fingers.

The folding chair squeaked as Alexa shifted.

"The journey, long and rugged, was through marsh and forest. He asked his whale Kewa to chew through the ground so water would rush in, and he could cross it by *waka*."

Alexa thought of the waves that had crashed over the ferry bow on her trip to the island. "By canoe? That could be dangerous."

Harata nodded. "*Hau-mate.*"

"Death wind," Alexa translated. *Thank you, Mary.*

"Let's get to the flensing," Kopae said. "We are in a hurry. The date was?"

Harata rummaged through a pile on the table. He pulled out a datebook, flipped through, then stopped. "The giving of second life began fifth of February."

"The what?" Alexa asked.

Harata observed her somberly as he fingered his fishhook. "We give the whales a second life through bone. Bone next to skin"—he dropped his pendant back down his shirt—"will change color. This represents the whale's spirit absorbing into my body, and mine into his."

"The day of the flensing?" Kopae reminded him.

"We landed at Mason Head where the beach was wide. A ranger led us inland, through marsh and bush, and back onto the beach." He focused on Kopae. "No need; we could have followed our noses."

"What did the ranger do when you got there?"

"The plane was waiting for him at Mason Head. He left right away. We camped three nights. We removed the skin, flesh, intestines, and blubber of twenty of the whales. The fresher whales were easy—the flesh cut like butter."

Alexa squeezed her eyes closed for a second.

"Who were you with?" Kopae asked.

"My team. Four of us from Auckland. On the third day a DOC helicopter dropped off bulldozers. The bones were buried, the graves marked, and we left." His tone changed. "Someone had butchered two whales before we arrived. The jaws were missing."

Kopae scribbled in her notebook.

Alexa thought of the charging sea lion. "Could it have been an animal?"

"A knife was used."

"Do you know who might have done it?" Kopae asked.

"No. Only Māori have the right to take the bone and teeth of whale."

Kopae handed Harata a group picture of DOC rangers. "Can you point out the ranger who led you to the whales?"

Harata regarded the photo, running a finger along the rangers—some male, some female, some old, some young. "This is him."

Alexa leaned in. Harata had picked out Stephen Neville, back row, third from right.

Kopae placed her hands on her knees as if she would stand. "Did you see the ranger finding something—maybe along the path?"

Harata answered quickly. "A radio in a patch of silver grass. He put it in his pocket. I prayed he would do the right thing."

"What do you mean? The right thing?" Alexa asked.

"Whales beach themselves because they are sick and fear drowning. They want to lie in shallow water with their spout out so they can breathe. They breathe the same air we breathe, and they value family and friends like we do. The pod expresses love and loyalty. When one grounds itself, others gather round. Then more. I prayed the drowning ranger would not beach himself."

Chapter Thirty-Two

As Kopae tried her phone, Alexa thought about the whales' loyalty to family and friends. In comparison—family strife and friendless—she was pathetic.

Kopae couldn't get service and used the portable radio to inform Sergeant Wallace that Harata confirmed Stephen's story about the personal locator beacon.

"Eh. That's what he's saying. And something else."

"What?"

"Supervisor Lowell said Stephen wasn't alone when he euthanized the whales. A temp helped him. But Stephen insists he was alone. Crikey—he's messed in the head."

This was big news. Alexa thought back. Stephen had never mentioned another ranger. Or a second shotgun. He probably felt alone, as if, Atlas-like, he carried the weight of whales on his young shoulders.

"Have you heard from the ballistics lab?" Kopae asked.

"No. But we just talked with Gray's crew member Squizzy Koch. He helped Gray haul up that shark. September first, he remembers, because it was his birthday. Next day the shark was gone, all the blood cleaned up. Lowell said Gray never reported it."

Kopae whistled. "Maybe he sold the shark and that's where the $5,000 came from. Maybe this is a black-market case."

"Eh. We're thinking the same. The deposit was cash."

"Hard to trace cash, Senior." They disengaged. Kopae turned to Alexa. "You heard that?"

She nodded. "People usually use cash for small transactions, not big ones."

"Yeah nah. I use my EFTPOS for everything," Kopae said.

A debit card. Alexa was used to the Kiwi term now.

Kopae drove the bumpy drive at a crawl. "If Stephen found the PLB near the whales, and not on King's body, that indicates King had been in the area." Kopae turned the car onto Pitiki Road, and the jostling ceased.

"Stephen told me that hunters often walk the perimeter of their hunting block when they first arrive," Alexa said. "I think the whales beached in part of Little Hellfire."

"Man," Kopae said, "we're shaking something loose. Do you think Robert King cut out the whale jaws? Maybe Stephen saw him, got mad, and shot him. There's our motive. Revenge for the whales. He had the means with his shotgun."

"But King's body was discovered a couple miles away," Alexa said. "No one would drag a body that far."

"Who butchered the whales then?" Kopae asked.

The wind pushing through Kopae's window wrestled with Alexa's hair, blowing stray locks into her face. She reset her pony-tail, pulling it tight. "If King didn't, and Stephen didn't, then we're talking about a third person." A single house, blue, flashed by. "The area is remote, right? Whoever did it took the jaws. They had to have a way to move them. Maybe it was someone with a boat."

Kopae smacked the dash with her palm and reached for the radio again. "Sarge," she said when Wallace answered. "Did Robert King's hunting pals mention seeing a boat in the area?"

"Hold on." The radio clacked and went quiet. In a few seconds Wallace was back. "All three said no."

"What about Stephen? Did he see any boats?"

"Don't know. He's gone now. Lowell is escorting him to Invercargill Prison. He's going to get a mental health screening."

Kopae accelerated, thrusting Alexa back into the seat. It felt like they were moving closer to answers.

"Lee Bay Road ends at the Rakiura National Park Visitor Centre," Kopae said a few minutes later. "After that, the road ends. McAdam's place is before the turnoff."

Alexa was curious to see the Facebook bully.

They parked behind a car in the sandy driveway and got out. A house by the sea—albeit humble—was a popular dream, Alexa thought, looking at the backyard bay spread like a turquoise palette. No dark clouds or stiffening wind yet. Alexa's heart sank when she noticed a fishing boat moored offshore. "Parked out front" as Kopae had said.

A man opened the door before Kopae knocked. A low growl came from behind him. "Hush, Jack," he said over his shoulder.

"I'm Constable Kopae, Stewart Island Police, and this is Ms. Glock from Auckland. Are you Ed McAdam?"

"That's me. What's wrong? The missus?"

"Nothing wrong, sir," Kopae said. "We'd like to ask you some questions."

"What about?" He had three days' beard growth and an oily bowl haircut.

Kopae stepped closer. "May we come in?"

"I'll come out." He stepped onto the stoop, pulling the door shut and forcing Kopae to back step. Jack barked frantically. Alexa could see his furry head through a window.

Kopae swallowed. "Do you own a Van Kees Stealth Glider trawling net?"

He frowned. "What is this about?"

"May I have your permission to see the netting on your boat?"

"What for?" McAdam looked confused.

"It's part of our investigation," Kopae said.

"What are you investigating? The shark attack? Don't think

I don't know." Sun spots freckled his weathered face. "Gray was shot and fed to the sharks. That outside DI—the one who thinks he knows anything about island life—told Stormy Parker."

Word had spread like an algae bloom, Alexa thought.

Kopae squared her shoulders. "If we could look at your nets, then we can be on our way."

"You tell me why, I might consider."

Jack's bark segued to howling.

"Ms. Glock has evidence that you threatened Andy Gray."

"Bugger. I've never even met him."

Alexa slipped the Facebook list from her pocket. She cleared her throat. "You made online threats toward Andy Gray, and the shark caging industry."

"That puts you under suspicion," Kopae said.

"What the hell are you on about?" McAdam bellowed.

"This appeared on the 'Ban the Cage' Facebook page: 'If the courts won't shut them down, we will.' That's the first one," Alexa said.

McAdam's face flushed. "Courts don't have the balls to shut 'em down. Meanwhile, we sit on our asses, twiddling our thumbs, pāua going to waste."

"Last week you commented directly to Andy Gray," Alexa said: "'I'd like to see a white keep you in check.'"

His face was cherry-red now. "Are you trying to pin his murder on me?"

"Showing us your trawling nets could potentially clear you," Alexa said.

"You'll have to go on a little trip." McAdam pointed to the boat attached to buoys in the bay. "The netting is onboard. I need to secure her for the storm anyways."

Kopae and Alexa eyed each other.

McAdam didn't wait for a reply. "I'll get my things." When he opened his front door, Jack stopped howling.

"I'll go," Kopae said to Alexa. "You wait here."

"DI Horne said we should stick together."

Kopae hurried to the sedan and opened the trunk, removed waterproof pants and gum boots. Alexa had a good pair of gum boots too, back in Auckland. She looked down at her Keds despairingly. At least the crime kit was in a water-resistant pack. She zipped up her jacket and headed to the beach, trying to gauge the distance to the fishing boat. It was close enough that she could read the name painted across the stern: *Pandora*. She looked left and right for sea lions before venturing onto the sand, stepping past a rowboat pulled safe from the sea's grasp.

McAdam, his PFD sun-bleached and tight against his chest-high waders, threw Kopae and Alexa life jackets, hauled the rowboat into the water, and barked for them to climb in.

Okay, Alexa thought. She and Kopae scrambled in the water and onto a bench seat facing McAdam, who rowed with practiced strokes from the center bench. He wore a cap and sunglasses and avoided eye contact. With each stroke, the rowboat jerked Alexa's chin into her orange life vest—the cheap kind summer camp kids wore. She cinched the waist belt tighter, reflecting that when water looked flat from a distance, that didn't mean it was close up. The cusp of the Pacific Ocean jumped and jiggled as if prodded by an electric current. Occasionally, a wave plunked over the side, further wetting her Keds.

"She's riding heavy," McAdam said.

"Fish and chips for lunch," Kopae laughed. "Look," she nudged Alexa. "Pāua on the rock."

They were directly over a reef. The water was so clear it was hard to tell how far down the reef was. Through the shadow of the tender, giant oysters were attached to rocks. Alexa figured those were pāua. She leaned over the side, rocking the boat, her nose close to the waves. Bubbles from the dip of the oar. The dart of small fish. A swirl of kelp straining for the surface. What if she spotted a shark? She sat up, scooched closer to Kopae. The thought of a white circling their toy boat gripped her windpipe, squeezed. She wanted to look for fins but couldn't bear the thought of seeing one. A ram, and they would flip. She clutched the bench, eyes wide, searching McAdam's face for signs of panic, understanding how the locals felt.

In five more minutes, they pulled along the fishing vessel, its broad navy flank in need of sanding and painting. McAdam told them to stay put as the rowboat nudged *Pandora*. He stood, gum boots planted wide, and threaded a rope attached to the rowboat through a metal ring on *Pandora*. When the rowboat was secured, he reached up to the side of the fishing boat and flipped down a folding ladder. It clacked against the side of the boat and settled. McAdam looked at Alexa. "You first. Lucky she's not pitching. Up you go."

As she stood, legs shaky, the rowboat shifted alarmingly, and the crime kit slid off her shoulder. She grabbed McAdam's extended hand.

"I'll take your pocketbook, toss it up to you."

She let the kit slide off her arm.

"Hold here." McAdam pointed to handholds on either side of the flimsy aluminum ladder lurching up and down with the small swells. She forced herself to release his beefy hand and grab the handles, pulling her body closer to the boat, thankful for years of push-ups and planks, and toed her wet Ked onto the first rung. She climbed fast, terrified of falling into the rowboat or water. The toughest part was hoisting herself over the rail and rolling onto the deck.

Kopae clapped.

Once they were all aboard, McAdam strode to the stern and pointed to a raised and rusted V-shaped contraption. "Called the gantry. Part of the net is attached on this side, the other here. Then I lower the beam with this winch and drag the net behind the boat."

Gobbling up everything in the ocean. "Do you ever catch sharks? Like by accident?" Alexa asked.

"Baby ones, eh. Throw 'em back overboard."

"Don't they drown first?" Alexa asked.

McAdam stayed quiet and opened a wooden box below the gantry. Netting lay in folds, faded blue and knotted in diamonds.

"What brand is it?" Alexa asked.

"Don't recall," McAdam said.

"I'm going to need to spread it out," Alexa said.

"Do what you want. I didn't have anything to do with Andy Gray's death."

McAdam busied himself as Kopae helped Alexa spread out the netting, which spanned the width of *Pandora*. The trawling net was cone-shaped—wide at the open end and funneled to a rounded sack. Only small fish could escape its clutches. She took out her magnifying glass and got on her hands and knees.

The net appeared in good shape. No holes, no blood.

"What do you think?" Kopae asked. "Is it Van Kees?"

Alexa peered at a segment through the glass. She could see eight individual plies. It was thicker and heavier than the fiber from Gray's fingernail. She set the glass down and grasped a section of netting in each hand and pulled in opposite directions. The net stretched. Van Kees had bragged that his netting was light and resistant to stretch.

"I don't think so. I'll snip a sample just to verify."

They folded and restored the net. The sky remained void of clouds, though Alexa thought the temperature was dropping. Her stomach churned at the thought of sitting in the small rowboat again. Why the hell didn't it have a motor? She stood on the deck, waiting for McAdam to finish storm prep, tapped her foot in the frustration of having wasted time, and checked the surface for fins.

McAdam was chatty on the way back, perhaps relieved that his net hadn't netted him. A breeze stirred up some chop, but he powered through it rhythmically. He was the one who spotted it.

Chapter Thirty-Three

McAdam whipped off his sunglasses, leaned forward, clunked the oars against the gunnels. "Got a shark coming to take a look," he said huskily.

Alexa's mouth went dry. She whipped around.

Kopae turned too, wobbling the boat. Off to the right, a dark fin sliced the surface, parallel to the rowboat, trailing a V wake. "Shit," Kopae said.

The enormous fin changed course, cutting the ocean in a straight menace to the rowboat, slow and unwavering. Alexa grabbed the bench, steeling herself for a ram. "Row," she yelled.

"Splashing attracts them," McAdam said.

"It's already attracted," Alexa screamed.

The fin disappeared. Alexa pushed her bottom off the bench and onto the floor of the rowboat. Any second they would be flipped into the water.

"Where's he gone?" Kopae asked.

Alexa hugged her knees, head bowed, nose against mildewed life vest.

"Goddamn," McAdam said. "He's circling."

"He's turning," Kopae whispered. "Coming around."

Alexa lifted her head, attracted, for dark reasons from her own deep depths, to the macabre. With slow-motion care, she unfolded and inched back onto the bench, the rowboat listing—"Watch it," Kopae screamed—her body shaking. The shark came alongside, first the white's head rippled by, flashing razor-teeth in a primeval smile, then miles of gill and torso, the triangular fin so close Alexa could touch the faded crescent scar near the tip and the ripped-flag notches on the grayish flesh, then the tail fin trailing a smaller wake. A full minute—or year, it was hard to tell—of muscle and terror, the shark's immensity spellbinding, and then it sank out of sight.

"Three and one-half meters," Kopae whispered, clutching Alexa's hand. "Maybe more."

Gulls circled the rowboat, screeching. Alexa couldn't breathe. "Is it...is it gone?"

"I don't think so," McAdam said.

They sat in silence, the boat turning in a slow tidal whorl, their heads swiveling to locate the fin again. Alexa thought it might be underneath them, planning a missile attack, but no, the fin resurfaced ten yards in front and circled back. This time the shark lifted its head out of the water and looked directly at her. Alexa cowered against Kopae and saw the shark's eyes were navy, not black. The shark flipped on its side, exposing a sea of ivory, and then its tail nudged the rowboat, the judder making Alexa scream as the shark veered into the deep.

"Holy hell," McAdam said. "Could have been a body slam."

The clink of waves hit them broadside. The wind was picking up. They had drifted closer to shore. McAdam picked up the oars but dropped them when the shark exploded from the water thirty feet behind them, flipped over, crashed back with an enormous splash that sent waves to swamp their boat.

"Jesus help us," McAdam said.

In two seconds, the shark breached again, a seal writhing in giant jaws. The screeching gulls flew at the commotion. Alexa looked to the shore. *Should she swim for it,* she thought crazily? *No.* "Row," she yelled and lifted the tip of an oar, thrusting it at McAdam's stomach. "Row before the wave hits us."

Either hours or minutes later, Alexa couldn't tell, the rowboat scudded into sand. McAdam dropped the oars in a clunk, hopped out, and pulled them in.

"The seal saved our lives," McAdam said. "Diverted the shark."

Alexa wanted to kiss the sand. Noticed she was holding Kopae's arm. Dropped it. Stumbled, caught herself.

The trudge to his house was silent.

They lectured McAdam about making online threats, but their heart wasn't in it—they were alive and for the moment that's all that mattered—and left McAdam hugging a frantic Jack. "Little tyke knows something almost happened to me," he said.

"Close one, that," Kopae said as they buckled up in the car. Her bronzed cheeks were splotched with red. "Had my hand on the radio, but who was there to call?"

They drove slowly away. Alexa finally broke the silence. "I don't know if this is how we should be spending our time."

"Almost dying?" Kopae said.

Alexa unfolded the trawler list, her hand trembling. "Checking this list of trawler owners. Kerry Gloden is next."

"I know Gloden," Kopae said. "I, well, went out with his son Graham couple a times."

Alexa let out a sigh.

"His place is on the drive back," Kopae said. "We can head to the station after Gloden's, see what's up. Maybe they'll have the ballistic reports." She took her cap off, ran fingers through her hair, and pulled it back on. "Can't stop shaking."

"No way I'm ever getting in a little boat again," Alexa said.

"Me either."

They reverted to silence, Alexa reliving the horror of being inches from those jaws. Rowing with the sharks instead of cage diving. Maybe she would tell Charlie.

Gloden lived in a single-story brown duplex close to town. After pleasantries about Graham "living the good life in Ozzie land," they learned Gloden's net wasn't on his boat. "I've had a change of mind about trawling," he said, unlocking a storage shed behind the duplex. "Too destructive to the seabed. I work on the salmon farm in Big Glory Bay now. Sustainability. That's forward thinking. Why do you want to see my nets?"

"Part of an investigation is all I can say," Kopae answered.

The trawling net, buried beneath musty tarp, was old and white.

"Ta," Kopae said, covering it back up and leaving the shed. "Are you ready for the storm?"

"They sent us home from work, that's why I'm here." Gloden's yard was on a rise above the harbor. He searched the sky. "Glad I'm not at sea."

"Me too," Kopae and Alexa said simultaneously.

An army of gray clouds stalked toward the island. They hadn't been visible from McAdam's place. It was past 4:00, and Alexa was antsy.

———

Wallace, alone in the station, was hanging up the landline when they rushed in.

"Hi, Senior," gushed Kopae. "We had a little adventure." She halted. Wallace's face was a canvas of confusion. "What's up?"

"That was Auckland ballistics." He shook his head. "Two things: The bullet damage in Robert King's skull came from an 870 Remington shotgun."

"Same gun Stephen had," Kopae said. "Clinches case one."

Alexa's heart sank.

"Wait. Here's the thing," Wallace said. "The shell doesn't match Stephen's Remington."

"What?" Kopae said. "How can they know that?"

Alexa didn't know how to unload a gun, but she had studied ballistics during her training and answered automatically. "It has to do with rifling, which is the unique spirals and grooves imprinted in the gun's barrel. These get imparted on the projectile."

"But they're wrong," Kopae said. "All the time in the weather probably eroded it."

Alexa's mind whirled, twirled, and landed on the temporary ranger who supposedly helped Stephen euthanize the whales. "Did Supervisor Lowell give you the name of the ranger with Stephen during the euthanasia? He probably had a checked-out Remington too. He could be the one who shot King."

"Lowell checked and the record book is misplaced or something," Wallace said. "He has ordered a full-out search. I'm waiting for his call. But he's en route to Invercargill with Stephen, flying before the storm hits."

"Where's the DI?" Alexa asked. "We have to let him know."

"He and Briscoe are following up on phone records. Gray called a landline number three times, twice the day before he made his cash deposit, and once the next day. Address is 7 Whips Way."

Kopae frowned. "Who lives there?"

"Sean and Missy Warren."

"I know Warren through his truck," Kopae said. "Nicest one on the island."

"That name sounds familiar." Alexa ran it through her cast of characters. The memory refused to solidify, but she remembered something else. "The American gal who measures kelp—Madalyn—she mentioned a truck passing her as she was leaving Golden Bay Wharf the afternoon Gray was killed." She rummaged through her tote for her notebook.

"Lots of trucks on the island," Wallace said, reaching for the phone.

Alexa found her notes. "A black Chevy."

"That's Warren's," Kopae said. "Wait a minute." She fiddled in her pockets, then looked at Alexa. "Where's our trawling list?"

Alexa found it and handed it over.

"Sean Warren is on our list, Senior," Kopae said. "He owns a trawler— *Darla Jo*—and it docks next to *The Apex*. He could be

Andy's killer. We better head over to Whips Way, see if the DI needs help."

"Hold on." Wallace dialed the DI's number.

"*Darla Jo* shows up a lot on the white-shark-sighting forms, too," Alexa added.

"Bloody hell," Wallace said. "Horne isn't answering." He dialed another number. "Briscoe? That you?"

Briscoe insisted he and Bruce were fine. They were having tea with Missy Warren and the kids. Sean Warren was on his way. "Five minutes," Briscoe said. "He'll be here in five."

"Have senior call us," Wallace said.

"He got back safe, then?" Kopae asked. "Briscoe? From the shark boat?"

"He came back babbling about where Gray was thrown overboard. Off Native Island. Three sharks pinged at the same time. He's a shark expert now, says they were fighting over prey."

Alexa's stomach churned. "Is that close to Ringaringa Beach?"

"Yeah nah," Kopae said. "You can see it from shore."

The radio blared, and Wallace jumped to answer. "Eh?" he said. "Speak of the devil." He played with some dials and turned the radio so the women could hear. "It's Shark Man, at the ferry terminal. His pronouncement."

Alexa was curious to hear what Kana Duffy had to say.

"...does not support culling of white sharks due to the...*bleep, garble*...on Ringaringa Beach."

The radio reception cleared.

"...indiscriminate killing of sharks does not increase human safety. No kill permits will be issued by Department of Conservation. The ban on water activities on Stewart Island is lifted. Proceed with caution as we share the waters with *Carcharodon carcharias,* mangō taniwha. Tune in next week for 'Critical Pings—One Shark's Journey.' This is Kana Duffy from Foveaux Strait."

The radio went dead. Alexa felt a tug of affection for Duffy; he'd made the right call.

"Nothing changed then, eh?" Wallace said, his eyes downcast. "I'm still not letting my boy near the water."

"We're down to one caging operator. That's something," Kopae said.

Alexa couldn't bear the waiting. "We need to do something." She looked out the window. The dark sky gave her an idea. "Let's hit *The Apex* before the storm gets bad and use BLUESTAR on the cleaned-up blood splatter. To prove Andy was killed on his own boat. The killer might even have left a footprint in the blood. It happens."

"I thought you needed darkness," Kopae said. "To see it glow."

"Total darkness isn't required. Low light like this works."

They turned to Wallace, whose brows had knit together. "Means, motive, and opportunity. *Darla Jo* parked next to *The Apex* gives Warren opportunity. Take the radio and keep it with you."

Kopae grabbed a yellow rain slicker from a coat hook. She looked at Alexa and pointed to another, navy blue and enormous, for her to grab. Alexa did gratefully.

A jolt of adrenaline flooded Alexa's veins as they jumped into the car and screeched off. The village already looked forsaken. A lonely light seeped from the Four Square grocery window. "Do you lose power during storms?" Alexa asked.

"No worries. We use diesel generators." A gust of wind tested her steering.

Alexa looked up the hill at Island Inn. Someone was retracting the patio awning. Battening down the hatches. She turned to the whitecap-ruffled harbor. The dark clouds that had been marching forward had now descended, angry and possessive. She could smell approaching rain through Kopae's cracked window and the sharp fresh scent of wind off faraway icebergs. Her phone, which she slipped in her pocket, had no bars.

Wallace's voice crackled on the radio. "DI called. He doesn't like this stuff about Sean Warren. Says to be ready to assist him. No word from Lowell yet."

"Yes, Senior," Kopae said. "The wharf is halfway to Sean's house."

Droplets dappled the windshield as they pulled into the empty Golden Bay Wharf parking area. Alexa opened the crime kit. First, she took out the camera and mini tripod. She disabled the flash and set the lens to manual. This was easier to do in the dry car. She hung the camera around her neck and tucked it down her coat. She retrieved her Maglite and tucked it into her pocket.

"Are you ready?" Kopae dropped the keys in her pocket, grabbed the radio, and cracked the car door.

"Hold on. Let me mix the BLUESTAR." Alexa dug around in the kit and pulled out a small spray bottle of distilled water and a BLUESTAR packet. She added two tablets, one beige and one white, to the water and gently swirled. *Science in all its glory,* she thought. She readied a second bottle too.

Kopae ogled the bottles. "It will react to blood, eh? What if it's fish blood? Like from that shark?"

"We'll do a quickie human blood check."

"What can I carry?" Kopae asked.

She looked like a kid in a candy shop, so Alexa gave her the tripod and spray bottles. "Don't shake them." The rain was light, but if it increased, it would dilute the BLUESTAR results. "Do you have an umbrella?"

"In the boot."

Alexa slipped the navy poncho over her jacket as Kopae found the umbrella.

From the rise they could see the three boats tethered to the pier: the water taxi, *The Apex,* and *Darla Jo.* Two additional boats were moored in the bay.

"Storm prep," Kopae said. "Boats are safer being moored than…"

Wind snatched the rest of her words away.

The hill gave them a vantage point, and Alexa scanned the area carefully. Both boat houses were shuttered, the beach was forlorn, and moody waves clapped the shore. She filled her lungs with air and started down the path, Kopae following, over the sand and onto the pier, the light rain making the wood slick.

The Apex, jostling the dock, was even with it. All they would have to do was jump over the guardrail.

"Lines should be let out." Kopae was breathing hard. "Boats in a storm need more line."

Andy Gray could no longer take care of his boat. Who would tend it, Alexa wondered?

Sean Warren's *Darla Jo* at the opposite end of the T-shaped pier looked abandoned: rust seeping from a porthole, chipping gray paint, a hulking winch with a stray cable clanking against a pole, a homely wheelhouse, and a rustic cabin. The fishing boat was half-again as long as *The Apex,* and an empty soda bottle, wedged by a wooden box, was the only indication that it wasn't a ghost town boat of yore. Alexa was tempted to snoop around, but she talked herself out of it. No probable cause.

Yet.

The distance between *The Apex* and dock was two feet. "Let's go," Alexa said. She held the crime kit to her chest and jumped the rail, the poncho parachuting behind her. Kopae landed lightly beside her, the spray bottles tucked in her pockets. Alexa dug out gloves and booties for each of them as *The Apex* heaved with a swell. A black band of heavier rain ruffed the entrance to the bay. It would descend shortly. "We better hurry," she said.

They wound up the spiral staircase, Alexa tugging the crime kit free of a rail. Up top—where someone had attacked her with the gaff—wind flared her poncho. She swallowed to moisten her dry throat, let the kit slide off her shoulder to the floor, and approached the gouged rail, stopping four feet shy. "That's where I saw the bullet," she pointed. "We'll spray this area."

Kopae turned in a billowing circle, taking in the scene, and then handed Alexa a bottle.

Alexa adjusted the nozzle to fine mist. She remembered the

thrill of the first time she had used the product: in a Raleigh parking garage. "You can spray it," she told Kopae magnanimously. "Stand with the wind to your back."

Kopae looked stricken and waved the bottle away. "I forgot the radio. I set it down in the boot when I was getting the umbrella. Sarge said to keep it with me. I've got to get it. What if he's…"

"Okay," Alexa shouted. "Go. I can't wait, though."

Kopae clattered down the spiral stairs, leaving Alexa alone on *The Apex*.

Chapter Thirty-Four

"Dammit."

Kopae had the tripod.

Alexa couldn't take photos and hold the umbrella at the same time. She would have to be quick in the drizzle.

Rookies sometimes douse. Alexa knew over-spraying could compromise DNA. She positioned her back to the wind, stepped a foot closer, and sprayed lightly. The wind carried the mist forward. Immediately, a light blue luminescence glowed in the dim light. She wished Kopae could see. She set the bottle down, whipped out the camera, and took several photos. Then she took a swab sample and stepped back and sprayed again. More glowing blue. She repeated, theorizing this was a blood trail. She stepped closer to the stairs and sprayed again. A blue-green Picasso abstract. Then she sprayed the top stair.

Blue.

She took a picture of the top rung before it faded. She listened for Kopae—where was she?—and scampered down the spiral. She judged the quickest path from the stair to the dock-side rail and sprayed again.

Bingo. Had Andy, bleeding from the gut, been thrown in the same cold water where she had been chummed? But what about Kana Duffy's theory that he had been thrown overboard near

Ringaringa Beach? She jumped nimbly onto the dock and sprayed the wood.

Jesus. A glowing smear.

Andy had been dragged along the pier. Her eyes rose to *Darla Jo* chafing at its lines. She had an ounce of spray left. Kopae had the spare bottle. She sprayed the dregs, leaving a glowing bread crumb trail to the rusting trawler.

A wave sent sea froth into her eyes. Andy Gray had been dragged from *The Apex* to the trawler. Warren was probably the murderer. She quickly took photos and then searched for Kopae's bright yellow slicker, but the dock was empty. Where the hell was the constable?

Raindrops pelted her slicker. The black band of clouds had arrived. Alexa swiped her eyes and cinched her hood. Free hands made her realize the crime kit was on *The Apex*. All she had was the camera looped around her neck and an empty spray bottle. No Kopae. No radio. They were making mistakes. A man shouted. She jumped and scanned the pier again.

No one was coming.

Then she heard a woman scream. From the bowels of *Darla Jo*. Kopae was in trouble. *Officer down, officer down!* She longed to shout. She jumped the three-foot gaping chasm onto the ghost town deck, fell to her knees, goddamned poncho heeding her frenzied crawl, and pressed beneath the porthole.

Angry voices.

A scuffle.

Another shout, followed by a blood-icing scream.

Then came only the sound of rain pelting her poncho.

Five terrified breaths broken by an engine belching to life. Alexa pivoted to see churning water fan from the twin motors. Blue smoke and diesel fumes wafted in the air. The trawler shuddered and the door to the cabin flung open, hitting Alexa in the forehead. A tall man emerged. Alexa bit back a cry and scooched behind the door, thankful her slicker was dark. She sank to a tight ball and listened to the clanking, muttering, and cursing trailing the man as he moved about the deck. When she heard him on the other side of the cabin, Alexa rose and peeked through the porthole. A dim light, an old-fashioned ship's wheel, a tattered stool, no Kopae.

Her phone. She had her phone. She struggled to remove it from her pocket and felt like tossing it overboard when she saw no service available.

Useless piece of crap.

A rope flew past, and the man came barreling to the dock side. She wedged behind the door and watched through the crack as he grabbed a pole and pushed the boat from the dock. He swept to the far end, loosened another rope, tossed it on board, and came straight at her. God almighty. Sean Warren was the tall fisherman who had given her a ride from the ferry *and* shown her around Grogan's boat this morning. He must have grabbed Kopae on her way to the car.

On a small island, everyone knows everyone, but no one recognizes evil.

He came straight at her. Alexa was doomed. But he swept by, entered the cabin, slammed the door.

Did he think Kopae had been alone? The thought gave her hope.

Exposed, Alexa flew to the rail, the poncho flapping like wings, the camera banging her chest. Dismay. Six feet of heaving seaweed between her and the pier. She glanced at the blurry beach, hoping to wave for help, flash the camera as SOS, but its gloomy desolation made her heart sink. *Jump*, she thought. She had survived the cold black water once. A clap of thunder and gust of wind chased her from the rail, made her flatten herself against the cabin, her gloved hands groping wood.

She whipped the gloves off, threw them to the ground, swiveled to the gleaming porthole, and risked another peek.

Jaw set, one hand on the wheel, Warren faced forward in the

three-sided glass wheelhouse as *Darla Jo* plunged through the bay. Behind him, Alexa made out a set of bunks, a small black stove, a clothesline with a towel swaying for attention. A ceiling light bulb. A ladder disappearing down a shadowy hatch. A hatch in a fishing boat was where the fish were stored.

Kopae. Down the hatch.

Alexa crouched, her stomach roiling as *Darla Jo* crested a wave. Warren was insane to be headed out in a storm. Ragged panic tried to paralyze her. She searched her brain for a plan. She was not helpless. *Think*, she commanded.

Her main advantage was Warren didn't appear to know she was here. Kopae had probably told him she was alone.

Smart.

Alexa, back against the cabin, was thankful a small eave sheltered her from the worst of the rain. Wallace knew their location. Well, their previous location. He'd probably checked in and was alarmed they had not answered the radio. And Bruce would by now realize Warren wasn't headed home for a cozy cuppa. They would search *Darla Jo*. Which would be missing.

Time was fleeting.

Warren had a plan. Alexa thought she knew what it was. Feed Kopae to the sharks. Like Andy Gray. She couldn't wait for rescue.

Her best bet was to overpower Warren. She crept backwards, to the bow, searching for a weapon. Her eyes went to the pole Warren had used to cast off, but it was narrow and long. Alexa was worried her swing would be off. She grabbed a rusting smoke-stack attached to a metal box, wrestled, but she couldn't pry it loose. She yelped when a gull—a storm-bird?—flew at her as *Darla Jo* hit a broadside wave and listed. She stumbled and stubbed her toe against a wooden hatch protruding from the deck. She studied it, her heart pounding, and decided it was a back door to the cargo area below. The hatch was straddled by a hand-cranked winch and pulley hook that looked as if it could lift a laden net from the sea.

She lunged for the trap door handle, pulled with might, her gaff wound gaping with the effort, the metal handle slick with rain.

Oof. It groaned open.

The stench of rotting fish flooded the air. There was no ladder, no light. Just a black hole.

Alexa sat on her butt, swatted the slicker out of the way, swung her legs so they dangled over the abyss, positioned herself, and dropped.

Thunk.

She landed on something rubbery and cold. Slid off. Scrambled to her knees. The keel listed. Alexa crawled forward, the damn camera swinging from her neck, her hands groping the slimy floor, until she felt the wooden side. She stood gingerly, hoping not to crack her head, and groped along the wall. Something sharp pierced her finger.

"Ow," she cried.

A muffled moan came from the opposite side. A flash of lightning through the hatch lit the hold. Alexa didn't know what was more horrifying: Kopae netted like a dead fish, or three monstrous shark jaws.

Chapter Thirty-Five

The Maglite was in her pocket. Would Warren see it if she turned it on? Another bolt of lightning lit the tombed enclosure and she saw she had landed on the carcass of a headless shark. Ten or twelve feet long. Bile rose in her throat: the shark, the stench, Kopae listless. She spotted the ladder leading to the cabin. If Warren took his eyes off the swelling horizon, he would see light.

She decided to risk it.

The net—blue, she noted—hung from a giant hook. Kopae was on her stomach, hovering a foot above the floor, her head and feet jerked into an upward arch. Alexa directed the beam into Kopae's closed eyes and was rewarded by them scrunching.

"I'll get you down," Alexa whispered, scuttling around the shark carcass to her side.

Kopae moaned. Her right fingers squeezed a handful of netting. Alexa thought of the fiber in Andy Gray's fingernail. Then she saw blood. Dripping from Kopae's head. She inhaled sharply. "You'll be okay, Elyse." She was thankful she remembered Kopae's first name. "You did good. I'll help you."

But how? The hull lurched and creaked as she directed the beam at the ceiling. She stretched her arms high, stood on tiptoes, but the hook was out of reach. She remembered what the trawler net had looked like spread across Ed McAdam's boat deck.

Triangular. A funnel at one end, wide and open at the other. All three corners must be hooked. She searched the hold for a knife, opened a large cooler, the beam illuminating a giant shark fin. Alexa slammed it shut, gagged. She dragged the cooler under the hook. Standing on top, she could just touch it. She grabbed a handful of netting, pulling and jostling Kopae, but couldn't get leverage. She stuffed the Maglite in her pocket and thrust up, trying to unhook the net. No luck. She grabbed another handful—its human cargo made it dead weight—and thrust again.

A thud made her stop.

Alexa fought to keep balance atop the cooler as *Darla Jo* heaved. The boat strained, the thrum of the engine changed. What was Warren doing?

When she tried again, thrust upward, part of the net swung loose, dumping Kopae to the floor in a yellow heap. Alexa unhooked the rest of the net, her arms full of it, and jumped down.

Kopae didn't sit up. Alexa scrambled by her head, shining the light at Kopae's eyes. They twitched but didn't open. Blood came from a gash at the back of her skull, matting her dark hair, snaking down her yellow slicker. Worse, blood seeped from her right ear. There was nothing to staunch the bleeding. Alexa whipped off her poncho and pulled her jacket over her head, which tangled in the camera strap. Now she was trapped. She fought her way loose, the camera hitting her lip, and tied the jacket tightly around Kopae's skull. She moaned, which Alexa took as a good sign. "Stay here," she whispered. "You're going to be okay."

Alexa pulled her poncho back on; the dark color helped her blend. She gathered the netting, bunched it to her chest, and crept to the ladder. Her knee hit something, another jaw. She expected her knee to be bloodied, ripped. But the teeth didn't pierce. Whale jaw.

Occam's razor.

Two could play the netting game. She climbed silently up the ladder, toward dim light, hanging on when *Darla Jo* pitched.

She knew how seals felt, popping their heads above water to scout for danger. What lurked above? She couldn't put it off. Kopae needed medical attention.

Her head eased past the last rung. Dammit. Warren wasn't at the wheel, his back to her, like she envisioned. She periscoped her head around. The cabin door was wide open, the cabin empty. What if Warren had found the open deck hatch and jumped down with Kopae? Her ankle tingled, anticipating a grab. She quickly climbed out, dropped the netting in a heap, got to her hands and knees, and crawled to the radio mounted by the ship's wheel. If Warren looked through the window, he might not see her. She grabbed the hand mike and pushed buttons. "Mayday. Mayday," she whispered.

It was dead.

She pushed buttons on the mounted part, but a gun nestled in the console snatched her attention. An electric charge transferred to her hand as she lifted the Ruger, surprised by its lightness. Warren had Andy Gray's gun. Her fingers gripped the handle as if she were a natural. When she felt her finger tighten at the trigger, she jerked. What if it was loaded and she shot herself? Or what if it wasn't loaded? Warren would know and laugh if she threatened him with it.

She stuck the gun in her slicker pocket and returned to the heap of net. What was Warren doing? Who was steering the boat? The roar of waves and wind deadened sounds of approach. She searched frantically through the net for the open end and stood, pressed against the wall next to the door, the net stretched wide in her spread hands. Rain poured in curtain torrents, and when Warren burst in, Alexa threw the net over his whole body and jerked with full might.

The netted man fell forward as she ran backwards, outside, pulling the net tight. Warren bellowed like the sea lion, rose to his knees, twisted her way—hands clawing and flailing. "What the fuck?" he roared.

Alexa jerked again, and he fell into the door frame. She jerked, pulled, walked backwards, death grip on the straining fiber, three yards, five yards, dragging Warren in a thrashing heap, and tripped on the open hatch, tumbled toward the hole, landed on her knees. Warren lunged at her, the netting distorting his face into a hideous spider. Alexa sprang up, twirled, and snared as many diamond weaves as she could around the hook above the hatch.

"You again," Warren yelled. "Get this goddamned…"

She lunged for the crank, turned as his webbed hand groped her arm.

Van Kees had said the net was as strong as steel. She cranked the handle a full turn, yanking Warren off his feet. Another crank and he flipped.

"Why did you kill Andy?" she screamed.

He thrust elbows against the weave, kicked, and heaved. "Get me out of here."

Alexa braced against the pitching deck, pulled as hard as she could, turned the crank a full rotation. Warren hovered, upside down, his curls flattened, his body contorted and swinging with the swell of the waves and his crimped exertions.

"Tell me why you killed him." She had a death grip on the crank, afraid if she let go, it would unreel, and Warren would flop into the hold with Kopae.

"Asshole Gray split the money for the jaws with me…" His voice was muffled as he kicked and jerked. "Then he didn't want to play nice. Said no more. Threatened to report me. Like that fuckin' cop. She's chum, like you'll be."

Her muscles shook violently.

"Let me down," he roared.

Thunder clapped. "What about Robert King?" she screamed. She couldn't hold on much longer.

Warren gave a mighty heave, then settled. "He came onto the beach. Asked what I was doing. Took pictures of me slicing out the whale's jaw. I hunted him down, took him out." He thrashed and kicked. "I'll hunt you down."

An explosion of noise came from a giant black bird. The beam of a searchlight hit Alexa in the face. She let go of the crank and fell backwards.

Chapter Thirty-Six

The Search and Rescue team and a senior sergeant from Invercargill loaded Kopae in a rescue basket as the deafening helicopter battled gusts to stay level. Alexa held her breath until the swirling, twirling basket with precious cargo disappeared into the belly of the bird.

A still-trussed Warren, squirming and handcuffed through the netting, was next. Alexa hoped he would flip the basket and sink to the bottom of the seething sea.

A wave broke over the bow, drenching her.

The senior sergeant, a woman, would leave last. Alexa gave her the Ruger, explained that it might have been the gun used in Andy Gray's murder. She watched the cop remove the magazine and eject a cartridge.

"So, it was loaded?"

"Yes."

The cop stepped into a complicated rescue harness, attached herself to the dangling rope, and gave three sharp tugs. "Your DI is waiting back on the island," she told Alexa. "He was wild with worry. Don will get you there." Alexa watched the cop be hoisted to the bay. As the copter took off, she rushed to *Darla Jo*'s side and puked into the ocean as the rain blew sideways. She hated this cargo of horrors.

"That's that, then," said Don, the man left behind. He patted Alexa on the back and cast a wary gaze at the heaving sea. "Let's get her home."

Like riding a bull, the trip back. Alexa barely held on. Twenty minutes later she spotted the Golden Bay pier, and when they were close enough for Don to cut the engine, her spirits lifted at the sight of Wallace, Briscoe, and Bruce pacing the dock.

"How's Kopae?" Wallace shouted as they neared.

"Airlifted to hospital," Don yelled.

Don grabbed a rope and tossed it over the waves toward him. As soon as they were close enough, Alexa jumped the rail. Bruce rushed to her, opened his arms, encircled her, held her tight, poncho to slicker, the camera pressing against her sternum. Too quickly he pushed her back, looked into her eyes. "When Kopae didn't answer the radio, we came as fast as we could."

She braced her legs when a gust tried to knock her down.

"The car was here, but *Darla Jo* was gone," Wallace said.

Briscoe, wrapping a line around a cleat, broke in. "We called Search and Rescue. They sent a copter and backup. Damn lucky they got through."

Bruce ordered Briscoe and Don to stay, tape *Darla Jo* off, start processing the scene. "We'll be back after we get Ms. Glock to safety and take her statement."

Her knees wanted to buckle, but she wouldn't let them.

Wallace's house was shelter in the storm. The two children barely looked up from the TV as Nina helped Alexa, whose arms hung like wooden blocks, out of the poncho and camera. "Your face," Nina said, brushing matted hair from her forehead. "All banged up."

Bruce cleared his throat and pressed by her into the kitchen.

"You can't stay out of harm's way, can you?" Nina fetched Alexa her own dry clothes from two days before, fresh and familiar, and ushered her into the bathroom. "You know where the towels are, eh?"

When Alexa saw her swollen forehead in the bathroom mirror, she remembered the cabin door slamming in her face. A mewl escaped from her mouth. She sat at the edge of the bathtub, head down, hair dripping onto the floor, until she could summon strength.

Nina was serving mugs of cocoa at the kitchen table when she entered.

"Here," Bruce said, pulling out a chair for her.

Wallace hung up his landline phone. "The rescue copter made it to Invercargill. I was afraid—what with the storm—but Kopae is in with a doctor now. I need to call her mother."

Alexa trembled as he made his call. Nina wrapped a throw blanket around her, and Spot pressed her muzzle on her thigh. She encircled the mug with her hands, startled to see a drop of blood where a shark tooth had pierced her finger. The jaws flashed in her mind.

Bruce cleared his throat again. "Supervisor Lowell said it was our man Sean N. Warren who worked as a temp ranger when he lost his job. Warren helped Neville shoot the dying whales. With a DOC shotgun."

Nina left the kitchen, shutting the door to the den.

"Bloody hell," Wallace said. "Why did Stephen say he was alone?"

"He felt alone," Alexa said.

Spot left her and whined at the door. Wallace let her into the den.

"Warren told me he killed Robert King." Alexa spoke through chattering teeth. "King saw him butchering whales. *Darla Jo* is full of jaws and fins."

"Losing his job, splitting up with Missy," Wallace said, sitting heavily. "Pushed him over the brink. No excuse, though. This lets Stephen Neville off the hook."

Alexa cringed at the word "hook." "But Stephen still messed up." *Andy Gray messed up too and paid the ultimate price*, Alexa thought, sad for Lisa Squires and her baby.

"Tell us what happened," Bruce said gently.

The cocoa sloshed as she brought it to her lips. The hot sweet chocolate burned her tongue, slid down her throat, warmed her belly. She took another sip, grateful the floor beneath her thick socks was stable, and told the men everything.

Chapter Thirty-Seven

She slept until eleven, and when she opened her eyes, feverish, she was surprised weak sunshine seeped between the curtains. The storm was gone. She rolled over, her body sore and stiff, and thought of Bruce, his blue eyes, the fact that the team had solved a double murder in four days. Victory was anchored by the weight of two bodies. Wearily, she climbed out of bed.

Her gaff wound looked worse in the bathroom mirror. She swallowed an antibiotic and two ibuprofen and studied her swollen forehead and bruised lip. Not her best look. She dressed as quickly as her lethargic limbs allowed, feeling guilty she'd slept so late. She didn't stop to eat but trudged from the inn to the station. The door was ajar, even though, according to her weather app, the post-storm temperature had dropped to fifty-two degrees. She wondered if she'd get her jacket back—she had used it to staunch Kopae's blood. And she had lost her cardigan to the gaff. All she had left for warmth was her bright red NC State sweatshirt. She entered the station and pulled the door shut. Wallace was hanging up the phone. She could see his computer screen and was surprised he was on Facebook.

"Miss Glock," he said, recoiling. "Er. How are you?"

"Fine."

"I'll call Joan at the medical center. Tell her you'll be stopping by."

"I'm fine, really. How's Kopae?"

His face went grave. "She's got a compound skull fracture. Hit with a blunt object. She'll be out a month."

"Will she fully recover?"

He shrugged. "The doc thinks so. Her mum is on her way."

"She was smart to let Warren believe she was alone."

"You did good, too." Wallace said and blushed. "I wish I could have seen Warren netted like a codfish. A bigwig from DOC is flying in to confer with Kana Duffy and take possession of the shark parts. They'll be used for research." He pointed to her crime kit stashed on a chair. "Briscoe found it on *The Apex*."

She was forever losing it. The evidence she had collected with the BLUESTAR would be crucial if there was a trial. "Where's DI Horne?"

"He and Briscoe flew out at first light to interrogate Warren in Invercargill."

Alexa's knees went wobbly. She sat at Kopae's cubicle.

"I just got off the phone with him. Senior said when he showed Warren that the fingerprint you lifted from Robert King's high-vis vest matched his, Warren caved, said he was desperate for money. He gave up a couple of names of middlemen at a shipping company in Bluff. It's an international port. They've been smuggling shark and whale parts to Taiwan."

"You've been busy," she said.

"New Zealand Customs Patrol has been informed." Wallace took his glasses off and apprised Alexa. "The DI said he'd see you back in Auckland. He called your boss, told him what an asset to the case you were, said you needed a few days off to recuperate. You could stay on at the inn. Have a hollie."

Why did she feel as if she'd been punched in the solar plexus? Must be she was feverish.

"Nina figured something out," he said, pointing to the computer screen. "Remember that comment from a Nathan Rawner? 'Pāua divers unite. Kill the cagers'?"

"I guess."

"Nathan is Sean Warren's middle name, and Rawner is an anagram of Warren."

"Okay." She didn't know what it meant.

"Warren was probably trying to pin Andy's death on an angry pāua diver."

———

She stood alone on the afternoon ferry deck, braving the wind, fingering the shark tooth she found in the crime kit, and watched as Stewart Island got smaller and smaller. She supposed cases were the same. Larger than life when you're in the middle, and then they recede.

She ran her fingers over the serrated edges and watched two mollymawks skim the ferry's wake. She might have the shark tooth made into a necklace and see if it changed color as it pressed against the flesh of her chest.

Mangō taniwha. She brightened, thinking the Māori words for white shark could be the title for the *Journal of Oral Pathology* article she would write. That's what she would do during her upcoming three-day medical leave her boss had insisted she take.

Nina had come to see her off and to return her latest batch of freshly laundered clothes. "Kip told me what a hero you are, netting that monster and saving Elyse's life."

"Wallace would have done the same thing." Alexa wanted to say more, to tell Nina to be grateful for what she had, to keep her children safe from harm, and to thank her for her kindness, but her throat clogged.

Stewart Island was obscured now. A mirage that had faded.

She was mad at Bruce. For pushing her away. For not knocking at her door at 2:00 a.m. For leaving without saying goodbye. He had left her a phone message, but she deleted it. Sharks should be left in peace, and she should too.

Alexa walked to the stern and leaned into the bracing future.

ACKNOWLEDGMENTS

Many thanks to the following people who helped shape *The Bones Remember*.

First to my agent, Natalie Lakosil of Bradford Literary Agency, who loves the Alexa Glock series and led me to the great Poisoned Pen Press/Sourcebooks team. My editor, Barbara Peters, provides astute guidance and loves New Zealand. Diane DiBiase, managing editor, and Beth Deveny, assistant content editor, are quick to respond, support, and guide.

The Bones Remember is a better book because of my writing group. A heartfelt thank you to our leader, Nancy Peacock, and my fellow writers, Lisa Bobst, Denise Cline, Linda Janssen, Mirinda Kossoff, and Ann Parrent.

Researching great white sharks was fascinating. Thank you to shark expert Warrick Lyon of New Zealand's National Institute of Water and Atmospheric Research for graciously checking my facts and sharing his tale of spotting "eleven white sharks in one spot in Stewart Island in one day." NIWA scientists are working to protect the white sharks by reducing fishing mortality.

The Department of Conservation rangers on Stewart Island are passionate about their work. Ranger Tanya Dann of Rakiura National Park Visitor Center was kind to answer my questions.

My brother, Ben LeFever, who knows weaponry, patiently answered my questions.

Triangle Sisters (and Misters) in Crime and the North Carolina Writers' network provided support and fellowship.

Some of the places in *The Bones Remember* are real and some are made up. All the mistakes are real and mine alone.

The Bones Remember exists because my husband one day said, "How would you like to live in New Zealand for a year?" Thank you, Forrest, for that and for being my best friend and best editor.

Don't miss a single adventure with Alexa Glock!
Read on for an excerpt from

MOLTEN MUD MURDER

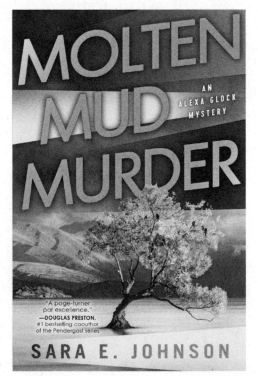

Chapter One

"Boiled? Boiled in mud?"

"No, ma'am. The chicken is sautéed, in chili-infused oil."

Alexa tore her eyes from the newspaper and stared blankly at the waiter of the Thai restaurant where she had stopped for lunch. She hadn't realized she had spoken aloud.

"More water?" the waiter added.

"Yes, please." .

A *New Zealand Herald* had been left behind on the next table over, and she had grabbed it to keep herself company. Now it was all she could do to finish her curry. She was so absorbed by what she was reading that the wet wad of rice and lemongrass held midway from bowl to mouth slipped from her chopsticks and landed on her white T-shirt.

"Dammit."

She dabbed at her breast with a cloth napkin dipped in water and resumed reading. The front page was filled with grisly details of a murder in Rotorua, the very place she was headed for her friend Mary's memorial service. She had planned to call on Mary's family this afternoon after checking in to a cottage she had rented for two weeks while she figured out a way to prolong her stay in New Zealand.

A body had been found yesterday half-submerged in a Waiariki Thermal Land of Enchantment mud pool.

Boiled. Boiled in mud. The urge to finger her scar, to reassure herself, flashed like neon. She drank the water instead.

Rotorua, on the North Island of New Zealand, lay smack in the middle of intense thermal activity, like Yellowstone National Park in the States. Alexa read that the temperature of the mud pools reached two hundred degrees Celsius. *Hotter than water at the boiling point.* What would be left of the body? Teeth? She ran her tongue across her own and thought back to three years ago at the North Carolina State Bureau of Investigation when she had completed a second master's in odontology. Teeth were what had brought her to New Zealand.

Maybe teeth would be the reason she would stay.

An aerial view of the geothermal park took up half the page.

"Terrible, eh?" said a man leaning toward her from an adjacent table. He pointed to the paper while his companion, a woman roughly Alexa's age, late thirties, nodded.

"Gruesome way to die," Alexa agreed.

"Are you a Yank?" he asked, only it sounded like "yeenk."

"I'm from North Carolina."

The couple eyed her like she'd said "I'm from Mars." The woman was wearing conflicting colors, and the balding man had on a tank and shorts that showed too much hairy leg despite the sixty-degree breeze wafting through the open restaurant door.

"I've been working in Auckland for the past six months," Alexa added.

"We went to Las Vegas, yeah," the man said.

"Choice," the woman said. "But wouldn't want to live there. Crazy people."

Alexa, thinking not all the crazies were in the States, went back to her newspaper, but the man wasn't done.

"The dead guy must have royally pissed off a Māori," he said, stabbing her paper with his thick pointer finger.

"A Māori?" Alexa knew who the Māori were, but she was taken aback by this man's brashness.

"A native, eh. They used to boil the heads of their enemies."

Alexa shoveled down a last bite, gulped more water, and tucked the paper into her tote. She rearranged her afternoon schedule on the spot. Check in to her rental cottage. Stop by the police station to offer her services. *Then* call on Mary's family.

Maybe she had found her way.

———

Trout Cottage was tucked down a gravel drive on the outskirts of Rotorua. Alexa climbed out of the ten-year-old Toyota Vitz hatchback she had purchased when she arrived in New Zealand and leaned back to stretch. The scent of lavender spiced the air; she located their purple heads bobbing in the breeze to the left of the weathered, single-story cottage. The hum of the Kaituna River and the dancing lavender made her close her eyes and give thanks for the opportunity to be in this faraway land of abundant beauty. Eight thousand, five hundred miles was a long way from home.

The key was under the mat, just as the owner had promised. Alexa walked into a living area: wicker couch covered in wide black-and-white striped cushions, tan leather easy chair with ottoman next to a reading lamp, full bookcase, soft gray carpet, fresh white walls. She smiled, dropped her tote and computer bag, and checked out the bedroom.

A queen bed covered by a muted gray-and-yellow floral duvet was flanked by nightstands. Cracking the single window, she then probed under the bedding—yes, an electric mattress warmer. Spring nights could dip into the forties.

Spring in October. *Crazy.*

A small table and two chairs were all the furniture that fit into the kitchen. A vase of lavender sprigs brightened the windowsill. Alexa leaned over to inhale and then checked the cupboards where she discovered pots and pans, an electric kettle—she'd have to be careful, the water boiled almost instantly—plunger, salt and pepper, tea bags, and a canister of coffee that she opened, sniffed, and dumped. No smell, no buzz.

A trip to the grocery store had to be squeezed into the afternoon. She had started a mental list when her cell phone rang.

"Hello?"

"Terrance Horomia," a voice said. "I am Mary's brother. We heard you were in town for the funeral, and we'd like to invite you for tea. Five o'clock?"

She had called Mary's family yesterday and told them she'd be coming to Rotorua and would like to pay her respects. Mary had befriended her at Auckland University, or uni, as the locals said, and during her six-month visiting professorship, they had become close. Mary, who had worked as a biotechnician in an adjoining lab, was always eager to gab about biosecurity and conservation and New Zealand's wonders. She had enticed Alexa to stay longer, to travel as soon as her fellowship finished. "I'll take you round," Mary had promised. "We'll have adventures."

"That's kind, yes," Alexa said. "I look forward to meeting you all."

Terrance told her that Mary had mentioned her. "She said you were *whānau*, like cousin, so come meet your family." He gave Alexa directions said *haere rā*, and the phone went silent. "*Whānau*." Alexa said it out loud, tasting it, hearing it, seeing Mary's bright eyes.

A short two weeks ago, Mary had popped into her office and invited Alexa to drive from Auckland to the tip of the North Island. "Cape Reinga. Talk about tidal rips. At the lighthouse, you can watch the Tasman Sea meet the Pacific, man-sea meets woman-sea." Mary had laughed. "You know how that goes." But then she had turned serious. "It's the leaping point for spirits, the place the soul departs."

Alexa shuddered. What had Mary meant, leaping place for spirits? It must have been another Māori saying.

A single, never-married friend her age was rare. Often when people discovered Alexa had never been married or had children, their eyes scrutinized her like a magnifying glass, searching for hidden faults, cracks. The assumption that she grieved for the Prince Charming husband she'd never found or the baby she'd never cradled was below the surface, ready to pounce. It infuriated her.

Alexa should have dropped everything and said "yes!" to Mary's invite. But she prided herself in never shirking work responsibilities and had had final exams to give and the six- month fellowship to wrap up.

Days later, Mary was dead in a one-lane bridge collision. Dead. *I could be, too. Who would mourn?*

Back home, she had blown it with her boyfriend, Jeb, when he mentioned marriage. "I like things the way they are," she'd answered.

Jeb had been incredulous. "We bought a couch together, and you won't commit? What's up with that?" He'd let it rip, and she knew she had hurt him. But Jeb hadn't been the right man. She doubted the right one existed, and when a colleague at the dental lab had posted the "Auckland University Seeking Odontologist Fellow" notice, she had thought "What the hell" and applied. Now she was here and determined to stay longer in New Zealand. Mary had had the right idea—explore. Why not? What else did she have back home? She'd never even been to Canada, and here she was in the Southern Hemisphere.

Alexa went back outside to unload the car, and after lugging in one large suitcase and one bulging backpack, she kicked off her Keds and sat on a porch chair in the sunshine to reread "Mud Pot Murder." According to the article, the body of a man, face and shoulders partially submerged in molten mud, was discovered by a busload of Chinese tourists at 8:50 Sunday morning. "We came from geyser and I was first here. I saw body sticking out but the head was in mud," one of the witnesses was quoted as saying. Police were declaring the death suspicious and asking for information from the public. At press time, no missing person had been reported. "The victim's identifying features are indistinguishable," said district medical examiner, Dr. Rachel Hill. "All we know is that the victim is male, Caucasian, and forty to fifty years of age."

Couldn't a tourist have just gone rogue? Right before she had left the States she had read about a visitor in Yellowstone National Park who had ignored warning signs and wandered off the designated boardwalk, stumbling into a hot spring. All that was left of the guy was a Boston Red Sox cap. No remains had been recovered.

Her work visa was good for six more months, as long as she found another job. No office or classroom. No man to anchor her. A sudden breeze wrestled the paper out of her hands. She looked up, surprised, at the swaying, limbless trees topped by green pom-poms along the driveway. They were having a bad hair day. An urge to explore New Zealand's wildness—glaciers, the Great Walks, locations from *The Lord of the Rings* films, the bubbling mud pots right here in Rotorua—struck like a bolt. And Mary had said there was even a thermal waterfall near her hometown.

Alexa scooped up the newspaper and padded back into the cottage, found directions for connecting to the internet, and set up her laptop. A quick search revealed directions to Rotorua Central Police Station and the name of the inspector in charge of the investigation: Bruce Horne. Alexa clicked on the inspector's bio: born in Wellington, 1973, bachelor of science, Auckland University, special agent in charge of improving police efficiency, promoted to detective inspector in 2012, held in esteem by Māori community, outreach coordinator, married, two daughters, yadda yadda. A dark-haired man with intense blue eyes did not smile from a studio portrait.

The police station was new and modern. A band of red wood Māori carvings—faces with protruding tongues, fish, birds, and canoes—wrapped around the exterior. Inside, the welcome desk in the high-ceilinged lobby was vacant.

Where was everyone?

Alexa waited three minutes, staring up at a lightly balanced Calder-like mobile of six large birds—albatross? They had huge triple-jointed wings and cast undulating shadows.

"Be with you shortly," said a no-nonsense voice belonging to a severely bunned woman with cat's-eye glasses perched on a sharp nose. The restrained hair was an unnatural black. The woman busied herself arranging steaming tea in a Save the Penguins mug and then several files. Her "Kia Ora! My name is Sharon Welles" name tag straightened, she finally spoke.

"How can I help you?"

"I'd like to see Inspector Horne regarding the mud pot case."

Her eyes sharpened. "Is the *detective* inspector expecting you?"

"No, but I think I can be of assistance. Is he in?"

"He's on his way back to the station now. Have a seat," she answered, pointing to an empty bench along a wall of windows. "I'll phone to let him know you're here. Whom shall I say is waiting?"

"Alexa Glock. Forensic odontologist."

"Odontologist?"

"Teeth."

"You got here quickly."

Alexa smiled and took a seat. It was three o'clock. She let the floating birds capture her attention, pondered her personal albatross, and then let her thoughts migrate to her career. Seven years she had been with the North Carolina State Bureau of Investigation in Raleigh. She fished out her curriculum vitae: criminal psychology, crime-scene processing, trace evidence analysis, courtroom testimony. Three years ago, ready for a change, she'd left to earn a second master's in forensic odontology. "Comes in handy when face recognition is…not possible," she'd explain to friends. Pearly whites had shifted her career to teaching, first at the dental school in Chapel Hill and then—a convenient relationship escape hatch—to Auckland, New Zealand.

A voice jarred her back to the present.

"Detective Inspector Horne, remember I told you someone from forensics is waiting to see you." Alexa could hear the receptionist's voice, gone a bit syrupy, but not the reply. The clock on the wall read 3:22. After a few seconds of listening, the receptionist gave Alexa a puzzled look. Putting her hand over the voice piece she said, "Now just who are you?"

"Alexa Glock. I'm a forensics odontologist."

"Detective Inspector Horne says he is not expecting you."

"I'd like to offer my services. I can help him with the mud pot case." As the receptionist began to speak into the phone again, a tall, fit man with dark hair graying slightly at the temples appeared in front of Alexa. Shrewd blue eyes assessed her as his hand extended down.

"DI Bruce Horne. How can I help you?"

"I thought I might be able to help you," Alexa replied, rising. She took the man's offered hand in a firm shake. He had aged pleasingly since his bio portrait. "I'm Alexa Glock from North Carolina. I mean, I've just finished a job in Auckland, and I am looking for work." She took a breath and continued before the man could stop her. "I'm qualified in forensics, odontology, and crime-scene investigation. I read about the mud pot death in the paper. I'd like…"

"Hold on. You aren't from Auckland CSI?"

"No."

"You're from North Carolina? That's across the pond," he said, his forehead wrinkling. "What brings you to Rotorua?"

"A funeral. But I have a work visa and I'm highly qualified."

"A funeral?" The man's glacier-blue eyes stared at her until Alexa felt her face get hot. He was disconcertingly handsome. She swatted that thought away like a pesky fly. "I'm expecting a forensics expert from Auckland in the morning. So I don't have any need of your services."

"In the morning? That's wasting time."

The detective inspector frowned as Alexa barreled on.

"I can ride out to the crime scene right now and do an initial analysis. I imagine safety is an issue." The number one rule in crime-scene investigation was to remove environmental hazards that could threaten investigators, but how could a bubbling mud pot be removed?

"As I said, we have someone coming. If you want a job, you need to apply online." He smiled briefly and started to turn.

"Here, take my résumé." She handed it to him but grabbed it back. "Oops. North Carolina number." Alexa dug for a pen and quickly drew a line through the number. "Just a sec. I can't remember what my new number is." She began to search her tote for the scrap of paper where she had written it, sure this would happen, removing sunscreen, an apple, and a scrunchie in the process. Horne stood patiently, watching her fumble around.

"Can I hold something?" he asked, one thick eyebrow rising in bemusement.

It was then she noted the curry stain front and center on her T-shirt. *Great.* "Yes, thanks." She handed him the apple. "Here it is." Number added, she traded her résumé for the apple and smiled into blue eyes. "I hope I hear from you."

Horne's left eyebrow flew up.

ABOUT THE AUTHOR

Sara E. Johnson lives in Durham, North Carolina. She worked as a middle school reading specialist and local newspaper contributor before her husband lured her to New Zealand for a year. Her novels *Molten Mud Murder* and *The Bones Remember* were the result.

Morgan Henderson Photography